HENRIETT

EIGHTEENTH-CENTURY NOVELS BY WOMEN

Isobel Grundy, Series Editor

Advisory Board

Paula R. Backscheider
David L. Blewett
Margaret A. Doody
Jan Fergus
J. Paul Hunter
John Richetti
Betty Rizzo

HENRIETTA

Charlotte Lennox

Edited by

Ruth Perry and Susan Carlile

THE UNIVERSITY PRESS OF KENTUCKY

Editorial and Sales Offices: The University Press of Kentucky
663 South Limestone Street, Lexington, Kentucky 40508-4008
www.kentuckypress.com

08 09 10 11 12   5 4 3 2 1

Library of Congress Cataloging-in-Publication Data

Lennox, Charlotte, ca. 1729–1804.
Henrietta / by Charlotte Lennox ; edited by Ruth Perry and Susan Carlile.
p. cm — (Eighteenth-century novels by women)
Includes bibliographical references.
ISBN 978-0-8131-2490-2 (hardcover : alk. paper)
ISBN 978-0-8131-9190-4 (pbk. : alk. paper)
1. Women domestics—Fiction. 2. Women—England—Social conditions—
18th century—Fiction. I. Perry, Ruth, 1943–   II. Carlile, Susan, 1967–   III. Title.
PR3541.L27H46 2008
823'.6—dc22
2008006154

This book is printed on acid-free recycled paper meeting
the requirements of the American National Standard
for Permanence in Paper for Printed Library Materials.

Manufactured in the United States of America.

Member of the Association of American University Presses

CONTENTS

INTRODUCTION

When Charlotte Lennox wrote *Henrietta,* she was in the thick of a very active London literary career. Already the author of a volume of poems, two novels, a remarkable work of literary criticism and history about Shakespeare in three volumes, a dramatic pastoral in verse, and three very well-received translations of historical memoirs from the French in ten hefty volumes, Lennox worked indefatigably to make a living from her writing, not only with her publications but also through her business dealings with booksellers and literati. Her correspondence shows her soliciting new books to translate, trying to arrange for new editions of her novels, and floating a subscription for her collected works. We have letters in which she enjoins her friend Samuel Johnson to reply in print to the few insufficiently positive reviews of her work; she also asks him to excerpt, reprint, and introduce sections of her translations in various literary magazines to bring them to the attention of the reading public. *Henrietta* was barely in print when Lennox wrote to John Boyle, Earl of Cork and Orrery, her patron and literary friend, asking him to speak to a bookseller—perhaps Andrew Millar, who published most of Lennox's work in the 1750s and 1760s and probably introduced her to Samuel Johnson—on behalf of *The Female Quixote* and *Henrietta,* to arrange for second editions. "If another edition of henrietta is prin[te]ed the proffits of it will be all my own," she told him.[1]

Boyle had offered to intercede for her with Rivington, another bookseller, to obtain for her the commission to translate Voltaire's new work, *Histoire de L'Empire de Russie sous Pierre le Grand.*[2] Translation, she remarked to Johnson, was "a great deal easier than Composition," and she was sure she could "make it as advantageous [financially] by industry" as by writing original works.[3] Nevertheless, despite her vigilance in seeking literary opportunities and her unflagging industry, she did not prosper. Two years after the publication of *Henrietta* (1758), having produced another massive French translation in the meantime and having arranged to publish a magazine called the *Lady's Museum* (1760–1761), she complained of her "present Slavery to the Booksellers, whom I have the mortification to see adding to their heaps by my labours, which scarce produce me a scanty and precarious subsistence."[4] One sign of her poverty in this most productive decade between 1755 and 1765, when she was writing and then revising *Henrietta,* putting out three multivolume translation projects, the verse pastoral *Philander,* the novel *Sophia,* and many pieces and translations for her magazine, the *Lady's Museum,* was that she moved seven times—probably a sign of keeping one step ahead of creditors.

The first edition of *Henrietta* in 1758 was "so hurried," she wrote to the Duchess of Newcastle, that she had not had time to ask Her Grace if she might dedicate it to her. But the favorable reception that it had met with, "both at home and abroad, where it has been translated several times," she wrote, had encouraged her to bring out a second edition, dedicated to the duchess.[5] Indeed, *Henrietta* did have a healthy eighteenth-century print life. Both the *Critical Review* and the *Monthly Review* praised it as the best novel in years; it was pirated immediately for a Dublin edition, and by 1760 several translations had appeared. In 1761 the second edition, the copytext used for the present edition, was issued. It was apparently still worth something when Millar sold his stock in 1769, for W. and J. Richardson bought it that June and in September sold a share to T. Lowndes, who printed a new issue right away as well as publishing *The Sister,* the play that Charlotte Lennox developed from a plot twist in the second volume.[6] *Henrietta* was translated into Swedish in 1781–1782, pirated by a different Dublin printer in 1786, reissued with plates in 1787, and included by James Harrison in his canonizing the *Novelist's Magazine* along with novels by Henry and Sarah Fielding, Smollett, Richardson, Sterne, Goldsmith, Swift, Haywood, Frances Sheridan, and John Shebbeare, among others.[7] A new French translation of *Henrietta* came out in 1789, and it was printed with new plates in 1798.

The edition we offer here, published in 1761, bore her own name, Mrs. Charlotte Lennox, whereas the first edition (1758) had only "The Author of The Female Quixote" on its title page. We have chosen to print this second edition because we believe that this is how Charlotte Lennox would have wanted her book to appear. She was undoubtedly responsible for the changes and emendations in this edition, which are many and meticulous, and are summarized in the "Note on the Text." Most of the changes in the second edition tone down the burlesque of the first version and elevate the diction to create a somewhat more realistic text as well as a more conventionally sentimental one. For example, the description of the "free-thinking woman" in volume II has been revised to be more negative in the second edition—possibly to make Henrietta look more conventionally "feminine" by contrast. This would-be intellectual woman is of lower birth in the second edition of the novel, ill bred and arrogant, and farcically scornful of other women "because they are subject to such weaknesses as tenderness and pity" (II: 172). Such alterations serve to intensify the reader's perception of Henrietta's good qualities by comparison— even though she has taken the drastic step of leaving her aunt's establishment and is recklessly living alone in the world. But we already know that Henrietta values her friendships with other women, has proven that she is faithful to her own religion, and is actively attempting to live an uncompromised life. More spirited and quick-tongued than the ideal recessive and modest heroine of the day, Henrietta nevertheless is easily distinguished from the pretentious and absurd imitation bluestocking that this foil represents. Lennox clearly wanted to make her text more "correct" to improve its salability in the second edition. She lived in London, in ready contact with her publisher, and was very focused on her literary career. So there is every reason to believe that she authorized the changes that went into the second edition.

Henrietta is a bildungsroman, the story of a young woman's education in the ways of the world, like Frances Burney's *Evelina* or Jane Austen's *Northanger Abbey,* although written long before either of them. But Henrietta's naïveté is shorter-lived and much less comic than that of these later heroines; she spends most of the book calmly but firmly telling an interesting assortment of men and women what she will and will not do for money. Thrown on the mercy of the world because an unreasonable aunt requires her to convert to Catholicism—which she cannot do in conscience—she tries to earn her living in a society that is repeatedly surprised by the spectacle of this young woman of quality without friends, family, or an establishment. This is the donnée of *Henrietta*—a setup that proved irresistible to Frances Burney in several of her novels.[8] Henrietta's refusal to change her religion in order to retain Lady Meadows's protection (not to mention to inherit her fortune) is only the first of many refusals this high-minded heroine makes because she will not compromise her moral position—her "delicacy," in the language of the day—for the sake of an inheritance, an establishment, or even just a situation. While her creator was hustling booksellers and literary friends from every possible angle just to survive, Henrietta was politely refusing offer after offer of fortune and position because she would not bend truth to suit venal purposes.

Henrietta is written with a sure hand and shows the pleasure of a seasoned writer in her craft. One glimpses the author behind the character when Mrs. Willis advises the heroine, who is writing to her aunt, in a self-reflexive moment: "There are some cases . . . in which simplicity is the greatest refinement of art; yours is one of them: be as simple and ingenuous as you can in the account you give your aunt, and let the facts speak for themselves" (II: 127). Reviewed positively when it first came out for its gentility, its satire, its spirited dialogue and probable incidents, its natural characters—"varied and well supported"—and its steady but delicate and unbigoted adherence to Protestantism,[9] *Henrietta* stands in a direct line in the development of the eighteenth-century novel:

between Fielding and Richardson, who came before her and Burney and Austen, who came after. The opening gambit of *Henrietta*—the appearance of a heroine without a class identity but expensively dressed, well spoken and well mannered, interestingly "oppressed" with "melancholy"—was later used by Frances Burney in *The Wanderer,* although she kept her heroine incognito for a good deal longer than Charlotte Lennox did Henrietta. The way Lennox keeps maneuvering her heroine into tight spots, morally speaking, to display her wisdom, wit, and incorruptibility, was used by Burney, among others, in the last decades of the eighteenth century as a standard fictional structure. But Lennox's delight in absurdities and her writerly relish were all her own.

Like the eponymous heroine of this novel, who had the example of a "scribbling" mother before her, Charlotte Lennox pays her respects in this novel to her predecessors, Fielding and Richardson. The brilliant opening scene of *Henrietta,* in which the assorted passengers of the Windsor stagecoach bicker about whether or not to make room for the unnamed but well-dressed heroine, is a feminized variation of chapter XII in Henry Fielding's *Joseph Andrews.* In that episode, after having been beaten, stripped, robbed, and left for dead in a ditch, Fielding's hero finds his rescue jeopardized by a carriage full of burlesqued characters—a falsely modest woman and several professional gentlemen who are afraid that he will bleed on their greatcoats. Lennox makes her debt to *Joseph Andrews* explicit in chapter VI when Henrietta prefers reading this novel—"one of the most exquisite"—to Delariver Manley's *New Atlantis* or one of Eliza Haywood's novels. "[Y]et I assure you," she tells her incredulous landlady, "I shall begin it again with as much eagerness and delight as I did at first" (I: 23). The chapter titles, too, of *Henrietta* are Fieldingesque, and the broad satire of types is reminiscent of his conception of the "comic epic."

But Lennox also broke new ground in her realistic satire of folly and vanity, psychological innovations in character development that Jane Austen took to subtler heights. As Henrietta explains wittily to Miss Woodby, "Politeness, my dear, is sometimes a great tax upon sincerity. . . . persons in a certain condition of life, make a science of hating one another with all the good breeding and complaisance imaginable" (I: 53). She might have been speaking of Lady Middleton in Jane Austen's *Sense and Sensibility.* Or there is the example of the mantua maker (i.e., a dressmaker) who "was above visiting her customers in a hackney coach [i.e., she traveled in a chair]: and this insolence was such a proof of her excellence in her business, that few ever scrupled to pay for it" (II: 136).

Richardson's influence can also be felt—first of all in the seriousness and danger of the instigating motive for our heroine's adventures, the way she is forced to leave the safety and protection of her home because she fears that she will be forced into marriage with a revolting old man. Richardson's inspiration is also visible in Henrietta's Clarissa-like sobering effect on an impudent libertine: her "mingled modesty and dignity struck him with awe" (I: 55); in the references to whether or not rakes make good husbands (I: 96; II: 153); and in the question of whether or not a woman may reject a suitor if she is not already prepossessed in favor of another (II: 190). There are echoes of Richardson's masterpiece in the way Henrietta finds herself lodged in the house of one who, if not an outright procuress, is one of those "convenient" persons who accommodates women who need to lie in (i.e., give birth) privately, or "a young wife whose husband, for certain family reasons, visits her only now and then" (I: 20). Although Lennox knew Richardson personally and admired him as a writer, Henrietta's trenchant remark about her selfish, libertine suitor, Lord B——, might be read as a comment upon his earlier, less morally well-developed novel *Pamela*. "The lover, who marries his mistress only because he cannot gain her upon easier terms, has just as much generosity as the highwayman who leaves a traveller in possession of his money, because he is not able to take it from him," remarks Henrietta to Mrs. Willis (II: 168).

Charlotte Lennox's admiration for and indebtedness to Richardson—he read the manuscript of *The Female Quixote,* gave her advice about Arabella's cure, and interceded with Millar to allay his doubts about printing the novel—would not have interfered with her criticism of *Pamela*. When the spirit was upon her, she could not forbear from sending up whatever seemed to her absurd or hypocritical. She is thought to have satirized her first patron, Lady Isabella Finch, in *The Life of Harriot Stuart* (1750) for promising favors and never delivering on them. Reading this, Lennox's first novel, Lady Mary Wortley Montagu was startled by the likeness.

> I was rouz'd into great surprize and Indignation by the monstrous abuse of one of the very, very few Women I have a real value for. I mean Lady B[ell] F[inch], who is not only clearly meant by the mention of her Library, she being the only Lady at Court that has one, but her very name at Length, she being christen'd Caecelia Isabella, thô she chuses to be call'd by the Latter. . . . It is one of the misfortunes of a suppos'd Court interest . . . even the people you have obliged hate you if they do not think you have serv'd them to the utmost extent of a power that they fancy you are possess'd of, which it may be is only imaginary.[10]

In *Henrietta,* Charlotte Lennox represents her heroine as skewering her aunt, Lady Meadows, in a letter with "some satirical strokes of my pen . . . I could not help humorously rallying upon some of her notions," she wrote, "and I placed them in the most glaring light" (I: 64). She soon repents her writerly vanity, however, when her aunt is persuaded that the letter is intended for a secret lover and its satirical contents leave Henrietta unable to disarm the accusation by showing her aunt what she has written.

It is precisely Lennox's bold and clear-eyed delight in human folly that makes this such an original book. Whereas the satire in *The Female Quixote* is pretty well centered on Arabella and her high-minded chivalric notions of women's supremacy, the satire in *Henrietta* extends in all directions—to the rich and to the middling classes, to aristocrats and tradesmen, to the young and old, to the ignorant and educated, to men and women. In the first edition of the novel, Henrietta mortifies an elderly suitor who is having trouble chewing his meat by "letting him perceive that I observed it," for she thinks he has no business courting her, old as he is, knowing that she does not want his attentions. The rudeness of this unladylike mockery was omitted in this second edition; but the misfiring conversation between the rich tradesman Mr. Cordwain and the earl who wants to marry his spendthrift son to Mr. Cordwain's only daughter (II: 152–54), or the pretentious deistical woman who holds forth on Epictetus on regulating the passions and then lashes out at her vulnerable maid "for accidentally hurting her with the comb" (II: 172), are subtler but no less effective indictments of human vanity. Like Elizabeth Bennet or her father in Jane Austen's *Pride and Prejudice,* Henrietta cannot help being diverted at the examples of human folly on display everywhere she turns.

Indeed, Jane Austen seems to have been influenced in a number of ways by this book. Although we do not have the same external proof positive that she read *Henrietta* as we do of her reading and enjoying *The Female Quixote,*[11] there is plenty of internal textual evidence of *Henrietta's* influence on Austen's three earliest novels. Miss Woodby, who meets Henrietta on the Windsor coach, swears an "inviolable attachment" to her just hours after meeting her (I: 11), in accents that remind one of Camilla Stanley in Austen's juvenile *Catherine; or, The Bower* or of Isabella Thorpe in *Northanger Abbey.* At the end of volume II, we learn that Miss Woodby, "who had always a violent passion for a redcoat" as well as a disregard for propriety reminiscent of Lydia Bennet, "married [a young cadet] in a week after their first acquaintance." But Lennox's outcomes are always more melodramatic than Austen's—they sometimes verge on slapstick— and in the case of Miss Woodby and her "lovely youth" we learn that he uses her fortune to buy himself a commission in the army and disappears with his regiment, leaving her to "bewail his absence, and sooth her love-sick heart with hopes that he would return more *passionate* than ever, and lay all his laurels at her feet" (II: 260).

Austen may have taken other hints from this novel. The improper arrangements Lady Meadows makes for transporting Henrietta from Bath to her country estate—thirty miles riding pillion behind the footman (I: 45)—may have translated in *Northanger Abbey* into General Tilney's sending Catherine Morland home alone. The scene in which Henrietta's dying father asks his brother to care for his helpless widow and child, only to have this uncle's avarice and resentment kept up by "the arts of his wife" so that he sends Henrietta's mother one hundred pounds, "declaring at the same time that it was all the assistance she must ever expect from him" (I: 41) recalls the famous second chapter of *Sense and Sensibility* in which Austen fills in the actual psychological workings of resentment and avarice. Miss Belmour's behavior when her lover ignores her might have been a prototype for Marianne's self-indulgent grief at Willoughby's defection in *Sense and Sensibility:* "She neglected her dress, took no pleasure in any amusement, avoided company, and spent whole hours in her closet, where she wept and prayed by turns" (II: 213).

And then there is the proposal scene in which Lord B—— offers his wealth and title to penniless Henrietta if only she will pretend to convert to Catholicism in order to qualify with her aunt as her heir while continuing to practice her own religion in secret. "A little dissimulation," Henrietta calls it scornfully. After listening to him with "great calmness" Henrietta says, "[I]f you had worlds to bestow on me, I would not be your wife," to which Lord B—— replies, "[T]his is too much: I have not deserved this treatment, but I thank you for it; . . . it has helped to restore my senses" (II: 192). The inequality of their situations, the way she cannot be bribed by his regard, his utter surprise at her rejection, and the way he struggles to regain his composure—all these elements remind one of Darcy's first proposal to Elizabeth Bennet in *Pride and Prejudice* and suggest that Lennox's treatment may have been a model for the later novelist. But Lennox's humor was broader, her characters more like Fielding's caricatures; she was less interested in plausibility than Austen and she could not resist turning her knife in her victims. So this scene ends by revealing Lord B——'s deeper venality rather than his deeper kindness.

Nor was Austen the only author who profited from Lennox's psychologically astute imagination. The scene between Henrietta and Lord B——'s mother, in which the countess admires the younger woman but fears her attractions because she has no fortune of her own (II: 157), was imitated by Frances Burney in *Cecilia* and by Charlotte Smith in *Emmeline*. This affectionate mutual appreciation between the heroine and the mother of the hero became a stock trope in later eighteenth-century fiction.

Indeed, Charlotte Lennox invented or developed a number of fictional formulas in this novel that became staples of later eighteenth-century fiction. Profligate sons of earls and dukes who needed to marry the fortunes of wealthy tradesmen to keep up their expensive habits, and wealthy "cits" (tradesmen's wives and daughters) who liked to humiliate the gentlewomen in their service but were really intimidated by their patent superiority, the contrast between characters like Henrietta, who rises early and dresses quickly, and those like the shallow Miss Cordwain, who takes five hours to dress—these stereotypes can be found fully fleshed for the first time in the pages of this novel. The oblivious vanity of the aging Mrs. Autumn and of the elderly Sir Isaac Darby, who dress as if they are much younger (Lennox was twenty-eight when she wrote *Henrietta*) and who behave foolishly as if no one can see their true ages, owes something to Fielding, but Lennox's characters are depicted with more attention to psychological realism than his grotesques.[12] And Lennox's spirited heroine, who would rather go into service than be a "toad eater" or a lady's companion—Henrietta, who does not have "too much pride to be a servant . . . [but] cannot so easily submit to be a dependent" (II: 172), who will not sell her soul or lie or flatter, although she will dress the hair or tend the clothing of her employer—Henrietta, who has no false pride but plenty of real pride, is Charlotte Lennox's own invention and not readily imitated by other writers. She is the spunky heroine who refuses to counterfeit Catholicism in order to inherit her aunt's fortune and whose retort to her uncle (the same who reneged on his deathbed promise) when he criticizes her for this scrupulousness plays on the eighteenth-century meanings of the word "friend": "'Friends! my lord,' replied Henrietta, rising in her temper; 'I have no friends, I have only relations'" (II: 186). Not until Elizabeth Bennet do we find another heroine with such gumption in the pages of English fiction.[13]

Lennox herself had a very strong sense of amour propre, visible in her own prickly dealings with others and in the lofty sense of personal dignity she always ascribes to her fictional heroines. Samuel Johnson, who thought Lennox "a great genius" and pronounced her superior even to Elizabeth Carter, Hannah More, Frances Burney, and Elizabeth Montagu, encouraged and helped her in her literary career so long as he lived.[14] Nevertheless, he remonstrated with her on several occasions for her testiness. "The Letter which you sent me some time ago, was rather too full of wrath for the provocation," he wrote in 1756, soothingly pointing out that the reviews in the *Monthly Review* and the *Critical Review* of her translation of *The Memoirs of the Countess of Berci* that had so irritated her referred to her with "great respect" although ostentatiously showing off their own "superiority of knowledge."[15] In another letter he writes, "I am sorry you misunderstood me" and urges her not to send him any more peevish letters, telling her that such letters can only "give mirth to your enemies" or "raise anger in your friends."[16] He tries to make up another quarrel in these words:

> When friends fall out the first thing to be considered is how to fall in again, and he is the best that makes the first advance, I have designed to come to you ever since half an hour after you ran from me but I knew not whither. I did not when I began intend to say more [than] the first sentence, nor when I left off, to have a final quarrel. Pray, my dear, think no more of it, but come to me or let me know when I can come to you, for the thought of driving you away will be very painful to
>
> Dearest Partlet,
Your most obedient &c
Sam: Johnson[17]

Further evidence that Lennox was quick to take offense is visible in the letter in which she tells a very close friend that she stopped writing to her, and did not tell her when she moved, because "not having received any answer to two or three letters which I wrote to you,—I thought I owd so much respect to my self, as to be silent for the future—"[18]

The heroines Lennox invents in her fiction exhibit an unusual degree of self-sufficiency and self-respect. Harriot Stuart, from the first novel, is proud of her beauty, proud of her wit, and confident of her literary gifts. At thirteen she writes extemporaneous verse in company and passes it around with smiling assurance. Arabella, in *The Female Quixote*, expects instantaneous obedience to her wishes from all the men around her. The romances that she has read and absorbed have taught her that women are powerful, unapproachable, magnetic, and noble. She imagines suitors dying for love of her, or silently earning the right to speak with her by patiently waiting for decades, or dueling with one another for her favors. And in *Henrietta*, as we have seen, the heroine writes a satiric letter about her aunt and then cannot show the letter to her. "How did I that moment inwardly regret my vanity, which had suffered me to rally the faults of a person on whom I so absolutely depended, merely to display my wit. I was so vexed at the dilemma to which I had reduced myself, that I burst into tears" (I: 65). Thus her sharp wit gets her in trouble—Lennox did not think women's intellectual capacity an unmixed blessing—and Henrietta is forced to leave her aunt's premises. Although gifted and willing to work, Henrietta's integrity and her sense of her own worth interfere with her ability to flatter and fawn and thus please her selfish employers. She conducts herself with dignity in all situations, as when defending herself against the reproaches of a jealous woman. "I am not used to scolding" she says, calmly withdrawing to her bedchamber (I: 111).

We do not know what caused Charlotte Lennox's breach with her first patron, Lady Cecilia Isabella Finch, although Lennox's satire of her undoubtedly made it irrevocable. She had originally interested Lady Finch, first Lady of the Bed-Chamber to Princess Amelia and Lady Isabella's sister, the Marchioness of Rock-ingham, when her misfortunes as a young woman left her without friends or resources—like the heroine of a novel. Charlotte Ramsay was born in Gibraltar, probably in 1729 or 1730, where her father was stationed at the time.[19] According to the *Edinburgh Weekly,* the family returned to England when she was still an infant. Her parents were Irish. Her father, Col. James Ramsay, "descended from the noble and ancient house of Dalhousie in Scotland," must have come of age in Ireland, where his father enjoyed "a very honorable post." Her mother was sister to the Reverend Dr. Tisdale of Ireland, a friend of Jonathan Swift.[20] When Charlotte Ramsay was about ten, her father accepted a lucrative military post in Albany, New York, and moved his family there; Lennox's accounts of life in a colonial outpost in *Euphemia* and *The Life of Harriot Stuart,* and of the treaties and trade with the Indians in both novels, probably came from recollections from this period. Her father dying a few years later, Charlotte Ramsay was then sent to her mother's sister, Mrs. Lucking of Messing Hall, a well-to-do widow in Essex. But bad luck dogged her steps, for she arrived in England, alone, at fourteen, only to learn that her aunt was very ill. Soon afterward the aunt died. Forced to live by her wits, Charlotte Ramsay managed to make some connections with these aristocratic patrons at some point, who admired her poetry. She was to have accompanied the Marchioness of Rockingham to her country estate in 1747 when she ran off instead with Alexander Lennox, "a young gentleman of good family and genteel education."[21]

When they met, Charlotte Lennox's prospective husband, Alexander Lennox, was employed by William Strahan, who was a partner of Millar the bookseller. Her husband seems to have supported her career wholeheartedly in the beginning. He understood the book trade and helped to preserve her respectability by accompanying her on visits to Samuel Johnson and Samuel Richardson, negotiating with booksellers, signing agreements, speaking with possible patrons and trying to arrange patronage, possibly making fair copies of her work, and even helping with the index to her translation of *The Memoirs of the Duke of Sully.*[22] It was he who in 1751 or 1752 made inquiries at the Orange coffeehouse for an Italian speaker when Charlotte Lennox felt that she needed to learn Italian for her work on Shakespeare's sources. Giuseppe Baretti eagerly presented himself, and he taught her Italian while she taught him English. The anecdote illustrates her gift for languages, because the first two volumes of *Shakespear Illustrated* were published not long after—1753—drawing on knowledge of texts in Italian, French, Latin, and Danish.[23] Her facility with languages is further attested to by how little she valued it: in *Henrietta,* the heroine disdains the pretentious pseudo-learned woman who peppers her discourse with French words and phrases. "Henrietta . . . began to conceive a very mean opinion of a lady who seemed to value herself so highly upon the knowledge of a language, which was now become a part of every cobler's daughter's education" (II: 170).

Charlotte Lennox's knowledge of French is visible in these pages—in the heroine's sneer at the provincial French of the woman hired by Lady Manning to be governess to her daughter and teach her French. Even Miss Woodby scorns the "low vulgar creatures" who, in Paris, would not qualify as "a chamber-maid to a woman of any fashion," but who, because they are French, are thought fit to form the manners of young English girls (I: 47).

Lennox's reading in French honed her literary sensibility. John Boyle, in his preface to *The Greek Theatre of Father Brumoy,* which Charlotte Lennox was working on at the same time as *Henrietta,* compares French novels with English novels which, "wandering from nature and probability, attempt only to represent persons who never existed even in imagination, faultless monsters, or aukward fine gentlemen." He adds that *The Female Quixote* and *Henrietta* "may claim an exception to this general remark"—exceptions that he suggests owed something to Lennox's familiarity with French fiction of the period.[24] Susan Staves has also made the point that English women writers learned from translating French women's texts that French women writers occupied respectable places in French culture as public intellectuals. In particular, Staves conjectures that Charlotte Lennox's four-volume *Memoirs for the History of Mme de Maintenon* (1757) demonstrated to her and to others how influential women could be a force for good and points out that the story of the founding of St. Cyr offered descriptions of a royal mistress's power as well as an exemplary model of virtue and intelligence.[25]

Undoubtedly Alexander Lennox's interest in his wife's literary career derived largely from the fact that it supported them both financially. The Duchess of Newcastle, who permitted Lennox to dedicate this second edition of *Henrietta* to her, arranged for apartments for the struggling writer in Somerset House and asked her husband to favor her.[26] But when the Duke of Newcastle offered her a pension for life, Charlotte Lennox asked instead that her husband be given a job, a decision that Alexander Lennox's subsequent selfishness led her to resent.[27] As a result, Alexander Lennox was given a position as tide-waiter in the Customs in 1761 or 1762, a job with a fluctuating salary but with opportunities for bribery and other forms of graft. Charlotte Lennox wrote to a friend in 1777 that her husband "for the present supplies my expenses—but how long he will be able to do it I cannot tell, for the American War has greatly reduced his income, while it has left him the same habits of expence."[28] Alexander Lennox's bid to inherit the title and property of the Duke of Lennox in Scotland in the 1760s was an ambitious attempt to secure the couple's financial stability—although it failed.

Married at seventeen or eighteen, Charlotte Lennox had no children with Alexander until she was thirty-five or thirty-six, after he had obtained his sinecure, at which point she gave birth to a daughter, baptized Harriot Holles on April 28, 1765 ("Holles" for Thomas Pellam-Holles, Duke of Newcastle, for by then the Duchess of Newcastle was her patron and godmother to the child). Six years later, at forty-one or forty-two, Lennox had a son, George Louis (Lewis) Lennox, of whom she was equally proud and fond. In 1777, in a letter to her friend Lady Lydia Clerke, she wrote, "[M]y dear little boy is always with me from Saturday till Sunday evening, when he returns to the Academy of which—young as he is, he is the ornament and delight."[29]

Having children slowed down her prodigious literary output and may have had something to do with her progressive estrangement from her husband. After the publication of *Eliza* (1767),[30] and the fiasco with *The Sister*—to which we will return—Lennox stopped turning out new work but tried repeatedly to reissue her works by subscription. Three times she tried to raise money to republish her work when the copyrights on her first editions ran out. She tried to sell subscriptions for an illustrated edition of *The Female Quixote* in 1773–1774, for her collected works in 1775, and for a revised edition of *Shakespear Illustrated* in 1793—all without success. By the 1780s, her husband was treating her badly. Samuel Johnson wrote a letter to an unidentified recipient asking for aid for her in July 1781: "I am desired by Mrs. Lennox to solicit your assistance. She is in great distress; very harshly treated by her husband and oppressed with severe illness. Do for her what you can. You were perhaps never called to the relief of a more powerful mind. She has many fopperies, but she is a Great genius, and nullum magnum ingenium sine mixtura."[31]

A draft of a letter that Lennox wrote to her husband in the late 1770s about their daughter's education shows their growing antagonism and her anxiety about money. In it she urges that Harriot Holles be sent to school in England rather than a convent in Bologne, which Alexander Lennox apparently favored. She writes that Dr. Johnson and "other persons of good sense and experience" had convinced her of the merit of English schooling—"and that is the cause they will never convince you" she continues bitterly; "therefore I submit to your despotick will, with this condition only, that I go with her, and see her settled—this point I never will give up." She then lists the clothes and linen necessary in "even the cheapest schools," as if Alexander Lennox had to be begged to give his daughter basic necessities.[32]

The portrait of the eponymous heroine's long, unhappy marriage to the ill-tempered and inconsiderate Mr. Neville in *Euphemia* (1790), her last novel, is thought to be autobiographical. Several letters of 1793 complete the picture of her enmity with her husband by then. One, to James Dodsley, the printer of two editions of *The Sister,* asking for "a trifling sum in my present necessities," complains that she is "reduced to an income of £40 a year, and out of that obliged to assist my son." She refers to Alexander as a "selfish father" and "the most ungrateful of men" who derived great advantages from her—presumably his sinecure at Customs as well as the profits of her literary labors.[33] Seven months later she appealed, more urgently, to Richard Johnson at the Royal Literary Fund for passage to America for her son, then twenty-one, driven "to desperation by a most unnatural father; and then deserted and left exposed to all the evils that may well be expected from the dreadful circumstances he is in." Here again she alludes to "the poor income I hold from a husband whose fortune I have made by the sacrifice of my own."[34]

Lennox lived in a literary world. She was admired by Fielding, Richardson, Johnson, Goldsmith (who wrote an epilogue for *The Sister*), John Boyle, Richard Farmer, the Shakespearean scholar, and David Garrick. She was painted by Reynolds. Always interested in the theater—in part because it was a more lucrative form of writing—she is supposed to have been friends with the tragedian Mrs. Mary Ann Yates, whom she thought a greater actress than Mrs. Barry, and whom she told Garrick she had in her mind's eye for the role of Roxana when translating Racine's *Bajazet.*[35] The Reverend William Beloe reports a gathering at Mrs. Yates's house soon after he came to London sometime in the 1750s where he met "Murphy, Home, the author of Douglas, Richard Cumberland, Hoole, . . . old Macklin, Mrs. Lennox, Mrs. Brooke, and various other eminent individuals."[36]

Not unusually for an eighteenth-century writer, Charlotte Lennox tried her hand at every literary genre, including literary criticism, poetry, essays, drama, fiction, translation, and even a verse pastoral. Ready in the late 1750s and 1760s to join the new magazine boom, she started the *Lady's Museum,* in which enterprise she may have been helped by the novelist Hugh Kelly.[37] Her very original work of feminist literary criticism, *Shakespear Illustrated: or the Novels and Histories, on which the Plays of Shakespeare are founded, Collected and Translated from the Original Authors with Critical Remarks,* was published in two volumes in 1753 by Andrew Millar, and with a third volume added in 1754. Johnson admired this work, wrote the dedication for it, and refers to it (a reference ventriloquized as if from Lennox herself) in his own edition of Shakespeare of 1765. Margaret Anne Doody associates it with *The Female Quixote,* published the year before, insofar as Lennox traces in Shakespeare's plays the romances he had read and whose plots he so often distorts. Lennox criticizes Shakespeare for stripping his women characters of the power and authority that they have in the original stories. She felt that he diminished "women into lovesick minxes or neurotic weaklings, taking from them the power and the moral independence which the old romances and novels had given them," according to Doody. His misreadings of these old stories, charged Lennox, tended "to humiliate his women."[38]

Lennox may have come to appreciate the power of women in these early romances, before Shakespeare went to work on them, from the work of another translator, Susannah Dobson. Dobson—along with Lennox and Sylvia Braithwaite Thornton—was part of a network of devoted friends centering on Lydia, Lady Clerke.[39] According to Susan Staves, Susannah Dobson had been drawn to translate the work of the great eighteenth-century scholar of the Middle Ages, Jean-Baptiste de La Curne de Sainte-Palaye, whose work explored the institutions and sensibility of chivalry, because she wanted to show that romances "were not merely the idle tales and useless fictions their English critics claimed and that their vision of women as heroines worthy of male worship was not merely a fictive illusion."[40] Dobson may have interested herself in these materials about French medieval chivalry several years before Lennox wrote *The Female Quixote,* for the work that she translated from Sainte-Palaye had been presented to the Académie des inscriptions et belles-lettres between 1746 and 1755.[41] Indeed, Charlotte Lennox may have learned about the cultural basis of chivalry—its emphasis on courtesy, its devotion to virtue—from Dobson's work, knowledge that fueled first her novel *The Female Quixote* and later *Shakespear Illustrated.*

Despite Johnson's idiosyncratic approbation, Lennox did not go unpunished for her feminist reading of Shakespeare's sources and for her contention that Shakespeare repeatedly sacrificed women's sense and virtue to heighten his dramatic effects.[42] Modern critics, too, find that her "catalogue of Shakespeare's 'absurdities' and 'improbabilities' grows wearisome by determined reiteration."[43] Her position made male writers and critics angry in her own day, although they did not attack her in print, possibly because of Samuel Johnson's protection. Both the *Monthly Review* and the *Gentleman's Magazine* damned *Shakespear Illustrated* with tepid praise.[44] Samuel Richardson said, "Methinks I love my Shakespeare, since this Attack, better than before."[45] And when Lennox asked Garrick (who had made his reputation playing Shakespeare, after all) to repeat to her the critical remarks about the first two volumes of *Shakespear Illustrated* that she had heard about secondhand, he wrote to her that he thought she had "betray'd a greater desire of Exposing his [i.e., Shakespeare's] Errors than of *Illustrating* his Beauties—there appeared to me (and to many others) a kind of severe Levity and Ridicule, which . . . is somewhat unjustifiable, when us'd against so great and so Excellent an Author—let me assure You of my best wishes for Your success in Every undertaking, & let me desire You in behalf of my best friend, & in ye words of an old saying, that as *You are brave, be mercifull.*[46] Garrick, however, forgave Charlotte Lennox for traducing his "best friend," for their relations continued cordial enough, and he later produced her play *Old City Manners* at the Drury Lane Theatre.[47]

The reprisals of the rest of the literary world came in the more damaging form of ruining the opening performance of her play *The Sister,* so that she had to withdraw it without making any profit from it. Before it opened, Oliver Goldsmith told Samuel Johnson that "a person had advised him to go and hiss it because she had attacked Shakespeare in her book called *Shakespear Illustrated.*"[48] On opening night, the audience was so loud and unruly that it managed to interrupt the play several times and at the beginning of the fifth act became so loud that the actors were unable to continue. George Colman, who wrote a prologue for the play and was theater manager of Covent Garden, wrote to Charlotte Lennox: "I am not ashamed to own that your Letter has brought tears into my eyes, and I do assure you that none of the many trials I have experienced in the direction of the Theater have given me more real uneasiness than the present event."[49] Nonetheless, when the play was published just two weeks after this debacle, it sold out within two weeks and a second edition was issued.[50] It was also published in Dublin that same year, then later in Hamburg (1776), Vienna (1776), Frankfurt (1777), Moscow (1788), and Regensburg, Germany (1802). Lt.-Gen. John Burgoyne thought it "one of the cleverest works of its class" and, without giving its author credit, borrowed much of it for his highly successful comedy, *The Heiress* (1786).[51]

The play *The Sister* differs from the novel *Henrietta,* from which it is adapted, in that it puts the dilemma of the brother (Courtney) at the center of the drama—his need to protect his charge (Lord Clairville in the play) from marrying his sister without permission from Lord Clairville's aristocratic father. Courtney, in the play, is in love with Charlotte, daughter of middle-aged Lady Autumn, who deludes herself that she is still young and beautiful and that it is *she* whom Courtney finds irresistible. Harriet (the character who is Henrietta in the novel), now merely "the sister" of the protagonist, is wiser, wittier, and more observant and vocal in the play than Henrietta is in the novel. Lady Autumn's absurdities draw the fire from Harriet's woman-centered critique of the patriarchal rules of society. Well made and fast paced, with entertaining dialogue and winning humor, the play would have succeeded had it not been for Charlotte Lennox's reputation as an overreaching woman. In addition to her hubris in criticizing Shakespeare, Charlotte Lennox was slightly ahead of the curve in offering this play to the public as a woman writer, before women playwrights became commonplace.[52]

Suspicions in the literary world of Lennox's proto-feminism were not misplaced. Charlotte Lennox cared deeply about women's power and agency—whether for good or ill—and she addressed these issues in everything she wrote. Whether in "The Art of Coquetry," *Shakespear Illustrated,* or *The Female Quixote,* Lennox's writing deals with customary attitudes toward women, the degrees of freedom they had in their lives, their ambitions and aspirations, and the means they had at their disposal for gaining power. She created women-centered worlds; most of the tyrannical villains and dangerous characters in Lennox's novels are women. Men may try to seduce the beautiful heroines, but they do not otherwise play games of benevolence and treachery, do not raise and dash hopes, and do not exercise arbitrary power over the fate of the protagonists. Women have the fortunes, hold the estates, and dominate the visible world. Mrs. Howard in *Sophia* is a case in point. She is charitable for show but ungenerous by nature; her treatment of her tenants or of the poor who come begging at her door proves her to be not merely frugal but selfishly grasping. Like other characters from the lower orders in Lennox's work, she exhibits not the largesse of aristocratic paternalism but the parsimony of the petite bourgeoisie in a newly capitalistic society. *Henrietta* continues this pattern: all of the heroine's encounters involve women with power, whether their prerogative comes from money, widowhood, social respectability, or shrewish passion. The structure of the narrative is to parade one powerful woman after another before the reader.

Unexpectedly, from a modern feminist standpoint, Lennox often exhibits ambivalence about learning in women, perhaps self-protectively. She seemed to believe that learning often made a heroine unacceptable to other women. In several of her fictions, an interest in books and poetry costs the heroine her mother's affection. Harriot Stuart remarks that her early "inclination to intellectual improvement"—encouraged by her brother—was "the ground of the indifference" her mother always expressed for her. Her delight in writing offended her mother, who preferred her more conventionally beautiful sister, who had no literary pretensions whatsoever. A story published by Lennox in the first issue of the *Lady's Magazine* under the pseudonym of "The Trifler" tells of a girl who alienates her mother because she loves to read. Her recourse to books only increases her mother's dislike of her. In *Sophia,* the sister who is the mother's favorite spends her time in amusement and adornment while the other, less favored sister reads. This theme is repeated, with variations, in *Eliza* (1767). In *Euphemia,* Miss Harley recalls that when she began to read to her uncle to take his mind off his gout—she mentions *Plutarch's Lives*—her new aunt began to plot jealously against her. In that novel, Clara Bellenden, the youngest of three sisters, is disdained by both her mother and her oldest sister for loving books. As for the literary mothers in Lennox's novels—such as Arabella's mother in *The Female Quixote,* whose legacy is the collection of romances in the library, or Henrietta's mother, who was "a scribbler" and a "woman of fine understanding and deep thinking" (I: 39)—they are dead, unable to protect or advise the daughters whose taste they helped to form. Thus Lennox warns that however much reading may enhance a woman's worth in the eyes of men, it separates a woman from her sisters and her mother.

Nor, despite her own wide reading, did Lennox praise or encourage women with more serious intellectual interests, but rather echoed the conservative attitudes of the day. In the *Lady's Magazine* she includes an essay, "Of the Studies Proper for Women," which advises women "to avoid all abstract learning, all thorny researches, which may blunt the fine edge of their wit, and change the delicacy in which they excel into pedantic coarseness."[53] The author goes on to say that Madam Daciers and Chatelets are rarely to be found; that no one wants a doctor in petticoats; that nothing is more "disgustful" than female theologians. Only history, belles lettres, and natural philosophy are appropriate subjects for women to explore; the rest should be left to men.

Lennox mocks women who pride themselves on their learning in all her fictions—possibly to draw fire from her heroines or from herself. In each of the novels, quite independent of the reading heroine, there is a cameo appearance of a bluestocking, devastatingly portrayed as selfish, egotistical, affected, and self-important. In *Henrietta,* it is the deistical lady mentioned earlier in this essay who shows up at the beginning of the fourth book in volume II, gratuitously lecturing everyone present about intelligent causes and moral attributes. She holds forth on all the most contested philosophical issues of the day—charity, Providence, the material body and the immaterial soul, the existence of evil and apparent inequity in the world—in a series of short, declarative statements that are meant not to open the subjects but to close them. Rude and intolerant, she is living proof that book learning can teach neither virtue nor self-restraint. This learned woman is bossy, self-regarding, thoughtlessly cruel, and so focused on her own thoughts as to be obtuse in social dealings with others. She is worse, not better, than other women; her intellectual explorations lead her only to feel contempt for others.

But, however Lennox tried to cover her tracks as an intellectual, to dissemble her learning, the literary world would not take her back into its embrace. Lennox's bad luck continued after her play *The Sister* was hissed off the stage. Her attempts to reissue her works by subscription failed; she appears to have separated from her husband and he began to grudge her support—and by now she had two children to feed, clothe, and educate as well. As a temporary respite, *Old City Manners* was staged with a lucrative benefit night and subsequently published. But her beloved daughter died, sometime between 1781 and 1783. Her own health suffered. She published her last novel, *Euphemia,* about an unhappily married woman, in 1790; reviewers thought the portrayal of the arrogant and disagreeable husband particularly well and realistically drawn. Then her son, George Lennox, got into trouble, by some contrivance of his "most unnatural father," and Charlotte Lennox appealed to the Royal Literary Fund for passage for him to America where, she said, her relations would receive him kindly. He appears to have sailed.

One sign of the esteem in which she was held, albeit a sad one, is the extent of support given her by the Royal Literary Fund at the end of her life. Very few women even dared to apply for support from this fund, a philanthropic venture sustained by private subscription, founded to relieve distressed writers; only fourteen of the successful applicants to the fund in the first twenty years of its existence were women writers, as compared to sixty-five male writers.[54] But Lennox's applications were accepted, and she was given eleven grants "on account of her urgent distress," amounting to more than eighty-five guineas, a substantial sum, between 1792 and 1804, when she died.[55] The records of Hookham and Carpenter, the booksellers who apparently shared *Euphemia* with Cadell, tell a similar story. They never billed her for the quires of paper, pens, and 150 copies of a folio-page prospectus for *Shakespear Illustrated* (March 21, 1796) that she charged to their account. They also paid for letters that they received for her; she apparently used their office as an accommodation address starting in March 1794, probably when her own residence became uncertain.[56] Altogether, they subsidized her to the amount of five pounds, ten shillings, and four pence—a sign both of her literary repute and of the hard times on which she had fallen. She died in terrible poverty, in 1804, in her midseventies.

Henrietta was written in happier times—before Lennox chose a salary for her husband over a pension for herself, before she had children, before she felt the disapproval of a faction of the literary world for her feminist criticisms of Shakespeare. She wrote this novel while she was still under the illusion that the approbation of Johnson, Boyle, Richardson, et al., together with her own industry, would bring her literary success and prosperity. Henrietta, the fictional heroine, has the energy and certainty that are missing from Lennox's later novels. Perhaps one needs security for satire. *Henrietta* represents an important moment in the history of eighteenth-century fiction as well as in Lennox's own life. Blending aspects of Fielding's and Richardson's methods for telling a story with a woman-centered consciousness and cast of characters, Lennox's novel led the way for the woman writers who came after her in the profession of letters that she labored in for so many years.

NOTES

1. Letter to John Boyle, October 10, 1758, Folger Library, Washington, D.C. We have profited throughout from access to Norbert Schürer's invaluable as-yet-unpublished collection of Charlotte Lennox's letters, for which we are most grateful.

2. The *Public Advertiser* ran an advertisement in 1760 announcing her translation of this book, but it never appeared.

3. Letter to Samuel Johnson, February 3, 1752, Chicago Historical Society.

4. Letter to the Duchess of Newcastle, June 10, 1760, BL Add. MS. 33067, f. 230, British Library, London. This letter may have exaggerated her poverty since she was seeking patronage from the duchess, but probably not by much. The French translation was *The Greek Theater of Father Brumoy*, 3 vols. (London: Millar, 1759–1760).

5. Letter to the Duchess of Newcastle, June 10, 1760.

6. *The Sister* was produced at Covent Garden February 17–20, 1769. For the

records of Millar's sale and Lowndes's share in *Henrietta,* see BL Add. MS. 38730 f. 148, British Library.

7. For a description of this magazine and Harrison's project, including a comparison to the list of novels included in the later *Ballantyne's Novelist's Library,* see Richard C. Taylor, "James Harrison, *The Novelist's Magazine,* and the Early Canonizing of the English Novel," *SEL* 33 (Summer 1993): 629–43.

8. Notably *Evelina* and *The Wanderer,* but also *Cecelia* to some extent.

9. These points are made in the reviews of *Henrietta* in both the *Monthly Review* and the *Critical Review.* For excerpts from these reviews, see Miriam Rossiter Small, *Charlotte Ramsay Lennox: An Eighteenth Century Lady of Letters* (New Haven: Yale University Press, 1935; repr., Hamden, Conn.: Archon, 1969), 136.

10. See Lady Mary Wortley Montagu's letter of March 1, 1752, to her daughter, Lady Bute, in *The Complete Letters of Lady Mary Wortley Montagu,* 3 vols., ed. Robert Halsband (Oxford: Clarendon, 1967), 3:8.

11. Writing to Cassandra on January 7 and 8, 1807, from Southampton, Austen says that the family is reading *The Female Quixote* aloud, "which now makes our evening amusement; to me a very high one, as I find the work quite equal to what I remembered it." *Jane Austen's Letters,* ed. Deirdre Le Faye (Oxford and New York: Oxford University Press, 1997), 116.

12. The libidinous widow or the old maid trying to attract a mate can be found in the Restoration comedies of manners—the ridiculous spectacle of an older woman with the bad taste to be ugly or to have sexual desire, although this figure had disappeared from the stage by the first decade of the eighteenth century. See Elisabeth Mignon, *Crabbed Age and Youth: The Old Men and Women in the Restoration Comedy of Manners* (Durham: Duke University Press, 1947). But Lennox's two characters, who are deluded about their appearance and who imagine that they have put one over on the rest of the world, seem quite original. Mrs. Autumn's perverse insistence that all men are in love with her is reminiscent of Arabella's delusions in *The Female Quixote,* but Mrs. Autumn has more vanity than Arabella and is a middle-aged, married woman.

13. Emily Ravensworth, in Ann Masterman Skinn's *The Old Maid* (1771), defends herself from an unwanted marriage, but her spunkiness is more limited than Henrietta's.

14. James Boswell, *The Life of Samuel Johnson,* 2 vols. (1791; repr., New York: Dutton, 1978), 2:510. Johnson is reported to have said of Lennox, "Mrs. Lenox writes as well as if she could do nothing else, and does every thing else as well as if she could not write." *Edinburgh Weekly Magazine,* October 9, 1783, 36.

15. Duncan Isles, "The Lennox Collection," *Harvard Library Bulletin* 19, no. 1 (January 1971): 44–45.

16. Ibid., 19, no. 4 (October 1971): 419.

17. Ibid., 419–20. Duncan Isles observes that "Partlet," the proper name one gives to a hen, sometimes refers to a woman, and that Shakespeare uses the name several times, including in the first part of *Henry IV* in "a mood of affectionate exasperation"

(420n194). But the usage goes further back: Dame Pertelote is the favorite wife among the harem of Chaucer's cock Chanticleer in the "Nun's Priest's Tale."

18. Letter to Lady Lydia Clerke, June 16, 1777; quoted in Temma Berg, "Charlotte Lennox and Lydia Clerke: Reflecting on Letters," in *Eighteenth-Century Woman*, vol. 2 (New York: AMS, 2002), 61–93. We want to thank Temma Berg for sharing this material with us before it was published and Norbert Schürer for sending xeroxes of the actual letter.

19. Susan Carlile, "Charlotte Lennox's Birth Date and Place," *Notes and Queries*, n.s., 51 (December 2004): 390–92.

20. These facts come from the *Edinburgh Weekly Magazine*, October 9, 1783, 34.

21. Ibid., 34.

22. Letter to Andrew Millar, August 1, [1755], Evelyn Papers, UP 10, British Library.

23. Small, *Charlotte Ramsay Lennox*, 15–17.

24. Quoted in ibid., 217.

25. See Susan Staves's invaluable book, *A Literary History of Women's Writing in Britain, 1660–1789* (Cambridge: Cambridge University Press, 2006), 293–95.

26. According to Norbert Schürer's explanation, Somerset House, owned by the queen, was a kind of almshouse for fallen aristocrats.

27. Philippe Séjourné, *The Mystery of Charlotte Lennox: First Novelist of Colonial America*, n.s., 62 (Aix-en-Provence: Publications des Annales de la Faculté des Lettres, 1967), 19.

28. Letter to Lady Lydia Clerke, June 16, 1777. Lydia Clerke was married to John Clerke, who was knighted in 1772 for his distinguished career in the Royal Navy. According to Temma Berg in her book on Lady Lydia Clerke's correspondence with her many devoted friends, *The Lives and Letters of an Eighteenth-Century Circle of Acquaintance* (Aldershot, U.K., and Burlington, Vt.: Ashgate, 2006), John Clerke was an adventurer, traveling to America, Africa, and India. He was also an adulterous and improvident man who trafficked in illicit wine, became a friend of Warren Hastings, and died in Madras in 1776. His younger brother, Charles Clerke, sailed around the world three times with Captain Cook. When Cook was killed in Hawaii, Clerke took over command of the *Resolution;* he died of consumption off the coast of Russia six months later.

29. Letter to Lady Lydia Clerke, June 16, 1777.

30. On Lennox's authorship of this previously unattributed novel, see Norbert Schürer, "A New Novel by Charlotte Lennox," *Notes and Queries*, n.s., 48 (December 2001): 419–22.

31. *The Letters of Samuel Johnson*, 3 vols., ed. R. W. Chapman (Oxford: Clarendon, 1952) 2:431–32. The Latin, from Seneca, means "great wit is to madness near allied."

32. Isles, "The Lennox Collection," *Harvard Library Bulletin* 19, no. 4 (October 1971): 426–28.

33. January 30, 1793. Again, thanks to Norbert Schürer.

34. Small, *Charlotte Ramsay Lennox,* 59.

35. Ibid., 41.

36. Ibid., 42. All of these people were connected to the theater. Murphy is probably Arthur Murphy (1727–1805), actor, playwright, and barrister, a friend of Samuel Johnson; John Home (1722–1808) was the Scottish author of the extremely popular tragedy *Douglas* (1756); Richard Cumberland (1732–1811), novelist, translator, and playwright, wrote a number of sentimental comedies including *The West Indian* (1771) and *The Brothers* (1769); John Hoole (1727–1803) translated Tasso and wrote three unsuccessful tragedies; Charles Macklin (1697–1797), actor and playwright, celebrated for playing Shylock and Mosca (in Jonson's *Volpone*), wrote the highly successful comedies *Love a la Mode* (1739) and *The Man of the World* (1781); Frances Brooke, née Frances Moore, novelist, playwright, translator, theater manager, essayist, wrote the tragedy *Virginia* earlier in the year that she married John Brooke (1756), who later became chaplain to Quebec.

37. Robert Bataille, in *The Writing Life of Hugh Kelly* (Carbondale: Southern Illinois University Press, 2000), addresses the question of Kelly's involvement in the *Lady's Museum,* claiming that "it is doubtful that Kelly did more than follow Lennox's directions" (5).

38. Margaret Anne Doody, "Shakespeare's Novels: Charlotte Lennox Illustrated," *Studies in the Novel* 19 (Fall 1987): 306.

39. Sylvia Braithwaite Thornton was married to Bonnell Thornton in 1768. In her will, proved in 1793, she leaves sentimental gifts to Lady Clerke, and to Charlotte Lennox several cloaks and garments and five guineas, as if she knew Lennox needed clothes. In a codicil, she leaves Lennox's picture to her sister. We are grateful to the invaluable and ever-generous Betty Rizzo for sending this information about Sylvia Braithwaite Thornton.

40. Staves, *A Literary History of Women's Writing in Britain,* 376.

41. Ibid., 375.

42. For example, Lennox objects to the way women's friendship is portrayed in *Othello.* Laura Runge catalogs the "legacy of irritated responses" aroused by Lennox's *Shakespear Illustrated* in her *Gender and Language in British Literary Criticism, 1660–1790* (Cambridge: Cambridge University Press, 1997), 137–47. See also Susan Green, "A Cultural Reading of Charlotte Lennox's *Shakespear Illustrated,*" in *Cultural Readings of Restoration and Eighteenth-Century English Theater,* ed. J. Douglas Canfield and Deborah C. Payne (Athens and London: University of Georgia Press, 1995), 228–57.

43. Brian Vickers, quoted in Runge, *Gender and Language in British Literary Criticism,* 137.

44. Ibid., 138; Small, *Charlotte Ramsay Lennox,* 17, 198.

45. Quoted in Runge, *Gender and Language in British Literary Criticism,* 138.

46. August 12, [1753], in Duncan Isles, "The Lennox Collection," *Harvard Library Bulletin* 19, no. 1 (January 1971): 40–41.

47. This play was adapted from *Eastward Ho!* by Ben Jonson, Marston, and

Chapman. When it was printed, Lennox acknowledged Garrick's help in the adaptation on the title page. Small, *Charlotte Ramsay Lennox*, 43.

48. Ibid., 37.

49. February 20, 1769, in Duncan Isles, "The Lennox Collection," *Harvard Library Bulletin* 19, no. 2 (April 1971): 167–68. Many believed that Richard Cumberland was behind the premeditated damning of the play. Small, *Charlotte Ramsay Lennox*, 172.

50. The first edition of *The Sister* was announced in the *London Chronicle* for March 4, 1769, and the *St. James Chronicle*, March 4–7, 1769, and the second edition was announced for March 19, 1769.

51. Small, *Charlotte Ramsay Lennox*, 174–76.

52. Ellen Donkin notes that there were two historical clusters of women writing for the stage, the first from 1670 (Aphra Behn) to 1718 (Susanna Centlivre) and the second from 1770 to 1800. *Getting into the Act: Women Playwrights in London, 1776–1829* (London: Routledge, 1995), 19.

53. This is chapter 2 of *L'Ami des femmes ou La Morale du sexe* by Pierre Joseph de Villemert, published in French in 1758. It was translated into English anonymously in 1766 by someone other than Lennox under the title *The Ladies Friend,* and this chapter was called "What Studies Are Proper for the Sex?" Thanks to Norbert Schürer for this information.

54. Jenny Batchelor, "The Claims of Literature: Women Applicants to the Royal Literary Fund, 1790–1810," *Women's Writing* 12, no. 3 (2005): 505–21. Of the fourteen women who applied to the fund under their own names, three were actresses, two were writers of educational works, one a travel writer, one a poet, and seven were novelists: Ann Burke, Phebe Gibbes, Elizabeth Helme, Maria Hunter, Charlotte Lennox, Eliza Norman, and Eliza Parsons.

55. The exact disbursements of the fund, including the weekly allowance paid Lennox in her last year, can be found in Small, *Charlotte Ramsay Lennox*, 57–58.

56. We are grateful to Jan Fergus for a copy of this page—the National Archives: PRO [Public Record Office] C104/75/1–3, Kew, U.K.—from the Hookham and Carpenter ledgers, and for helping to interpret its meaning.

CHRONOLOGY

1729/1730	Born to James and Catherine Ramsay, between March 11, 1729, and March 9, 1730, in Gibraltar. The family returns to England while Charlotte is still an infant.
1739	Ramsay family moves from England to Albany, New York, where James Ramsay is captain of an independent company.
1742	James Ramsay dies in Albany, New York (March 10). Soon after, Charlotte returns to England and is patronized by Lady Cecilia Isabella Finch and the Marchioness of Rockingham.
1746	Plays Lavinia in *The Fair Penitent*.
1747	Marries Alexander Lennox at St. George's Chapel, Mayfair, London (October 6). *Poems on Several Occasions* published in London (November). "Charlotte Ramsay" appears on the dedication page.
1748	Acts in a play at Richmond.
1750	*The Life of Harriot Stuart,* "written by herself," published in London (Dublin, 1751; Amsterdam, 1752; London, 1771). Stars as the main protagonist, Almeria, in Congreve's *The Mourning Bride*. "The Art of Coquetry" reprinted from *Poems on Several Occasions* and "The Birthday Ode to the Princess of Wales," by "Mrs. Lennox," in *Gentleman's Magazine* (November 20).
1752	*The Female Quixote* published in London (London, 1752; Dublin, 1752; Hamburg and Leipzig, 1754; Amsterdam, 1762; Dublin, 1763; Lyon, 1773; London, 1783; London, 1799; London, from Paris, 1801; Madrid, 1808; and in *British Novelists* 24 and 25, 1810 and 1820).

1753–1754   *Shakespear Illustrated* (3 vols.) published in
                 London (Philadelphia, 1809).
1756   *The Memoirs of the Duke of Sully*, translated
                 from the French, published in London (London,
                 1757; Edinburgh, 1760; London, 1761; London,
                 1763; Edinburgh, 1770; Edinburgh, 1773;
                 London, 1778; London, 1778; Dublin, 1781;
                 London, 1805; London, 1810; London, 1812;
                 Edinburgh, 1812; Philadelphia, 1817; Edinburgh,
                 1819; London, 1819; London, 1856).
                 The Memoirs of the Countess of Berci, translated
                 from the French, published in London.
                 The Memoirs of Count de Cominge, translated from
                 the French, published in London.
1757   *Memoirs for the History of Madame de Maintenon*,
                 translated from the French, published in London
                 (Dublin, 1758).
1758   *Philander* (dramatic pastoral) published in
                 London, but never performed (Dublin, 1758).
                 Henrietta published in London and in Dublin
                 (Lausanne and Paris, 1760; London, 1761;
                 London, 1769; London, 1770; Frankfurt, 1771;
                 Paris, 1775; Stockholm, 1781–1782; Dublin,
                 1786; London, 1787; Paris, 1789; London, 1798).
1760   *The Greek Theater of Father Brumoy*, translated
                 from the French, published in London.
1760 (March)–   *The Lady's Museum*, monthly periodical published
1761 (February) in London. This included the serialized novel
                 "The History of Harriot and Sophia," later the
                 novel *Sophia; The History of the Count de Cominge;*
                 "History of the Dutchess of Beaufort" from *The
                 Memoirs of Sully;* and some of Lennox's poems.
1761   Lennox's portrait painted by Sir Joshua Reynolds,
                 which is later engraved by Cooke and Bartolozzi.
1762   *Sophia*, previously "The History of Harriot and
                 Sophia," published in London (Paris, 1770).
1764   Names and ending changed in *The History of the
                 Count de Cominge* and published as *The History of
                 the Marquis of Lussan and Isabella.*

1765	Lennox's daughter, Harriot Holles Lennox, baptized (April 28).
1767	*The History of Eliza* published in London.
1769	*The Sister* staged by George Colman (February 18) and published twice that year in London and once in Dublin (Hamburg, 1776; Vienna, 1776; Frankfurt, 1777; Moscow, 1788; Regensburg, Germany, 1802).
1772	Lennox's son, George Louis (or Lewis) Lennox, born.
1774	*Meditations and Penitential Prayers* translated from the French, published in London.
1775	*Old City Manners* staged in London (November 9), followed by seven more performances and publication in London.
1778	Appears in Richard Samuel's portrait *The Nine Living Muses of Great Britain,* which also includes Elizabeth Carter, Anna Laetitia Barbauld, Angelica Kauffman, Frances Sheridan, Catherine Macaulay, Hannah More, Elizabeth Montague, and Elizabeth Griffith.
1781–1783	Lennox's daughter, Harriot Holles, dies.
1783	George Lennox's short fiction "Annette: A Fairy Tale" serialized in the *British Magazine and Review* (October and December) and reprinted in the *Edinburgh Weekly Magazine* (1783–1784), the *New Novelist's Magazine* (1786), the *Hibernian* (1783–1784), and the *Gleaner* (1805).
1787	George Lennox's short novel *The Duke of Milan* printed in the *New Novelist's Magazine* (April–May) and *Weekly Entertainer.*
1790	*Euphemia* published in London.
1792	Subsidized by the Royal Literary Fund until her death.
1793	George Lennox emigrates to Baltimore, Maryland (August).
1804	Dies in Dean's Yard, Westminster, and is buried in Broad Chapel.

NOTE ON THE TEXT

The first edition of *Henrietta* was advertised on February 2, 1758, and the second, corrected edition, which we have used as the copytext, was first announced on March 17, 1761, in the *London Chronicle*. We have listed variations between the two editions in appendix I. We chose the second edition as a copytext for this modern edition because it was probably corrected by Lennox, who was living in London at the time, with access to the bookseller's (Millar) premises where the second edition was produced. The second edition consistently represents a more polished version of the novel, probably Lennox's attempt to attract a wider audience. In this edition spelling has sometimes been modernized in such changes as *catholick* to *catholic* and *raillying* to *rallying*, and a more modern use of semicolons and commas makes for easier reading. A more elevated style has replaced simpler, more direct language, such as the change from "nothing" to "a trifle" and from "anxious to get out" to "desirous of leaving." These alterations represent an inflation of tone and diction, an attempt to be more elegant. Type names (both male and female), such as Bale (a merchant), Measure (a mantua maker), Fig (a grocer), Haggle (a broker), Steam (a soap boiler), Traffik (a baronet), Supple (a sympathetic waiting woman), Vellum (a clerk), and Echo (a gossip), have been replaced by more plausible and realistic names in this second edition: Damer, Cary, Jennings, Collins, Rogers, Harris, Smith, Jones, and Ellis. Details about the passage of time and sums of money have been corrected, making them more realistic and less arbitrary. For example, Henrietta's brother is described as having been abroad for ten years in the first edition. However, in the revised version he has been gone for "several years." Given their young age and the story line, "several years" is a much more likely time span than ten. Roughly 20 percent of the original plates were reset to accommodate these improvements.

Although most details of the plot have been left entirely as they were in the first edition, the omission of one passage suggests a shift in the depiction of the character of Henrietta. In the first edition, Henrietta's description of her elderly suitor, Mr. Danvers, suggests a slightly more malicious and spirited character than is portrayed in the second edition of the text: "When we were placed at table, I found myself opposite to him; and observing that he chewed his meat with great difficulty, for want of teeth, I was resolved to mortify him, by letting him perceive that I observed it, looking at him several times with a kind of sensibility for this so unavoidable a misfortune." This passage is omitted in the second edition, creating a more conventionally decorous picture of Henrietta, and one aligned more completely with her otherwise high-toned behavior. This change, together with alterations in diction, makes the novel less of a burlesque and more conventionally sentimental. Although Henrietta is still adventurous and opinionated in the second edition, she is not saucy. Henrietta has been slightly tamed; perhaps Lennox thought this would satisfy her audience.

There are several factors that point to the probability of Lennox's hand in these corrections. During 1760–1761 she was regularly involved in the publishing world. On February 21, 1760, her translation of *The Greek Theatre of Father Brumoy* was published (*London Chronicle*). On August 1–2, 1760, the *Public Advertiser* advertised her translation of a text by Voltaire named "Histoire de CZAAR Pierre le Grand. Par M. De VOLTAIRE. The English Translation being made by Mrs. Charlotte Lennox." to be published "In a few Days," although nothing more was heard of this work. During this time Lennox was also editing the periodical *The Lady's Museum,* which ran from March 1760 to February 1761. To be this active as a woman in the London publishing market suggests that she was her own greatest advocate. The meticulous correction of this edition of *Henrietta* reveals a care that its author might be more inclined to give than a printer. After the first edition was published, a letter she wrote to Lord Orrery on October 29, 1758, indicates her concern for the second, corrected edition and how she looked forward to her full share in its profits, explaining that this time the profits "will be all my own." Her financial compensation translated into a greater feeling of ownership over this revised and corrected edition. She may have also desired to improve it, since she complained in a letter on October 6, 1760, that the first edition was "so hurried." The edition of 1761 is the first to bear Lennox's name, both on the title page and at the end of the dedication. Instead of reading, as does the 1758 title page, "The Author of The Female Quixote," the 1761 title page reads "By Mrs. Charlotte Lennox." Lennox corresponded with the Duchess of Newcastle, to whom she dedicated this edition, just a little over a month (October 6, 1760) before the date of the dedication (London, November 20, 1760), complaining of her "incessant slavery to the booksellers," which is another indication of how hard she was working this year.

In editing this text, we have sought to remain faithful to the 1761 spelling and punctuation. For example, this edition maintains spellings such as "to-morrow" and "visiter" and the inconsistent use of apostrophes. We have made alterations in the following instances: eliminating running quotes, regularizing dashes and the number of spaces to indent paragraphs—since any variation is typographical rather than intentional—modernizing the long s, and regularizing opening and closing quotes. In cases where typographical errors impair the meaning we correct them and list them in appendix II. Our notes include explanations of eighteenth-century words that do not appear in a standard dictionary of today.

HENRIETTA.

BY

Mrs. CHARLOTTE LENNOX.

IN TWO VOLUMES.
VOL. I.

The SECOND EDITION, Corrected.

LONDON:

Printed for A. MILLAR, in the Strand.

MDCCLXI.

TO HER GRACE

The Duchess of Newcastle.

MADAM,

The condescension and benignity with which your Grace has hitherto favoured my performances and attempts, have at last given me boldness enough to entreat your patronage for a little novel.

Those to whom this book is new, will expect the name of such a patroness to be followed by some work of deep research and elevated dignity; but they whose nearer approaches to your Grace, have enabled them to distinguish your private virtues, will not be disappointed when they find it recommended only by purity and innocence. To obtain the approbation of a judgment like yours, it is necessary to mean well; and to gain kindness from such benevolence, to mean well is commonly sufficient.

Had your Grace resolved only to countenance those who could have enlarged your knowledge, or refined your sentiments, few could have aspired to the honour of your notice, and far had I been removed from all hope of the favours which I have enjoyed, and the expectations which I have been permitted to indulge. But true greatness is always accessible, and pride will never be confounded with dignity by those who remember that your Grace has admitted this address from,

MADAM,

Your Grace's most obliged, and
Most devoted Servant,

London,
Nov. 20, 1760.

Charlotte Lennox.

CONTENTS.

BOOK I.

BOOK II.

HENRIETTA.

BOOK THE FIRST.

CHAP. I.

*Which introduces our Heroine to the Acquaintance of the Reader in
no very advantageous Situation.*

About the middle of July, 17———, when the Windsor stage-coach with
the accustomed number of passengers was proceeding on its way to
London, a young woman genteely dressed, with a small parcel tied up in
her handkerchief, hastily bolted from the shelter of a large tree near the road;
and calling to the coachman to stop for a moment, asked him, if he could
let her have a place? The man, although he well knew his vehicle was already
sufficiently crouded, yet being desirous of appropriating this supernumerary
fare to himself, replied, that he did not doubt but he could find room for her;
and, jumping off his box, begged the company to sit close, and give the young
woman a place.

"What do you mean?" said a jolly fat woman, with a face as red as scarlet,
"Have you not got your usual number of passengers? Do you think we will be
stifled with heat to put money into your pocket?" "There is room enough for such
a slender young body as this," said the coachman, "if you would but sit closer."

"Sit closer!" repeated the dame, and spreading her cloaths, "Don't you see
we are crouded to death: how dare you pretend to impose another passenger
upon us, when your coach is already full?"

"Well," said a tall lean woman, who sat next her, "This is the first time
I ever travelled in a stage-coach, and truly I am sick of it already. There is no
bearing the insults one is exposed to in these carriages. Prithee, young woman,"
pursued she, with an air of great contempt, "Go about your business, you see there
is no room for you—And do you, fellow, get on your box, and drive on."

"*Fellor* me! no *fellors*," said the coachman, in a surly tone, "I won't drive
till I please. Who are you, pray, that takes so much upon you to order me?"

"Who am I, you fancy Jack-a-napes," said the lady, "a person that—but I shall not demean myself so much as to tell you who I am: it is my misfortune to be stuffed up in a stage-coach at present—what I have never been used to, I assure you."

"Good lack-a-day!" said the fat gentlewoman, with a sneer, "A great misfortune truly—I would have you to know, madam, your betters ride in stage-coaches. Here's a coil indeed with such would-be-gentry."

"Good woman," said the other, with an affected calmness, "Pray don't direct your impertinent discourse to me, I have nothing to say to you."

"No more a good woman than yourself," said the plump lady, with a face doubly inflamed with rage; "I scorn your words."

"Very likely;" said a grave man, who sat on the opposite side, "but I wish it was possible to make room for the young gentlewoman."—"Ah! God bless your honour," said the coachman, "I thought you could not find in your heart to let such a pretty young woman as this walk."

"Pretty!" exclaimed the haughty lady—"You are a fine judge of beauty indeed—but I will not submit to be crouded, fellow: so you and your pretty passenger may ride on the coach-box, if you please."

"Nay, since you come to that," says the fat gentlewoman, "I am resolved you shall not have your own way—The young woman may be as good as you; and she shall not be obliged to ride on the coach-box—So open the door, coachman," said she, shoving her antagonist at the same time with all her force—"Here is room enough."

A young gentlewoman in a riding-habit, who sat on the same side, but next the widow, declared that she was willing to give part of her seat to the stranger; and begged the haughty lady to yield. "Poh," said the rosy matron, "don't stand begging and praying her; since you are on my side, we will be too hard for her, I warrant you." Saying this, she put one of her huge arms round the young woman's waist; and thus reinforced, shoved her neighbour so forcibly against the other window, that she cried out with pain and vexation.

The young lady without, who had been the occasion of this contest, and who had hitherto stood silent, with her hat over her eyes, alarmed by the screams of her foe, raised her head; and in a tone of voice so sweet, as immediately fixed the attention of the whole company, intreated them not to quarrel upon her account: it was indeed, she said, of great consequence to her to be admitted, but she would not continue to desire it, since her request had produced so much uneasiness among them.

The passengers who occupied the other side of the coach were two men and a woman big with child; which circumstance had made it impossible for the men to offer her a seat with them, for fear of incommoding the pregnant woman. But the youngest of the men having now got a glimpse of the stranger's face, declared that the ladies might make themselves easy, for he would resign his seat; adding, that he was extremely glad he had an opportunity of obliging such a handsome lady. He then jumped out of the coach, and taking the stranger's hand to help her in, stared confidently under her hat, which put her into a little confusion: however, she thanked him very politely, and accepted his offer; but not without expressing some concern for the manner in which he would dispose of himself.

"Oh! madam," said the coachman, "the gentleman may sit upon the box with me, and he will have the pleasure of viewing the beautiful prospects all the way we go."—"I shall see none so beautiful," said the young fellow, "as what they who remain in the coach will behold."

The fair stranger now blushed more than before, and being willing to avoid any farther speeches of this sort, she hastily got into the coach, thanked the young man a second time, who having seen her seated, placed himself by the coachman on the box, and they proceeded on their journey.

Chap. II.

The commencement of a violent friendship between two young ladies, which has the usual consequences, a communication of secrets, by which the reader is let into part of Henrietta's story.

A profound silence now prevailed among the company in the coach; the eyes of all were fastened upon the fair stranger, who appeared wholly insensible of the scrutinizing looks of her fellow-travellers. Something within herself seemed to engross all her thoughts, and although by her eyes being constantly turned towards the windows of the coach, it might be imagined the passing objects drew her attention, yet their fixed looks too plainly indicated that they were beheld without observation. Her person, though full of charms, and the easy gracefulness of her air, impressed less respect for her on the minds of the women, than the elegance of her morning-dress, which they were now at leisure to consider. Her gown was a white sprig'd muslin, extremely fine, through which shone a rich blue Mantua silk petticoat: her cap, handkerchief, and ruffles were trimmed with fine Brussels lace: her apron had a broad border round it of Dresden work; and a white lutestring hat shaded her charming face, which she was solicitous to conceal from view.

The melancholy with which she seemed oppressed, conciliated to her the good-will of her female fellow-travellers, though from very different senti-ments. The haughty lady, who had refused to let her have a place in the coach, found her envy and ill-nature insensibly subside, by the consideration that this stranger was probably more unhappy than herself.

The lusty matron, pleased that by insisting upon receiving her, she had con-ferred an obligation on one who appeared to be of a rank above her own, enjoyed her present superiority, and pitied her from the overflowings of gratified pride.

The young lady in the riding-habit, whose vanity had been a little morti-fied at seeing herself associated in a journey with persons whom she conceived to be very unfit company for her, thought herself very happy in the acquisition of so genteel a fellow-traveller; and as she had not deign'd to open her mouth before, from an opinion of the meanness of her company, she now made herself amends for her silence, by addressing a profusion of civil speeches to the fair stranger, who replied to every thing she said with extreme politeness, but with an air that showed her heart was not at ease.

The passengers being set down at different places, miss Courteney, for that was the name of our fair adventurer, remained alone with the young lady in the coach. This circumstance seemed to rouze her from a deep revery, in which she had been wholly absorbed during the last half hour; and looking earnestly at her companion, "Ah! madam," said she, in a most affecting accent, "and when am I to lose you?" "I shall leave you in a few minutes," said the lady; "for I am going no farther than Hammersmith."[1] "Lord bless me!" said miss Courteney, lifting up her fine eyes swimming in tears, "What shall I do? what will become of me?"

This exclamation gave great surprize to the other lady, who from several circumstances had conceived that there was some mystery in her case. "You seem uneasy," said she to miss Courteney, "pray let me know if it is in my power to serve you."

This kind request had such an effect on the tender heart of miss Cour-teney, that she burst into tears, and for a few moments was unable to answer; when the lady pressing her to speak freely, "I am an unhappy creature, madam," said she, sighing; "and am flying from the only person in the world upon whom I have any dependence. I will make no scruple to trust you with my secret. Did you ever hear of lady Meadows," pursued she, "the widow of Sir John Meadows?"

"I know a lady who is acquainted with her," said the other, "she is a woman of fashion and fortune."

"Lady Meadows is my relation," resumed miss Courteney; "she took me, a poor helpless orphan, under her protection, and during some time treated me with the tenderness of a mother. Within these few weeks I have unhappily lost her favour, not by any fault of mine, I assure you, for I have always loved and reverenced her. Nothing should have obliged me to take this step, which has no doubt an appearance of ingratitude, but the fear of being forced to marry a man I hate."

"O heavens! my dear creature," exclaimed the lady in an affected tone, "What do you tell me! were you upon the point of being forced to a detested match?" "Yes, madam," replied miss Courteney; "and to this hard lot was I doomed by her to whom I owe all my past happiness, and from whom I expected all the future."

"You have obliged me excessively by this unreserved confidence," interrupted the lady; "and you shall find me not unworthy of it. From this moment I swear to you an inviolable attachment. Sure there is nothing so transporting as friendship and mutual confidence! You won my heart the moment I saw you. I have formed a hundred violent friendships, but one accident or other always dissolved them in a short time. There are very few persons that are capable of a violent friendship; at least I never could find one that answered my ideas of that sort of engagement. Have not you been often disappointed? tell me, my dear: I dare say you have. Your sentiments, I believe, are as delicate as mine upon this head. I am charmed, I am ravished with this meeting! Who would have imagined that by chance, and in a stage-coach, I should have found what I have so earnestly sought for these three months, a person with whom I could contract a violent friendship, such as minds like ours are only capable of feeling."

"I am extremely obliged to you, madam, for your good opinion," said miss Courteney; "I hope I shall never be so unfortunate as to forfeit it; indeed I have reason to think that in my present distressed situation, a friend is a blessing sent from heaven."

"Well! but my dear Clelia," said this flighty lady, "you have not told me all your story—I call you Clelia, because you know it is so like common acquaintance to address one another by the title of Miss such a one—Romantick names give a spirit to the correspondence between such friends as you and I are; but perhaps you may like another name better than Clelia; though I think that is a mighty pretty one, so soft and gliding, Clelia, Clelia—tell me do you like it, my dear?"

"Call me what you please," said miss Courteney, smiling a little at the singularity of her new friend; "but my name is Courteney."

"Courteney is a very pretty sirname," said the lady; "I hope it is not disgraced with any odious vulgar christian name, such as Molly, or Betty, or the like."

"I was christened Henrietta, after my mother," said miss Courteney. "Henrietta is well enough"—returned the other; "but positively, my dear, you must assume the name of Clelia when you write to me; for we must correspond every hour—Oh! what a ravishing pleasure it is to indulge the overflowings of one's heart upon paper! Remember to call me Celinda in your letters; and in all our private conversations, we shall have a thousand secrets to communicate to each other. But I am impatient to know all your story; it must needs be very romantick and pretty."

"Alas!" said the charming Henrietta, "this is no time to talk of my misfortunes; we are entered into Hammersmith, and there you say you must leave me: give me your advice, dear madam, tell me in what manner I must dispose of myself."

"*Dear madam*," repeated the lady—"is that the style then you resolve to use; have you forgot that we have contracted a violent friendship, and that I am your Celinda, and you my Clelia?"

"I beg your pardon," said Henrietta; "I did not think of that name: well then, dear Celinda, what would you advise me to do? I am going to London, there to conceal myself from the search that lady Meadows will doubtless make for me when she hears I have left her house: all my hope of a reconciliation with her is through the interposition of a friend. I have a brother, who has been abroad several years, and whom I every day expect to hear is arrived; but I dare not show myself to any of lady Meadows's acquaintance, lest I should be hurried back, and sacrificed to what she calls my interest. I know so little of the town, that I am afraid I may take up my residence in an improper house, among people where my honour, or at least my reputation, may be in danger. Direct me, dear madam—My dear Celinda, I would say, direct me what to do in this dreadful dilemma." Here she paused, anxiously expecting the answer of her new friend, which will be found in the following chapter.

Chap. III.

Which illustrates an observation of Rochefoucault's, that in the misfortunes of our friends there is always something that does not displease us.[2]

I protest, my dearest Clelia," said the lady, your fears are very natural upon this occasion. I should in your situation be almost distracted. Even our parents' watchful cares are hardly sufficient to guard us against the attempts of insolent men: how much more then are those attempts to be dreaded, when we are left defenceless and exposed. Believe me, my dear, I sympathize truly with you in this misfortune. Good Heaven! I think I should die with apprehension were I in your case."

"Don't terrify me," said miss Courteney, trembling. "I have taken an imprudent step, but I must make the best of it now: Providence, I hope, will be my guard."

"I would not terrify you, my dear," said the lady; "but I must repeat, that were I in your case, I think my fears would distract me. Thank Heaven! I am protected by watchful parents, cautious relations, and prudent friends; yet hardly thus can I think myself secure from these enterprising wretches the men."

This young lady had indeed a stronger protector than all these, which she did not mention, or perhaps was insensible of; and that was the extreme disagreeableness of her whole person. Her features, it is true, could not be called irregular, because few faces were ever distinguished with a set more uniformly bad. Her complexion, which was a composition of green and yellow, was marvellously well suited to her features. Nor was it possible to make any invidious comparisons between her face and her shape, since it was hard to decide which was worse.

Miss Courteney, who had burst into tears, occasioned by her reflections on her own helpless situation, compared with the advantages her friend enjoyed, and which she had so ostentatiously enumerated, was upon the point of soliciting her advice again; when the lady joyfully exclaimed, "Oh! there is my aunt's house, my dear Clelia, we must part immediately."

"Sure," said Henrietta, sighing, "you will not leave me till you have advised me what to do."

"Lord! my dear," said the other, "one young creature is not qualified to give another advice upon such occasions. I wish it was in my power to give you proper advice; you know I have vowed to you an inviolable friendship. And,"—

Here the coachman, as he had been directed, stopped before a large handsome house; and a well-dressed footman immediately appearing, came forwards to open the coachdoor.

"Hear me one word," cried miss Courteney, perceiving this tender friend was actually going to leave her without any farther solicitude for her safety— "upon the strength of that inviolable friendship you have vowed to me, I will venture to ask a favour of you: it is, pursued she, that you will recommend me to some person of your acquaintance in London, who may direct me to a decent house, where I can remain in safety till my brother's arrival."

"I vow this is a lucky thought," said the lady; "I believe I can serve you, my dear Clelia; but you must step in with me to my aunt's. John," said she to the servant, "is my aunt at home." The man told her his lady was just gone to take an airing.

"That's well" said the lady, "we shall have an opportunity to settle this matter: but, my dear Clelia, I think it will be best to discharge the coach, the fellow possibly will not wait. I'll send my aunt's servant to take a place for you in the Hammersmith stage, which I know does not set out this half hour."

Henrietta readily complied, overjoyed that she had really found a sincere friend in the person of this whimsical lady; who, having led her into a large well-furnished parlour, ordered some tea to be brought, and then told her, that she would give her a letter to her millener, who was a very good sort of a woman, and where she might depend upon being absolutely safe.

"When I was last in town," pursued she, "which was about three weeks ago, her first floor was empty; and in this season of the year, I believe she will let it to you for two guineas³ a week."

"A single room will do for me," said miss Courteney; "my circumstances do not entitle me to magnificent lodgings, and my business is to keep myself private."

"Well, well, my dear, be that as you please." said the other; "I will write the letter without mentioning what lodgings you require." Saying this, she called for pens and paper; and having wrote the following billet, gave it to miss Courteney for her perusal.

> Dear Mrs. EGRET,
> THE lady who will deliver you this, is one for whom I have the most violent friendship imaginable. You know how ardent my friendships are; but I think I never had any so firmly rooted as this, though our acquaintance commenced but a few hours ago. This dear friend having desired me to recommend her to some person to lodge with, I thought of you, knowing you can accommodate her with genteel apartments. I am, dear Mrs. Egret,
> Your humble servant,
> E. WOODBY.

Henrietta having read the letter, returned it again into the hands of her friend, gratefully acknowledging the favour, although she had some objections to it; for she did not approve of the words genteel apartments, being resolved not to exceed a very moderate price: but she rightly conceived that miss Woodby rather listened to her own pride than her conveniency, by throwing in that circumstance, and therefore took no notice of it.

The letter being sealed and directed, miss Courteney carefully deposited it in her pocket, and the two ladies were preparing to drink their tea, when the footman entered, and said the stage-coach was just going off: our fair traveller instantly rose up, and took leave of her friend, who having prevailed upon her to drink a glass of sack[4] and water, since she was disappointed of her tea, parted from her with an affectionate embrace, and a promise that she would see her in town very shortly.

Miss Courteney finding only one passenger in the coach, who was a grave elderly woman, she resumed her journey with some kind of chearfulness, having thus happily got over her apprehensions of falling into bad company, where chance might have directed her to lodge.

CHAP. IV.

In which our heroine, through inattention, falls into the very difficulty she had taken such pains to avoid.

But this cessation from uneasiness did not last long: for the mind which can fasten with violence but upon one circumstance of distress at a time, and being suddenly relieved from that, is sensible of a calm, which, compared with its former feelings, may be called pleasure, yet soon selects another object to engross its attention, and fixes on it with equal anxiety and sollicitude. Thus it fared with our lovely heroine, whose others cares had all been swallowed up in reflections on the danger to which her honour was exposed. Eased of these apprehensions by the good offices of miss Woodby, she was happy for a few moments, till the consequences of her flight rush'd full upon her mind: lady Meadows's favour irrecoverable; her fortune ruined; her reputation blasted. This last thought, which, from the delicacy of her sentiments, gave her the deepest regret, dwelt most upon her mind; and forgetting that she was not alone, she clasped her hands together in a violent emotion, and burst into tears.

The old gentlewoman, who had been eying her very attentively, not a little surprised at the seriousness that appeared in the looks and behaviour of so young a creature, eagerly asked her, What was the matter?

Henrietta, rouzed by this question, which, (so absent had she been) first informed her she was observed, wiped her eyes, and composing her counte-nance, said she was often low-spirited.

"Don't tell me of low spirits," said the old gentlewoman, "such young bodies as you are not low-spirited for nothing. What! I warrant you, there is a sweetheart in the case."

"Oh! no, madam," said miss Courteney, blushing, "no sweetheart, I assure you."

"No really," resumed she; "well then, I suppose you have lost a friend."

"I have indeed lost a friend," said the young lady, hoping that acknowledgment would put an end to the questions of her fellow-traveller.

"Indeed!" said the old woman; "and this friend—is it a father, or mother, or sister, or—"

"All, all," interrupted miss Courteney; bursting again into tears.

"How all?" repeated the old woman. "Have you just now lost all these kinsfolks?"

"I lost them all in losing that friend, madam," said Henrietta; vexed that her sensibility, wakened by such questions, had made her too little guarded in her expressions.

"Oh, Oh, I understand you, child," said the good gentlewomen: "this person, I don't ask you whether it was a man or woman, was to you both father and mother. Well, and so I suppose you have just heard of the death of this good friend, and are going to town on that occasion."

Miss Courteney finding that the inquisitive temper of her fellow-traveller was likely to lead her into a discovery of her situation, chose rather to be silent than violate truth, by feigning circumstances, to deceive her; and, fortunately for her, she was prevented from suffering more disagreeable interrogatories, by the coach suddenly stopping at an inn in Piccadilly, where it put up.

The old gentlewoman, however, at parting, asked her what part of the town she was going, to, and offered, if it was in her way, to accompany her; but Henrietta evaded the question and the offer, by telling her, that she intended to take a chair.[5] The coachman accordingly called one for her, which she entered immediately; and being asked by the chairman where she would please to be carried? she recollected with great confusion, that miss Woodby had not told her where her millener lived.

She now sought for the letter, hoping there was a full direction upon that. But what was her grief and perplexity, when she found the superscription contained only these words "For Mrs. Egret." "Good Heaven!" exclaimed the fair unfortunate, "what shall I do now?"

The chairman repeating his question, she told him that she had forgot a direction, and asked him, if he knew where Mrs. Egret, a millener, lived? The fellow replied in the negative; but added, that he would enquire. He accordingly stepped into the nearest shop, which was a haberdasher's, and making a small blunder in the name, which the person he spoke to mistook for Eccles, he was told, that the millener for whom he enquired, lived in Charles street.

The fellow returned, extremely pleased with his success, and relieved the young lady from her anxiety, who bid him carry her directly to Charles street; and she soon found herself at the door of a millener's shop, where she discharged her chairmen; and entering, asked a young woman, whom she saw at work, if her mistress was at home?

The girl desired her to walk into a parlour, where she was met by an agreeable well-dressed woman, who received her with great politeness, and desired to know her commands.

"I have a letter for you," said Henrietta, putting it into her hands, "from a young lady, a customer of yours: the contents will acquaint you with my business."

The millener took the letter, and having read it, returned it again with a smile, saying, "She was not the person to whom it was addressed."

"No! madam," said miss Courteney, excessively surprised, "Is not your name Egret?"

"My name is Eccles, madam," said the millener. "Bless me!" cried miss Courteney, "the chairmen have made a mistake: I bid one of them enquire where Mrs. Egret, a millener, lived, and he was directed hither. I shall be obliged to you," pursued Henrietta, "if you will let your maid call a chair."

"To be sure, madam," said the millener; "but do you not know where this Mrs. Egret lives?"

"I have unfortunately forgot to get a direction," returned the young lady; "but I hope you can inform me."

"I wish I could, madam," said the millener; "but really I know no such person as Mrs. Egret." "Surely I am the most unfortunate creature in the world!" cried Henrietta.

"I hope not, madam," said Mrs. Eccles, with a look of great complacency: "there are more persons, besides Mrs. Egret, who would be glad to accommodate you with lodgings. I wish mine were good enough for you."

"Oh! they are good enough, no doubt," replied miss Courteney; "but I was recommended to Mrs. Egret, and"—"Pray, madam, walk up, and look at my first floor," said Mrs. Eccles; and, without waiting for any reply, immediately led the way.

Henrietta followed in such perplexity of mind, that she hardly knew what she did; and, while the officious millener led her from room to room, expatiating at large upon the conveniencies, she continued silent, revolving in her thoughts the dilemma to which she was reduced.

The evening was so far advanced, that she could not think of going in quest of Mrs. Egret, of whom she could get no information here; yet she was not able to resolve upon taking lodgings in the house of a person, to whom she was an absolute stranger: a misfortune which she had vainly endeavoured to avoid by the application she had made to miss Woodby.

"I am afraid you don't like this apartment, madam," said Mrs. Eccles; who observed her look pensive and uneasy. "I have no objection to it," said miss Courteney; "but that it is rather too good. I do not propose to go to a high price; a bedchamber and the use of a parlour will be sufficient for me."

The millener looked a little dissatisfied at these words, but told her she could accommodate her with a large handsome bedchamber up two pair of stairs, but added, that she had no other parlour than that which she kept for her own use.

Miss Courteney desired to see the room, which was indeed very handsome and convenient; and the millener perceiving she liked it, told her, that she should be welcome to the use of the dining-room till her first floor was let.

The young lady thought this an obliging proposal; and being pleased with the woman's countenance and behaviour, ventured to make an agreement with her, and every thing being settled upon very easy terms, "there is but one difficulty remaining," said she, with an engaging smile, "and that I know not how we shall get over; we are strangers to each other."

"Oh, madam," interrupted Mrs. Eccles, "though it is not my custom to take in lodgers without having a character, yet I can have no scruple with regard to a lady of your appearance. As for me, I have lived a great many years in this neighbourhood, and am not afraid of having my character enquired into."

She spoke this with a little warmth, which made Henrietta imagine she expected the same degree of confidence she had shown: so making a merit of necessity, she appeared very well satisfied, and immediately took possession of her new apartment.

Chap. V.

Which contains nothing but very common occurrences.

Mrs. Eccles being summoned into her shop by a customer, miss Courteney desired her to send up pen, ink, and paper, being resolved to write to miss Woodby that night, and acquaint her with the disappointment she had met with. The maid soon appeared with candles and all the materials for writing; delivering at the same time her mistress's compliments to the young lady, and a request that she would favour her with her company to supper. Miss Courteney promised to wait on her, provided she was alone; and, sitting down, wrote the following letter to her new friend.

YOU will no doubt, my dear miss Woodby, be both surprised and grieved to know that your kind intentions have been frustrated; and that by forgetting to give me a direction, your recommendation to Mrs. Egret has proved useless to me. By a mistake of the chairman, who I desired to enquire where Mrs. Egret lived, I was brought to another millener's, and she not being able to direct me where to find her, I am obliged to take up my lodging with a stranger. It was my apprehensions of what has befallen me, that induced me to trust you with my secret, a secret of the highest importance to me; and most generously did you repay my confidence by your ready assistance. It was my ill fortune which ordered it so, that I should not profit by your kindness. However, my gratitude is equally engaged, and since I observe nothing disagreeable in the behaviour of the person in whose house I now am, I shall endeavour to make myself easy till I hear from you. I long to see you, to tell you my unhappy story, to have your compassion, or rather to be justified by your approbation of what I have been compelled by circumstances to do. Oh! my dear miss, how unhappy is that mind, which, with right intentions, feels a consciousness of something wrong in its resolutions! Direct for me by the name of Benson, at Mrs. Eccles's, millener, in Charles street. Adieu. I sign the pretty name you gave me.

CLELIA

Henrietta had just sealed her letter, when somebody tapp'd at her door; she opened it immediately, and, seeing Mrs. Eccles, asked her pardon for not waiting on her before. Mrs. Eccles told her, that her little supper being ready, she came to see if she was at leisure.

Miss Courteney found the cloth spread in the parlour, and an elegant supper was served up. Mrs. Eccles did not fail to apologize frequently for the meanness of her entertainment, and was gratified with as many assurances from her fair guest, that no apology was necessary. During the repast, Mrs. Eccles entertained her with an account of the newest fashions, the most celebrated performers of the opera and playhouses, little pieces of scandal, and the like topics of conversation, which Henrietta had often heard discussed among her more polite acquaintance, and indeed almost the only ones that engage the attention during the recess of the card-table.

The millener then turning the discourse to the accident that procured her so agreeable a lodger, artfully pursued her hints till the young lady found herself obliged to satisfy in some degree her curiosity concerning her situation.

Though she was naturally communicative, even to a fault; yet she did not think proper to disclose herself farther, than to tell her, that she had been obliged to come to London upon some affairs of consequence, which could not be settled till the arrival of her brother, who was every day expected from his travels.

This account was so near the truth, that miss Courteney, in the simplicity of her own heart, thought it could not fail of being believed. However, the millener who knew the world very well, conceived there was something extraordinary in the case—nothing less than a love-intrigue: nor did this suspicion give her any uneasiness. She was one of those convenient persons with whom a lady, upon paying a certain sum of money, might lie-in[6] privately, and be properly attended. She made no scruple of accommodating with lodgings a young wife, whose husband, for certain family reasons, visits her only now and then; and as she generally found her account in such sort of lodgers, she seldom desired, and indeed was seldom encumbered with any other.

The youth, beauty, and elegance of miss Courteney, the introductory letter so oddly conceived, her apparent perplexity and concern upon her disappointment of the lodgings she had expected, raised suspicions, which the story she now heard, confirmed; and not doubting but this affair would prove beneficial to her, she exerted her utmost endeavours to please her fair lodger, and engage her to an entire confidence.

When the clock struck eleven, Henrietta rose up, in order to retire to her own chamber, to which Mrs. Eccles officiously attended her; having taken leave of her at the door, she bolted it on the inside, and, after recommending herself to the protection of Heaven, went to bed, but not to rest. A thousand disquietudes kept her waking till the morning, when she sunk into a slumber that lasted till eleven o'clock.

As soon as she opened her eyes, she was informed, by the strong light in her chamber, that the morning was far advanced; and, finding by her watch, which lay on a chair near her bed-side, how much she had exceeded her usual time, (for she was a very early riser) she hurried on her cloaths, and went down stairs, being extremely anxious to get her letter sent to miss Woodby: she went directly into the shop, supposing she should find Mrs. Eccles there; but was excessively surprised to hear from the apprentice, that her mistress was not yet up.

"I suppose," said miss Courteney, "she rested no better than myself last night, which was the cause of my lying so late this morning."

"La! ma'am," replied the girl, "my mistress is never up before eleven or twelve." "Indeed!" said the young lady, dissembling her concern at a circumstance which gave her no favourable opinion of her landlady. "But, madam," added the girl, "you may have your breakfast whenever you please to order it." She then called the maid, whom miss Courteney ordered to fetch a porter, being determined to have her letter delivered into miss Woodby's own hands, if possible. A porter was soon found, who undertook to carry the letter to Hammersmith as directed; and this affair being dispatched, Henrietta ordered some chocolate[7] for her breakfast, and retired to her own chamber.

CHAP. VI.

In which miss Woodby again makes her appearance.

In about a quarter of an hour, Mrs. Eccles appeared in a long loose linen sack, being her morning dress, and insisted upon miss Courteney's breakfasting with her; who at length consented, having agreed to pay at the rate of a guinea a week for her board, during the time she stayed, which she inly determined should not be long.

After the tea-things were removed, she went into the shop to make a purchase of some ribbons and gloves; and while she was amusing herself with looking over a great variety of fashionable trifles, which the apprentice officiously shewed her, a young gentleman, who had been attracted by her appearance, came into the shop, and asked to look at some Dresden ruffles. Henrietta, blushing at the earnestness with which he gazed on her, retired immediately, telling Mrs. Eccles, as she passed through the parlour, that there was a gentleman in the shop. The millener, upon this information, lifted up her hands mechanically to her head to adjust her hair, and hastened to attend her customer; while her fair lodger, taking a book that lay in the window, went to her apartment, with an intention to amuse herself with reading till the longed-for return of her messenger.

The book however, which was a volume of the New Atlantis,[8] did not suit her taste; she threw it away, and abandoned herself to her own melancholy reflections, which were at length interrupted by her landlady, who entered the room with a smiling air, telling her, she had had a very good customer.

"I am glad of it," said Henrietta.

"Truly," said Mrs. Eccles, "I believe I am obliged to your fair face for my good luck this morning." "How!—" returned the young lady, with a countenance graver than before.

"Nay, never wonder at it," said Mrs. Eccles, "the gentleman laid out twelve guineas with me; but I don't believe he wanted the things he bought. You were the loadstone," added she smartly, "that drew him into the shop.—He asked me a hundred questions about you."

"I am sorry for it," said miss Courteney, "I wish I had not been in the shop." "And why sorry? pray," resumed Mrs. Eccles, "I warrant you are sorry you are handsome too—However, I have another thing to tell you, to increase your sorrow, and that is, that you have certainly made a conquest of this fine spark; and, to overwhelm you with affliction," pursued she laughing, "I verily believe he is a man of quality."

"Do you know him then," said miss Courteney; who could not help smiling a little at her vivacity.

"I only judge by his appearance and manners," replied Mrs. Eccles, "that he is a man of rank; but I dare say, we shall hear more from him." "Sure—Mrs. Eccles!" interrupted miss Courteney, with some emotion.

"Nay, nay, child," exclaimed Mrs. Eccles, "don't put yourself into a flurry; I don't know that I shall ever see him again—But, pray what book have you got here?" "One I found in your parlour," said miss Courteney. "Oh, I see what it is," cried Mrs. Eccles, opening it; "it is a charming pretty book. If you love reading, miss, I can furnish you with books; I have a very pretty collection—" "I should be glad to see your collection," said the young lady, who was apprehensive of her renewing a conversation that had been very disagreeable to her.

Mrs. Eccles immediately led her into a little room on the same floor, and opening a closet, in which there were about two dozen books ranged on a shelf, she bid her take her choice, for there was variety enough.

Henrietta soon examined the so much boasted collection, which she found chiefly consisted of novels and plays. "Well," said Mrs. Eccles, "how do you like my books? are they not prettily chosen?"

"I assure you," replied she taking down one, "you chose very well when you chose this; for it is one of the most exquisite pieces of humour in our language." "I knew you would approve of my taste," said Mrs. Eccles, "but what have you got?—O! the Adventures of Joseph Andrews—Yes; that is a very pretty book, to be sure!—but there is Mrs. Haywood's Novels,[9] did you ever read them?—Oh! they are the finest love-sick, passionate stories; I assure you, you'll like them vastly: pray, take a volume of Haywood upon my recommendation." "Excuse me," said Henrietta, "I am very well satisfied with what I have; I have read this book three times already, and yet I assure you, I shall begin it again with as much eagerness and delight as I did at first."

"Well, as you please," said Mrs. Eccles, leaving her at the door of her own chamber, "I won't disturb you till dinner is ready."

Miss Courteney sat down to her book, which agreeably engaged her attention, till she was interrupted with the pleasing news of her porter's being returned: she flew down stairs; he delivered her a letter, the seal of which she eagerly broke, and found it as follows.

CELINDA to her dearest CLELIA.
NO words can describe the excess of my grief at the news of your disappointment: but, my dear, how was it possible for your chairmen to mistake the house so egregiously—not know where Mrs. Egret lived! Foolish fellows! she is one of the greatest milleners in town, and employed by persons of the first rank. But don't be uneasy, I shall see you this afternoon: your messenger found me preparing to set out for town with my aunt—Adieu, my Clelia, and believe me with the most unparallel'd affection, ever your's,
                                                        CELINDA.

The hopes of seeing her friend, and being settled in more agreeable lodgings, gave Henrietta such a flow of spirits, that when she was summoned to dinner by her landlady, she appeared less reserved than usual, and even kept up the conversation with some kind of chearfulness. Mrs. Eccles, finding her in so good a humour, introduced the subject which ran most in her head—The fine young gentleman, who had been her customer in the morning, was praised in raptures of admiration—so genteel, so well bred—such sparkling eyes, such an air of distinction—Every now and then exclaiming—"Well, you have certainly made a conquest of him—we shall see him again, never fear—he'll find his way here again, I warrant him."

Miss Courteney, to put an end to this discourse, told her landlady, that she expected a lady to drink tea with her that afternoon; Mrs. Eccles immediately gave orders for the dining-room to be put in order, and thither miss Courteney retired in expectation of her visiter. At six o'clock a footman's rap at the door anounced the arrival of miss Woodby; Henrietta ran to the head of the stairs to receive her.

"O Heavens! my dear creature," cried miss Woodby, "What trouble have I been in upon your account!—but even the disquiets of friendship are pleasing; I would not be insensible of that charming passion, nor without an object of it for the world."

Miss Courteney thanked her in very obliging terms, while her sentimental friend adjusted her dress in the glass, and then throwing herself into a chair, declared that she was all impatience to hear her history.

"Permit me," said miss Courteney, "to inform you first, that I am not easy here, I do not greatly like my landlady, and I wish I could remove this very night." Miss Woodby told her it was impossible, because she had not yet seen Mrs. Egret, but that she would go to her in the morning, and prepare her for her coming. Henrietta, being now at ease, complied with her friend's request, and began her little history in this manner.

CHAP. VII.

In which Henrietta relates the story of her parents, introductory to her own.

It is no wonder, my dear miss Woodby, that at these early years I am precipitated into distresses and dangers; my very birth was a misfortune to my parents, and intailed upon them those miseries which began by their unhappy passion.

"My father was the youngest of three brothers, but so great a favourite of his father the earl of ———, that it was thought he would make his fortune very considerable, having a very large estate, and a very lucrative employment, out of which he every year laid by large sums to provide for his younger sons, of whom my father, as I have already said, was the best beloved.

"It happened one day, that the widow of an officer in the army came to solicit the earl's interest towards getting her a pension. She was accompanied by her daughter, a young woman about sixteen years of age, and who must at that time have been exquisitely handsome, since, after a long series of troubles, and in an age more advanced, she appeared to me one of the most beautiful women in the world.

"The widow, by a certain method of persuasion which operates powerfully on the domesticks of men in place, got her petition sent up to the earl.

It imported that her husband, after having served near fifty years in the army, had obtained leave to sell his commission[10] for the benefit of his wife and child; that the money arising from it had been deposited in the hands of an agent who had broke a few months afterwards, by which unhappy accident all the money was lost, and this loss had so greatly affected the old gentleman, that he died a few weeks afterwards, leaving his wife and child wholly unprovided for, and made wretched by those very means that were calculated to secure them a genteel subsistence; since by the sale of her husband's commission, the widow was no longer intitled to a pension, which however she hoped to obtain, in consideration of his long services, and the peculiar circumstances of her misfortune.

"The widow, who knew it was in this nobleman's power to put her immediately upon the list of pensions, conceived great hopes of the success of her application, when, after waiting two hours in the hall, she was ordered to attend his lordship in his library.

"The nobleman received her with civility enough; but his first words destroyed those expectations with which she had flattered herself.

"I am sorry it is not in my power to do you any service, said he; your husband sold out, therefore you have no right to the pension. I pity your misfortune; but in this case there is nothing to be done.

"The widow was a woman of sense and breeding: she was sensible that the earl paid no regard to her plea, otherwise he would not have urged that as an argument against granting her petition, without which no petition would have been necessary: intreaties she found would be fruitless, therefore she would not descend to the meanness of a suppliant, but curtsy'd in silent anguish, and withdrew.

"The earl's youngest son, who was present at this scene, and who had beheld the decent sorrow of the mother with reverence, the innocent beauty of the daughter with tender admiration, impelled by an emotion which yet he knew not the cause of, hastily followed them, and offered his hand to the widow to lead her down stairs.

"She, who from a natural dignity of sentiment, had been enabled to endure the supercilious behaviour of the father without betraying any signs of discomposure, burst into tears at this instance of unexpected attention and respect in the son.

"Mr. Courteney, as he led her down stairs, had his eyes incessantly turned towards the young lady, who followed blushing, to see herself so earnestly beheld. He found they had not a coach waiting for them, he ordered a servant to call one; and in the mean time desired they would walk into a parlour, where he took occasion to express his concern to the widow for the disappointment she had met with; but assured her, that he would employ his good offices in her favour, and from the influence he had over his father; he said he hoped he should succeed. He then desired to know where he might wait upon her, in case he had any good news to bring her.

"The widow, charmed with his politeness, astonished at his kindness, and full of hope and pleasing expectation, gave him a direction in writing, which she had brought with her.

"Mr. Courteney received it, bowing low, as if she had conferred a favour on him; a favour it was indeed, for, by this time, he was lost in love for the charming daughter, whose looks discovered such soft sensibility of her situation, such conscious dignity, which misfortune could not impair; such calm resignation, as if, superior to her woes, that her beauty seemed her least perfection; and he was more captivated by the graces of her mind that shone out in her person, than with her lovely person itself.

"The coach was now come; he sighed when he took leave of them, rivetting his eyes on the young charmer, who modestly looked down, unable to bear his ardent glances. Again he assured the widow of his services; and, suddenly recollecting himself, he put a purse into her hand, begging her to accept that trifle as an earnest of his friendship.

"The lady was so much surprised at his behaviour, that she was at a loss in what manner to answer him; and, before she could form any, she found herself in the coach, to which he had accompanied her with great respect. When the coach drove from the door, she examined the contents of the purse, and found five and twenty guineas in it: a present, which, if it had been less, would have mortified her pride, and being so considerable, alarmed her prudence. She recollected every circumstance of the young gentleman's behaviour, and all contributed to persuade her, that he was actuated by some motive more forcible than meer compassion.

"She remembered that she had caught him gazing earnestly at her daughter; she reproached herself for taking her with her, for accepting the money, for giving a direction. She dreaded the consequence of having exposed her child to the attempts of a young man formed to please, and by his rank and fortune enabled to pursue every method that could gratify his passions. She began now to be solicitous about the effect such uncommon generosity had on the mind of her daughter. She asked her what she thought of the gentleman, who so kindly interested himself in their affairs, notwithstanding the cruel denial his father had given?

"Miss, whose gratitude had with difficulty been restrained from rising from her heart to her tongue, eagerly seized this opportunity to praise their benefactor. Her expressions were so lively, she showed so tender a sensibility of his kindness, such a blushing approbation of his person and manners, that the good widow thought proper to check her vivacity by a little reproof, and attributed all the respect he had shown them to his natural politeness, and his offers of service, and the present he had forced on her, to a sudden sally of compassion which young unexperienced persons are liable to. However, her apprehensions were now increased; and when Mr. Courteney came to see her, in consequence of his promise, which was two days afterwards, she had already taken her resolution.

"She took care that her daughter should not be in the way when he sent up his name; and notwithstanding the politeness with which he accosted her, she observed that he was disappointed, and that his eyes involuntarily sought out an object which he more wished to see than her.

"I don't know whether these little particulars may not seem tedious to you, my dear miss Woodby; but I have often heard my mother repeat them with delight; declaring that these first tokens of my father's affection for her made so deep an impression on her heart, fluctuating, as it then was, between hope and fear, that she ever retained the most lively remembrance of them, and could never relate them without feeling in some degree the same pleasing emotions with which she was at that time agitated.

"Mr. Courteney began the conversation with assuring the widow, that he had been mindful of her affairs; that his solicitations had not yet indeed had the desired effect; but that he hoped shortly to bring her better news. The widow thanked him with great politeness, for his kind interposition in her favour, which she declared would always have a claim to her sincerest gratitude, whether he succeeded or not in his applications. She then drew the purse out of her pocket, and putting it respectfully into his hands, told him, that not being in any immediate necessity, she begged he would not take it ill if she declined accepting a present which would lay her under an unreturnable obligation.

"Mr. Courteney blushed with surprize and disappointment—but the dignity with which she looked and spoke, making it impossible for him to press her any farther, he received the money back again with a low bow, apologizing at the same time for the liberty he had taken.

"The widow, seeing him disconcerted, politely recommended her interests to him; and Mr. Courteney, charmed that she would allow him to be her friend on any terms, retired with a promise that he would take as much care of them as of his own.

"This interview," continued Henrietta, "confirmed the widow in her suspicions, that her daughter was not indifferent to their new benefactor—he had observed her scrupulous reserve with regard to the young beauty, and hoped to remove it by affecting a total neglect of her; so that he did not even enquire how she did.—Whatever is done with design is always overdone: the widow was persuaded that a man of Mr. Courteney's good breeding would not have passed over one of the common forms of politeness, but to answer some secret purpose. Her vigilance increased in proportion to her fears; and although he made her several visits, under pretence of enquiring more minutely into the circumstances of her case, yet he never was so fortunate as to find her daughter with her.

"This conduct, while it stimulated his passion, gave him a high opinion of the virtue and prudence of her, who, in such unhappy circumstances, showed such extreme attention to the honour and reputation of her child. Hitherto he had not been at the trouble to examine his own views and designs upon this young beauty. Hurried away by the violence of his passion, he had assiduously sought opportunities of seeing and conversing with her; but the difficulties he met with made him look into his own heart, that he might know if he was still sufficient master of it to give over a pursuit which was likely to prove fruitless.

"Amazed to find that what he took for a transient inclination, was a passion immoveably fixed; that he had formed resolutions, when he believed he had only entertained desires; that the whole happiness and misery of his life was in the power of a young woman, destitute of friends, fortune, hopes, and expectations, and rich only in beauty and virtue—for virtuous he was sure she must be, under the care of so wise and prudent a mother. He was alarmed at his own condition; dreaded the consequences of a passion so placed as that it could never procure the sanction of his father's consent, and resolved to expose himself no more to the danger of seeing her.

"However, he did not fail to solicit his father very earnestly in behalf of the unfortunate widow. The earl, who had taken notice of his officious respect the day she was introduced to him, and attributed it rather to the beauty of the daughter than any sentiment of compassion, began to be uneasy at his so frequently pressing him on that subject, and forbad him to mention it any more.

"Mr. Courteney was obliged to be silent, lest he should confirm those suspicions which he saw his father had conceived; and finding his mind in a very uneasy state, he hoped that, by removing himself to a greater distance from the object he loved, he should remove the thoughts of her likewise; he obtained his father's consent to his retiring for a few weeks to their seat in the country, under pretence of a slight indisposition; but he could not resolve to go without endeavouring once more to force a present upon the widow, which might prevent her being exposed to any distress during his absence.

"He therefore wrote to her, and acquainting her with the ill success of his mediation with his father, expressed the highest concern for it, and assured her that nothing could alleviate it but her acceptance of the bank note which he inclosed, and which was for fifty pounds: he told her, he was going into the country, that she might not suppose he had any design of inducing her by such a present to admit his visits; and concluded with assuring her, that she might at all times command his services, and rely on his friendship.

"He did not send away this letter till he was ready to take horse; and being now more composed, from the belief that he had silenced the scruples of this good woman, and secured her and her lovely daughter from any immediate necessity, he pursued his journey—full of pleasing reflections on the disinterestedness of his love."

Chap. VIII.

In which Henrietta continues her history.

Absence (says a certain writer) increases violent passions, and cures moderate ones; just as the wind extinguishes a small flame, while it makes a great one burn more fiercely.[11] Mr. Courteney's passion was of this kind; he had loved with violence from the moment he began to love. In vain he had recourse to books, to company, to field sports, and rural amusements; it was not possible for him to call off his thoughts a moment from that object from whom he fled with such care. Two months he wore away in a constant perturbation of mind, still flattering himself that he was nearer his cure, while his disease gathered strength every day.

"It happened that one evening he fell into company with some officers, whose regiment was quartered in that part of the country; and one of them mentioned colonel Carlton, and the unhappy situation his widow and daughter were left in.

"Mr. Courteney, rouzed to attention by that name so dear to him, pretended to be wholly ignorant of those ladies case, that he might indulge himself in the pleasure of talking of her he loved.

"The officer gave him a circumstantial detail of what he knew as well as himself; concluding with many commendations of Mrs. Carlton's good sense, prudence, and virtue; and such rapturous praises of the young lady's beauty and uncommon qualifications at such early years, that Mr. Courteney, for the first time sensible of the tortures of jealousy, could with difficulty conceal his emotions.

"You speak so feelingly, said a gentleman in company, of this young lady's perfections, that I fancy you are in love with her: come, here is her health; is it to be a match?

"I should be but too happy in such a wife, replied the officer; but she deserves a better husband: it is not for a poor lieutenant, added he, smiling, to marry for love; but if I was a man of fortune, I would prefer miss Carlton to all the women I have ever seen.

"Mr. Courteney afterwards declared that he suffered inconceivable anguish during this conversation. He quitted the company with some precipitation; and when he was at liberty to reflect, he reproached himself a thousand times for his folly in leaving such a treasure for another to obtain. Every man he thought would look upon miss Carlton with the same eyes as that young officer; and among them might not one be found blest with a fortune to make her happy, and above all narrow considerations which could hinder him from making himself so?

"Resolutions are easily formed when the heart suggests them. Mr. Courteney, who had so long fluctuated between his passion and his prudence, was, by the fear of losing what he loved, determined in an instant to put it past the possibility of losing her. His father's anger, which at first appeared so formidable to him, was now considered as a trifle, that would be easily got over: he was not going to introduce any stale mistress into a noble family, nor to give a comedian or singer for a sister to his sisters, and a daughter to his mother; alliances so much in fashion with the present race of nobility and people of fashion: in miss Carlton he should marry birth, beauty, virtue, every perfection but riches, but unhappily that, in the estimation of his father, was worth them all.

"His fortune indeed was undetermined; it might be great, it might be very inconsiderable, since it depended upon the will of his father. His father would never consent to his marriage with miss Carlton; but though disobliged, yet loving him as he did, was it likely that he would always continue inexorable? Besides, he had a certain, though a remote prospect of a large estate, to which he was to succeed at the death of a relation, who was old, and had been married twenty years, without having ever had a child.

"Should he find it impossible to reconcile his father to his marriage, yet he was at least of a genteel provision; but with such excellencies as miss Carlton

was possessed of, how could it be imagined that she should not in time concili-
ate his father's affections, and make him approve of his choice?

"There is no logick, my dear miss Woodby, like the logick of the heart.
Mr. Courteney, as is usual on such occasions, having taken his resolution before
he reasoned upon the matter, reasoned afterwards in such a manner as to be
soon persuaded his resolution was right.

"Early the next morning he ordered his horses to be made ready, and he
returned to London with all imaginable expedition. He alighted at the house
of a friend, where he dismissed his servants and horses, and then taking a
hackney coach, was driven to the street in which Mrs. Carlton lived. Upon
stopping at the house, and enquiring for Mrs. Carlton, he was told that she
had left it five weeks before, and being greatly indisposed, had taken lodgings
at Chelsea for the air.

"Mr. Courteney, who now thought every moment an age till he saw miss
Carlton, and had acquainted her with his passion and his honourable intentions, procured as full a direction as could be given him; but notwithstanding
his impatience to be with his mistress, he obeyed the dictates of his duty, in
first going home to pay his respects to his father.

"The earl received him a little coldly; an expression of displeasure was
on his countenance, which however wore off by degrees, as he enquired concerning his health, his studies and amusements, during his absence. At length
seeming to recollect something, he went to his cabinet, took out a letter, the
seal of which had been broke, and delivered it into his son's hand, assuming
the same angry countenance as before.

"Mr. Courteney, not able to imagine what all this meant, opened the
letter hastily, and found it was from Mrs. Carlton, dated the very day of his
departure, and in it was inclosed the bank note he had sent: the purport of
her letter was to refuse in a genteel but steady manner all pecuniary assistance
from him; however, she thanked him for his civilities, and acknowledged herself
greatly obliged to him.

"When Mr. Courteney had read this letter, which he did with much
confusion, the earl asked him sternly, what was his design by engaging in such
a commerce? You are in love with the daughter, added he, no doubt—but if
you corrupt her, you are not an honest man; if you marry her, you are no
longer my son.

"He left him as he pronounced these words; and Mr. Courteney, who,
while he beheld it at a distance, thought his father's displeasure might be sustained, was overwhelmed with the first effects of it, and relapsed into all his
former doubts, anxiety, and irresolution.

"He retired to his own chamber to consider on what he ought to do; but unable to bear the cruel war which such contrary interests, such opposite wishes, such perplexed designs, raised in his mind, he hurried out of the house to lose reflection in a variety of objects, and took his way to the Park.

"He walked down the Mall: it was crouded with company which did not in the least engage his attention; he continued his walk, and finding himself at Buckingham-gate, his steps mechanically pursued the road that led to Chelsea.

"As soon as he saw himself near the place where his mistress resided, all other thoughts were absorbed in the transporting reflection, that he should see her within a few moments; his father's threats were forgot, the loss of his favour filled him with no uneasy apprehensions. To how many revolutions is the human mind subject, when passion has assumed the reins of government which reason ought to hold! Mr. Courteney had almost imperceptibly to himself resumed his first design of offering his hand to miss Carlton.

"With very little difficulty he found out the house where her mother and she lodged; the door was opened to him by a girl, who, upon his enquiring if Mrs. Carlton was at home, told him she was sick in bed, and, showing him into a little parlour, ran up stairs to acquaint miss, as he supposed, that a gentleman was there.

"In a few minutes a venerable old woman appeared, who had so fixed a concern upon her countenance, that Mr. Courteney, shifting his thoughts from the illness of the mother to the apprehension of some possible misfortune to the daughter, (for love if it hopes all, fears all likewise,) asked her with great emotion if any thing extraordinary had happened to the ladies!

"The good woman, pleased with his solicitude, which she thought promised some relief, told him plainly, that Mrs. Carlton was in the utmost distress; that she had been ill several weeks; that she had not been able to procure proper advice; and added she, bursting into tears, she has even wanted common necessaries."

"O my God! exclaimed Mr. Courteney, with a deep sigh; but miss—what is become of miss? Alas! Sir, replied the old woman, the dear child is almost dead with fatigue and grief; she has watched by her mother these ten nights successively, there is no persuading her to quit her for a moment. I left her in an agony of sorrow, for it is believed poor Mrs. Carlton cannot live three days.

"Conduct me to her, cried Mr. Courteney eagerly; I may possibly be able to comfort her; let me see her, I conjure you, immediately.

"Stay a moment, sir, said the old woman, stopping him, for he was making towards the door; I will go up first and inform the ladies. There is no occasion for that, said Mr. Courteney, Mrs. Carlton knows me very well; she will not I am sure be sorry to see me, I have something to say to her.

"The good woman, seeing his obstinacy, permitted him to follow her up stairs; she gently opened the chamber-door, and, approaching the bed where the sick lady lay, told her there was a friend of her's, who desired to see her. Mr. Courteney entered that moment, and beheld a sight which called for more fortitude than he was at that time possessed of to support without tears.

"Mrs. Carlton lay extended on her bed, supported by a heighth of cushions to facilitate her breathing, which she seemed to do with great difficulty. Death appeared in her languid countenance; and an expression of the tender anguish of a mother for the child whom she was so soon to leave exposed to the insults of a barbarous world, mixed with the pious resignation of a christian, was impressed on every line of it.

"Miss Carlton was kneeling at the bed-side, and held one of her mother's hands, which she was bending over in an agony of grief: upon hearing what the old woman said, she raised her head; and, directing her streaming eyes to the place where Mr. Courteney stood, showed him a face pale, emaciated, but lovely still; at sight of him a faint blush overspread her cheeks, and hastily turning to her mother, it is Mr. Courteney, my dear mamma, said she.

"Oh! Sir," said Mrs. Carlton, perceiving him, you are very good to seek out affliction thus. I shall shortly be past all my cares; but what will become of this poor helpless orphan? The tears that streamed from her eyes prevented her further utterance.

"Mr. Courteney threw himself on his knees at the bed-side, and almost sobbing with the violence of his emotions at this affecting language, Oh! madam, said he, What must you not have suffered? why would you not accept what little assistance it was in my power to offer you? I know your delicate scruples—I come to beg you will give yourself a right to all my future services—I have something to communicate to you—But, added he, looking at the old woman who had introduced him, we are not alone.

"Speak freely, sir, said Mrs. Carlton, this good woman is my daughter's nurse; she knows all my affairs; I am much indebted to her kindness and affection for my child.

"What I have to say, proceeded Mr. Courteney, relates to that dear, that lovely daughter: I loved her from the first moment I saw her; such innocence, such beauty, could not suggest any impure desire. As soon as I knew the force of my passion, which absence first made me know, I fixed its purpose. Permit me to offer her my hand; I cannot be happy without her.

"What do you say, sir? said Mrs. Carlton, excessively surprised: would you marry my daughter? Then after a little pause, No, pursued she, this can never be, your father will not consent to it.

"I own freely to you, madam, said Mr. Courteney, that I have no hopes of gaining my father's consent; but when the affair is irretrievable, he will be softened, I am sure he will. Let not this scruple hinder you from giving your daughter a protector. Surely, said Mrs. Carlton, lifting up her eyes, the hand of Providence is here; and it would be impious to oppose its will. You have my consent, sir, said she to Mr. Courteney; would it pleased God that you had his also, whom it is your duty to consult on this occasion, and to obey if you can.

"Mr. Courteney assured her he would solicit his father's consent; but that he could not be happy without miss Carlton, and was already determined.

"That young lady had retired into another room at the beginning of this discourse, in perturbations which may be better imagined than described. Mr. Courteney, by her mother's permission, attended her: he approached her with a timidity, which the inequality of their circumstances considered, may seem surprising; but those who know the nature of a sincere and violent passion, will easily account for it: for fear, says an elegant writer,[12] always accompanies love when it is great, as flames burn highest when they tremble most. He took her hand, and kissing it respectfully, told her that Mrs. Carlton had begun his felicity, by permitting him to offer himself to her acceptance as a husband, but that she only could complete it by her consent.

"Miss Carlton blushed, turned pale, and blushed again: at length she replied, that she had no other will than her mother's. But this offer, added she, in an accent that expressed at once her surprise and gratitude, is so generous, so unexpected, so unhoped for—The last words seemed to escape her; she blushed more than before. Mr. Courteney took in all their tender meaning: he kissed her hand again in a rapture of joy, and was beginning to make her some passionate declarations, when they heard the nurse crying out for help.

"Surprise and joy at what had so lately happened, operated so powerfully on Mrs. Carlton's almost exhausted spirits, that she had fallen into a fainting fit. Miss Carlton eagerly flew to her assistance, Mr. Courteney followed her with an anxious concern. As soon as she recovered, he told her he would instantly return to London, and dispatch a physician to attend her, and would be with her again the next evening.

"He took a tender farewel of his mistress, and calling the nurse aside, gave her twenty guineas to provide whatever was wanting, and hastened back to London.

Chap. IX.

The story continued.

Mr. Courteney's first care was to send a physician to the sick lady; and that performed, he deliberated in what manner he should acquaint his father with his intention. He knew him too well to hope for his consent to his marriage with miss Carlton, and he had not courage enough to stand the reproaches of a parent, whom he was predetermined to disobey. He chose therefore to write to him, supposing he should, when unawed by his presence, be able to find arguments strong enough to make some impression on his mind, and to plead his excuse.

"As he dreaded extremely a private interview with his father, he was glad to find at his return home, that a great deal of company was expected that evening; he did not appear till they were all met, having purposely wasted a good deal of time in dressing. The earl was still ruffled with what had passed before between him and his son; and Mr. Courteney observed that his looks and behaviour were less kind than usual.

"As soon as he retired to his apartment, instead of going to bed, he sat down to compose a letter to his father. He began with the highest expressions of grief for having, by an irresistible impulse, engaged his affections without his concurrence: he justified his choice by every argument that love could suggest in favour of the beloved object; he implored the continuance of his father's affection; and promised in every future action the most perfect submission and obedience.

"This difficult task performed, he found his mind much easier and composed, as if in reality he had obtained the pardon he was soliciting for, and now resigned himself to all the pleasing reveries of successful love.

"After a few hours rest, he rose under pretence of going out to ride; and, leaving orders with a servant to deliver his letter to his father at his hour of dressing, he went immediately to the Commons, procured a licence, and flew to Chelsea; he found Mrs. Carlton much worse than when he left her; yet joy at seeing him again, seemed to give her new life and spirits. She called him to her bed-side; he acquainted her with what he had done; she had some scruples, but the fear of leaving her daughter destitute overbalanced them all.

"I am dying, said she, pressing his hand; the physician you sent was too sincere to flatter me. I die contented, since I leave my child under your protection. Let the ceremony be performed in my presence; after that is over

I shall have no farther business with the world. Miss Carlton, drowned in tears, and almost sinking under the violence of her grief, was with great difficulty persuaded to give her hand to her lover at so shocking a time; but her dying mother conjured her to give her that last satisfaction.—A clergyman was instantly provided by the faithful nurse: the clerk acted as father to the weeping bride; and Mr. Courteney's servant and the good nurse were witnesses.—Never sure was there a more melancholy wedding—the bridegroom's joy was checked by simpathising concern—the bride's tender sensibility lost in agonising woe—the service was performed with the solemn sadness of a funeral.

"As soon as it was over, Mrs. Carlton collected all her remaining strength and spirits to pronounce a blessing on the new-wedded pair; and straining her daughter with a weak embrace, declared that she was now easy, and should die in peace. Mr. Courteney made a genteel present to the clergyman and the clerk, and dismissed them: he took an affectionate leave of Mrs. Carlton, who desired to be left to her private devotions; and earnestly recommending his bride to the care of her nurse, he went back to town with a resolution to declare his marriage to his father; his sentiments being too delicate, and his notions of honour too just to permit him on any consideration of interest to conceal the engagements he had entered into, and suffer the woman whom he thought worthy to be his wife to live under a doubtful character.

"On his return home he found his letter had been delivered to the earl. His mother, being informed of his arrival, sent for him to her dressing-room, where he found her in tears. She told him that his father had been in the most violent transports of anger, upon receiving his letter; and she conjured him, if he valued her peace, to proceed no farther in a design that must inevitably be his ruin.

"Mr. Courteney sighed, and was preparing to answer her, when the earl himself entered the room; the impression of his first fury was still visible on his countenance. As soon as he saw his son, he poured a torrent of reproaches on him, inveighing against his meanness and ingratitude; then suddenly, and with great vehemence, uttered the most dreadful imprecations on him, if he followed the dictates of his despicably-placed passion, and married a beggar.

"Oh, hold my lord! cried Mr. Courteney, throwing himself at his feet; curse me not, for I am already married. The earl, almost mad with rage at this confession, spurned him rudely with his foot, and flung out of the room, declaring that he renounced him for ever.

"Mr. Courteney, stung with indignation at this treatment, rose up, and uttered some words of resentment, when his attention was called off from the affront he had suffered, by the condition in which he observed his mother, who, from surprise and terror, had swooned, and lay motionless on the couch, where she had thrown herself. Mr. Courteney, excessively shocked at this sight, rung the bell for her woman, while he applied himself to give her all the assistance he was able. As soon as he saw her recovering, he staid not to increase her disorder by his presence, but retired to his apartment; and after he had taken all the money he had in his cabinet, he left that house which was now become dreadful to him, and went to the lodgings of a young gentleman who had been his fellow-student at college, and whom he had reason to believe his friend, if friendship can be acquired by conferring obligations.

"To this young gentleman he unloaded his heart, but found not the consolation he expected. He expressed the utmost astonishment and concern for his indiscreet marriage; and, instead of offering him any advice in his perplexed situation, or consoling him, oppressed as he was by the displeasure of his father, manifested in so contemptuous a manner, he maintained that the earl's anger was just and reasonable, and exclaimed at his imprudence in ruining himself for a woman.

"Before the mischief was done, remonstrances might have been seasonable; but nothing could be more unkind than to insist upon an error which was already committed, and could not be repaired. Mr. Courteney was at first surprised at this behaviour in a man who had always shewn so deep a sense of his kindness, and professed the most tender friendship for him: but he had still temper enough left to consider, that most people follow their own interests, and are at one time grateful for their convenience, and at another ungrateful for the same reason.

"He left him without taking any notice of the disgust he had conceived; and after he had hired lodgings for the reception of his wife, he hastened to Chelsea, where he arrived time enough to moderate the first agonies of her grief for the loss of her mother, who had expired a few moments before.

"Having given directions concerning the funeral, he forced Mrs. Courteney out of that mournful house, and carried her to London, applying himself with the tenderest assiduity to alleviate the sense of her loss, all his own just causes of uneasiness being forgot, and his anxiety for the melancholy future lost in his contemplation of the happy present: so true it is, that wedded-love supplies the want of every other blessing in life; and as no condition can be truly happy without it, so none can be absolutely miserable with it.[13]

Chap. X.

A farther continuation of her story.

In the mean time Mr. Courteney corresponded privately with his mother, whose gentle nature had, with little difficulty, been softened into a forgiveness of her son's imprudent marriage; but all her endeavours to reconcile the earl to it had proved ineffectual. He continued inexorable, and peremptorily commanded her never to mention that undutiful son to him more, whom he reprobated for ever.

"The countess durst not hazard an interview with her son, while his father's resentment continued unappeased; but she allowed him two hundred pounds a year out of her pin-money,[14] and upon this moderate income they lived with more happiness than is often to be found in the highest affluence."

"And why not," interrupted miss Woodby here, "a cottage, with the person we love, is to be preferred to a palace with one to whom interest and not affection has joined us. I know I could be contented to keep sheep with the man I loved. Speak truth, my dear Clelia, would you not like to be a shepherdess? O, what a delightful employment, to watch a few harmless sheep! to wander thro' groves and fields, or lie reclined upon the flowery margin of some murmuring stream, and listen to the plaintive voice of the nightingale, or the tender faithful vows of some lovely and beloved shepherd!"

"What a romantic picture," said miss Courteney laughing, "have you drawn! It is a mighty pretty one it must be confessed, but there is no resemblance in it. I remember, when I was about fourteen, I had the same notions of shepherds and shepherdesses; but I was soon cured. I happened to be at the house of a country gentleman, who managed a large farm of his own; one of the servants saying something about the shepherd, my heart danced at the word. My imagination represented to me such a pretty figure as we see on the stage in the dramatic pastoral entertainment of Damon and Phillida, in a fine green habit, all bedizened with ribbons, a neat crook, and a garland of flowers. I begged to be permitted to go into the fields to see the shepherd, and eagerly enquired if there were no shepherdesses likewise; but how was I disappointed!—The shepherd was an old man in a ragged waistcoat, and so miserably sun-burnt, that he might have been mistaken for a mulatto: the shepherdess looked like a witch; she was sitting under a hedge, mending old stockings, with a straw hive on her head, and a tatter'd garment on, of as many colours as there were patches in it. How diverting it would have been to have heard this enamour'd swain sigh out soft things to this lovely nymph!"

"Oh! ridiculous," cried miss Woodby—"I am sick at the very thought; but, my dear Clelia, go on, I beseech you, with your story."

"I have not come to my own story yet," said miss Courteney; "all that you have heard has been only an introduction to it; and I have given you the history of my parents in the words, as near as I can remember, of my mother; for she loved scribbling, and committed the principal incidents of her life to paper, which for my instruction she permitted me to read: I say instruction, for she was a woman of fine understanding and deep thinking; and she had interspersed through her little narrative many beautiful and just reflections, and many observations and useful maxims, such as her reading, which was very comprehensive, and her experience furnished her with."

"Proceed, my dear Clelia," said miss Woodby, observing Henrietta paused here, "I am impatient to hear more." "If you please," said miss Courteney, "we will drink tea first." "I have just two hours to stay with you," replied miss Woodby, looking at her watch; "if I am at home by nine o'clock, which is my aunt's hour for supper, it will do." Henrietta then ordered tea, which was soon dispatched, and she resumed her story in this manner:

"My father, who was very desirous of conciliating his elder brother's affections, at least wrote to him, he being now upon his travels, and gave him an account of his marriage; but his letter, though conceived in the most tender and respectful terms, produced a cruel and supercilious answer, which not only took away all hope of his proving a mediator between him and his father, but proved that he had in him no longer a friend or brother.

"His affairs were in this desperate situation when my mother became pregnant; a distant relation of my father's now took an interest in this event, and being very rich and ambitious of making a family, he declared that if the child was a son, he would adopt him and make him his heir. You may imagine this design was received with great joy; the old gentleman was very assiduous in his visits to my mother during her pregnancy, and seemed extremely happy in the thoughts of perpetuating his name; an ambition very common to persons of low extraction, who, by industry and thrift, have risen to great riches: for he was only by marriage a relation to my father, and had been too much neglected on account of the meanness of his original. But all these flattering expectations were destroyed by my birth, which I had reason to say proved a misfortune to my parents. The capricious old man was so greatly chagrined at his disappointment, that he transferred all his favours to another cousin, who was so lucky as to present him with a son to succeed to his fortune, and continue his obscure name to posterity.

"My brother's birth happened a year afterwards, and unfortunately for him a year too late. My father still continued to draw his whole income from the bounty of his mother, who was a constant but fruitless mediator in his behalf: her death, which happened about three years after his marriage, was an irreparable loss to him; for it was not improbable but the lenient hand of time, which weakens the force of every passion, joined to her tender solicitations, might have effected a reconciliation between his father and him; but this hope was now no more: the countess bequeathed my father all the money she had saved, which was but a very small sum; for she had always given with a liberal hand to the poor, though with so little ostentation, that it was supposed she had saved some thousands out of her pin-money, for she was less expensive than any other woman of her rank in England; but it was not till after my father's marriage, that she began to save, and then only for him.

"Six hundred pounds was all that was found in her cabinet, which some months after her decease was paid to my father with every circumstance of contempt.

"These repeated calamities were so far from lessening the love of my father and mother, that they seemed to redouble their tenderness; seeking in each other that happiness which fortune denied them, and which they were always sure to find in their own virtue and mutual affection.

"My father, who had had a very liberal education, employed the greatest part of his time in the instruction of his children: under his tuition I acquired the French and Italian languages; by my mother I was taught every useful accomplishment for a young woman in my situation; nor did my father's narrow circumstances hinder him from procuring me those which were suitable to my birth. My brother had no other tutor but this excellent father, who qualified him for an university; and at fourteen years of age he was sent to that of Leyden, and I have never seen him since.

"In the mean time the earl my grandfather, who still continued inexorable, was taken off suddenly by an apoplectick fit; and having never altered his will, which he made immediately after the marriage of my father, he found he was cut off with a shilling. This stroke, as it was always expected, was less sensibly felt than another which immediately followed it. That relation, to whose estate my father was to succeed, having buried his wife, married a young woman, who, in a year afterwards brought him a son to inherit his fortune.

"My father, now seeing no prospect of any provision for his children, fell into a deep melancholy: he had by the interest of some of his friends, obtained a place which brought him in between three and four hundred a year; but out of this it was impossible to save much. The uneasiness of mind which he laboured under corrupted his blood; he was seized with a decay which carried him off in a few months, and deprived his wife of the best husband, his children of the best father that ever was.

"In his last illness he had wrote to his brother, and recommended his helpless family to his compassion; but that nobleman, whose avarice was his strongest passion, and whose resentment against his brother was kept up by the arts of his wife; her family, though noble, being very poor, and therefore dependent upon him, took no other notice of my father's last request, than to send my mother a bank bill for an hundred pounds; declaring at the same time that it was all the assistance she must ever expect from him; and with this heroick act of generosity, he silenced the soft pleadings of nature, and persuaded himself that he had done his duty.

"My mother, being young with child when my father died, miscarried; and by that accident, together with her continual grief, she fell into a languishing illness, which threatened a short period to her days. Eight hundred pounds was all that my father left: from this small sum a widow and two children were to draw their future subsistence. What a melancholy prospect! however my brother, who was then about seventeen, had made such great proficiency in learning, that, notwithstanding his youth, he was recommended by the professors of the university to have the care of some English youths who studied there, which afforded him a decent subsistence.

"My mother having placed eight hundred pounds in the hands of a rich merchant a man of birth and liberal education, who had been a friend of my father's, and gave her very good interest for it, she disposed of all her furniture, and with the money arising from the sale, set out with me for Bath, the waters being prescribed to her by her physician.

"Not being able to support the expence of living in the town, she took lodgings in a pleasant village, about three miles distance from it; and here, feeling her distemper daily gaining ground, she prepared for death, with a resignation that was only interrupted by her anxiety for me.

"It was not indeed easy to form any plan for my future subsistence, which would not subject me to a situation very unfit for my birth. Had my brother been provided for, she would have made no scruple of sinking that small sum that was left, into an annuity for my life, which with economy might support me above necessity and dependence. She wrote to my brother, and desired his advice with regard to me. My brother, as if he had entered into her views, in his answer conjured her to have no solicitude about him, since, with the education he had received, he could not fail of supporting himself in the character of a gentleman, but to dispose of that money in any manner which might be most for my advantage.

"My mother shed tears of tender satisfaction over this letter, so full of duty to her, and affection for me; but the more generous and disinterested appeared her son, the less was she capable of taking a resolution, which, if any disappointment happened to him, must leave him without any resource.

"You may be sure, my dear miss Woodby, I was not very forward to fix her purpose; for I could not bear the thought of being the only person, in our little distressed family, to whom a subsistence was secured. While my mother was thus fluctuating, she was visited in her retirement by lady Manning, a widow lady of a very plentiful fortune, with whom she had been in some degree of intimacy during the life of my father.

"This lady showed great fondness for me; and my mother imparting to her her difficulties with regard to settling me, lady Manning begged her to make herself quite easy, for that she would take me under her own care.

"Miss Courteney, said she, will do me honour by accepting my house for an asylum, and I and my daughter will think ourselves happy in such an agreeable companion. My mother was extremely pleased with this offer; and lady Manning pressed me to go with her to London, for which place she was to set out in a few days.

"I was so much shocked at the proposal of leaving my mother in the dangerous condition she was judged to be, that I did not receive lady Manning's offer with that sense of her intended kindness which she doubtless expected; and when my mother, wholly governed by the consideration of my interest, urged me to go with lady Manning, I burst into a violent passion of tears, vehemently protesting that I would never leave her; and lamenting her causeless distrust of my affection, in supposing that I could be prevailed upon, by any prospect of advantage to myself, to separate from her.

"I observed lady Manning redened at these words, which she understood as a reproach for her making so improper a proposal, and which I really desired she should: for I was highly disgusted with her want of delicacy, in desiring me to leave my mother, and her believing it possible that I could consent.

"I saw pleasure in my mother's eyes at this artless expression of my tenderness for her; but at the same time I thought I could perceive by the turn of her countenance that she was apprehensive I had disobliged lady Manning: therefore I endeavoured to remove her fears by the strongest assurances of gratitude to that lady. She received those assurances with a little superciliousness at first, but that presently wore off; and at parting she renewed her professions of friendship to my mother, and promises of a parent's care of me.

"She left Bath three days afterwards, so that we did not see her again, which made my mother a little uneasy; but we had soon a very kind letter from her, in which she repeated all her former offers, and expressed great tenderness for me.

"At her return from London, she passed through Bath in her way to her country-seat; and, finding my mother much worse, she redoubled her professions of affection for me, and was so lavish in her promises, that she left her quite easy on my account. Indeed, notwithstanding what I have suffered from lady Manning, I shall ever think myself obliged to her for contributing so greatly towards that composure of mind which my mother felt, from the time that she thought me secure of a retreat, till it would suit with my brother's circumstances to take me under his own care.

"I will not, my dear miss Woodby, enlarge upon the last three months of my mother's life, which was spent in a constant preparation for her end. Indeed the innocence of her manners, and the unfeigned piety that shone through her conduct, made her whole life one continued preparation for that awful moment, so dreadful to the wicked; so full of peace, confidence, and holy joy to the good. In fine, I lost this excellent mother, and my bleeding heart still feels her loss."

The tears, which at this tender remembrance flowed from miss Courteney's eyes, made a pathetick pause in her relation; but recovering herself, she proceeded, as will be found in the following Book.

HENRIETTA.

BOOK THE SECOND.

CHAP. I.

In which Henrietta enters upon her own story, and shews, that to confer benefits, is not always a proof of benevolence.

The worthy merchant," resumed miss Courteney, "whom I mentioned to you, had the goodness to come to Bath, upon the news of my mother's extreme danger. He arrived time enough to receive her last intreaties, that he would continue his friendship to me. I was then entered into my twentieth year, and chose him for my guardian; he would have taken me with him to his house, but my promise being engaged to lady Manning, I was obliged to decline his obliging offer.

"I sent her an account of my mother's death; Mr. Damer, so was the merchant called, would not return to town till he saw me safely disposed of.

"About three days after I had written to lady Manning, I received a letter from her, which was brought by one of her servants: in which, after the usual compliments of condolence, she desired I would set out immediately with the person whom she had sent to attend me. My guardian, for so I used now to call Mr. Damer, coming in, I told him I must prepare to be gone immediately, and gave him lady Manning's letter to read.

"How are you to go, miss? said he, after he had looked over the letter. As I never doubted but lady Manning had sent her post-chaise or chariot for me, I told him I supposed there was a carriage come with the messenger.

"O yes, replied Mr. Damer, there is a very good pillion, and you are to ride behind the footman. I took notice of the equipage as I came in, but I shall not permit you to perform a journey of thirty miles in that manner: therefore, miss, I would have you send a letter to the lady by her messenger, and inform her that your guardian will convey you safe to her seat.

"I was as much pleased with this kind attention in Mr. Damer, as I was shocked and surprised at the ungenteel manner in which lady Manning had sent for me: however, I concealed my thoughts of it, and wrote such a letter as my guardian desired me. The next morning at eight o'clock, a post-chaise was ready at the door, and Mr. Damer attending; all my cloaths had been packed up the night before, and we set out immediately.

"Lady Manning received us very politely, and detained Mr. Damer to dinner. I thought I could observe something forced in the respect she seemed to pay me; and I was particularly disgusted with her using the words *Your guardian* every moment, as if in derision of the title I had to one.

"When Mr. Damer went away, he took an opportunity to speak to me apart, and made me promise him, if I should have any reason to be displeased with my situation, that I would write to him plainly, and he would come himself and fetch me away. This tender solicitude in the good old man affected me very sensibly, and I could not help shedding tears when I saw him drive away.

"Lady Manning was extremely inquisitive about his connexion with me, and asked me a great many questions. I am very glad, said she, your affairs are in the hands of so wise a man; for surely he who can raise a large estate out of a trifle, as has been the case with Mr. Damer, must needs be a very wise man, and I don't doubt but he will manage your *fortune* to the best advantage.

"I was greatly displeased with the first part of this speech, and particularly with the manner in which the word Fortune was drauled out.

"The poor trifle I have, madam, replied I, does not deserve to be termed a fortune.

"I assure you, said she, it was very kind in a man of Mr. Damer's substance to trouble himself with such inconsiderable matters; and it is a great thing for you to be permitted to call such a man guardian.

"Very true, madam, replied I, with some warmth; and I believe Mr. Damer thinks it no discredit to be called so by a child of Mr. Courteney's, whatever her fortune may be.

"I observed lady Manning to reden at this reply, which at that time surprised me, and I could not conceive the reason of it; but I soon found that it was a mortal crime in her eyes to pretend to derive any advantage from birth. There was nothing which she seemed to hold in greater contempt than family-pride, and indeed, when unseasonably exerted, it is contemptible; but it was plain that lady Manning did not think meanly of the fortuitous advantage of being well-born, because she envied those who possessed that advantage; and tho' the daughter of a soap-boiler herself, she was extremely fond of being thought to have ancestors; and it was to gratify her pride, that her husband, who was a rich citizen,[15] by trade a brewer, got himself knighted, that, together with a very large jointure, he might leave his wife the title of lady."

"Surely," interrupted miss Woodby, "this woman had no good intentions when she invited you to her house; it is impossible that such low creatures can have any notion of friendship or generosity."

"You have guessed truly," replied miss Courteney; "it was to gratify her pride, to have the daughter of a gentleman subjected to her caprice, and dependent on her bounty, that made her so solicitous to have me with her; but although I did not make these reflections immediately, yet I was so disgusted by this first conversation, that I could not promise myself any great happiness in such society.

"Her daughter was now introduced to me, a tall aukward thing about seventeen: she was an heiress; and being taught to believe that riches give birth, beauty, wit, and every desirable quality, she held every one in contempt who was not possessed of this advantage, and because she had it herself, she supposed she had all the others.

"Whatever documents were given her, they were always introduced with—Consider, miss, what a fortune you are—a young lady of your fortune. — How was it possible for a girl thus tutored, not to derive insolence from the consideration of her fortune?

"The governess, who had the care of this young lady, was not very likely to enlarge her notions—Her only recommendation to such a trust was, that she could jabber corrupted French without either sense or grammar, and miss was taught to *parler françoise* in a broad provincial dialect; for this governess had never seen Paris, and perhaps had never been out of the little village where she was born and bred, and conversed only with peasants, till she came to England to teach language and fine breeding to a rich heiress. It was very natural for lady Manning to make such a choice, who doubtless thought it a great distinction to have a foreigner for governess to her daughter."

"Nay, my dear," interrupted miss Woodby, "lady Manning in this particular does not differ from many persons of the first quality, who commit the education of their daughters to low vulgar creatures, meerly because they are French; creatures that in Paris, or in any of the chief cities in the provinces, would not be thought qualified for a chamber-maid to a woman of any fashion, yet when driven into England on account of their religion, as they all pretend, though perhaps it is for want of bread in their own country, derive such distinction from their flimsy sacks, their powdered hair, and their speaking French, that they are thought the fittest persons in the world to form the manners of young girls of quality.[16] How absurd should we think it in a French woman of quality to entertain an aukward Yorkshire girl with a coarse clownish accent, as English governess to her daughter, to teach her the language, and correct her pronunciation? and yet not one in twenty of the Mademoiselles in the houses of our nobility and our French boarding-schools are better qualified for such an office.—But I beg pardon, my dear, for interrupting you so long: I long to hear what sort of a life you lived in this rich despicable family."

"Truly," said miss Courteney, "it was not very agreeable: when lady Manning and I were alone, she used to entertain me with an account of her forefathers; she reckoned up among them half a dozen sheriffs, three lord-mayors, and a long train of aldermen. She lamented the death of her husband most pathetically; for if he had lived two years longer, he would have been elected lord-mayor, and she would have lived in the Mansion-house, and been queen of the city—These were her words.

"When we were at table and the servants attending, she used to turn the discourse upon the misfortunes of my father, lament the sad condition to which my mother and I were reduced by his death, express great anxiety about my brother, and enter into a minute discussion of our affairs.

"When there was company present, she would take notice that I was melancholy, and tell me that I must not take misfortunes to heart, and then sigh as if she was extremely affected with them herself; by which she recommended me to her visiters as an object of compassion, and never failed by that means to produce some instances of neglect towards me; so powerfully did that consideration operate upon most minds.

"She would sharply reprehend her daughter for any supposed want of civility to me, and pass over in silence any real one; telling her that if miss Courteney had not a fortune, yet she was a gentlewoman as well as herself, and that no body should be despised for being poor.

"Such were the continued mortifications that I was obliged to endure from this generous benefactress: yet I ought not to call them mortifications, because they only excited my contempt. About that time I received a letter from my brother, in which he informed me that he was going to travel with a young English nobleman, whose governor had died suddenly at Leyden, and whom he was appointed to succeed upon a very advantageous footing, on account of his birth; he desired me to draw upon him for what money I had occasion for.

"I received these insults with the more indifference, as I knew I could put an end to them when I pleased, by quitting lady Manning's house, which I could now do without any inconvenience to myself; and foreseeing that this indelicacy in her treatment of me, must necessarily end in something too coarse for me to dissemble my resentment, I was willing to stay till she shewed herself in her true colours, which would be my justification whenever I quitted her."

Chap. II.

Wherein family-pride awakens those natural affections which family-pride had suppressed.

It was not long before I had this opportunity. She desired me one day to walk with her in the garden, having something to communicate to me greatly to my advantage; and, after a profound silence of about ten minutes, she looked archly at me, and asked me if I could guess what she had been doing for me? Indeed I cannot, madam, replied I. Well then I will tell you, said she, nothing less, I assure you, than providing you a husband. Indeed! said I, laughing, and pray, madam, who is this intended husband? Come, come, said she gravely, before I tell you who he is, you must promise me to make no silly objections; such as age, not being a fine gentleman, and the like. The person I have in my eye for you is a sober staid man, and blessed with means to support you handsomely, without depending upon any body. That indeed is something, replied I; but who is this person, madam? I have a good mind, said she, to tantalize you a little, by keeping you in suspence;—but in short the person I mean is honest Mr. Jones.

"Although I expected some very absurd and impertinent proposal, yet my imagination had never reached any thing so ridiculous as this Mr. Jones; for I had had his history from himself some time before. He had been taken by her father out of a parish-school, because he understood writing and accounts, to keep his books for him. Upon his young mistress's marriage, he was advanced to be a clerk in her husband's office; and here, having scraped up a little money, he made some successful ventures in trade, and had acquired about two thousand pounds. After Sir John's death, my lady made him her steward, with a salary of fifty pounds a-year; and he was in this honourable and lucrative post, when she proposed him as a husband for me.

"My surprise was succeeded by a strong inclination to laugh, which, indeed, I took no pains to suppress; and pray, madam, said I, has this grave personage expressed any good liking to me?

"I hope you are not jesting, said she.—Why, did you expect me to be serious, replied I, upon such a proposal?

"Such a proposal, miss! repeated lady Manning colouring: if my daughter was in your circumstances, I should not be sorry such a proposal was made to her. Very likely, madam, returned I, and it might be more proper than to Mr. Courteney's daughter, and the niece of the earl of ——

"This may look like vanity, my dear miss Woodby; but I confess I was excessively shocked at her levelling me with her daughter, when riches were out of the question; for I was contented to allow her all the superiority she could derive from them. Lady Manning made me a smarter answer, and delivered with more calmness than I expected from her.

"If the earl of ——, said she, behaved more like an uncle to you, miss, it would be oftener remembered that you are his niece; but, as it is, I do not know whether it may not be an advantage to you, to have it forgot; for there are very few gentlemen of small fortunes who would choose an indigent woman of quality for a wife.

"I hope however, madam, said I, that none but a gentleman will presume to offer himself to me; and I shall take care not to justify my uncle's neglect, by encouraging any improper address.—You are very much in the right, miss, said lady Manning, one unfortunate marriage in a family is enough.

"'Tis well, madam, replied I, bursting into tears, you mean my father's, no doubt; but it was no otherwise unfortunate than that it had not the sanction of my grand-father's consent; my mother's excellencies justified his choice; and she might have had a fortune too, though not equal to what he might have expected, if it had not been trusted in the hands of a villain, who broke to leave his own children fortunes, as many other villains have done.

"This last hint threw lady Manning into some confusion; for it was suspected that her grand-father, who was a corn-factor,[17] had done the like: and, whether it was that she was afraid of my speaking still plainer, or that she was really concerned for having given me such just reason to complain of her, she thought fit to beg my pardon for what was past, and assured me, that whatever I might think of her, she was unalterably my friend.

"In my first emotions of resentment, I had resolved to write to Mr. Damer, and acquaint him with the treatment I had met with, which I knew would bring him immediately to my relief: but I considered that my leaving lady Manning in disgust might have disagreeable consequences; for she would not fail to represent every thing in such a manner as to make me appear in the wrong, and the world seldom espouses the part of the oppressed, because they who oppress have that on their side which is sure to exculpate them; they are rich: besides, the summer was now almost past, and she talked of going soon to London, where I could take an opportunity of leaving her without any noise, and of putting myself immediately under my guardian's protection; but I was delivered from this disagreeable situation sooner than I expected, and by means which I had then no reason to hope for.

"Lady Manning was desirous of spending a few weeks at Bath before she returned to London. A lady happened to be there at that time, who, I afterwards learned, was my great aunt by my father's side, and had followed the example of every branch of his family, in taking no notice of him after his marriage.

"This lady, lady Manning became acquainted with; and not knowing the relation in which she stood to me, she began one day to exclaim against the pride and folly of people in low circumstances, who expect to be considered on account of their birth, producing me as an instance, and relating how I had refused an honest man whom she had proposed to me for a husband, because he was not a gentleman, repeating my own words with a sneer; and therefore—*Not a proper match for Mr. Courteney's daughter.*

"This being the first time she had named me, lady Meadows (for it was her) cried out in some astonishment, what, madam, is that pretty young lady (so she was pleased to say) that I saw with you once in the rooms, Mr. Courteney's daughter?

"Lady Manning answering in the affirmative—good heaven! said lady Meadows, and have I lived to hear one of my family spoken of with such contempt?

"One of your family, madam! interrupted lady Manning, surprised.

"Yes, said lady Meadows, one of my family, who has done you too much honour to accept of an obligation from you; how could you presume to propose your scoundrel steward for a husband to my niece? but I will take her out of your hands immediately; you shall be paid for her board; my nephew's daughter shall not lie under an obligation to any upstart cit.[18]

"It is not to be doubted that lady Manning replied with great bitterness; but lady Meadows, from whom I afterwards had these particulars, was in too much emotion to listen to her. She immediately quitted the walk, for they were on the Parade;[19] and getting into her chariot, told lady Manning, that she was going to her lodgings to fetch me away.

"Thus, my dear miss Woodby, did I recover a relation, a friend, a benefactress, in a woman, who for many years, had had no intercourse with my father, and disclaimed him, as the rest of his relations had done, on account of his marriage: she whose resentment could not be softened by time; whose compassion could not be awakened by distress; she who had silenced the soft pleadings of nature, yet listened to the voice of pride; and from a sense of the affront that had been offered her family, in the husband proposed to me, she did all that a better motive could have suggested her to do.

"You may imagine I was greatly surprised, when a servant informed me, that lady Meadows was at the door in her chariot, and desired I would come to her. I had often heard my father mention this aunt of his, from whom, before his marriage, he had great expectations. I went down stairs in much confusion of mind, not knowing what this summons could mean, yet presaging some good; and as soon as I appeared, lady Meadows let down the glass, and desired me to come into the chariot. Her footman instantly opening the door, I got in, and placed myself by her, expecting when she would speak, and anxiously longing for an explanation.

"Lady Meadows gazed at me in silence, during some moments; then taking my hand, My dear, said she in a tender accent, you are very like your father. Poor Ned! added she with some emotion, he was not kindly used.—The tears streamed from my eyes at this mention of my father. I observed lady Meadows was greatly affected. Oh nature! thought I, why were thy tender feelings suppressed so long? Don't weep, my dear, said she, I will be both father and mother to you.

"Had I been in another place, I should have thrown myself at her feet, to express my gratitude for this affectionate promise. I could not speak at that moment; I took her hand, kissed it, and wet it with my tears. She kindly wiped my eyes with her own handkerchief; then looking again in my face, as if with pleasure, you are like your mother too, I suppose, said she: I never saw her, but I have heard that she was very handsome.

"This obliging manner of mentioning my mother, which I so little expected from her, quite subdued me. My dear, said she, what is past cannot be helped; you are my daughter now; you shall be no longer obliged to lady Manning.—That woman, pursued she, rising in her temper as she spoke, has herself told me the insolence of her treatment of you; she then gave me an account of what had passed upon the Parade, as I have already related to you.

"Lady Manning thought to have injured me in your opinion, said I, and she has made me happy, by awakening your tenderness for me: I now forgive her for all her insults.

"But I never will forgive her, interrupted lady Meadows.—As soon as we come to my lodgings, you shall send for your cloaths, and never more enter her doors.

"I was very unwilling to part with lady Manning in this manner, and

pressed my aunt to allow me to go and take leave of her civilly; but she positively refused, and I found she could not endure the least contradiction, which
is indeed one of her foibles. I therefore contented myself with writing to her,
and acquainted her with lady Meadow's resolution in my favour; I made the
best apology I could for leaving her so suddenly, and expressed some concern
at the misunderstanding there was between lady Meadows and her, which
made it impossible for me to wait on her.

"Politeness, my dear, is sometimes a great tax upon sincerity. Lady Manning had certainly treated me very ill, and in strict justice I was not obliged
to shew any respect to a woman who had violated all the laws of hospitality
with regard to me; but custom decides arbitrarily in these cases; and persons
in a certain condition of life, make a science of hating one another with all
the good breeding and complaisance imaginable.

"Lady Manning, according to this rule, returned a civil answer to my
letter, wished me all happiness, and wherever she went, let loose all the asper-
ity of her tongue against me. One calumny propagated by her hurt me more
than the rest: she confidently reported that I had sacrificed my conscience to
my interest; and that upon my aunt's promising to settle her whole fortune
upon me at her death, I had turned Roman catholick: for lady Meadows had
been perverted to that religion by her husband, and, like all proselytes, was
extremely bigotted to her new principles.

"I thought it became me to discountenance this report as much as possible; therefore I was more regular than ever in my attendance at church; and
although my aunt, after we came to London, would often have engaged me
to go to mass with her, intending no doubt to work me to her purpose by
degrees; yet I constantly and steddily refused to gratify her in this particular,
though in every other I studied to oblige her as much as possible. She would
often engage me in arguments upon the subject of religion, which I generally
strove to evade; and when I found that would not do, I defended myself with
great courage, and with so much success, that she would tell me with an air,
half smiling, half angry, I was too hard for her, and that she would consign
me over to her chaplain.

"This chaplain, whose name is Danvers, is a priest of the order of the
Jesuits: he had been recommended to lady Meadows by her late husband, whose
memory she adored; and this powerful interest, joined to the jesuit's insinuating
manners, acquired him so great credit with lady Meadows, that she governed
herself wholly by his advice; and that the great work of her salvation might be
perfected, and her every word and action be under his direction, he lived in
the house with her, where he ruled in a most arbitrary manner; his absolute

empire over the conscience of my lady, rendering his dominion over all that had any dependance on her as uncontroled as he could desire."

Here Henrietta stopped, observing her friend to look at her watch, which produced an exclamation that the reader will find in the following chapter.

Chap. III.

Which introduces a Jesuit to the acquaintance of the reader.

Oh! my dear," cried miss Woodby, "I am in despair to find it is so late, I must leave you now; but I am so impatient to hear the rest of your story, that if you will give me leave, I will breakfast with you to-morrow, and as soon as my eager curiosity is satisfied, we will go together to Mrs. Egret's."

She then desired a chair might be sent for; "and in the mean time," said she, "we will step into the shop, I will make a little purchase on purpose to see your landlady, whom you seem to dislike so much."

"Indeed I do not like her," replied Henrietta, "and yet she is mighty civil." "Well," said miss Woodby, tripping down stairs, "I'll give you my opinion of her when I have studied her a little."

Miss Courteney was following her into the shop, when perceiving the young gentleman, who was there the day before, in discourse with Mrs. Eccles, she pulled miss Woodby by the sleeve, whispering, "Don't go in now, there is somebody with her." "Indeed, but I will," replied miss Woodby, who saw the glimpse of a laced coat, for which she had always a violent passion, "and so shall you likewise."

Saying this, she pulled miss Courteney in, and, swimming up to Mrs. Eccles, bid her with a lively air show her some ribbons and blond laces.

The young gentleman, as soon as the ladies appeared, made them a profound bow; and, fixing his eyes on Henrietta's face, seemed to contemplate it with astonishment and delight.

Mean time miss Woodby was playing over a thousand fantastick airs, and uttering as many pretty absurdities, which she had heard admired coming from the mouths of beauties, without reflecting that she herself was no beauty—Mrs. Eccles perceived her foible immediately, and took occasion, when she was showing her some new-fashioned caps, to tell her, that such a one would suit the air of her face; that this coloured ribbon was most proper to shew the lustre of her eyes; observed that she had wonderful fine hair, and begged to know who cut it.

Henrietta, a little in pain for her friend, to whom personal compliments were by no means proper, endeavoured to relieve the confusion she supposed she was under, by diverting her attention to something else, and asked her opinion of some Dresden work that was lying before them. But miss Woodby had no leisure to answer her; for the gentleman, conceiving that it was easier to introduce some conversation to her than to miss Courteney, whose mingled modesty and dignity struck him with awe, addressed a trifling question to miss Woodby, which she answered with such an affected sprightliness as encouraged him to talk to her with the familiarity of an old acquaintance.

Miss Woodby was excessively delighted with his address to her, and played off all the artillery of eyes, air, and wit upon him.—Happy was it for the young gentleman, who courageously bore all her attacks, that this fire was given from two little grey eyes, over which her forehead hung like a precipice; and that this form which was thrown into a thousand different attitudes to strike him, was so distorted by nature as to leave little more for affectation to do.

The chair had been waiting half an hour without miss Woodby's perceiving it, when Henrietta, who was not at all pleased with the figure her friend made, told her, smiling, "that she would not let her stay any longer for fear she should by that means be disappointed of her company at breakfast the next day."

"I vow, my dear, you are in the right," cried miss Woodby, "to send me away; for my aunt is waiting supper for me—I am a giddy creature."—She then desired Mrs. Eccles to put up the things she had bought; for, in the gaiety of her heart, she had bought a great many. Mrs. Eccles obeyed, telling her she hoped she should have the pleasure of serving so agreeable a lady again.

The gentleman would hand her into her chair, which miss Woodby accepted with a very gallant air, after she had assured miss Courteney aloud, that she would be with her in the morning, and told her in a whisper that her landlady was a very pretty behaved woman.

Henrietta went up to her chamber directly, to the great disappointment of the young gentleman, who, finding there was no probability of seeing her again that night, went away disburthened of a heart which he had left with the charming stranger.

She was now summoned to supper by Mrs. Eccles, who was full of praises of the young lady her visiter. "This has been a lucky day, to me," said she, "for I have let my first floor, at a very good price, considering the season of the year." "I am glad of it," said the young lady. "That is very obliging of you, my dear miss," said Mrs. Eccles, "and you may still have the use of the dining-room when you have company; for my lord will be seldom at home in the day, these lodgings are only to sleep in. But how do you like him? Is he not a mighty agreeable man? Dear soul! not a bit of pride in him—."

"Do you mean the gentleman I saw in the shop?" said miss Courteney. "Yes," returned Mrs. Eccles, "he is a lord, I assure you." "Well," said miss Courteney, "I am glad you are not to lose one lodger without getting another, for I must leave you to-morrow." "How!" replied Mrs. Eccles, with an altered countenance, "I hope you are only in jest." "Upon my word I am in earnest," said miss Courteney. "I am sorry for it, madam," resumed she, "but this is very short notice."

Henrietta was a little surprised at the peevishness with which she spoke these last words, so different from her usual complaisance: but she would not seem to take notice of it, and only told her, that it was not her design to stay more than a few days at this end of town, having affairs to transact in the city, which would oblige her for her own convenience to take lodgings there.

Mrs. Eccles appeared satisfied with this answer, tho' a cloud hung upon her brow during the whole time they were at supper, which miss Courteney shortened as much as possible, and retired to her chamber, with new prejudices against her landlady, that made her rejoice in the prospect of getting away the next day.

Miss Woodby came according to her promise to breakfast, in a world of spirits, and had scarce taken a seat, when she asked after the charming fellow who entertained her so agreeably in the shop.

Henrietta told her, she saw no more of him; "for the moment you was gone," said she, "I went up stairs; but really, my dear, I wonder you seemed so pleased with his conversation, methought it was very silly and trifling."

"Oh!" exclaimed miss Woodby, "there is an inexpressible charm in the trifling chat of a pretty sensible fellow, when we know he submits to it only to please us women." "Truly," said miss Courteney, "your sex is not obliged to you for that compliment. Must a man then talk nonsense to be acceptable to us." "Lord, how grave, you are! my dear," said miss Woodby—"why don't you know that I am the veriest coquet in nature, and take an infinite pleasure in making a wise man look and talk like a fool."

"A coquet, my dear!" interrupted Henrietta, surprised, "no, surely." "Indeed but I am," replied miss Woodby; "and I verily think I should not be in the least concerned to see a hundred men dying of love for me." "Indeed!" said miss Courteney. "Yes, indeed," repeated the other; "but why that stare of astonishment? are these notions so new to you?" "Why, no—" hesitated miss Courteney (whose astonishment arose from the contemplation of the figure which uttered all this extravagance) "I have somewhere met in my course of reading with such fantastical notions, but I cannot say that I ever thought I should hear them avowed by a young lady of your good sense." "Oh! your servant for that compliment," returned miss Woodby, bowing; "but on the article of vanity we are all fools.—But come, my dear, make your tea, and then resume your story; for I die with impatience to hear it."

"I wish you would excuse me," said Henrietta, "till I am got to Mrs. Egret's, for I shall not be easy till I am out of this house." "Why have you such a dislike to this house?" said miss Woodby, "I protest I think your landlady a mighty civil, obliging woman." "Well, I don't like her," replied Henrietta, "she has let her first floor all on a sudden to the gentleman we saw in the shop." "And how does that affect you?" interrupted miss Woodby.

Henrietta blushed at this question; she was not willing to own that she thought there was some design in his coming, and expected her friend would have made that inference herself; but finding she did not, she endeavoured to divert her attention from the hint she had dropped, by saying she had set her heart upon going to Mrs. Egret's, and had told Mrs. Eccles that she was to leave her to-day.

"That was very imprudently done of you," said miss Woodby, "before you knew whether Mrs. Egret could accommodate you with lodgings; but own the truth now," pursued she, "did you not put yourself into a flutter upon hearing the gentleman had taken lodgings here?"

"Why, I cannot help saying I was startled at it," replied Henrietta, "and the more when I heard he was a man of quality; for surely these lodgings are much too mean for a person of that rank."

"Is he a man of quality?" exclaimed miss Woodby—"Oh! the dear creature—I protest I am quite in love with him now; I doat on a man of quality—And pray why should his coming fright you away.—Ah! my dear," said she, smiling archly, "had I not reason for saying a moment ago, that on the article of vanity we are all fools? Now are you ready to imagine here is a plot between this young nobleman and Mrs. Eccles against your fair self. Poor lady," pursued she, laughing, "this presumptuous knight will certainly carry you away."

"You are in a gay humour to-day," said miss Courteney, blushing, "but raillery a-part, it imports me greatly not to be known: this lord, as Mrs. Eccles says he is, will no doubt have a great many persons coming after him; I may be seen and discovered; and, if you knew what I have to dread in that case, I am sure you would think it reasonable for me to be desirous of leaving this house."

"You will be in more danger of a discovery at Mrs. Egret's," said miss

Woodby; "her house is much larger than this, and she is very seldom without people of fashion in it." "But I can keep in my chamber," said Henrietta. "And what hinders you from doing so here," said miss Woodby—"Ah! it is as I suspected; you are certainly apprehensive of being conveyed to some island in an immense lake."

"But, my dear miss Woodby," said Henrietta, laughing, "why, have you changed your mind about my going to Mrs. Egret's?" "I have not changed my mind," replied miss Woodby; "I am ready to do what I promised, but it is my opinion that if Mrs. Egret cannot furnish you with a lodging, you will be very safe here, and I will be with you as often as I can." "Ah, my dear," said miss Courteney, mimicking the tone she had used to her; "but come write a line to Mrs. Egret to know if she has a single room to spare, and I shall be satisfied."

Miss Woodby immediately complied with her request, and a porter was dispatched to St. James's-street, who soon returned with a billet from Mrs. Egret to miss Woodby, expressing her concern that she could not accommodate her friend.

"Well," said Henrietta, when she heard this, "I find I must be contented to stay here a few days longer; but remember I claim your promise to be with me as often as you can." "That you may depend upon," said miss Woodby; "and now I claim your's to finish your history, I am impatient to hear how you came off with this doughty chaplain."

Chap. IV.

In which our heroine engages herself in a very unequal contest.

I must confess," said miss Courteney, resuming her narrative, "that I had no inclination to engage in a religious dispute with a man whose learning and abilities furnished him with so many advantages over me; therefore whenever he gave the conversation that turn, I generally took refuge in silence, not being willing to hurt a cause I had so much at heart, by defending it weakly.

"However, I was often drawn in to answer by some apparent absurdity advanced by him, which it seemed mighty easy to refute. On these occasions Mr. Danvers would listen to me with wonderful attention, observe the most minute exactness in his reply, as if what I had urged had indeed great force: nay, he would sometimes seem a little prest by my arguments; pause for a few moments, as if he found it necessary to collect all his strength against so potent an adversary; and after a well-turned compliment on my understanding, he would resume the argument, in which he never failed to puzzle, though he could not convince me; but always concluded with a declaration that I was too hard for him, and it was well he had the best side of the argument, for nothing but truth could stand against such subtilty of reasoning.

"These praises always left me in a very good disposition to renew the subject whenever an opportunity offered. I began to be extremely fond of disputing with the chaplain; and, instead of shunning it, as I used to do, I even invited his opposition.

"I have heard it observed that vanity cheats many a woman out of her honour, I am sure it was well nigh cheating me out of my religion; for this jesuit, by his insidious praises, had given me such a confidence in my talent of reasoning, that I began to believe if he did not make a proselyte of me, I should certainly make one of him; and, in my eager pursuit of victory, I sometimes engaged myself beyond my strength, and received such checks, that if my faith was not overthrown, yet it was strangely staggered: but some disgust which I took to the manners of the chaplain preserved me from the poison of his doctrine, and made me lose all my relish for arguing with him.

"My aunt, who was certainly very desirous of my conversion, was much pleased with her chaplain's zeal to forward so great a work; and that she might give no interruption to our discourse, she would often leave us alone for several hours together.

"At such times, the jesuit would be very lavish of his compliments and praises; of which my person would even come in for a share—He would gaze on my face till he lost the chain of his discourse, and, by his inattention to what he was saying, gave me many advantages over him; and often, while he was pursuing his argument with great warmth, he would lay his hand on mine, hold it for several minutes together, and press it so violently, that I could hardly help crying out.

"All this, however, would not have startled me; but one day, taking occasion upon something I had said to break into an exclamation of surprise, at my prodigious understanding, he kissed my hand in a kind of rapture; and having once taken this liberty, he repeated it several times, to my great confusion and surprise.

"These are suspicions, my dear, which, against persons of a certain character, one dare not even avow to one's self. I was shocked, yet would not venture to examine why; I could never endure to be alone with him, yet never asked myself the reason; my eyes, as it were, mechanically avoided his; his civilities were odious to me. If he enquired after my health, I answered him coldly, without knowing I did so; and when he launched into any of his usual praises, I was downright rude to him, yet scarce perceived it myself.

"I now so carefully shunned being alone with him, that notwithstanding he sought opportunities of engaging me in private, which heightened my disgust, yet he never could find any. This conduct, if he had any guilt in his heart, must certainly give him cause to think I had detected it; and indeed I soon found, by my aunt's altered behaviour, that he was endeavouring to undermine me in her affection.

"The little peevishness I observed in her towards me, I imputed at first to her chagrin, at my having disappointed her wishes in not becoming a convert to that religion she professed; but I soon found that she had been made to conceive strange notions of me. She objected to the gaiety of my disposition; she did not like that crowd of lovers, as she phrased it, that followed me, and were encouraged by my coquet airs, and the pleasure I shewed in being admired.

"It is certain, that the report of the fortune my aunt designed for me, procured me addresses from several men, whom as she did not approve, so neither did I encourage; having, in reality, none of that sort of vanity which is gratified by a great many pretenders of this kind, nor did I feel the least partiality to any one of them; so that I told her it would give me no uneasiness if she forbid their visits for the future, which, since I found they were disagreeable to her I would have done myself, if I had thought it became me to take that liberty in her house. This declaration would not satisfy my aunt: she had further views; I must marry, and she must choose a husband for me, without leaving me in an affair that so nearly concerned my happiness, even a negative voice.

"I have no doubt but that the person she pitched upon was recommended to her by the chaplain; he was a Roman catholic baronet, had a large estate, was not much above sixty years of age, his person just not horrible, and he was not quite a fool. This was the man whom my aunt proposed to me, or rather commanded me to accept; for he had modesty enough not to try to engage my affections, till he had secured her consent, and was admitted in form to make his addresses to me.

"My aunt indeed allowed that there was some disproportion in our years; but then he had a good estate, and I was wholly dependent upon her; his person, she acknowledged, was not very amiable, but he was a baronet, and could give me a title; to be sure, she said, he was not a man of bright parts, but he would make a good settlement on me; and concluded with assuring me, that my chearful consent would greatly endear me to her, which I should find by the disposition she would make in her will.

"My aunt, having thus anticipated every objection I could make, and, in her opinion, fully answered them all, I thought it would be to no purpose to dispute with her on points already decided; I therefore contented myself with declaring, that I could not like Sir Isaac Darby (for that was his name); that I should be miserable if I married him; that I was extremely happy in my present situation, and had no wish to change it.

"Lady Meadows, I perceived, was a little offended at this so positive a declaration; but, I had nothing for it but steadiness. I expected, said she, more compliance from that sweetness I have been fond of supposing in your temper, and from your good sense, a greater attention to your own interest. I assured her, that it was and ever should be my sincerest endeavour to avoid offending her; that I would admit no offer but such as she should approve; and that I would guard my heart against any preference which was not authorised by her; more than this I told her was not in my power to promise, for no consideration of interest could prevail upon me to give my hand to a man, whom it was impossible for me either to love or esteem.

"Finding she listened to me patiently, I urged every argument my imagination could furnish me with, to prove to her that such an engagement, entered into upon pecuniary motives only, could not be happy, and might be very miserable. I begged she would not think of disposing of me in marriage, till I seemed less satisfied with my present happy lot; and that, by giving me no superior duties in domestic life to fulfil, she might entitle herself to all my undivided cares, affection, and assiduity.

"My aunt seemed affected with what I said: she told me she had no intention of forcing my inclination; that, loving me so well as she did, it was natural for her to wish to see me settled; that Sir Isaac Darby was a very advantageous offer; she recommended to me to consider well what I refused, and to conquer my unreasonable dislike of him, if possible.

"If it were possible, madam, replied I, your command would make me attempt it, but—No more buts now, Henrietta, interrupted my aunt—Sir Isaac dines here to-day; remember I expect you will treat him civilly at least, since he has so great a regard for you.

"I smiled, courtesied, and went out of the room where this long conversation had been held; for I heard the chaplain's step in my aunt's dressing-room; and this being the hour when he generally joined us, I chose to avoid seeing him then, for fear he should prevail upon her to exact something more than civility from me to the odious wretch, who had thus bartered for me without my consent.

"I did not appear in the dining-room till dinner was ready to be served; my antiquated lover approached with a janty air, and a sliding bow; and O!

don't you pity me, my dear, kissed my hand, as he led me to my seat. Nothing but the respect I owed my aunt could have hindered me from laughing at this ridiculous display of gallantry in the old man; for age has no claim to our reverence, if not accompanied by those qualities from whence it derives its worth. Wisdom, gravity, experience, the triumph of reason over passions, prejudice, and folly: all these we expect to find in fulness of years, and these make its wrinkles not only respectable but even lovely.

"In Sir Isaac Darby, age was contemptible as well as unlovely; he wanted to be young, in spite of time; he talked and laughed aloud; he strutted about the room; he adjusted his bag, for he was drest up to five and twenty; he hummed a tune: I sat staring with astonishment at him.[20]

"From what had passed between my aunt and I in the morning, I had no reason to imagine that Sir Isaac would be treated as a declared and authorised lover; but some time after dinner was over, Mr. Danvers withdrew, and my aunt, upon some trifling pretence, following him, I was left alone with the old baronet. I would instantly have quitted the room; but, remembering that my aunt had required civility of me at least, I resolved not to affront him, by leaving him to himself; and since I was obliged to stay, I would draw some amusement from the ridiculous scene before me.

"I know not whether it was from any particular archness in my looks just then (for I had composed my countenance to a kind of forced gravity) or whether the old man was at a loss in what manner he should form his address; but it is certain, that all his confidence seemed now, for the first time, to forsake him, and he sat silent during several minutes, stealing a glance at me every now and then: while I, with a formal air, played my fan, and increased his confusion by my silence. At length he quitted his own chair for that which my aunt had sat in, and which was next me; and drawing it still nearer to me, he made a motion to take my hand, which I withdrew as hastily as if a snake had touched it.

"This action a little disconcerted him; but taking courage again, after a preluding hem, he began, Charming miss Courteney, I don't doubt but lady Meadows has informed you of the violence of my—Here an unlucky cough interrupted his speech, and held him so long, that he grew black in the face; his endeavours to suppress it having, as I believe, almost choaked him. I rose up in a seeming fright, as if I had designed to call for assistance; but finding his cough had ceased, I sat down again at a greater distance than before.

"I fancy the town air does not agree with you, sir, said I, it is certainly very bad for asthmatical disorders.

"Oh, madam! said he, this is no asthma. I got a slight cold the other night at Spring-Gardens;[21] for we staid very late, and the ground was damp: but I came off better than any of my companions, two or three of whom are still laid up with colds. But tell me, dear miss Courteney, did you receive favourably the declaration your aunt made in my name? may I hope, or am I doomed to despair? whined out the superannuated enamorato, with an hideous ogle, which he designed for a languish.

"Oh, good sir, replied I, excessively shocked at his folly, these Arcadian strains do not become your wisdom and gravity. My aunt did mention your proposals to me, but I cannot accept them; I have no inclination to change my condition.

"How admirably this pretty seriousness sits on those sweet features! said the wretch, looking confidently at me, without being in the least mortified with my rebuke. But, my dear miss Courteney, you must change your mind—indeed you must—and your condition too, my fair one.

"Perhaps I may, sir, said I.

"Oh, that charming perhaps! said he, it restores me to life.

"Was there ever any thing so provoking, my dear, I protest I could hardly help abusing the ridiculous old man.

"I really think, sir, said I, looking at him with infinite contempt, that my seriousness would become your age, as well as my youth; but, pursued I, rising, to put an end to all your hopes, be pleased to know, that I am determined never to give my hand till I can give my heart with it; for I have no notion of being perjured at the altar, and of vowing to love, honour, and obey, when it is impossible for me to do either.

"I went out of the room when I had said these words, leaving the baronet to mumble the ends of his fingers with his gums; for he affected to bite his nails, as some persons who really have teeth do, when they are angry.

"I met my aunt as I was going to my own chamber: What, Henrietta! said she, have you left Sir Isaac alone?—I suppose you have treated him rudely; but come, you must return with me—I will, if you insist upon it, madam, said I, but I had much rather be excused—Indeed! said my aunt, looking a little angrily on me, and with that grave face too, but I shall not insist upon it, miss, and so you may go up to your own room, if you please.

"Although I was very glad to be at liberty to retire, yet my aunt's permission was given in such a manner that I saw she was offended with me for desiring it. I had experienced the obstinacy of her temper on several occasions; and I was convinced that if she set her heart upon marrying me to the baronet, she would use her utmost endeavours to carry her point, and the loss of her favour might probably be the consequence of her disappointment."

Chap. V.

Containing an account of some difficulties our heroine was involved in, arising from an old exploded notion, that interest ought not to be the sole consideration in marriage.

Full of these melancholy reflections, I resolved to write to Mr. Damer, acquaint him with what had passed, and intreat his advice in the uneasy and perplexed state of my mind. Not that I had the least intention of being governed by it, if he recommended to me compliance with my aunt's commands in favour of the baronet; but this I was well assured, from his good sense and natural rectitude of mind, he would not do, since it could never be supposed that such a man could be my choice; but I was willing to stand clear in his opinion, and pay him the deference that was due to the quality of guardian which he had so kindly assumed.

"I had been writing near two hours, for I had given him a circumstantial detail of every thing that had passed with regard to the baronet, whose character I treated with great contempt; but what was worse, my aunt herself did not escape some satirical strokes of my pen for her ready concurrence with the old man's proposals; and although I mentioned her (as it was my duty) with all imaginable love and respect, yet I could not help humorously rallying upon some of her notions, which were really odd enough, and I placed them in the most glaring light.

"The prodigious length of my letter first gave me notice that I had been a long time thus employed; and, looking at my watch, I found it was past our usual hour for tea, and wondered that I had not been summoned down stairs. I therefore made haste to conclude my letter, that I might send it to the post, when my aunt unfortunately entered the room. I started up from my chair when I saw her; and, hastily crushing the letter all in my hand, I put it into my pocket, not without betraying some signs of confusion.

"So, Henrietta, said my aunt, have I caught you? Caught me! madam, said I, considering whether she might not have been looking over my shoulder while I was writing so saucily about her; for guilt like love makes every thing seem possible that we fear. Yes, said she, have you not been writing? Nay, don't deny it, pursued she (for I hesitated and knew not what to say, lest she should desire to see my letter) it is no wonder that poor Sir Isaac Darby was rejected with so much scorn, when there is a favoured lover with whom you correspond privately.

"Bless me, madam, cried I, who has told you so? I correspond privately with a favoured lover!—This is some cruel calumny invented by an enemy to deprive me of your good opinion. Well, said my aunt, shew me the letter you conveyed so hastily into your pocket upon my appearance, and then I shall know what to think.

"You never, madam, replied I, used to desire to see my letters; nor would you now, but in consequence of some suspicion very unfavourable to me. That suspicion, interrupted my aunt, whatever it is, will be greatly strengthened by your refusing to shew me what you have been writing.

"Surely, madam, replied I, that is not just, I may have been writing to Mr. Damer, or to my brother. To your brother, said my aunt, I am certain you was not writing, because you have not heard from him for several months, and don't know how to direct to him (which indeed was but too true). It is possible that you were writing to Mr. Damer; but why refuse to shew me your letter? you can have no transactions with him that I ought not to be acquainted with: but I am persuaded that letter was not designed for Mr. Damer; and there needs no more to convince me that you are carrying on a private, and therefore an improper correspondence, than your thus obstinately refusing to shew it me.

"My aunt had reason for what she said: nothing was more easy, if I was really innocent, than to shew her the letter, which would remove her suspicions; but this, as I had managed that fatal letter, it was impossible for me to do. By not shewing it, I confirmed those suspicions she had so unjustly conceived, which might indeed have disagreeable consequences; but by shewing it, I was sure to incur her resentment for the liberties I had taken with her.

"How did I that moment inwardly regret my vanity, which had suffered me to rally the faults of a person on whom I so absolutely depended, merely to display my wit. I was so vexed at the dilemma to which I had reduced myself, that I burst into tears.

"Oh! I see how it is, said my aunt, keep your letter, Henrietta, I am convinced sufficiently. She hurried out of my chamber at these words. Shocked to the soul at having thus incurred the imputation of entertaining a secret lover, I went after her, resolving in that first emotion to shew her the letter, and rather be thought ungrateful to her, than guilty of an imprudence so disadvantageous to my character; but she was already at the bottom of the stairs, and I had time to make new reflections which prevented my former purpose.

"I considered that since there was no foundation for her fears of my listening to a private address, I might easily find means to undeceive her, and justify myself; but if I shewed her a letter, in which she was mentioned with so great freedom, I might possibly never be able to remove those ill impressions of me which she would doubtless receive, and I should be all my life branded for ingratitude.

"I was so terrified at this thought, that I resolved to put it out of my power to expose myself to such a misfortune, by destroying the fatal letter, which I did with a precipitation that left no time for second thoughts. When this was over, I expected to have found myself more calm and easy, but it was quite otherwise. I had given foundation to believe that I was engaged in a love-intrigue; for surely all clandestine addresses may be termed so, since there is too much mystery, contrivance, and little arts, necessary to them, not to give great pain to a delicate mind. I burst into tears at the reflection. My aunt's woman, who had a very tender regard for me, came into my chamber, and, finding me so disordered, begged to know what had happened.

"I related every thing that had passed between my aunt and I, but did not own to all the little freedoms I had taken with her in my letter; yet said enough to convince her, that I could not well show it to my aunt.

"Mrs. White, for that was her name, was very much concerned for my situation: she told me, that her lady and Mr. Danvers were in close conference. It is certainly he, said she, who has infused these suspicions into my lady, which, by this unfortunate circumstance of the letter, are now confirmed: she gave me such plain hints of the chaplain's selfish dispositions and designs, that it seemed highly probable he would spare no artifices to lessen my aunt's affection for me; for, since he had failed in making me a convert, which perhaps might have answered other views, he was desirous of keeping my aunt entirely to himself, and so manage her conscience, which he had the direction of, as that holy mother-church and he might divide her spoils.

"All this considered, my condition seemed so dangerous, that I begged Mrs. White to send a porter with a message from me to Mr. Damer, desiring to see him; for I resolved to regulate my conduct on this occasion wholly by his advice. She left me to do what I had desired her; and I remained alone in my chamber till nine o'clock, at which time I was summoned to supper.

"I found only my aunt and Mr. Danvers: I was a little confused; for knowing what suspicions I laboured under in my aunt's mind, I thought I had the air of a guilty person, and I felt that I blushed, and blushed the more for that reason.

"My aunt looked very coldly upon me; Mr. Danvers had the appearance of one that was very much concerned that all was not well between us: my aunt scarce spoke three words during supper; it was not my part surely to talk much; and Mr. Danvers accommodated himself to the present temper of my aunt; so that this was a very gloomy meal.

"When the cloth was removed, I was going to withdraw, for it seemed as if my presence was a restraint upon my aunt; but I considered that such a step being unusual, would imply a consciousness of something wrong in me, and that being innocent, it was my part to seek an explanation. I therefore addressed myself to my aunt, and begged she would give me an opportunity of clearing myself, by telling me who had poisoned her mind with suspicions to my prejudice.

"The chaplain was about to leave the room upon my entering on this subject. There is no necessity, sir, said I, for your retiring; I dare say the cause of my aunt's displeasure against me is no secret to you. My aunt has been told that I receive addresses from some man in private, and that I correspond with him; I declare this to be absolutely false, and I beg to know from whom you had your information, madam, said I, again directing myself to her, that I may refute this calumny; I am very confident the person who has thus maliciously injured me, will not dare to maintain the falshood to my face.

"Whether the chaplain thought this was meant for him, I know not; but although he had continued standing, as if he intended to leave us to ourselves, yet I had no sooner uttered these last words than he resumed his seat immediately, as if he would shew me he was not in the least affected by them; but I observed that he fixed his eyes upon my aunt, and expected her answer with some emotion.

"Before I comply with your condition, said my aunt, do you, Henrietta, agree to mine; let me see that letter you wrote to-day. I looked at the chaplain; I saw an alteration in his countenance, he was evidently more composed. Oh! thought I, sighing, how great would my triumph be, if I had this letter to show, and could show it without fear!

"You hesitate, Henrietta, pursued my aunt, why, if that letter was not to a lover, why do you refuse to produce it? I declare, madam, said I, upon my word and honour, that the letter was to Mr. Damer—Well, let me see it, said my aunt, and I shall be satisfied—I cannot show it to you, madam, replied I, in a faultering accent (for I dreaded the inference that would be drawn from what I was going to confess) I have torn it. Well, said my aunt, with a calmness that cost her some pains to maintain; and why did you tear it? it was not written to be torn, that is certain—But I will answer for you, niece, you tore it that I might not see it; and why might not I see it if it was to Mr. Damer—Again I protest, said I, that it was to him; but I did not chuse to let you see it, it was a long letter, full of impertinences: you would have thought I was very free in my observations on some particular persons, more free than became me perhaps—You might have been offended, and I tore it to prevent your seeing it.

"My aunt looked down, paused, and seemed not wholly dissatisfied with my manner of accounting for the reluctance I shewed to deliver my letter to her; but before she would declare herself, it was necessary she should consult her oracle, and that could not be done before me. She therefore put an end to the conversation, by ringing the bell for her woman. I attended her to her chamber, at the door of which she bade me good night, telling me, she would talk further with me in the morning.

"I endeavoured to make Mrs. White comprehend, by a look I gave her unobserved, that I wished to speak to her; and accordingly she came to me, after my aunt was in bed, and delivered the answer the porter had brought from Mr. Damer; he was out of town, but expected back in a week or two, was what the servants told him.

"Mrs. White repeated her offers of service to me, but dropped some expressions which shewed she would be glad to be assured that I really had no secret engagement which might justify my aunt's concern.

"These doubts, hinted with great respect, were so far from being resented by me, that I conceived the better opinion of her discretion, and confided absolutely in her sincerity. I made her quite easy with regard to the subject of her fears; and she repaid this condescension with the kindest assurances of attachment to me and care of my interests.

"I went to bed, full of hope that I had in part removed my aunt's suspicions, and relying on my innocence, I was persuaded I should soon restore myself to her good opinion; but innocence is not always a security to its possessor, because malice attains its ends by arts, which a good mind cannot conceive, and therefore is unable to guard against.

"Mrs. White informed me in a whisper, as I was going into my aunt's dressing-room next morning, where we always breakfasted, that her lady and the chaplain had been talking together for half an hour. I drew no favourable omen from this intelligence, nor from my aunt's looks, which were very cold and constrained.

"When breakfast was over, and Mr. Danvers had withdrawn, I expected she would enter into some conversation with me on the subject of the letter; but finding she talked of indifferent things, I took occasion to mention it myself, and begged to know if she had any doubts still remaining in her mind.

"Surely, replied my aunt, you think I am a person that can be very easily imposed upon. Then you are resolved, madam, said I, with some peevishness (for indeed I was horridly vexed to find her so strongly prejudiced) to believe I encourage a clandestine address, notwithstanding every appearance to the contrary.

"No indeed, interrupted my aunt, I am not so unreasonable, miss; it is because there are very strong appearances against you, that I am forced to believe what you would not have me—that letter, Henrietta—but no more on this subject at present, I am going to my house near Windsor forest tomorrow; we shall there have leisure enough to talk over this affair, and there I shall open my mind freely to you. I curtesied and was silent.

"My aunt took me with her to pay some morning visits, and seemed to be in very good humour; but her words, that she would open her mind freely to me at Windsor, gave me a great deal of anxiety. I did not doubt but I was to be prest again on the subject of sir Isaac Darby, and I was prepared for an obstinate resistance; but I was apprehensive that this resistance to my aunt's will, meeting with the unaccountable suspicions she had entertained, would infallibly ruin me with her. O my brother! thought I, why are you not here to countenance and protect me; or why have you so long neglected me, as to leave me in suspense whether I have a brother or not!

"This thought, and several others no less painful, spread an air of pensiveness and melancholy on my countenance, which my aunt, as I perceived, by some hints that dropped from her, interpreted to my disadvantage. In short, my dear, she imputed my pensiveness to the concern I was under at leaving town, as I could not expect to have many opportunities of seeing at Windsor this lover who had possession of my heart.

"You cannot imagine, miss Woodby, how much I suffered in being obliged to restrain my indignation at being thus treated; to have a phantom of a lover conjured up to teaze me with, and to combat suspicions which had not the least foundation, but in prejudice and caprice, against which plain truth and reason were very unequal arms: for how should reason remove what would never have been admitted, if reason had not been first set aside? Nothing was ever more improbable than that I should have a secret lover: I never went any where without my aunt; her visiters were mine; I could see no body without her knowledge: how was this engagement formed? But her chaplain had doubtless assured her, that I had a secret engagement, and she piously believed him, in contradiction to her own judgment: this was one of those cases that required an implicit faith; and in matters of faith, you know, Roman catholics are not permitted to exercise their reason.

"We set out next morning for Windsor: the chaplain and my aunt's woman being in the coach, the conversation was wholly upon indifferent things. After dinner was over, my aunt took me into her closet, and entered into a long discourse, which it would tire you to repeat—but the substance of it was my unhappy situation, when she took me out of the hands of lady

Manning—her tenderness for me; the great things she designed to do for me, nothing less than making me her sole heir; the folly of marrying for love, exemplified in my father's marriage; her fears that I was going to throw myself away on some young fop, who would make me miserable; sir Isaac Darby's generous passion for me, his great estate, the handsome settlements he proposed to make; and lastly, the pleasure I would give her, by suiting in this case my inclinations to my interest.

"To all this I answered very particularly; I acknowledged she had shewn a parental tenderness for me, and I had paid her, and ever would pay her, I said, the duty and obedience due from a child to a parent: that in the article of marriage, my natural parents would certainly have allowed me a negative voice, which was all I claimed now, since I was absolutely resolved not only never to marry without her consent, but not to admit of any address which she disapproved. I begged her never to propose sir Isaac Darby to me again, because my heart wholly rejected him; though at the same time I protested (as I might well do) that my affections were entirely disengaged.

"All your asseverations, replied my aunt (who had listened to me with many signs of impatience) signify nothing without you marry sir Isaac Darby; and by that only shall I be convinced that your head does not run upon some wild showy fellow, who will make your heart ake.

"Here (continued she) is a baronet of an ancient family, a large estate, of good morals, not disagreeable in his person—but what is person in a man? who loves you, who will make you a large jointure,[22] who gives you a title, place, equipage, all that a prudent sensible woman can desire, and you refuse him; grant that he is older than you, he has the more wisdom—(O my dear, how difficult it was for me to forbear laughing here); but you are not in love with him—let me tell you, Henrietta, that is not a plea for a young woman of delicacy—What, is it not possible for you to make a good wife to an honest gentleman, without bringing with you all that romantic passion which forces girls to jump out of windows to get to their fellows! and, for the sake of a man who possibly a few weeks before was an absolute stranger to them, break through every tie of natural affection, and, to be a wife, be contented to be neither daughter, sister, nor niece?

"I was going to speak—My aunt in a peremptory manner laid her hand on my mouth. I will not hear a word more, said she, on this subject; if you refuse to give your hand to sir Isaac, I know what I am to think—I allow you two days to consider of it. Hitherto I have treated you as my own child; if you comply you shall find me a mother, if not I am only your aunt; and you know how some who stand in that degree of relation to you behave. This was pretty plain, my dear; I was so shocked that I suffered my aunt to go out of the closet without making any answer; and retired to my own chamber to weep in freedom."

Chap. VI.

In which our heroine is very reasonably alarmed.

It was indeed true that my father's family took no notice of me, notwithstanding the applications that had been made to them; and when my aunt Meadows introduced me at my uncle's the earl of ———, I was received so coldly by him and his lady, that I inly resolved never to expose myself to such a mortification again; and my aunt entered so far into my just resentment, as never to press me to make them a second visit.

"My brother was abroad; if living, he neglected me; and perhaps I had no brother; for how else could I account for so long a silence in one who seemed to have such tender affections? I had no resource but in Mr. Damer's friendship, and he was at this time unluckily at too great a distance to be of any use to me. I saw plainly that I must either accept sir Isaac Darby, or be thrown back into by former indigence and dependence—Dreadful alternative!—But the man considered, was there room to pause long?

"My imagination suggested to me every possible ill consequence of the loss of my aunt's favour; but, weighed against the misery of such a marriage, they all seemed light—Yet would you think it, my dear, amidst the many real evils I had reason to apprehend by disobliging my aunt, one trifling circumstance dwelt strongest upon my mind, and that was the occasion of triumph I should give to lady Manning, who would exult over my fallen expectations and return to indigence. I was ashamed of my own weakness when I found this thought capable of giving me so much pain; and in the contemplation of greater misfortunes which were likely to be my lot, I sought to blunt my sense of these lesser ones, which were the necessary consequences of them.

"Towards evening Mrs. White threw herself in my way, as I was walking pensive in the garden. She told me that my aunt was full of hopes that I would comply: that sir Isaac was to be invited the next day; and that it was expected the generosity of his proposals with regard to settlements, the rich presents of jewels which he would offer, and his resolution to agree to every thing I desired, would make such an impression on my mind, as to induce me to give a free and willing consent. Mrs. White added, that since my aunt was so determined upon concluding this match, she wished I could conquer my aversion to it; for she feared that my absolute refusal would so irritate her, that she might be easily persuaded to take some violent resolution against me; and there is one, said she, who will spare no pains to bring that to pass.

"I replied, that nothing which could befal me from the loss of my aunt's favour, was to be dreaded so much as being the wife of sir Isaac Darby, and that my resolution was fixed. Mrs. White sighed, shrugged her shoulders, and hastened from me for fear of being observed, seeming, as I thought, to believe my case desperate.

"When she was gone, I considered, that if I accepted of the two days my aunt had given me to come to a resolution, I should be exposed during that time to the odious courtship of sir Isaac, whose presence was, it seems, judged necessary to influence me; I therefore determined to declare myself immediately, and plunge at once into the distresses that awaited me.

"I left the garden instantly, and went in search of my aunt; as soon as I entered the room where she was, she laid down a book she had been reading, and looked earnestly at me, seeming, by my countenance, on which I believe was impressed the agitation of my mind, to expect something extraordinary.

"You have indulged me, madam, said I, with two days to consider of your proposal with regard to sir Isaac Darby; but so long a time is not necessary: were any thing less at stake than the future happiness of my life, you should find me incapable of opposing your will; but in this case it is not possible for me to obey you. Judge of my aversion to that man, when I protest to you, that if death or his hand was an alternative that I must chuse, I would without hesitation prefer death as the lesser hardship.

"This determined speech seemed to surprise my aunt, though I think she had no reason to expect I could ever be prevailed upon to marry sir Isaac.

"You are an undone girl, said she, after a pause of near three minutes; I believe your father's folly is hereditary to you—I have done my duty—Your obstinacy be upon your own head.

"I confess I was greatly affected with her calm resentment, so likely to be lasting: I burst into tears; she went out of the room, I followed her into another, where Mr. Danvers was sitting. As soon as I perceived him, I hastily withdrew, for I was not willing to be seen by him in that state of dejection—I retired to my own room, and there, after I had relieved my mind by another flood of tears, I endeavoured to soften my own apprehensions of what might be the effects of having disobliged the only relation who would own me, and collected all my fortitude to enable me to bear the worst that could happen.

But that worst, my dear, proved so terrible to my frighted imagination, that to avoid it, I have taken a very imprudent and dangerous step, and whither it will lead me, Heaven knows; for my heart forebodes some fatal consequence from it."

"Lord bless me!" said miss Woodby, "after escaping such an odious husband as sir Isaac, was any thing worse to be feared!"

"Ah!" cried miss Courteney; "but it was not certain whether I should escape him; for if my aunt's scheme had taken place, I had every thing to fear." "What could your aunt's scheme be?" said miss Woodby impatiently. "Mr. Danvers's rather," said miss Courteney, "and its being his made it more formidable.

"My aunt seemed so easy and chearful at supper, and spoke to me so kindly, that all my gloomy apprehensions vanished, and I was happy in the thought that I should preserve her favour without becoming the wife of sir Isaac Darby; but I was soon undeceived. Mrs. White tapp'd at my door, after she had put my aunt to bed; I let her in, and told her, in a rapture of joy, how favourably my aunt seemed disposed, and that I should no longer be persecuted about the odious baronet. O miss! said she, I am afraid this calm foretels a storm. A storm, repeated I, what do you mean?

"I always dreaded, said she, that Mr. Danvers would use his power with my lady to your disadvantage; but who could have imagined that he would prevail upon her to send you to France, and lock you up in a nunnery?

"How! exclaimed I, almost breathless with terror and surprise—Confine me in a nunnery! Is it possible—How came you to know this?

"By the strangest chance in the world, replied Mrs. White. I am not used to listen, I scorn it; but some words that fell from the chaplain, alarmed me on your account, and I resolved, if possible, to know what he was driving at. This evening, pursued she, I went to my lady to take her directions about some laces I was making up for her. I found the chaplain with her: they seemed to be in deep discourse; and my lady, as if angry at being interrupted, bid me, in a hasty manner, come to her another time. I went away immediately; and just as I shut the door, I heard the chaplain say, Depend upon it, madam, there is no other way to preserve her from ruin. Certainly, thought I to myself, this must concern miss Courteney; I put my ear to the key-hole, and heard my lady answer, But shall I not be called a tyrant, for sending my niece to a convent contrary to her inclinations?

"The chaplain made a long speech, which I could not distinctly hear; but he told her she must make a sacrifice of such idle censures to God; that it was her duty to endeavour to save a soul; that you were in a state of perdition;

and oh, my dear miss! but that I cannot believe, he assured her you would throw yourself away upon the idle fellow (those were his words) that you were in love with, if not prevented by bolts and bars.

"In the end my lady seemed determined, and they consulted together about the means they should use to entrap you into a convent. My lady proposed making a tour to Paris, by way of amusement, to take you with her, and leave you in some monastery. Mr. Danvers, I found, objected to that; he desired she would leave the affair wholly to his management, and said he would think of some expedient that would be less troublesome to her. I did not stay to hear any more; for I was apprehensive of some of the servants coming that way, and discovering me at so mean a trick as listening.

"Good God! cried I, what shall I do? what shall I do? repeated I passionately, in the anguish of my mind. My guardian is not in town! to whom shall I apply for advice and assistance in this extremity! I may be hurried away to this horrid confinement, when I least expect it.

"That is impossible, said Mrs. White; forewarned forearmed, as the saying is. Since you know what is intended against you, you must be upon your guard; you cannot be carried away against your will.

"Mrs. White did not appear to me to have a very just sense of the danger I was exposed to; for what will not bigotry attempt! I was glad, therefore, when she left me to my own reflections; which she did, after begging me to be composed, and not to discover the manner in which I came by the intelligence she had given me.

"The latter part of her injunction I faithfully promised to perform; but, oh! my dear miss Woodby, how was it possible for me to be composed amidst such dreadful apprehensions?—To be locked up in a gloomy monastery, perhaps for ever, exposed to the persecutions of superstitious zeal: but this was not the worst of my fears—To be consigned over, perhaps, to the care of a wolf in sheep's cloathing, who had already shocked my delicacy with freedoms, that, proceeding from such a man, in such a character, might well awaken the most frightful suspicions."

"Truly," said miss Woodby, "that seemed to be the worst part of your danger; for I don't like this jesuit at all, every thing may be dreaded from a hypocrite: but, as to the being shut up in a convent, there is no great matter in it. Such beauty as yours would have soon engaged some adventurous knight in your cause, who would have scaled the walls to have delivered you—Oh, what a charming adventure! I protest I would submit to a few months confinement in such a place, for the pleasure of being delivered from it in so gallant a manner."

"Sure you are not in earnest," said Henrietta. "Indeed but I am," replied miss Woodby. "Well," resumed miss Courteney, "you have very whimsical notions; but I assure you none of these entered into my head: the loss of liberty seemed to me so frightful a misfortune, that I was almost distracted with the idea of it.

"The first thought that occurred to me, and which indeed was the most natural, was to prevent my aunt from carrying her designs into execution, by leaving her. I might well imagine she would use violence to detain me, if I attempted it openly; therefore it was necessary to steal myself away, and this has the air of an adventure you must own; but as I had no confident in this design, no gallant youth to assist me in my escape, and did not even make use of a ladder of ropes, or endanger breaking my neck, I am afraid this adventure is not in a taste high enough for you."

"Oh, you are rallying me!" said miss Woodby; "but I long to know how you escaped; no confident! how could you manage so arduous an undertaking by yourself?"

"With great ease, I assure you," said miss Courteney; "and I don't think you will allow it to be an escape, when I tell you I walked peaceably out of a door, not without some trepidation however, which arose less from the fear of a pursuit, than the consciousness that I was taking a step which every young woman of delicacy will if possible avoid.

"As I have already told you, I instantly resolved upon leaving my aunt; but where should I seek an asylum? Mr. Damer, whose protection I might have requested with honour, was not in town; my brother was abroad; none of my father's relations would receive me; I had no acquaintances but such as were my aunt's, to whom any application would have been very improper, as I should have found very strong prejudices to combat with; it being a received maxim among persons of a certain age, that young people are always in the wrong; besides, one seldom meets with any one who has not that littleness of soul which is mistaken for prudence, and teaches that it is not safe to meddle with other people's affairs, which narrow notion prevents many a good office, many a kind interposition; so that we seem to live only for ourselves.

"My perplexed mind could suggest no better expedient to me, than to seize the first opportunity that offered to go to London, and there conceal myself in a private lodging till Mr. Damer's return, who I doubted not would take me under his protection. Before I had fixed upon this resolution, great part of the night was wasted; so that I lay later than usual the next morning. When I went down to breakfast, I found my aunt dressed, and her coach ordered. She took notice that my eyes looked heavy; I told her I had a violent head-ach, which indeed was true: she said it was a cold, and bid me keep myself warm.

"I am going to Richmond, added she, it will be late before I return to dinner; therefore let the cook get you a chicken when you chuse to dine, and don't walk out to increase your cold.

"My heart leaped so when I found I was to be left at home, that I was afraid my emotion was visible in my countenance. My aunt, however, did not observe it; for, apparently, she had no suspicion that I knew any thing of her design to send me to a convent: and therefore she could not possibly guess my intention to leave her. But she certainly overacted her part, all on a sudden to drop her favourite scheme, the marrying of me to sir Isaac Darby; and when I might reasonably expect that my obstinate refusal to comply with her desires, would create some coldness in her towards me, to find her not only free from all resentment, but even particularly kind and obliging. Sure this was sufficient to raise doubts in my mind, that something more than ordinary was at the bottom of all this affability.

"It often happens that cunning over-reaches itself; for it seldom hits a medium, and generally does too much or too little. My aunt's behaviour would have led me to suspect that some design was forming against me; but if it had not been for Mrs. White's information, I should never have been able to discover what it was, for my own penetration would have gone no further than to suggest, that some scheme was laid to bring about my marriage with sir Isaac Darby; but this fear would have been sufficient to have winged my flight, so that the arts my aunt made use of to lull me into security, proved the very foundation of my doubts.

"I had a new palpitation of the heart when I saw the chaplain follow my aunt into the coach. Sure! thought I, Heaven approves of my design to get away, since so many circumstances concur to make it practicable. It was natural, my dear, as my religion was in danger from the persecutions preparing for me, to think Heaven interested in the success of my intended escape.

"There is certainly something very pleasing in supposing one's self, on certain occasions, the peculiar care of Providence. A Roman Catholick would have made little less than a miracle of so favourable a concurrence of circumstances. However, I suppressed this rising sally of spiritual vanity, and employed my thoughts in contriving how to get to town with convenience and safety, without expecting any supernatural assistance."

Here miss Woodby broke in upon the fair narrater, with an exclamation that will be found in the following chapter.

CHAP. VII.

In which Henrietta concludes her history.

"Oh! my dear," interrupted miss Woodby, laughing, "you have given an excellent name to a species of folly, which at once excites one's laughter and indignation. I know an old lady who is a constant frequenter of the chapel in Oxford-road, that has arrived to such a heighth of spiritual vanity as you justly term it, that she fancies Providence is perpetually exerting itself in miracles for her preservation, and that her most inconsiderable actions are under the immediate direction of Heaven; for she will tell you with surprising meekness and humility, that unworthy as she is, she is in high favour with God; if she happens to stumble against a stone without falling, she says, with a smile of conscious satisfaction, To be sure God is very good to *me*. According to her, *God acts by partial, not by general laws.* And should it cease raining immediately before she is to go out, either to church or a visit, it is all one, she supposes that Providence is at that moment at work for her, and has cleared the skies that she may walk with conveniency; for she cannot always purchase a coach or a chair, half of her little income being appropriated to the preachers, from whose doctrine she has imbibed these self-flattering ideas."

"Oh!" said miss Courteney, laughing, "you have heightened the colouring of this picture exceedingly."

"Upon my word I have not," said miss Woodby, "and—but that I am not willing to interrupt your story so long, I could give you an hundred proofs of this odd species of pride; for I assure you, my dear, the haughtiest beauty in the drawing-room, amidst a croud of adorers, and in the fullest display of airs and graces, has not half the vanity of one of these saints of Whitefield's or Wesley's creation."[23]

"I really pity the poor woman you mentioned," said Henrietta; "she appears to me to be very far from attaining to any degree of perfection: for may it not be supposed that this unreasonable confidence will lead her to neglect many duties very essential to a good christian? For I have heard it observed, that the preachers of that sect chiefly declaim against fashionable follies; and, according to them, to dress with elegance, to go to a play or an opera, or to make one at a party of cards, are mortal sins; mean time poor morals are wholly neglected, and superstition is made an equivalent to a virtuous life."

"Yet a writer," replied miss Woodby, "who is greatly admired by our sex, and who in his works pays court to all religions, carrying himself so evenly amidst them, that it is hard to distinguish to which he most inclines, has introduced these modern saints reclaiming a woman who had led a very vicious life, and doing more than all the best orthodox divines had done; and he has not thrown away his compliment: I dare say this numerous sect has bought up an impression of his book; and is not the third edition upon the title-page a very good return to it?[24] Oh! my dear, there is no vanity like the vanity of some authors: it is not to be doubted but if there were mussulmen[25] enough in the kingdom to add a unit more to the account of those editions, but we should find him introducing the alcoran,[26] making proselytes from luxury.—But how have we wandered from your story—You are still at Windsor—I long to hear the rest."

"I assure you, my dear," said miss Courteney, sighing, "I have not been sorry for this little interruption: it has given some relief to my mind; for I know not how it is, but the recollection of this period is painful to me; and yet under the same perplexity, and with the same apprehensions, I should certainly act again as I have done. I think I told you that Mr. Danvers went in the coach with my aunt; a circumstance with which I had reason to be rejoiced, as it greatly facilitated my escape. I was still lingering over the tea-table, uncertain in what manner I should perform my little journey, when Mrs. White came into the room: she was apprehensive that I should be uneasy at my aunt's and the chaplain's excursion together, as supposing it was to settle something relating to their scheme; and therefore made haste to inform me, that my aunt had been summoned to Richmond, by a message from a Roman catholic friend of her's, who was dangerously ill there; and desired to see her, together with Mr. Danvers, who was her ghostly father, as they term it.

"Mrs. White continued to talk to me on the subject of my aunt's design, while I was considering whether it would be proper to make her the confident of my intended flight to London, and engage her to procure me some vehicle to carry me thither. But it was possible she might not approve of my leaving my aunt so suddenly, in which case I should find it difficult to get away: besides, I did not think it reasonable to involve her in the consequences of my flight, by making her privy to it; and that the only way to enable her to justify herself to my aunt was not to make her guilty. I therefore resolved to steal out of the house, and go as far as I could on foot, not doubting but chance would throw some carriage in my way, in which I might finish my journey; and to gain all the time I could, I told Mrs. White, that my anxiety had hindered me from sleeping all night; that I was not well, and would go to my chamber and try to get some repose, desiring her not to disturb me.

"Having thus got four hours at least before me, I resolved to write a short letter to my aunt before I went. In this letter I told her, that having accidentally discovered her intention of sending me to a convent abroad, my terrors of such a confinement had forced me to throw myself under the protection of Mr. Damer; that I hoped, through his mediation, to convince her I had been guilty of no imprudences which could merit such severe usage as a punishment, and was not so unsettled in my religion as to be perverted by that or any other means. I begged her to believe, that except in that article, and in marrying contrary to my inclinations, I would pay her the same obedience as to a parent; but that I would rather submit to the lowest state of poverty, than marry a man whom I could neither love nor esteem; or change the religion in which I was bred, and with which I was entirely satisfied. I concluded with earnestly intreating to be restored to her good opinion, which I assured her I would always endeavour to deserve.

"Having sealed and directed this letter, I put it into one of my dressing-boxes, not doubting but as soon as I was missing, every thing that belonged to me would be searched for letters, in hopes of further discoveries. I next tied up some linen in a handkerchief, and with an aking heart, sallied out of my chamber, and crossed a passage-room which had steps leading to the garden. As soon as I had got out of the back-door, which opened into the forest, I concluded myself safe from discovery: and mended my pace; having no difficulty in finding my way, because I pursued the road which I had often traversed in a coach or a chaise.

"You will easily imagine my mind was full of melancholy reflections, and indeed so entirely was I engrossed by them for near an hour, that I did not perceive I was tired, till I grew so faint I was hardly able to move a step farther. I had now got into the open road, and it being about the time when I might expect to see some of the stage-coaches from Windsor pass that way, I sat down under the shade of a large tree, at some distance from the road, impatiently wishing for the sight. All this time I had not been alarmed with the fear of meeting with any insult, for I had seen no one from whom I could apprehend any such thing; but I had scarce enjoyed this comfortable shelter three minutes, when I perceived two ill looking fellows, as I thought them, making towards me with all the speed they were able. I started up in inconceivable terror, looking round me to see if any help was near if they should assault me, when I fortunately discovered the stage-coach; and being now eased of my fears, I resumed my station, till it was come near enough for me to speak to the driver. The two fellows who had given me such a terrible alarm, stopped short upon seeing the coach, and I really believe I had an escape from them.

"I called out to the coachman as soon as he could hear me. You know, my dear, the difficulties I found in getting admission. Little did those good women, who refused it, imagine that to avoid a slight inconvenience to themselves, they were consigning me over to the greatest distress imaginable."

"Wretches!" exclaimed miss Woodby, "I cannot think of them without detestation; but, my dear, (pursued she) did not you wonder to see a person of any figure in a stage-coach? As for you, I soon discovered there was something extraordinary in your case: but what did you think of me with such company, and in such an equipage?"

"Indeed, my dear," said miss Courteney, "at that time a stage-coach appeared to me a most desirable vehicle, and I had not then the least notion of its being a mean one; so greatly do our opinions of things alter with our circumstances and situations: besides, a difficulty then occurred to my thoughts, which, amidst the hurry and precipitation with which I quitted my aunt's house, had not been sufficiently attended to before, and that was how I should dispose of myself for a few days, till Mr. Damer's return; for it was necessary I should conceal myself with great care, having so much to apprehend from my aunt's bigotry and prejudices, and the (perhaps) interested officiousness of her chaplain.

"Under what strange disadvantages had I lodgings to seek for! by an assumed name, with an immediate occasion for them; and no recommendation to any particular house, which I could be sure was a reputable one. Your politeness, and the unexpected offer of your friendship, encouraged me to communicate my distress to you, and to intreat your assistance; and I must still regret the unlucky mistake that brought me hither instead of Mrs. Egret's. And now, my dear, you have my whole story before you. Have I not been very unfortunate? and am I not in a most dreadful situation? But what it chiefly concerns me to know, does your judgment acquit me of imprudence and folly in this precipitate flight from my aunt, to whom I owed so many benefits, and on whom I depended for support?"

"Approve your flight!" cried miss Woodby; "Yes certainly, child: who would not fly from a bigot, a priest, and an old hideous lover? I protest I would in your case have done the same thing." "Well, that is some comfort," replied miss Courteney; "but every body will not think as you do; and to a mind of any delicacy, sure nothing is so shocking as to have a reputation to defend; and the step I have taken will no doubt expose me to many unfavourable censures."

"And do you imagine," said miss Woodby, "that with a form so pleasing, and an understanding so distinguished, you will be exempted from the tax that envy is sure to levy upon merit? Don't you know what the most sensible of all poets says:

Envy will merit as its shade pursue,
And like a shadow proves the substance true.[27]

"Take my word for it, it is no great compliment we pay to persons, when we tell them that all the world speaks well of them; for those who are remarkable for any shining qualities will be more envied than admired, and frequently more calumniated than praised. But, child," pursued the volatile miss Woodby, assuming a sprightly air, "how do you intend to dispose of yourself to-day; it is late: I must go home to dress."

"Dispose of myself," repeated miss Courteney, "even in this solitary chamber; for I am determined, since I must stay here a day or two longer, to be as little with my landlady as possible."

Miss Woodby then fluttered down stairs, followed by her fair friend, who took that opportunity to tell Mrs. Eccles, that she should not leave her so suddenly as she had imagined, which was very agreeable news to the millener; who had no other objection to her beautiful lodger, but her extreme reserve, which did not at all suit her purposes.

CHAP. VIII.

Containing nothing either new or extraordinary.

Miss Courteney, after having traversed her chamber several times in great restlessness of mind, at length resolved to take a hackney coach and drive to Mr. Damer's, supposing she should know from his clerks or servants the exact time when he was expected home; at least they could give her a direction where to write to him, and it would be some comfort to acquaint him with her situation, and have his advice.

She had no sooner formed this design than she hastened to put it in execution; and having made a slight alteration in her dress, she went down to Mrs. Eccles, and desired her to send her maid for a coach, telling her she was obliged to go into the city upon business, and desired her not to wait for her at dinner. Mrs. Eccles insisted upon waiting till four o'clock at least, and attended her to the door, less out of complaisance than to hear where she ordered the coachman to drive; for the enquietude, irresolution, and pensiveness, which she discovered in her fair lodger, extremely heightened her curiosity to know her affairs.

Henrietta, though she did not suspect the motive of her officiousness, yet not thinking it proper to let her know where she was going, only bid the coachman drive to St. Paul's church-yard, and when there, she gave him a fuller direction. Alas! sighed she, when the coach stopped before the great gates of her guardian's house, were the hospitable master of this mansion at home, here should I find a secure asylum.

As soon as a servant appeared, she asked if Mr. Damer was at home, that she might with greater propriety introduce her farther enquiries; but was most agreeably surprised to hear him answer her in the affirmative, while he opened the coach-door: however, she ordered the coachman to wait, and then followed the servant, who introduced her into a large parlour, and retired to acquaint his master with her being there.

Immediately a young gentleman, of an engaging appearance, entered the room, and desired to know her commands. Henrietta seeing, instead of her guardian, a young man whom she was quite a stranger to, blushed at first, but a more painful sense of her disappointment soon spread a paleness over her fair face.

"Is not Mr. Damer at home, sir!" said she, in an accent that shewed her concern, "my business was with him?"

"My father, madam," said the young gentleman "is in Holland, from whence I came myself but lately; he has affairs to settle there which will detain him three or four weeks. But cannot I serve you, madam," added he; his voice becoming insensibly softer while he gazed on a form which it was not possible to behold without some sensibility. "Pray let me know, it will give me great pleasure if I can be in the least degree useful to you."

"I shall be obliged to you, sir," replied miss Courteney, "if you will forward a letter from me to Mr. Damer. It is a great unhappiness to me that he is abroad at this time: he is my guardian, and at present I have need of his advice and assistance."

"Pardon me, madam," said young Mr. Damer, "is not your name Courteney." "It is, sir," replied she.

"Dear miss," said he, looking on her with a tender sympathy; "I wish my father was at home, since you wish so—And yet, perhaps—all parents are alike," added he, after a pause and sighing, "they are too apt to imagine that happiness consists in riches. But are you in a place of safety, miss—Are you sure you are in no danger of being discovered? I wish it was in my power to offer you an asylum—but—"

"Bless me, sir!" interrupted Henrietta, in great astonishment, "you seem to be perfectly well acquainted with my situation."

"Yes, madam," said Mr. Damer, "I know something of your affairs, and from my soul I approve of your courage and resolution. A gentleman, named Danvers, was here yesterday to enquire for you; your aunt's chaplain, is he not?"

"Yes, sir," replied miss Courteney, "and my persecutor—but what did he say? I suppose he represented me in strange colours."

"You need only be seen, madam," said Mr. Damer, "to undeceive the most prejudiced: yet what he said was not disadvantageous to you, unless," added he, with a soft smile, "you think it a fault to have a tender heart."

"Ah! the wretch," interrupted miss Courteney, not able to contain her indignation; "I see he has been propagating falshoods injurious to my reputation; after having poisoned the mind of my aunt with suspicions that were the cause of my losing her affection, he is endeavouring to deprive me of every friend I have in the world—But this, sir, is the plain truth: he suggested, as I have no reason to doubt, a preposterous match for me to my aunt; I rejected it; he found means to persuade my aunt, that I listened privately to the addresses of some man who was an improper husband for me. My aunt, in order to prevent my ruin, as she supposed, insisted upon my accepting the person she had chosen for me; and, upon my obstinate refusal, was prevailed upon by her chaplain to resolve to confine me in a nunnery abroad. I had intelligence of this design, and I secretly left my aunt's house, to prevent her executing it; but I am so far from having any secret engagement, that if I could be sure my aunt would not pursue her scheme of entrapping me in a convent, I would instantly return and bind myself by the most solemn oaths never to marry any one whom she does not approve.

"You see, sir," proceeded miss Courteney, "what need I have of your father's assistance; he is my only friend and protector; through his mediation I might expect to be restored to the good opinion of my aunt."

"Well, madam," said Mr. Damer, "if you will write to him, I will take care of your letter; and if it be ready to-morrow, I will attend you myself for it; I hope you have no objection to my knowing where you are: in my father's absence I shall be proud to act as your guardian; though he has had the happiness of knowing you longer, yet his concern for your interest cannot be greater than mine. Shall I wait on you to-morrow morning, miss?" added he. Henrietta, by his manner of urging this request, and his frequently casting his eye towards the door, as if afraid of some interruption, concluding that she detained him from business of more importance, rose up immediately, and, giving him a direction to her lodgings by the name of Benson, told him, she would have her letter ready; but asked if it would not come safe inclosed to him by the penny-post, being unwilling, she said, to give him the trouble of coming for it.

"I beg, madam," said he, as he took her hand to lead her to the coach, "that you will believe I can have no greater pleasure than that of serving you. It is necessary that I should have an opportunity of talking to you at leisure, that I may know how I can be farther useful to you."

Having helped her into the coach, he bowed low, and retired hastily, with such an expression of tender concern on his countenance as any woman, less free from vanity than miss Courteney, would not have failed to observe; but she making no other reflections on his behaviour, than that he was more polite than persons usually are who are bred up to business, congratulated herself on having found a friend, through whom she could securely correspond with her guardian, and receive his advice, so that she might now consider herself as being under his immediate care and direction, though absent; a circumstance that greatly alleviated her uneasiness.

Mrs. Eccles, who had waited dinner for her longer than had been agreed on, expressed great pleasure at seeing her look so chearful. "To be sure (said she) you have heard some unexpected good news, I am heartily glad of it—Well, now I hope you will have more spirits." Henrietta smiled, but made no answer; for an ingenuous mind can only evade indiscreet curiosity by silence.

The cloth was scarce removed, when the young lord, who had now taken possession of his apartment in Mrs. Eccles's house, came into the parlour. Henrietta immediately rose up to retire to her own chamber, when he starting back, and standing at the door as if to obstruct her passage, "I came, (said he) Mrs. Eccles, to beg you would make me a dish of coffee; but since my presence drives this young lady away, I will go up stairs again."

"Oh, by no means, my lord," said Mrs. Eccles, "I am sure miss Benson will not let you think so. You are not going, miss, are you?" added she, turning to Henrietta.

"I have letters to write," said the young lady, "that will take me up the whole afternoon."

"Well," said my lord, "I will drink no coffee then; for unless you stay, miss, I shall be persuaded that my coming has driven you away. Let me intreat you," pursued he, entering and leading her to a chair, "to allow me the pleasure of drinking a dish of coffee with you; you will have time enough afterwards to write your letters."

Miss Courteney, who was willing to avoid the appearance of singularity, sat down again, tho' with some reluctance, telling his lordship, that she would not be the means of disappointing him of his coffee; but that she must insist upon being permitted to withdraw in half an hour, having business of consequence upon her hands.

The young nobleman gave little attention to what she said, but gazed on her with an earnestness that threw her into some confusion. The millener going out of the room to give orders about the coffee, he began in most vehement language to declare a passion for her, and called in the assistance of poetry, to express his admiration of her charms.

Henrietta, who in her own character would have treated this manner of address with ridicule and contempt, thought it became her, in her present circumstances, to resent it seriously; therefore rising, with some signs of indignation, she told him, that since his lordship thought proper to entertain her with such kind of discourse, she would immediately retire. My lord, who saw she was angry in good earnest, was excessively afraid of her leaving him; therefore taking her hand, which he forcibly held, till he had sealed a vow upon it with his lips, that he would not say another word to offend her, he brought her back to her seat, which, upon seeing Mrs. Eccles enter, she resumed.

The conversation then took another turn; but Henrietta was too much chagrined to mix in it with any degree of chearfulness: besides, the party seemed to her to be but ill assorted, a nobleman, a millener, and a young woman in obscure circumstances. Her delicacy was shocked, and all the politeness she was mistress of was scarce sufficient to hinder her from shewing how much she was displeased with herself and her company.

As soon as the tea-equipage was removed, she looked at her watch; and seeming apprehensive that she should not have time enough to write her letters, she withdrew with such precipitation, that they had no opportunity to solicit her longer stay.

"This is a strange girl," said the young lord, throwing himself into his chair, from whence he had risen to return the hasty compliment she made at her departure, "but divinely handsome! who can she be? I vow to God I believe I shall be in love with her in earnest: have you made no discovery yet, Mrs. Eccles," pursued he; "there is certainly some mystery in the case, and a love mystery it must be; for women are not even faithful to their own secrets, unless an amour is the business, and then they are impenetrable."

"Your lordship may be sure," said Mrs. Eccles, "that I have spared no pains to discover who she is; but she is excessively reserved, and talks so little, that there is no probability of intrapping her: yet I think there is one way by which your curiosity may be satisfied. Your lordship has seen a gay flighty lady with her, of whom she is very fond."

"What, that ugly creature!" said my lord, "that fastened upon me in your shop; do you mean her? is miss Benson fond of that thing?"

"Oh! very fond," replied Mrs. Eccles, "They were shut up together four hours this very morning."

"Then depend upon it she is the confident," said his lordship. "Oh! I guess your scheme; you would have me bribe her."

"Bribe her, my lord," repeated Mrs. Eccles; "she seems to be a woman of some fashion. I dare say you would affront her extremely, by offering her a bribe."

"I am very sure," interrupted his lordship, "that she will not be able to resist the bribe I shall offer her: I will flatter her, my dear Mrs. Eccles, till I not only become master of all her friend's secrets, but even her own; but how shall I get an opportunity of talking to her alone?"

"I will engage," said Mrs. Eccles, "that it will not be long before she is here again; and, if your lordship should happen to be below when she comes, I fancy you would not find it difficult to detain her a little while from her friend."

"Well," said my lord, "I leave it to you to manage this interview for me: when I know who this miss Benson is, I can make my approaches accordingly; but when do you expect her down stairs again?" "Not till supper-time," said Mrs. Eccles; "she is never weary of being alone." "Ah, that is a bad sign!" said he, "I doubt I have a rival—Well I will look in upon you at ten o'clock; perhaps I may find her with you."

Mrs. Eccles assuring him she would engage her till that time, if possible, he went away humming an opera air, but with less vacuity of thought than usual, miss Benson being so much in his head, that, if he had been accustomed to reflection, he would have concluded she was in his heart also, and that he was in love with her in earnest.

Henrietta in the mean time was employed in writing her letter to Mr. Damer, to whom she gave a faithful account of all that had happened to her, and earnestly intreated his good offices towards effecting a reconciliation between her aunt and her. The inconveniencies she saw herself exposed to in her present situation made her so desirous of this happy event, that her letter was almost a continued repetition of solicitations for that purpose. She begged him, in case he did not return to England, to write to her aunt, and endeavour to soften her, assuring him that she pretended to no greater liberty than what an obedient daughter might expect from a parent; being resolved to obey her will in every thing, provided she might not be compelled to marry the old baronet, nor confined in a nunnery with a view to the change of her religion.

She expressed her satisfaction in the polite behaviour of his son to her, whom she would consider, she said, as her guardian in his absence, and would take no step without his advice and concurrence.

She had finished her letter long before the millener's usual hour of supper; but being resolved to go down no more that evening, she spread letters and papers upon the table, as if she still continued extremely busy. Mrs. Eccles, upon entering her chamber to know if she was ready for supper, found her with the pen still in her hand; and was a good deal mortified to hear her say, That, having dined so late, she would not sup that night, but would finish her letters before she went to bed.

Mrs. Eccles did not think proper to press her; for her extreme reserve inspired her with a kind of awe, that made her cautious of giving her the least disgust; and Henrietta taking leave of her at her chamber-door for the night, she went away in great concern for the disappointment his lordship would meet with.

It was indeed a very mortifying disappointment to him; for his impatience to see miss Courteney had brought him back much sooner than he had intended, and Mrs. Eccles, when she came down stairs, found him already in her parlour. When he heard the young lady's resolution, not to appear again that night, he took an unceremonious leave of his complaisant landlady, and joined his company again at White's,[28] wondering to find himself in so ill an humour, on so slight an occasion, and that dice and Burgundy were scarce sufficient to call off his thoughts from this coy unknown, whom yet he did not despair of gaining.

CHAP. IX.

A very short chapter.

Henrietta, upon her coming down next morning to breakfast, was informed by Mrs. Eccles, that a gentleman had been enquiring for her that morning; but hearing she was not up, had left word that he would call again. She did not doubt but it was Mr. Damer, and was a little confused that his punctuality should so much exceed hers in an affair that immediately concerned her; but the truth was, the young merchant's impatience to see her had outstripped time, and he came much earlier than she had reason to expect him.

She retired immediately after breakfast, desiring that the gentleman might be shewn up stairs when he came again; for Mrs. Eccles, at her request, had made a small alteration in her apartment, and put her bed in an adjoining closet, that she might with more propriety receive a visit in her own room.

She was scarce got up stairs, when Mr. Damer was introduced: she apologised for the trouble he had in calling twice; and delivering him her letter, recommended it to his care with extreme earnestness, assuring him, she should be very unhappy till she had an answer. She then enquired more particularly concerning the visit Mr. Danvers had made him, anxious to collect from what he said what impression her flight had made upon her aunt.

"I will not flatter you, miss," said Mr. Damer. "Lady Meadows is extremely enraged—Mr. Danvers mentioned nothing of a design to put you into a convent; but owned that your aunt had a very advantageous match in view for you, which you rejected—and—"

"Pray go on, sir," said Henrietta, observing that he hesitated.

"Your aunt will have it, madam," pursued he, "that your affections are engaged—I cannot believe that a young lady of your good sense would make an improper choice—I should be very glad to be able to convince my father that nothing of this kind is the case—Excuse me, miss, I am very anxious for your happiness; it would give me infinite joy to find that your aunt is mistaken."

"My aunt has no reason, sir, for her suspicions," replied Henrietta; "but if my affections were engaged, why should she think I had made an improper choice?" "Ah! miss—" eagerly interrupted Mr. Damer.

"I hope, sir," said miss Courteney, gravely, "you will believe me, when I declare that my aunt's fears are without foundation; it concerns me greatly that your father should not entertain the same idle suspicions; and, were he here, I am sure I could convince him."

"Dear miss," interrupted Mr. Damer, "I cannot suffer you to go on; do not imagine that I am not convinced. I had doubts, but you will excuse them; my great concern for your happiness was the cause—Rely upon me, I beg you; I will take care my father shall not be prejudiced, and till his return I am your guardian."

Henrietta, upon a little reflection, was more pleased than offended at the doubts he so candidly acknowledged; in so young a man, such plainness and sincerity were far more agreeable than the refinements of compliment and flattery, and more suitable to the character in which he desired to be considered, and in which she did consider him. She thanked him for a solicitude, which she said was so advantageous to her; and to shew him that she wished to give him all imaginable satisfaction with regard to her conduct, she entered into a particular detail of the situation she had been in with her aunt, whose views with regard to her, she explained: she slightly touched upon the character of the chaplain, and imputed to his great influence over her aunt, the rash and severe resolutions she had taken against her.

She was proceeding to justify herself for having left her aunt's house; when

Mr. Damer interrupted her with some emotion: "every reasonable person, miss (said he) that knows your motives for taking this step, will not only hold you excused, but will even applaud you for not sacrificing yourself to riches."

"I am sure," said Henrietta, "my aunt would hear reason, were it not for that invidious chaplain, who fills her with suspicions, and animates her resentment. Oh, that Mr. Damer was come!"

"I hope," said the young merchant, "that we shall see him shortly; but in the mean time, miss, let me know how I can be useful to you: do you like your present lodgings? are the people such as you approve? Let me know if you have any inclination to remove, and I will endeavour to settle you some-where that will be agreeable to my father; I suppose you would have no objection to lodge with an acquaintance of his, and where you will be near him."

"No, certainly," said miss Courteney, "it would be highly agreeable to me." "Well, miss," said Mr. Damer, rising, "I will wait on you again in a day or two: but perhaps you have occasion for money, I have brought some with me; pray do not put yourself to any inconveniency, but draw for what sums you have occasion."

"The trifle, sir," said Henrietta, blushing, "that is in your father's hands, will not admit of my drawing very largely; however, I will venture to take up twenty pounds, because I have occasion to purchase some trifling things; for all my cloaths are at my aunt's, and I am in great hopes she will not send them after me: that would look indeed," said she, sighing, "as if I must never expect to return again; and I am resolved not to send for them, that it may appear I do expect and wish it."

Mr. Damer, upon hearing this, pressed her to take forty guineas; but she said, twenty would do, having some money by her. He then took leave of her, with a promise to see her again soon; and left her greatly pleased with his friendly behaviour, and with the prospect of being soon with persons less obnoxious to her than Mrs. Eccles.

She had scarcely deposited her money in her desk, when miss Woodby bolted into the room with her usual robust liveliness. Indeed her spirits were particularly exhilarated that day, having had the dear delight of conversing a whole hour with a beau, who said the civilest things to her imaginable; a piece of good fortune she did not often meet with, and for which, though her vanity did not suffer her to find it out, she was wholly indebted to her fair friend, the beau being no other than the young lord who lodged in the house, with whom she had been engaged in conversation great part of the time that Mr. Damer was with miss Courteney. And if the reader is curious to know what passed between them, he will be fully informed in the next chapter.

Chap. X.

Which gives the reader a specimen of female friendship.

Mr. Damer had been about half an hour with miss Courteney, when miss Woodby came to pay her a morning visit. As soon as Mrs. Eccles saw a chair set her down at the door, she flew up stairs to aquaint her noble lodger with her arrival; he instantly followed her down, and meeting miss Woodby at the bottom of the stairs, affected a joyful surprise at his good fortune in seeing her so unexpectedly again.

"The lady you are going to visit," said he, "is engaged with company, I believe; but I am resolved you shall not go away," pursued he, taking her hand and leading her into the parlour, "I was so charmed with your conversation the first time I saw you, that it is not probable I will lose this opportunity of renewing our acquaintance."

"Oh! your lordship is very obliging," said miss Woodby, suffering herself to be led into the parlour, while her transport at finding herself treated with so much gallantry, and her passionate desire of pleasing, threw her into such ridiculous affectation, that every limb and feature were distorted. Compliment, to which she was very little used, acting like strong liquors upon a weak head, she became so intoxicated, that she hardly knew what she did, which, joined to a natural aukwardness, produced the most absurd blunders in her behaviour; so that, endeavouring to trip with a lively motion to her seat, she overturned a light mahogany table that was in her way, and heard the crash of the china that was on it with very little emotion: the pleasure of shewing herself to the greatest advantage, absolutely engrossing her; and so unseasonably did she return his lordship's polite bow, when he had seated her in her chair, that their foreheads struck against each other with a force like the concussion of two rocks; but this accident, no more than the former, disturbed miss Woodby's enjoyment of her present happiness; and, wholly insensible to the pain of her forehead, she immediately entered into conversation with his lordship, asking him, with the liveliest air imaginable, if he had been at Ranelagh[29] last night; never once making the least reflection upon what he had told her of her friend's being engaged with company, which, as she knew her situation, might well have raised her curiosity.

The beau told her, he was not there; "but you and miss Benson were, I suppose," added he.

"Now your lordship mentions miss Benson," said she (without answering his question) "pray tell me how you like her; is she not very handsome?"

"Yes," replied my lord, "she is handsome; but," added he, looking full at her, "she wants a certain lady's agreeable vivacity."

"Oh! your servant, my lord," said miss Woodby, making the application immediately; "but really, as your lordship observes, she wants vivacity; there is something heavy and lumpish in her."

"Yet she is genteel," said my lord. "Oh! extremely genteel," cried miss Woodby; "but does not your lordship think she is rather too tall? being so slender as she is, does not that heighth give her a certain aukwardness?—But I really think she has one of the finest complexions in the world!"

"Has she not rather too much bloom," said my lord. "Why, yes," replied miss Woodby, "I think her complexion wants delicacy; but no objection can be made to her eyes, you must own, except that they are rather too large, and roll about heavily."

"Upon the whole," said my lord, "miss Benson is tolerable; but I perceive you are extremely fond of her by your partiality."

"Oh, my lord," said miss Woodby, "we are the greatest friends in the world; I conceived a violent friendship for her the first moment I saw her—You cannot imagine how ardent my friendships are."

"That is bad news for your lover," said my lord; "for love and friendship (the wise say) exclude each other; but I hope miss Benson makes a proper return to so much affection."

"Oh! we are united in the strongest bands of friendship," said miss Woodby; "the dear creature has not a thought that she conceals from me: and though I have not been aquainted with her a week, she has intrusted me with all her affairs."

"Indeed!" said my lord, "not acquainted a week, and so communicative! are you sure, my dear miss Woodby, that this young lady is not a little silly."

"I cannot say," replied miss Woodby, "that her understanding is the best in the world; but she has a very good heart."

"Your own is very good, I do not doubt," said my lord, "which leads you to make so favourable a judgment of another's—However, as she has laid open her affairs to you, you may, from the conduct she has avowed, collect your opinion of her."

"Very true," said miss Woodby; "and I do assure your lordship, that I cannot help approving of her conduct, because her motives were certainly just: though the ill-judging world may perhaps condemn her for running away from her aunt; and, from her hiding herself in a lodging, assuming another name, and such little circumstances, may take occasion to censure her, yet I am persuaded in my own mind that she is blameless."

"Benson is not her name then," said my lord, affecting great indifference. "Oh, no, my lord," said miss Woodby, "her name is Courteney.—But bless me—what have I done! I hope, my lord, you will be secret; I did not intend to tell your lordship miss Benson's true name—I would not for the world violate that friendship I have vowed to her."

"Depend upon it, madam," said my lord, "I will be secret as the grave. It is of no consequence to me to know her name; I shall never think of it again—But to be sure the poor girl is to be pitied—And so she ran away from her aunt; who is her aunt, pray?"

"Her aunt's name is Meadows," said miss Woodby, "lady Meadows; do you know her?"

"Not I," said my lord, throwing himself into a careless posture, and humming an air as if his attention was wholly disengaged; when suddenly turning again to miss Woodby with a smile—

"Why (said he) should not you and I be as good friends as miss Benson and you are; our acquaintance is not of a much shorter date, and perhaps commenced nearly in the same manner?"

"I protest," said miss Woodby, "and so it did; for I first saw your lordship in Mrs. Eccles's shop, and I happened to meet miss Benson in a stage-coach about four days ago."

"And there your acquaintance began?" said my lord; "you have improved it well since, if she has really been ingenuous enough to let you into the true state of her affairs. I suppose there is a lover in the case."

"A lover there certainly is," said miss Woodby; "but he was of her aunt's chusing; and it is from this lover she fled."

"O brave girl!" said my lord; "but is she not fled to a lover of her own chusing?" "No, I believe not," said miss Woodby.

"Well," said my lord, "I fancy she has deceived you, and that the gentleman who is with her now is her lover; he is a plain sort of man, Mrs. Eccles says, and looks like a merchant."

"Oh!" said miss Woodby, "it is Mr. Damer her guardian, I suppose." "But this is a young man," said my lord. "Then perhaps it is her brother," said miss Woodby, "who was abroad with a nobleman, and is now returned."

"I think I hear him coming down stairs," said my lord, "I have a mind to see him as he goes out." Saying this, he bowed and ran into the shop, leaving miss Woodby a little confused at his abrupt departure; and now, for the first time, she reflected that she had been indiscreet, and revealed too much of her friend's situation: but being incapable of taking any great interest in the concerns of another, this thought did not affect her much; her spirits had been put into such a violent flurry by my lord's complaisant address to her, that she only considered her own satisfaction in holding him in conversation; and if he had come back to her again, she would have given him all the remaining part of miss Courteney's history, without reflecting upon the baseness of the part she was acting, and only sensible to the pleasure of engaging the attention of a man: for, by the fatal concurrence of a disagreeable figure, and much affectation, she was generally neglected by that sex, whom she took all imaginable pains to please.

His lordship, at his going out of the room, had not otherwise taken leave of her than by a running bow, which left her some faint hopes of his return; but seeing him put on his hat and go hastily out of the shop, she concluded that he did not intend to come back: therefore she went up stairs to pay a visit to her friend, to whose account of her meeting with young Mr. Damer, and his friendly behaviour to her, she gave so little attention, her thoughts being wholly engrossed by the agreeable young nobleman, that when she left her, which was but a very short time afterwards, she scarce remembered any thing that had passed between them.

CHAP. XI.

In which our heroine is in great distress.

In the mean time the young lord, having an extreme curiosity to see the man whom he suspected to be his rival, followed Mr. Damer down the street, and had a full view of him as he crossed into another; he found he was young, and had an agreeable air, but there was a kind of pensiveness on his countenance, that did not seem to suit with the condition of a favoured lover. He readily admitted this thought, because it favoured his own wishes; he reflected on what he had heard from the communicative miss Woodby, and concluded he had no reason to despair.

A young woman eloped from her relations, with no body about her of authority enough to control or direct her actions; these were very favourable circumstances for a man of intrigue: and he resolved to be no longer kept at a distance by a reserve, which he imputed either to affectation or artifice, and which a suitable share of boldness could only overcome.

Having settled the plan of his operations with Mrs. Eccles, whom he had strongly engaged in his interests, he retired to his own lodgings; for those he had at the millener's were only hired to facilitate his designs upon miss Courteney.

That young lady finding herself free from his intrusion, and being less disgusted with Mrs. Eccles's behaviour than usual, who was very much upon her guard, and had her reasons for being so, passed the day with more tranquillity of mind than her situation had hitherto permitted, and condescended, at Mrs. Eccles's intreaty, to spend two hours with her after supper at piquet.[30]

In the mean time his lordship had conveyed himself into a closet in her apartment, and about eleven o'clock saw the unsuspecting fair one enter with a candle in her hand, and, after cautiously fastening the door, sit down composedly to read.

Her beauty, which was of that sort, which inspires respect as well as love, the innocence of her deportment, her security amidst that danger which threatened her, excited sentiments that made him half ashamed of his design. Charmed with beholding her in so agreeable an attitude, her fair face reclined on one of her hands, her elbow leaning on the table, her book in the other hand, which she seemed intently to read, he opened the closet-door a little way, that he might have the pleasure of contemplating her at leisure.

This motion was not unobserved by Henrietta; she raised her eyes off her book, which made him hastily pull the door close again. Henrietta, now convinced that there was somebody in her closet, started up, and, dropping her book, cried out aloud for help. His lordship immediately rushed out of the closet, threw himself at her feet, and begged her not to be frightened. Indignation succeeded to terror; her face, which was all pale and wan before, was now crimsoned over; her eyes shot indignant flashes at the insolent invader; but, in a moment, recollecting the danger she was exposed to, again her face was overspread with paleness, and an universal trembling seized her. The young lord, who observed the beautiful emotion, and was beginning to be shocked at the boldness of his attempt, again conjured her not to be afraid, and vowed he would leave her room: but Henrietta, on whom these assurances made no impression, sprung from him to the window, and, throwing up the sash, cried out as loud as she was able.

"Miss Courteney," said he, rising, but keeping at a distance for fear of alarming her more, "do not indiscreetly expose yourself, I swear by Heaven I will leave your room."

"What!" cried she, amazed to the last degree to hear him pronounce her name; "you know me then, and yet have dared to insult me thus—But leave me, my lord, this instant leave me, or I will raise the neighbourhood by my cries."

"Charming creature," said his lordship, looking on her with tenderness and awe, "I do know you, and I know your virtue now; I will leave you: believe me I am sorry for the terror I have put you into; grant me a moment's audience to-morrow; I have something to say to you that will convince you I am desirous of meriting your pardon."

He then bowed respectfully, and, unlocking the door, went down stairs; Henrietta all the time keeping close to the window, that she might be ready to call for help, if he shewed any design of staying in her apartment; nor till she heard him enter his own, and shut the door after him, durst she venture from her post to secure her door, which she did with the utmost precipitation, making it as fast as she could; and then shutting her window, for her cries had not been heard, she passed the night in a chair, resolving not to go to bed any more in that house.

The dangers she was exposed to, made her almost repent of having fled from her aunt's tyranny; and mortified as she was by such shocking insults, she thought it would have been a less misfortune to be the wife of sir Isaac Darby, or the inmate of a gloomy convent, than the avowed object of a libertine's passion.

Surprised as she was that my lord was acquainted with her name, and anxious to know by what means he had made the discovery, yet it never once occurred to her that miss Woodby had betrayed her. Her generous mind was incapable of suggesting such a suspicion, and she was even doubtful whether Mrs. Eccles was privy to his insolent attempt: so difficult it is for innocence to fathom the depths of guilt.

Amidst the melancholy reflections which her situation gave rise to, she drew some consolation from Mr. Damer's friendly concern for her. She resolved to go to him in the morning, and claim his promise of settling her immediately with one of his father's friends, yet without revealing the mortifying treatment she had been exposed to, and from which she had extricated herself: for true virtue blushes to own its conquests, because those conquests are proofs of its having been attempted. These various thoughts kept her waking the whole night; but towards morning she fell into a slumber, from whence she was roused by a loud knocking at her chamber-door. She rose instantly from her chair, where she had past the night; and perceiving the day was far advanced, opened the door, and let in her landlady; who excused herself for disturbing her, being apprehensive, she said, that she was ill, from her continuing so long in her chamber.

"It would not be surprising," said Henrietta cooly, "if I should be ill, considering the fright I was in last night. Did you not hear me cry out, Mrs. Eccles?"

"Dear heart," said Mrs. Eccles smiling, "hear you cry out! why what was the matter? some groundless apprehensions of thieves, I suppose; but there is no danger: my house has very good fastenings; I have lain it many a night by myself, I assure you."

"That may be," said miss Courteney; "but I am resolved never to lie in it another night; it would be well, Mrs. Eccles, if you were a little more cautious to whom you let your lodgings: rakes are dangerous company."

"I hope I have no such persons in my house," said Mrs. Eccles. "I have been insulted in your house," said Henrietta, "which obliges me to hasten my departure from it; pray let your maid get me a coach to the door."

"Why, you are not going, madam, are you?" said Mrs. Eccles pertly. "Not immediately," replied miss Courteney, "but I shall go to-day; at present I am going out upon business."

"And why pray will you go to-day, madam?" said Mrs. Eccles still more saucily. "Because," said miss Courteney, who did not like the accent in which she spoke, "I do not chuse to stay in a house where I am liable to be insulted."

"I hope you intend to cast no aspersions upon my character, madam," said Mrs. Eccles: "I would have you to know that I value my character as much as any body, though I am not so prudish as some folks."

"Will you order your maid to get me a coach?" said Henrietta, who was extremely apprehensive of some further rudeness from this woman; "I am in haste."

"Insulted, indeed!" repeated Mrs. Eccles: "fine airs for folks to give themselves, when no-body knows who they are, or what they are." Henrietta, finding that her insolence increased, told her she would go down herself, and send the maid for a coach, and was passing by her for that purpose; but Mrs. Eccles placed herself between her and the door, "No, no, my fine scrupulous young lady," says she, "you shall not stir, I assure you."

"Sure," said miss Courteney trembling, yet endeavouring to seem very courageous, "you will not dare to detain me!" "Indeed but I will," said Mrs. Eccles, "till I am paid; I know nothing of you but your airs and affectation; I may never see you again perhaps."

The young lady immediately pulled out her purse, blushing at the new indignity that was offered her; and taking out a guinea, "I agreed with you, Mrs. Eccles," said she, "for a guinea a week: here is a guinea for you, and now am I at liberty to go out?"

"Perhaps not," said Mrs. Eccles; "you have aspersed me with scandalous reflections, and I can tell you, madam, I will have satisfaction." "Lord bless me," said miss Courteney, who was now frighted out of her seeming courage, "what shall I do! what will become of me?"

This exclamation immediately brought up his lordship, who had been listening at the door of his apartment, and heard part of what had past.

As soon as Henrietta saw him her terror increased, not doubting but he came as an auxiliary to her landlady; but the contemptuous look he gave Mrs. Eccles, removed her apprehensions.

"What do you mean," said he, in an angry tone, "by treating this young lady in such a manner. Miss Benson do not be uneasy: if you are going, you shall meet with no hindrance; I ask your pardon for being the cause of your fright last night; I do assure you I am sincerely sorry for it."

"I hope you are, my lord," said miss Courteney, "and I thank you for this seasonable interposition." Saying this, she hastened down stairs, and dispatched the maid for a coach; while she stepped into the millener's parlour to settle her dress a little, and to put on her hat and cardinal,[31] which she had brought down in her hand.

Chap. XII.

In which the history goes forward.

Henrietta was waiting impatiently for the coach, when the young nobleman entered the room; "You are going then, miss?" said he sighing, "I waited at home all this morning for an opportunity of seeing you, that I might recommend such a resolution, as I find your prudence has suggested to you. Mrs. Eccles is not a proper woman for you to lodge with, and this I believe her behaviour to-day has convinced you of; had she not made the discovery to you herself, I should have done it, partly to repair the affront I have been so unhappy to offer you, and partly to secure you against the like, by letting you know that you are in the house of a woman of doubtful character."

This language bore the marks of so much prudence and sincerity, that Henrietta could not help being affected with it; and accordingly she expressed a grateful sense of his concern for her.

"I have something else to say to you," said he, "which possibly will surprise you more; but it is necessary you should know it, to avoid further inconveniencies, by a misplaced confidence: it was your friend miss Woodby that informed me of your true name and circumstances. I see you are shocked; she has indeed betrayed you, but less from malice I believe than folly. I am master of your secret miss Courteney," said he, speaking lower, and taking her hand; "but you may depend upon it, I shall make no other use of it, but to serve you in whatever way you shall direct; command my utmost services; dearest creature, dispose of me, my life, and fortune: never did I feel a real passion for any of your sex before."

"My lord," interrupted miss Courteney, concerned to find him again upon this strain, which destroyed the hope of his disinterestedness; "since you know my situation, you must also know that such discourse is extremely embarrassing to me. I am at present under the displeasure of my friends, without whose consent I will never admit of an address of this kind." She looked at him here; and observing him in some confusion, for indeed his intentions were not of that sort that could be communicated to her friends, she blushed at the humiliating idea that apparent confusion raised in her mind; but recovering herself,

"I am contented (said she) that your lordship should know my name, since chance has ordered it so, and I depend upon your honour not to mention me. I must also acknowledge myself obliged to you for the discovery you have made of miss Woodby's treachery; it is a very useful discovery, for otherwise I should still have confided in her, and been again betrayed." His lordship was going to reply with great eagerness, when the maid came in, and informed miss Courteney, that a coach was at the door.

"You are going then?" said he, with a melancholy look; but, 'ere he could proceed, Mrs. Eccles entered, and, with a countenance and voice altered to great obsequiousness, told Henrietta, that the gentleman who had been there yesterday, enquired for her. "O how lucky is this!" exclaimed miss Courteney: "let him be shewn up stairs, I'll wait on him." The millener having withdrawn, the young lord catched hold of Henrietta's hand as she was leaving the room,

"And can you be so cruel (said he) to quit me thus without giving me the least hope?" "Pray, my lord," said miss Courteney, drawing her hand from him with an air disdainful enough, "no more of this idle gallantry."

"Who is this gentleman that enquires for you?" said he, with a beseeching air.

"My lord," replied miss Courteney, "the gentleman is my friend." "Say rather your lover," said he: "oh! what joy you discovered when you heard he was come." "I had reason for being rejoiced, (interrupted she) he is my guardian, who has the care of my affairs." "Your guardian (repeated his lordship) may I not know his name?"

"He is the guardian of my person rather than my fortune," said Henrietta; "the poor trifle that I can call my own, does not deserve the name of fortune—It is my unhappiness," added she, sighing, "to be in a situation that exposes me to unworthy suspicions, and subjects me to humiliating explanations. You know my name, my lord, therefore you may know the name of the person, under whose protection I shall be for the future; Mr. Damer is my guardian, he is a considerable merchant in the city."

"Enough," cried the lover, kissing her hand in a rapture, while she was struggling to be gone from him, "I know him—Say only," pursued he, still endeavouring to detain her, "that you will permit me to see you again." "Excuse me, my lord," said Henrietta, breaking from him, "I cannot grant your request; tho' I must repeat the one I made to you, take no notice of your having met with me, and suffer me to be obliged to you for your secrecy."

"O! doubt me not," said he, following her to the stairs, and taking a passionate leave of her with his eyes, "I will obey you."

Henrietta answered no otherwise than by a courtesey, and hastened up to Mr. Damer, wondering at this unexpected visit, and indulging a flattering hope that his father was returned.

Mr. Damer met her as she entered the room, and, bowing more gravely than usual, told her, that he was afraid he kept her at home, being informed by her landlady that she was just going out.

"I was going out," said miss Courteney, "but it was to you." "Were you!" replied he, with a smile of pleasure that beamed over his countenance, "have you any new commands for me? I am glad I came so seasonably."

"But tell me, sir," said miss Courteney, "is my worthy guardian come back; have you any news for me? this visit was unexpected."

The young merchant was a little disconcerted at this question; for he had reasons which he did not care to own for visiting her so soon again: he had a glimpse of the young lord, as he passed by the parlour the day before; he saw him come out of the house; observed that he followed him, and looked at him with an inquisitive eye—He began to suspect that this gay gentleman had some design upon miss Courteney, and that she might have an inclination for him. He therefore resolved to take her immediately out of his way, and had already secured to her a safe retreat.

"I wish (said he) that I had any better news to bring you, than that I have provided you a lodging with the wife of one of my father's factors;[32] she is a sensible woman, and will treat you with great respect—I am persuaded my father will be pleased to find you there." "And I am ready," said Henrietta, eagerly, "to go immediately; for my intended visit to you to-day was to press you to find some suitable lodging for me—I don't know the person with whom I am at present; and she has no woman-lodger in the house but myself."

"You have a great deal of prudence, miss," said Mr. Damer, who was indeed excessively pleased to find her so desirous of going; "I fancy you can soon settle with your landlady; and we will make use of that hackney coach which stands at the door, and which you sent for, it seems." "I have settled already with her," said miss Courteney, "and this small parcel you see will be all my luggage, except the money you paid me yesterday," added she smiling, and unlocking her desk to take it out.

Mr. Damer very politely took up her little parcel, and carried it down stairs. Mean time miss Courteney was so much mistress of her resentment as to take a civil leave of Mrs. Eccles; and Mr. Damer, who was waiting for her at the door, handed her into the coach, and came in himself, after he had given the man directions where to drive.

The young nobleman, who was standing at one of his windows, saw her depart with great uneasiness. She was now in the hands of her guardian, and consequently his approaches would be more difficult; but youth and fortune think every thing attainable. His passion for Henrietta was violent enough to make him run all hazards to obtain her on any terms but marriage. Nothing is more easy than for love to conquer reason; its greatest triumph is when it is victorious over interest. The earl of ——, father to this young lord, was negotiating a match for him with a young woman of very great fortune, the daughter of an eminent packer[33] in the city. The noble youth, stimulated by forty thousand pounds, had pleaded his passion with such success, that the lady preferred him to all his titled rivals, and he had a great many, from the baronet up to the duke. The honest packer, sacrificing his ambition to his daughter's inclinations, chose rather to let her follow her taste and be only a countess, than become father-in-law to a duke by crossing it: an admirable instance of humility it must be confessed, and scarce to be equalled but by that of the nobleman, who, with such generous contempt of hereditary honours, solicited his alliance; but, happily for the reformation of manners, such instances are not now very rare.

This marriage therefore being in great forwardness, it behoved the young lord to be cautious in prosecuting his scheme upon miss Courteney. He was convinced she was virtuous; and that the only way to undermine that virtue was to make himself sure of her heart, before he discovered that his repentance was but feigned, and his intentions not honourable; when the passion she had for him would excuse, if not justify, an attempt that passion forced him to make; firmly depending on the poet's maxim, that, *the faults of love by love are justified.*[34]

The great point was to bring her to admit of his addresses without the knowledge of her friends, for which he could urge reasons sufficient; and when that point was gained, he might securely reckon upon success: for a young woman who engages in a private correspondence of that kind, deprives her-self of the suggestions of prudence, the caution of experience, the counsels of wisdom, and the restraint of authority; her whole conduct is then influenced by the passion with which she is actuated, which is at once her impulse and her guide.

Our lover, having given some sighs to the departure of his mistress, comforted himself in the hope of seeing her soon, with more advantage, since he had in some degree secured her confidence by the disinterested advice he had given her with regard to Mrs. Eccles; and having now no farther occasion for the apartment he had hired in that house, he quitted it immediately, not without discovering in his behaviour to her at parting some part of that contempt, which even the greatest libertines feel for such as assist their criminal designs.

Mean time Henrietta, extremely pleased with the care and attention of her new guardian, was by him conducted to a large well-furnished house in the city, and received with great respect by the mistress of it, who was a middle-aged woman, with a benevolent aspect and an easy agreeable behaviour.

"Mrs. Willis," said Mr. Damer, leading in miss Courteney, "permit me to introduce you to this young lady, my father's ward, and at present under my care: I hope you will make every thing agreeable to her during the time she stays with you. Miss Benson (added he) I need not give Mrs. Willis any other recommendation to you, than that she is a friend of my father's, and very much esteemed by him."

Henrietta, though in some confusion at being introduced under a feigned name to a friend of Mr. Damer's, saluted her with a graceful air, and replied to the compliments she made her with great politeness; but took the first opportunity of her withdrawing, to ask Mr. Damer, why he concealed her true name from a friend of his father's?

Mr. Damer asked her pardon for not having consulted her before on that subject; but said, that by still continuing the name of Benson, she would be more secure from the search her aunt might make for her.

"Alas! sir," said miss Courteney, "I am afraid my aunt is too much offended to be at any pains to find me out—I am more apprehensive of the contrivances of Mr. Danvers; he no doubt has strong reasons for putting her upon such harsh measures. While I was alone and unprotected, I thought it necessary to conceal myself, since it was not impossible but I might have been forced away; but I am sure no such attempt will be made, when it is known that I am under my guardian's protection. I think therefore this gentlewoman ought to be aquainted with my name. I would avoid as much as possible the appearance of mystery. I shall never recollect, without pain, the sad necessity that has reduced me to it."

"It will not be prudent," said Mr. Damer, "to alter our measures now:

I have called you miss Benson; the discovery of your true name will come with more propriety from my father, when he has accommodated matters between your aunt and you: we may expect a letter from him in a day or two, in which he will probably fix the time of his return. In the mean while I hope you will find yourself agreeably situated here—I have agreed for your board and lodging."

"At a moderate price, I hope," said miss Courteney, "my circumstances do not entitle me to great expence." "I have taken care of that," said Mr. Damer. Mrs. Willis coming in that moment, he recommended miss Courteney to her care, promising, when he heard from his father, to come immediately with the news. He then took his leave, and Mrs. Willis conducted her fair lodger to another parlour, where the cloth was laid for dinner, and introduced two pretty children to her, a boy and a girl, with whom the young lady was extremely pleased.

There was in the countenance of this woman so much sweetness and complacency, and such an unaffected politeness in her behaviour, that Henrietta found herself insensibly disposed to like her, and was pleased to hear her fall naturally into an account of herself with a frankness and simplicity that denoted the goodness of her heart.

From what she said, miss Courteney collected that she had made a marriage of choice rather than of prudence, and that industry had supplied the place of fortune. She found she was under great obligations to the elder Mr. Damer, who had settled her husband in an advantageous way at Leghorn, where he acted as his factor, and had enabled her to furnish that large house, in a very genteel manner, for the reception of such merchants as came from abroad, and were by him recommended to lodge with her. Her extreme tenderness for her husband, which had hurried her to Leghorn upon hearing that he was ill, that she might have the satisfaction of attending him herself, and her anxiety for her children, which brought her back as soon as he was recovered, that she might re-assume her care of them, were qualities which won her the esteem of miss Courteney. She marked with what becoming reserve she slightly touched upon her family and connections, which were very genteel, and by which Henrietta accounted for the easy politeness of her manners and behaviour, so seldom found in persons of her rank.

The young lady then turned the discourse upon her guardian's son, whose character she was desirous of being acquainted with. Mrs. Willis told her, that he was a sober diligent young man, and though the heir of immense riches, yet applied himself to business with as much industry as if he had had his fortune to make: that he had for several years transacted his father's business in Holland, from whence he was but lately returned; and that he traded largely for himself.

"Before I went to Leghorn (added she) there was some talk of his being to be married to the daughter of a very rich citizen; but since my return, which was about a week ago, I have heard nothing of it, not having seen Mr. Damer till the day that he came to tell me I should be so happy as to have you, madam, for my lodger."

Miss Courteney having passed this day more agreeably than she had done any since she had left her aunt, was at night conducted by Mrs. Willis to a genteel apartment, consisting of a bed-chamber and dressing-room. She dismissed the maid whom Mrs. Willis ordered to attend and undress her; and being greatly fatigued for want of rest the preceding night, lost all her cares, her anxieties, and resentments, in the sweet oblivion of a calm and uninterrupted sleep.

CHAP. XIII.

The history still advances.

Henrietta, though an early riser, and though she rose next morning earlier than usual, yet found, upon her going down, Mrs. Willis had waited breakfast for her some time.

As soon as the tea-equipage was removed, she retired to leave Mrs. Willis at liberty to go about her domestick affairs; and, when alone, was again assaulted with all those cruel reflections which had almost incessantly filled her mind since her flight from her aunt. Among these, miss Woodby's treachery suggested none of the least painful: she was ashamed of her credulity, of her ill-placed confidence; indignation for the shocking treatment she had met with from her succeeded. She was upon the point of sitting down to write to her, and to express the deepest resentment of her malice and treachery; when, recollecting the extreme levity of that young woman's temper, her ridiculous affectation, her folly and insensibility, she thought it would ill become her to make serious remonstrances to one who only merited contempt; that by taking no further notice of her, that contempt would be best expressed, and her own consciousness of the part she had acted would account for it.

While she was thus ruminating, Mrs. Willis's maid introduced two porters bringing in a large trunk to her apartment. They delivered her the key sealed up, and a letter from Mr. Damer, in which he informed her, he would wait on her that afternoon.

She opened the trunk trembling; it contained all her cloaths, linen, and all the trinkets her aunt had given her. She searched eagerly in it to see if there was a letter for her; but finding none, she threw herself into a chair, and burst into a flood of tears.

While her aunt retained her cloaths, she had formed a feeble hope that she was anxious for her return, and would facilitate it, by assuring Mr. Damer, that she would no more press her to the hated marriage, nor think of confining her in a convent; but now what could she conclude, but that she had abandoned her for ever, and that a reconciliation was not to be expected. The most gloomy prospects offered themselves to her view, poverty, dependence, neglect; but what was worse than all, the loss perhaps of reputation. How should she be able to excuse herself to the world for her late action; the world which judges actions only by their success: and when it beheld her unhappy and reduced to indigence, would not fail to conclude her guilty.

In these melancholy apprehensions did she wear away the hours till summoned to dinner by Mrs. Willis, who, with tender concern, perceived that she was afflicted, but would not discover that she perceived it; and used her utmost endeavours to amuse her, yet without any apparent solicitude, lest it should alarm her sensibility with a fear that her uneasiness was observed.

Mr. Damer came according to his promise in the afternoon: his arrival gave almost as much satisfaction to Mrs. Willis, as to her fair anxious lodger, from a hope that it would produce some comfort to her. The young merchant instantly discovered that Henrietta had been weeping; and, as soon as Mrs. Willis withdrew, he tenderly approached her, and taking her hand, asked her if any thing new had happened to give her disturbance? Henrietta replied with a hasty question, "Have you any message for me from my aunt, sir?"

"I cannot say I have a message for you, miss," answered Mr. Damer; "your aunt has indeed wrote to me." "May I not see her letter?" asked miss Courteney again, eagerly. "To be sure," said he, taking it out of his pocket, and presenting it to her, "I wish it was conceived in more favourable terms." Miss Courteney read it trembling, and found it as follows:

SIR,

I HAVE given directions that every thing which belongs to that unhappy girl my niece should be sent to you, that if you know where she is, they may be conveyed to her. She has, by her scandalously running away from me, ruined her own character, and brought aspersions upon mine; since even those who condemn her most, will likewise blame me, as if I had acted unkindly towards her.

May the loss of my affection be the least of her misfortunes; though
the worst that can possibly happen are likely to be the punishment
of her ingratitude and folly.

Henrietta returned the letter to Mr. Damer with a sigh. "I have indeed
(said she) irrecoverably lost her affection: but, sir, it is fit my aunt should know
where I am, and that I solicited your protection as soon as I could. This will
preserve me from some of those unfavourable suspicions which she mentions
so severely. I will write to her instantly."

"Oh! no, by no means," said Mr. Damer, "I think it will be best for me
to make a visit to lady Meadows, and tell her, that you are under my care, and
that I have placed you here."

"And will you take the trouble to go to Windsor, sir," said miss Courteney, extremely delighted with this expedient. "I would go any where," said
Mr. Damer, "to serve you. Pray make yourself easy."

"I shall be easier," said miss Courteney, "when my aunt knows that this
scandalous runaway is under proper protection, and is accountable for all her
actions to your father. Perhaps she may relent when she is convinced I am not
so indiscreet as she imagined, and that I had no other motive for leaving her
but the fear of being confined in a convent. If you find my aunt absolutely
resolved not to be reconciled to me, I must then consider how to dispose of
myself in a way more suitable to my circumstances."

"Remember, miss," said Mr. Damer, with some emotion, "that you are
under my care—I hope you will take no resolution without acquainting me."
"No certainly," replied Henrietta—"but, sir, I have no fortune; I am lodged,
attended, and treated, as if I had a very considerable one. This expence I shall
not be willing to support a great while longer, it will break in too much upon
that trifling sum, which was put into your father's hands, for my brother's use
as well as mine. Heaven knows (said she, sighing) whether he is alive; if he is,
he will probably need it; if he is not, it will go but a very little way in supporting me in the manner in which I now live."

While Henrietta was speaking in this manner, Mr. Damer seemed ready
to interrupt her several times, but checked himself as if upon better recollection; when she was silent, he walked about the room, musing; then suddenly
turning towards her,

"These considerations, miss, (said he) ought at least to be postponed
till my father's return, and I think you may rely upon his prudence: he will
certainly take care that your expences shall not exceed your income; in placing
you here, I have done what I thought would be agreeable to him."

Henrietta, observing that he was in some confusion, was concerned that she had spoke so freely, being apprehensive that he understood what she had said as a distrust of his prudence. She therefore told him, that if he found her aunt implacable, she would be extremely well satisfied to continue with Mrs. Willis as long as Mr. Damer should think it necessary.

This assurance satisfied the young merchant, who left her with a promise to see lady Meadows the next day, and to wait on her as soon as possible, with an account of the success of his visit.

She passed this interval in a state of anxiety and suspence, that doubled every hour. As soon as she saw Mr. Damer again, she endeavoured to read in his countenance, before he spoke, the news he had brought her.

"Well, miss (said he) I have seen your aunt." He paused; and Henrietta, in a faultering accent, begged him to tell her in one word, whether he had succeeded or not?

"Indeed I have not: (said he) lady Meadows seems resolved never to forgive you for running away from her; but don't despair, my father may have more weight with her." "It is at least some comfort (said she) that she knows I am under your protection." "I have a letter from my father," said Mr. Damer, "he has got the gout in his right hand; he dictated it to one of his clerks, and therefore speaks with reserve of you. He desires me to tell you, that he hopes to be in London in three weeks at farthest, when he will use his utmost endeavours to reconcile you to your aunt; and, in the mean time, recommends you most affectionately to my care."

This account of her guardian's kind concern for her, gave some relief to the depressed spirits of miss Courteney, who, although she had not flattered herself with any hope from the young merchant's mediation with her aunt, was as much shocked at the confirmation of her continued displeasure, as if she had not expected it. However, she expressed a grateful sense of his services, and disposed herself to wait with patience for the arrival of Mr. Damer, who alone could determine her destiny.

Chap. XIV.

Containing several mysterious circumstances.

Henrietta had been about a fortnight in the house of Mrs. Willis, whose good sense and polite behaviour, had entirely won her esteem, when, on a sudden, she became reserved and thoughtful, and often failed in those little attentions which mark respect, and an extreme willingness to oblige. She, who had avoided the least appearance of curiosity to know more of her affairs than what she pleased to disclose, now asked questions with an inquisitive air, and seemed to seek for occasions of collecting a fuller knowledge of her from her conversation.

Henrietta had insisted upon her being made acquainted with her true name and circumstances, from the time that Mr. Damer had acknowledged to her aunt that she was under his care, which had then produced no other alteration in Mrs. Willis than rather an increase of respect towards her, which she conceived due to her birth.

The young lady, whose extreme sensibility was not the least of her misfortunes, observed her increasing coldness, and suffered great uneasiness. She had willingly indulged a tenderness and esteem for her; and was concerned to find from her altered behaviour, that either she had failed in her endeavours to acquire the friendship of Mrs. Willis, or that the woman whom she had conceived so good an opinion of, was in reality not deserving of hers.

However, she was determined not to let Mr. Damer perceive that she was dissatisfied with her behaviour; and she continued to live with her in the same easy manner as formerly, notwithstanding the coldness and constraint with which she was now treated.

Mr. Damer scarce ever failed to call and see her once a day; but one day he returned about an hour after he had been with her, and told her he had just received letters from his father, in which he acquainted him that Mrs. Willis would in a few days have several foreign merchants in her house, whom he had recommended to lodge with her; and that, his stay in Holland being protracted for some time longer, he thought it would not be proper for miss Courteney to reside with Mrs. Willis till his return, as her house would be full of men.

"My father," added Mr. Damer, "desires me to ask you, miss, whether you have any objection to go into the country for a few weeks. He has a distant relation, a widow, who lives at Hampstead, with whom he says he will be glad to find you at his return; he begs you will excuse his not writing to you, having the gout still in his hand, and desires me to assure you of his tenderest concern for your welfare."

A week before, Henrietta would have thought it a misfortune to have left Mrs. Willis to go into any other lodging; but she was so piqued by her behaviour, that she heard this news without any uneasiness, and told Mr. Damer she would implicitly follow her guardian's directions.

He said he would conduct her to his cousin's himself; and took leave of her, after he had desired her to be ready for her little journey the next day.

Mrs. Willis came up to her apartment soon after Mr. Damer went away. "I hear I am soon to lose you, miss," said she, entering. "Yes," replied miss Courteney cooly, "such is my guardian's pleasure; but," added she smiling, "you will not miss me; you will have other company." "Other company!" repeated Mrs. Willis.

"Mr. Damer tells me," said miss Courteney "that your house will be full soon; some gentlemen recommended by his father will be here."

"It is strange," said Mrs. Willis, "that I should know nothing of it; have you had a letter from your guardian, miss?"

"No," replied miss Courteney; "but his son has heard from him—But," pursued she, after a little pause, "it is strange, as you say, that you should not know you are to have new lodgers."

Mrs. Willis looked at her attentively, as she spoke these words, "May I ask you, miss," said she, "the cause of your sudden removal?"

"I know of none," replied miss Courteney; "but that, my guardian thinks it will not be proper for me to stay among so many gentlemen as will shortly be your lodgers."

"I wish there had been a better reason than that," said Mrs. Willis; "for I am very sure I am to have no lodgers recommended by the elder Mr. Damer, otherwise I should have known it."

"Has not his son told you so?" asked miss Courteney, in great confusion of thought.

"He told me nothing," replied Mrs. Willis, "but that you are to leave me to-morrow."

"Lord bless me," cried the young lady, in great emotion, "what can this mean!"

"Suffer me," said Mrs. Willis, looking on her with tenderness and concern, "to ask you a few questions: when you know my motives, I am sure you will not think that it is an impertinent curiosity which makes me take this liberty, but my anxiety for you."

"Dear madam," interrupted miss Courteney, "ask me what you please: you alarm me excessively."

"I would not alarm you," said Mrs. Willis; "but I will own to you that I have fears, nay more, that I have had doubts; but I see I have been to blame with regard to the latter: has Mr. Damer shewn you his father's letters, miss?"

"Shewn them to me!" repeated Henrietta, "no—but sure—dear Mrs. Willis explain yourself—I am ready to sink with the apprehensions you have raised in my mind."

"Compose yourself, my dear," said Mrs. Willis, drawing her chair nearer to her, and taking her hand tenderly. "I mean you well; be assured I do: and now I will tell you all that has been upon my mind for several days past. Never did I imagine that I should entertain unfavourable suspicions of the son of my benefactor; but indeed, my dear miss, I am afraid he has not acted ingenuously with you."

That moment a loud knocking at the door interrupted Mrs. Willis. She started from her chair. "Who can this be?" said she in some surprise; "I will go and see." She ran hastily out of the room; but returning again instantly, "Possibly," said she, "it may be Mr. Damer: remember, miss, that it is my advice to you, not to leave my house, if he should desire you, at least till you have heard what I have to say."

She uttered these words with extreme earnestness and concern, and went immediately down stairs, leaving Henrietta in an agony of doubt, anxiety, and astonishment.

Her surprise kept her motionless in her chair, till she was roused by the voice of a woman upon the stairs that led to her apartment, whom she heard say, with great haughtiness of accent, "No, there is no occasion for that ceremony; I shall go in without introduction, I assure you."

She suddenly started from her chair, and was going towards the door, when she saw it flung open with some violence, and a lady of a very disagreeable figure but richly dressed, and in the utmost extremity of the fashion, appear at the entrance.

Miss Courteney, recovering a little from her surprise, looked at the lady, in order to recollect whether she had ever seen her before; but being wholly unacquainted with her features, and observing that she stood still and gazed at her without speaking, she concluded the visit could not be designed for her.

"I fancy, madam," said she, approaching her, "you are mistaken; I am not the person you seek."

"No, *madam*," returned the lady with an emphasis, "I am not mistaken;" then throwing herself haughtily into a chair, "I shall not ask your leave," said she, with a malignant smile, "to sit down in this apartment; I may take that liberty with what belongs to Mr. Damer—Do you know me pray, *madam*."

"Not I, truly," replied miss Courteney, indignation at this insolent treatment having banished her former terror and surprise, and seating herself, with a careless air, just opposite to her, "Pray let me know what is your business with me," said she.

"Pert creature!" said the stranger affecting contempt, while her lips quivered with rage, and her whole frame seemed convulsed with the violence of her emotions: "What! you would have me understand you to be a woman of fortune, would you not?—Upon my word," said she, looking round her, "this is a very handsome apartment. Your dressing-room forsooth! You have your forms, no doubt, and receive company in your dressing-room in a morning. A very genteel dishabille, too; and your face varnished over so nicely!—Who would not conclude that white and red to be natural?"

"You are come here to insult me, I find," said Henrietta, her fine face glowing with indignation.—"I cannot imagine what cause I have given you for this strange rudeness. I never, as I can remember, ever saw you before; and insist upon your quitting my apartment. You can have no business with me, I am sure."

"Indeed but I have, minx," said the stranger, with the pale rage of a fury; "and my business is to turn you out of this apartment: my fortune shall not be wasted in supporting such wretches."

"Your fortune!" cried miss Courteney, in astonishment: "What have I to do with you, or your fortune?—Who are you?"

This moment Mrs. Willis entered the room: "Excuse me, ladies," said she; "I heard high words between you."

"Ladies!" interrupted the stranger: "how dare you, woman, join me with such a creature?—What business have you to intrude?"

"Madam," replied Mrs. Willis, "I came to inform this young lady, my boarder, who you are: she does not know you.—Miss, this is young Mr. Damer's lady."

"What!" cried Henrietta, in the utmost astonishment, "is Mr. Damer married?"

"Oh—you are surprised then," said the lady, with a sneer: "disappointed too, perhaps.—You had the confidence, I suppose, to think he would have married you one of these days!—Tell me, you wicked thing, did he ever give you such hopes?—Oh I could tear his eyes out!" said she, rising, and walking about the room like one frantick, while the enormous length of her negligee swept the room, like the train of a tragedy-queen.—"A wretch, to use me thus! me, who has brought him such a fortune! but I'll be revenged: he shall never have a quiet moment. I'll make him know what it is to slight a woman of virtue."

All this time Henrietta continued silent, rooted in her chair, and with difficulty restrained the anguish of her heart from rising to her eyes, lest this outrageous woman of virtue should exult in her distress, yet she saw that she was betrayed; that Mr. Damer had acted weakly, if not basely: her reputation was ruined, yet she would not stoop so low as to enter into any justification of herself to a woman who had treated her so cruelly, upon a bare suspicion. The pride of affronted virtue came to her aid, against that torrent of overwhelming grief, which had for some moments absorbed all her faculties: she rose from her chair, and approaching Mrs. Damer,

"The error you are in," said she, "would have moved my compassion, had you treated me with less insolence. I scorn to undeceive you.—Go, learn from your husband who I am; and blush if you can, for the injurious language you have given a person as much your superior by birth, as in that virtue perhaps of which you boast, and which has not withheld you from such indecent transports of jealousy, as it would become a virtuous woman to suppress."

The superiority with which she spoke, the dignity of her air and manner, struck her mean-souled adversary with such awe, that she continued silent for some moments, with her haggard looks fixed on her. Envy, at the view of so lovely a form, added new stings to her rage and jealousy. At length, she poured forth a torrent of reproaches, with such eagerness of malice, that her words were scarce intelligible.

"I am not used to scolding," said miss Courteney, calmly, retiring towards her bedchamber, "and you, Mrs. Damer, seem to be an excellent scold."

The lady, provoked at this appellation, employed the coarsest language imaginable to express her resentment of the injury; but miss Courteney took shelter in her bedchamber, the door of which she double-locked.

"Insolent trollop," said Mrs. Damer, raising her voice that she might hear her, "call me scold! I scorn your words, you saucy, impudent, audacious hussy: I never could scold in my life,—no, you dirty puss:—I am a woman of breeding; I am none of your beggarly quality: I had forty thousand pounds to my portion, you proud paltry minx.—Scold! call me a scold—"

"Pray, madam, compose yourself," said Mrs. Willis, "and do me the favour to walk down into my parlour.—Here is some mistake. I am pretty certain you have injured this young lady by your suspicions."

"Young lady!" interrupted Mrs. Damer, "What makes her a lady?—A fine world it is, now-adays, when beggars are called ladies. I would fain know what fortune she has to put her upon a footing with ladies."

"I know nothing of her fortune, madam," said Mrs. Willis.

"Fortune! poor wretch!" said Mrs. Damer: "a few paultry hundreds.— Such ladies! Suppose her grandfather was an earl, has she a fortune? answer me that."

"I don't know, really," replied Mrs. Willis. "Well then," said Mrs. Damer, "why do you give her a title she has no right to? But why do I talk to you, vile wretch? you are my husband's confident."

This thought renewed all her rage, and she loaded Mrs. Willis with such shocking invectives, that the poor woman could not refrain from tears.

"Your husband's father, madam," said she, "has been a generous benefactor to me: I consider that, and will be patient under your abuse."

The word *abuse* was such a charge upon this lady's want of breeding, that she called Mrs. Willis a hundred saucy jades, for daring to say that she was capable of abusing any body; and having almost exhausted her spirits with the violence of her passions, and finding that Mrs. Willis sat silent, and took no farther notice of what she said, she flounced out of the room, declaring, that her father-in-law should know that she acted as procuress for his son, and that she should return to her rags and poverty again.

Mrs. Willis thought her behaviour dispensed with her from treating her with that respect, which she would have otherwise paid to Mr. Damer's daughter-in-law, and therefore did not offer to wait on her down stairs, but rung the bell for somebody to attend her, and, locking the door after her, she tapped gently at miss Courteney's chamber-door, telling her, that Mrs. Damer was gone.

"Who is this fury?" said the young lady, as she came out. "You have been treated very ill by her, Mrs. Willis, I am sorry for it." "And I am sorry for what you have suffered, my dear miss," replied Mrs. Willis; "but Mr. Damer is to blame for it all. I am now sure you are entirely innocent."

"Innocent!" repeated miss Courteney, with a sigh—"How low am I fallen, when that could ever be doubted! But Mrs. Willis, you knew, it seems, that Mr. Damer was married, I am surprised you never mentioned his wife to me."

"And are you not surprised, miss," said Mrs. Willis, "that Mr. Damer never mentioned her to you?"

"To be sure that is very strange," replied Henrietta, "what could he mean by it?"

"Ah! miss," said Mrs. Willis, "a very little reflection on Mr. Damer's behaviour might have informed you that he was in love with you."

"In love with me!" cried Henrietta, blushing with shame and resentment.

"Yes," said Mrs. Willis, "in love with you; if that can be called love which seeks the ruin of its object. I saw it in his looks, his words, cautious as they were, his whole behaviour shewed it but too plainly."

"And this man married too!" cried Henrietta, lifting up her eyes. "To what have I, by one rash step, reduced myself! But still Mrs. Willis, my first difficulty recurs, why did you avoid speaking of his wife to me?"

"Hear me, my dear, with patience," interrupted Mrs. Willis, "I shall be very free; but my plainness ought not to offend you, since it is a mark of my sincerity." Mrs. Willis paused here a moment, and then proceeded, as will be found in the following chapter.

CHAP. XV.

In which those circumstances are partly explained.

You may remember I told you, soon after you came here, that before I went to Leghorn, I heard Mr. Damer was courting the daughter of a rich citizen; I had been returned but three or four days, when he came to me to know if I could accommodate a young lady, a ward of his father's, with lodging and board; to which I readily consented.

"It is no flattery, miss, to tell you, that when I saw you, I was charmed with your person and behaviour: your beauty and Mr. Damer's extreme assiduity, made it seem highly probable that he loved you. I set myself to examine his behaviour, and the observations I made on it confirmed my suspicions. I had then heard nothing of his being married, having upon my return been so taken up with my domestic affairs, that I had no leisure to make or receive visits, from which I could receive any information concerning what had happened in my absence.

"I was a little surprised to find that you had been introduced to me under a feigned name, and that you were not called Benson, but Courteney. However, I made no reflections upon that circumstance, till, about two days afterwards, I accidentally heard that Mr. Damer had been married two months; then it was, that in my astonishment at his so cautiously avoiding any mention of his wife, I was led to reflect upon what you yourself had informed me of your situation; your flight from your friends, Mr. Damer's apparent tenderness for you, awakened suspicions, I own it, disadvantageous to you.

"I waited impatiently for the hour of Mr. Damer's visiting you, and the moment I saw him wished him joy on his marriage, expressing my surprise that I should not have heard of that event from himself. He coloured, and seemed in great confusion; and, after a little pause, Have you said anything of it to miss Courteney? said he.

"I replied that I had heard the news but an hour before, and had not seen you since.

"You will oblige me (said he) if you will not mention it to her—I stared—My wife (continued he) is the most unreasonable woman in the world; she has taken it into her head to be horribly jealous of me, though we have been married so short a time—It was a match (and he sighed) of my father's making—but I assure you I am very unhappy.

"I am sorry for it, sir (interrupted I) but what reasons have you for concealing from miss Courteney that you are married?

"It is a sad thing, Mrs. Willis (said he) when a man is not master in his own family. I hope that is not your case, sir, answered I. Indeed but it is, he replied. Miss Courteney, you know, is agreeable. Oh! very agreeable, said I. My wife is of such an unaccountable humour (resumed he) that I durst not offer miss Courteney, though my father is her guardian, an asylum in my house, till her relations were reconciled to her, lest I should be teazed with jealousy and suspicions.

"I am persuaded, sir (said I) that miss Courteney has too much good sense to take it amiss that you did not invite her to your house, as things were circumstanced. She has more reason to be displeased at your concealing your marriage from her, which every body knows, and which she would soon know if she lived less retired.

"Let me intreat you, Mrs. Willis (said he) not to mention it to miss Courteney. I would not upon any account that she should know I am married, yet could not offer her an apartment in my house.

"Indeed, sir (said I, smiling) you make this matter of more consequence than you need to do; miss Courteney will not consider it as any slight to her.

"She must either think herself slighted (resumed he, with quickness) by my not inviting her, or she will divine the reason, which would be worse; for in that case her delicacy is so extreme, that she would never allow me to see her.

"Ah, thought I, is it so! He perceived he had almost betrayed himself; and changed the discourse, asking me many questions about my husband, whose diligence and fidelity he highly extolled, dropping hints of designs in his favour; and indeed it is in his power to be of great service to him.

"But I had no satisfaction, pursued Mrs. Willis, in what he said; for, to my apprehension, it appeared as if he sought to bribe me into a concurrence with his designs, whatever they were. Therefore I sat silent, and I believe discovered by my looks, that I did not like his proceedings; for he rose up, and, with an air of some resentment, said,

"That his father would be in town in a few days, and would then dispose of you properly; and that in the mean time he must insist upon my being silent with regard to his marriage, since it would throw him into great confusion if you knew it; and added, that he thought he might reasonably expect this instance of my complaisance.

"I told him that I was very glad to hear his father would be in town so soon, and would take the young lady under his own care: that since he desired it, I would not be the first to acquaint you with his marriage; I owned his reasons appeared to me very whimsical: but that it was not my business to be impertinently curious; and that I should concern myself no farther about it.

"He seemed pleased with this indifference, and went up stairs to see you. I had already taken my resolution, my dear miss Courteney, which was to write to his father, and acquaint him with the whole transaction. I was willing to leave the young gentleman in a false security, that he might not suspect my design, and take measures to render it useless; and not being sure how far even you might be trusted, for my suspicions of you, though weakened, were not yet removed, I thought it best to say nothing that could alarm you, till I had received the old gentleman's advice how to act; but my measures were broke by Mr. Damer's resolving to take you from my house.

"He came into the parlour to me to-day, before you saw him, and told me, that he had directions from his father to send you into the country, because he did not expect to return for some time yet, and he did not approve of your residing in London till he came.

"You may easily imagine, miss, that I was not satisfied with the cause he assigned for this sudden resolution. I was now alarmed for you; and judged it necessary to acquaint you immediately with Mr. Damer's being married, that you might not fall ignorantly into his snares. I began with asking you questions, to which the openness and simplicity of your answers convinced me that you were imposed upon greatly by Mr. Damer. I was going to explain myself clearly, when Mrs. Damer's arrival interrupted me. You know with what earnestness I intreated you not to leave my house; I was apprehensive that he was come to hurry you away, and I trembled for the danger to which you were exposed.

"When I left you, I met Mrs. Damer upon the stairs; and, not knowing her, I asked, who it was she desired to see? The young woman that lodges with you, said she, in a tone of voice that surprised me. I told her, I would go and acquaint you that there was a lady wanted to speak to you: but she rushed by me, saying, there is no need of that ceremony, I shall introduce myself.

"Her behaviour recalling to my mind what Mr. Damer had said of his wife's jealousy, I suspected this was the lady; and, to be assured, I enquired of a servant, who attended her, who she was. The moment I knew it was really her, I flew up stairs, being full of concern for you; for I saw a storm in her countenance, and dreaded the consequence—The poor young man is indeed plagued with a jealous wife; and in that particular he told the truth. But, my dear miss, I see plainly that the mystery he has made of his connexions with you has rouzed her suspicions."

"It is all an incomprehensible mystery to me," said Henrietta, sighing: "Mr. Damer has certainly deceived me, for what purposes I know not; but I know that I will never see him again, but in the presence of his father, to have this dark affair cleared up.

"But, my dear Mrs. Willis, how shall I express what my heart feels for you, who have shewn so tender a regard for my honour and quiet—How miserable might I have been, had you been less good—I am sure I may rely upon your prudence—Advise me then what to do: you know my story; you see my present situation—I have no friend, no protector."

"My dear miss," interrupted Mrs. Willis, "there is but one thing for you to do, and that is, to return to your aunt."

"How can I appear before her?" said Henrietta, "after having so greatly disobliged her by my flight; a flight which has had such disgraceful consequences. Besides, do not the same motives that obliged me to leave her, still subsist? and are they not equally strong against my returning?"

"I would not pain you, my dear miss," said Mrs. Willis, "with the recollection of a past error, were it not to make it useful to you in your present circumstances—Warned as you were of your aunt's designs, it was impossible to carry them into execution without your concurrence: your flight therefore was not necessary, and, if not necessary, surely it was highly imprudent; and, in my opinion, can only be repaired by a voluntary return.—Need I tell a young lady of your delicacy, that imputations, however unjust, sully, if they do not stain a character. Do you think this woman's frantic jealousy will be silent? how can you otherwise prove the falshood of her assertions, than by returning to your aunt, and making yourself accountable to her for all your actions? Nothing can be more unfortunate for youth and beauty, than to be left to its own guidance and discretion. The world seldom attributes too much prudence to youth: however regular our conduct may be in that gay time of life, it is supposed to be owing to the care and attention of our parents or relations, rather than to our own circumspection. Can a young woman, who voluntarily sets herself free from that restraint, hope to escape unfavourable censures, when those who owe it to chance only that they are not subjected to any control, suffer perhaps in the opinion of the world, because they are possessed of a liberty which they may make an improper use of?

"You see, my dear, to what inconveniencies you have been exposed: these are the necessary consequences of your unprotected state; there is no doubt but you would repel every attempt to the prejudice of your honour: but does not modesty, if not virtue, suffer by such attempts? and can you acquit yourself of imprudence, when you reflect that you have thrown yourself into a situation which renders you liable to them?"

"It was indeed," said Henrietta, who, by her blushes and confusion, acknowledged the strength of her reasons, "imprudence to throw myself into this situation, but it would be guilt to continue in it. Oh! that I had had such a friend as you to advise with at Windsor, I should never have taken a step, which I blush to think of now. I will return to my aunt, Mrs. Willis, I will throw myself upon her mercy; and if I must be made a sacrifice of—"

"Indeed, my dear (interrupted Mrs. Willis) these fears are groundless: you cannot possibly be married against your consent; and you have it always in your power to refuse. As for the convent, you cannot be cheated into it, that is certain, since you know she had such a design, and may guard against it."

"But suppose (said miss Courteney) that she should not receive me again; Mr. Damer found her inexorable."

"Ah! my dear," replied Mrs. Willis, shaking her head, "Mr. Damer was not a fit person to be trusted with such a negotiation: but, however that may be, I am sure, when your aunt knows in what manner he has acted, and the reasons you have to distrust him, she will think it necessary to take you out of his hands. Your return to her will remove her suspicions against you, and convince her that it was from a sudden impulse of fear only, that you left her; and that you had no desire of disposing of yourself contrary to her inclinations."

"But I have one favour to beg of you (said miss Courteney) and that is, that you will go along with me to my aunt; resentment may shut her ears to all that I can say to her, but I think she cannot resist your pleas, urged with that good sense you possess in so high a degree."

"Doubt not, my dear (said Mrs. Willis) but I am ready to do you any service in my power."

"What hinders us then from going directly?" cried Henrietta, eagerly; "we can get a post-chaise, and—"

"The day is too far advanced (replied Mrs. Willis) we will, if you please, set out early to-morrow morning, I will take care to have a post-chaise in readiness; in the mean time you may depend upon being secure from any disagreeable visits here, neither Mr. Damer nor his fury of a wife shall see you, unless you desire they should."

"Notwithstanding the treatment she gave me (said miss Courteney) I would rather see her than him; but you may well imagine, Mrs. Willis, that I do not wish to see either of them."

"Make yourself easy, my dear (said Mrs. Willis) you shall meet with no insult of any kind in my house."

Henrietta embraced her with tears of gratitude, which the good woman returned with a parental tenderness, and then left her to give the necessary directions for their little journey the next day.

END of VOL. I.

HENRIETTA.

BY

Mrs. CHARLOTTE LENNOX.

IN TWO VOLUMES.
VOL. II.

The SECOND EDITION, Corrected.

LONDON:

Printed for A. MILLAR, in the Strand.

MDCCLXI.

THE CONTENTS OF
THE SECOND VOLUME.

BOOK III.

BOOK IV.

HENRIETTA.

BOOK THE THIRD.

CHAP. I.

In which our heroine meets with a new disappointment, and some farther instances of miss Woodby's friendship.

Henrietta, being now left to her own reflections, beheld her late conduct in a light in which it had never appeared to her before; the sense of blame so justly incurred, filled her with remorse and shame. Hitherto she had industriously aggravated the cause of her fears, that she might not stand self-condemned; which to an ingenuous mind is of all others the greatest evil: but Mrs. Willis had stated her case too justly.

What force could give her unwilling hand to the old baronet? How could she be cheated into a convent, when she was forewarned of the design? From her obstinate opposition to her aunt's will, nothing worse could have happened than the loss of her favour and protection, which by her flight she had anticipated. She now wondered at the unreasonableness of her fears, and looked back with the deepest regret upon the errors they had occasioned.

These melancholy thoughts, and her anxiety about the reception her aunt would give her, kept her waking almost the whole night. As soon as it was light, she rose, and dressed herself, impatient to be gone; Mrs. Willis at her summons made haste to join her, and, when they had breakfasted, set out immediately upon their journey; Henrietta full of perturbation and inquietude, Mrs. Willis with that serenity which attends the consciousness of doing what is right.

The young lady, as she drew nearer her aunt's dwelling, found her emotions increase; one while her imagination represented lady Meadows as kind and indulgent, ready to forgive her error, and to restore her to her affection; and, immediately after, she would tremble with the apprehension of her severe reproaches.

Mrs. Willis perceived her uneasiness, and used her utmost endeavours to compose her: but when the chaise stopped at the door, she was near falling into a fainting fit; and her friend was obliged to ask if lady Meadows was at home, for Henrietta was not able to speak.

The servant-maid who opened the door, having got a glympse of the young lady as she sat in the chaise, eagerly flew to the side of it—"O my dear miss!" said she, in a transport of joy, "is it you?"

"How do you do, Jenny?" said miss Courteney; and trembling, added, "is my aunt at home?"

"My lady," said the girl, "set out two days ago for her seat in Devonshire. Oh! miss, here has been sad doings, poor Mrs. White is turned away; there came an ugly mischief-making lady from London, and told my lady a heap of stories about you, and so Mrs. White was turned away: but won't you please to alight, miss?"

Henrietta looked at Mrs. Willis, for she knew not herself what to resolve on, the news she had heard having thrown her into the utmost perplexity—"I wish we could see Mrs. White," said Mrs. Willis to her in a whisper.

Miss Courteney immediately enquired of the maid, how long Mrs. White had left her aunt, and where she was to be found? The girl told her she had been gone above a week, and that she believed she was at her sister's in Windsor. Henrietta had often heard her mention her sister, who was married to a tradesman in Windsor; and, after she had taken leave of the poor affectionate girl, who wept to see her depart again, she gave the post-boy directions where to drive.

Mrs. White, when the chaise stopped at the door, heard from a little parlour where she was sitting, the voice of miss Courteney enquiring for her, and flew with trembling eagerness to meet her.

"Oh! miss," said she, taking her hand, and leading her into the room, "I am rejoiced to see you: where have you been all this time?—What an unfortunate creature was I to be the means of your taking such a rash resolution—Oh! that I had kept what I knew to myself—But surely, it was very unkind in you not to acquaint me with your design, not to ask my advice. I might have prevented all this trouble; but thank Heaven you are safe and well—well I see you are."

Henrietta then interrupting the good woman, who, between chiding and fondness, had taken no notice of Mrs. Willis: "That I am safe (said she) I am obliged to this gentlewoman; for some strange treachery was preparing for me, I believe, but her care has prevented it."

"Treachery!" interrupted Mrs. White—"Aye, you have met with enough of that, I suppose: there was your new-found friend and acquaintance, miss—I forget her name, whom you told all your secrets to; you made no scruple to trust her, miss, though you was so reserved to me; she was the occasion of my losing my place. Ah! miss, but I will not upbraid you; I see you are concerned: God forbid I should add to your uneasiness; I have suffered greatly upon your account. It was very unkind in you to put it in the power of a stranger to do me so much mischief: surely, I did not deserve such a return from you. But God knows my heart, I would not upbraid you for the world; no, I scorn it; but I have been the greatest sufferer, I am sure, and yet I meant well."

"Was not the lady's name Woodby?" interrupted Henrietta, impatient to hear the particulars of this new act of treachery and baseness.

"Aye, Woodby," replied Mrs. White, "a disagreeable creature as ever my eyes beheld. I shall never forget how she sidled into my lady's dressing room, and, half out of breath, told her, she had taken the liberty to wait on her to bring her some news of her niece. I could not hear distinctly all she said, for my lady ordered me to withdraw; but I put my ear to the key-hole, as I had done once before for your service, miss, which I have reason to repent, Heaven knows—but what is past cannot be helped—it is not my way to *rip* up things that are past."

"Well," said Henrietta, "but what did you hear?"

"Nay, for that matter," resumed Mrs. White, "I may draw myself into another *premune*[1] perhaps: after what I have suffered I ought to be cautious; but I love you, miss, and must tell you every thing, whatever it cost me, and that you have experienced already. Well, she made up a horrible story, that you had gone away suddenly from lodgings where she visited you, and notwithstanding the friendship there was between you (and a great clutter she made with that word), you went away without giving her any notice of your intention; and this she said had a strange appearance."

Miss Courteney lifted up her eyes here, in astonishment at what she heard.

"As for me," continued Mrs. White, "she did my business in an instant; for as soon as she was gone, my lady sent for me, and, in a violent rage, told me I should not stay another night in her house. She was informed, she said, that I had been the cause of your running away, by filling your head with notions of her designing to confine you in a convent. She would hear nothing that I could say in my own defence; and dismissed me that very evening."

"I am excessively sorry," said Henrietta, "that you should suffer so much on my account—It was indeed very imprudent in me to be so communicative to miss Woodby, but I could not imagine she was capable of so much treachery."

"But how have you been able to conceal yourself so well, miss, from the enquiries of all your friends?" said Mrs. White. "Mr. Damer, it seems, your guardian's son, knew not where to find you."

"Did Mr. Damer say, he knew not where I was?" cried miss Courteney, in astonishment.

"He told Mr. Danvers so," replied Mrs. White, "who went several times by my lady's orders to enquire for you."

"Was there ever such complicated treachery!" said Henrietta, looking at Mrs. Willis with tears in her eyes. "Well, my dear," said the good woman, "there is at least this advantage in misfortunes, that they bring us at last to wisdom. You will for the future be more cautious how you engage in such perilous enterprizes."

"Ay, miss" said Mrs. White, "and how you trust false friends to the prejudice of your true ones—You see what it has cost me—but no more of that—I can forget and forgive."

"Well, and what is now to be done?" said miss Courteney, folding her hands with an air of despondence.

"It is easy to answer that question," said Mrs. Willis; "you must write to your aunt, my dear, and give her an account of all that has happened to you. There is certainly something to condemn in what you have done; but in what you have suffered, there is much to be pitied. I am persuaded her tenderness will silence her resentment. I hoped to have left you with your aunt, miss," continued Mrs. Willis; "but since that cannot be, you will return with me, I suppose."

"To be sure I will," said miss Courteney, "with whom in my present situation can I be so happy as with you?"

Mrs. White desired she might be permitted to come and see her, to which Henrietta readily consented; promising, if she was reconciled to her aunt, to use her utmost endeavours to reinstate her in her place.

Chap. II.

Which throws new lights upon Mr. Damer's behaviour, and contains a very improving conversation.

The two ladies being again seated in their post-chaise, Mrs. Willis kindly applied herself to comfort her fair companion, whose affecting silence shewed a deeper sense of her new disappointment than any words could express. However, miss Courteney felt in reality fewer perturbations and less anxiety in her return, than when she began her journey. So true it is, that when we hope little, we fear little likewise.

She now looked upon her aunt's affection as irrecoverable; miss Woodby's vile insinuations had strengthened her suspicions: Mr. Damer, when he found himself detected, would doubtless account for his behaviour in a manner unfavourable to her; her unhappy flight had given such a colour to her succeeding actions, as rendered any justification of herself hopeless; and the insidious chaplain might now with ease confirm those prejudices he had raised.

In this manner she reasoned herself into a belief that her misfortune was irremediable: despair, as an ingenious writer[2] observes, being that ease to the mind which mortification is to the flesh, Henrietta found some relief in being freed from that vicissitude of hopes and fears which had so long held her mind in the most racking suspence; and, with a kind of gloomy satisfaction, resigned herself to all the bitterness of her fate.

Mrs. Willis, who knew not the peculiarities of lady Meadows's temper, or if she had, would not perhaps have considered, that obstinate people are ever most obstinate in error, thought all things might be set right again, by miss Courteney's giving a candid narrative of what had happened to her since her leaving her; she therefore pressed the young lady to delay writing to her aunt no longer than the next day.

"There are some cases," said Mrs. Willis to her, when she saw her sitting down to write, "in which simplicity is the greatest refinement of art; yours is one of them: be as simple and ingenuous as you can in the account you give your aunt, and let the facts speak for themselves."

Henrietta followed her advice, and related every part of her conduct since she had left her, and the treachery and deceit that had been used towards her, with the utmost plainness and sincerity, and saw that she had made her letter more affecting by its simplicity, than she could have done by the nicest touches of art. Mrs. Willis read it, and approved of it; and it was immediately dispatched to the post.

Scarce was this little affair over, when Mr. Damer sent in his name.

"I like this piece of ceremony," said Mrs. Willis; "it looks as if the man was ashamed of what he has done: do you chuse to see him, miss?"

"Oh! no," replied Henrietta; "it would be strange, indeed, if I was willing to see a man whom you suspect of having such shocking designs, and who I am sure has not acted honestly."

"Well then," said Mrs. Willis, "I will go down to him, and hear what he has to say."

She returned again in less than an hour, smiling. "This young man," said she, "does not want sense: what would you say, miss, if I was to tell you that he has persuaded me he has acted very right, and with the best intentions in the world."

"I should say that I am less unhappy than I thought I was," replied miss Courteney; "for surely it is a great misfortune to meet with persons who abuse our confidence and the good opinions we have of them."

"That misfortune," said Mrs. Willis, "will in time become so common, that you will feel it less sensibly than you do now. The only way to avoid being deceived, is to be always upon your guard against deceit."

"That is to say I must be always suspicious," said Henrietta; "this may be a very prudent maxim, but my heart disavows it."

"Alas! my dear," replied Mrs. Willis, "we all enter upon the world with high notions of disinterestedness, friendship, sincerity, and candor: but experience shows us, that these qualities exist not, or among so very few, that it does not fall to the lot of one mortal in a thousand to meet with them in those we contract friendships with. The frequent disappointments we suffer in the search of them, make suspicion grow into a habit of thinking, which if it lessens our enjoyments lessens our inconveniencies likewise."

"Then I," said miss Courteney, "shall be always exposed to inconveniencies; for I am sure I can never bring myself to suspect persons who appear deserving of my good opinion: and indeed I think it is more honourable to be often deceived, than to be always doubting."

"But it is not so safe," replied Mrs. Willis, smiling: "however, my dear, in unexperienced youth like yours this way of thinking is meritorious: the faults of the world can only be learned by a long acquaintance with it, and by suffering from that acquaintance. Those who derive this kind of knowledge from the heart rather than the head, are indeed safe themselves, but dangerous to all others.

"But I will keep you no longer in suspense with regard to Mr. Damer. He has glossed over his behaviour so as to make me appear satisfied with it, which indeed it is necessary I should, if I would not wish to make an enemy of him; and a very powerful one he might be to my husband.

"He asked for you as soon as he saw me, and did not seem surprised at the very slight excuse I made for your not seeing him. He expressed great concern for the treatment you had received from his wife; for in her frantic rage it seems she told him all that had passed between you."

"You find," said he, "I did not exaggerate my wife's failing."

"It is a great misfortune," replied I; "but, sir, I think if you had not made a secret of your connections with miss Courteney, Mrs. Damer's jealousy would not have had so plausible an excuse, nor would the young lady have had any reason to complain of you."

"I should have found it absolutely impossible," said he, "to have concerned myself in miss Courteney's affairs, or been of the least use to her, had my wife known any thing of the matter; the very sight of miss Courteney would have roused her suspicions, and have put it out of my power to act either as a friend or guardian by her; and, in her unhappy situation, she had great need of my care and attention."

"However, sir," replied I, "it was certainly ill judged to conceal from miss Courteney, that you was married: what must she think of such a strange conduct?"

"Why, Mrs. Willis," resumed he, "I have already told you, that I could not own my marriage to miss Courteney, without letting her into my reasons for not being able to offer her an asylum in my house, during her aunt's displeasure, an offer she had great reason to expect. I was unwilling to expose my wife's foible, and to raise scruples in the young lady's mind, which might prevent her from receiving those little services from me which she had so much need of: I hope you will represent all this to her, and let her know how greatly I am afflicted at what she has suffered."

"To be sure I will," replied I; "but miss Courteney tells me you have received letters from Mr. Damer, in which he acquaints you that there are some foreign merchants coming to reside in my house, and that she was to be removed for that reason. I surprised her greatly by saying I had heard nothing of it; and, indeed I am a good deal surprised myself at it."

"Why, to be plain with you, Mrs. Willis," said the young gentleman, "this was only an invention."

"Indeed!" said I, looking very grave: "to be sure you had some good reason for it."

"Doubtless I had," pursued he, "and you yourself shall be judge of my reason— This is a bad world, Mrs. Willis, a very bad world: nothing but stratagems and designs, fraud and cunning. Our sex, Mrs. Willis, is in a state of war with yours, our arms are sighs and vows, and flattery and protestation, and (as in all other warfares) we fight to destroy."

"Bless us!" interrupted Henrietta, half smiling, "what could this fine preface lead to?"

"I protest," resumed Mrs. Willis laughing, "it was with the utmost difficulty I composed my countenance to a look of grave attention; while he uttered all this with a solemn accent, and an air of infinite importance."

"Truly, sir," replied I, "for so young a gentleman you think very gravely of these matters: it is highly commendable in one of your years."

"Heaven forbid, Mrs. Willis," said he, "that all men should be libertines; but in short it was to preserve miss Courteney from falling into the snares of one, that I formed an excuse for sending her into the country."

"Vile dissembler!" exclaimed miss Courteney again, glowing with indignation; "preserve me from falling into the snares of a libertine! I hope my own discretion, without any aid from him, was sufficient to guard me against any snares that a libertine could lay for me."

"I hope so too," said Mrs. Willis.

Henrietta blushed a little at this expression, which seemed, she thought, to imply a doubt, but would not interrupt Mrs. Willis again.

"I told you that this gentleman was very artful," continued the good woman, "as you will be convinced by the story he related."

"You must know," said he to me, looking extremely wise, and lowering his voice, "that when I waited upon miss Courteney at the lodgings she had taken after she left her aunt, I observed a fine gay young man there, who followed me when I went out, and looked at me in a manner that shewed great curiosity and attention. It came into my head that this might be the spark[3] of whom miss Courteney's aunt was apprehensive: I discovered that he lodged in the house with the young lady; and this circumstance I liked by no means. I resolved to remove her immediately, and place her with you: she so readily consented to my proposal, that I doubted whether I had not been extremely mistaken in my conjectures concerning this young gentleman; but a day or two after she was settled with you, my spark came to enquire for her at my house: now it was plain that miss Courteney held some correspondence with him, otherwise he could not have known where to come after her.

"I happened not to be at home, and the servants told him, that no such person was there. He came several times, and was always answered in the same manner. His enquiries at length reached the ears of my wife; she desired he might be shewn up to her apartment when he came next; and it was from him that she learned miss Courteney was under my care.

"To one of her temper it was enough to know that I had the management of a lady's affairs, to make her suspect that I had a more than ordinary interest in the lady herself. But she concealed her thoughts from me: and I, who was wholly ignorant that this gentleman had seen my wife, was only concerned at the connexion there seemed to be between miss Courteney and him; and therefore fixed upon that stratagem, to remove her out of his reach, without giving her any suspicions of the cause.

"I have since enquired about the gentleman; and I hear that he is a man of quality, and that he is shortly to be married to a great fortune. Judge now whether his designs on miss Courteney could be honourable; and whether I had not reason to act as I did with regard to sending her away?"

"And now, my dear," added Mrs. Willis, smiling, "did you ever hear a more plausible tale?"

"I have somewhere read it observed," replied Henrietta, "that we are better deceived by having some truth told us than none. Mr. Damer has put this maxim in practice; his tale is plausible, because part of it is true: but his inferences are all false; and their cause lies too deep for me to discover it."

She then related succinctly all that had passed in the house of Mrs. Eccles, and that she had earnestly intreated Mr. Damer to dispose of her elsewhere, being resolved, after the affront that had been offered to her, to remain there no longer. She added, that the young lord having hinted his suspicions that Mr. Damer was her lover, she thought herself obliged to tell him his name, and explain the nature of his connexions with her, that she might not, by going away with a person unknown, leave room for calumny to slander her.

Mrs. Willis was charmed with this candid account of her conduct, which overthrew all Mr. Damer's insinuations. She embraced her with great tenderness. "All will soon be set right (said she) your aunt will receive you with redoubled affection." Miss Courteney sighed; but having already taken her resolution, she was prepared for whatever events might happen.

CHAP. III.

Which we are afraid will give some of our readers a mean opinion of our heroine's understanding.

Two days afterwards a letter was brought by the post for miss Courteney; the direction was in her aunt's hand: she opened it with some trepidation, and found it as follows:

HENRIETTA,

FOR niece I cannot, after what has happened, call you—If you had not, by the highest imprudence that any young woman could be guilty of, given too much colour for the shocking censures that are cast on you, I might perhaps have been deceived by your plausible account of things. I am sorry to find you have acquired so much art, it is but too sure a proof that you are less innocent; yet it would be easy for me to take to pieces every part of your defence, and shew you the absurdity of it: but this is needless; for whether you are innocent or guilty, you have greatly wounded your reputation, and I can no longer with honour consider you or treat you as my niece.

There is but one way left by which you can retrieve your fame and my affection; motives which ought to have some weight with you, but infinitely less than the desire of securing your salvation.

I hoped and believed your conversion was near completed, and doubtless it would have been, had not your passions intervened.

If you will retire to a convent, and put yourself into a way of being instructed in the true religion, I will pay your pension largely; and the day that sees you reunited to the faith, shall see you restored to my fondest affection, and made sole heiress to my whole estate. Consider well before you determine; and know, that upon any other terms than these, you must not hope for farther notice from me.

F. MEADOWS.

Although several parts of this letter were extremely shocking both to the delicacy and pride of Henrietta, yet the shining bribe that was offered her to procure her apostasy, made a large compensation. She had now an opportunity given her of making a worthy sacrifice to the religion she believed and professed; a circumstance that exalted her in her own opinion: for her self-love had been deeply wounded by the humiliations she had undergone; and as great delicacy always suffers most, so it enjoys most from its own reflections.

She was not free from a little enthusiasm that told her it was glorious to suffer in the cause of religion, nor so disinterested as not to feel great pleasure in the thought of being able to free her moral character from injurious suspicions, by so firm an attachment to her religious principles.

Her impatience to answer her aunt's letter, would not allow her time to communicate to Mrs. Willis the contents of it: but as soon as she had done writing, she sent for the good woman, and put lady Meadows's letter into her hands, with such an air of conscious satisfaction, as persuaded her the so much desired reconciliation was effected; but when upon reading the letter, she found her mistake, she threw it down, and, in a melancholy accent, and a look that expressed the most anxious curiosity, asked her how she had resolved?

"Read this," said Henrietta, giving her the letter she had written; "I am sure you will not disapprove of what I have done." Mrs. Willis read it eagerly, and found it as follows:

MADAM,

It is a great grief to me to find that your affection is irrecoverable, for at the price you have set upon it, I must ever deem it so. If my defence seems absurd, madam, it is because truth is too weak to combat prejudice: I leave it to time and my future conduct to clear my innocence, and am resolved never to give a confirmation to those aspersions which are cast on my character, by sacrificing my religion to my interest.

That poverty, which happily is become my choice, will be my best vindication; and if it affords me no other blessing but that of a good conscience, it will bestow on me the highest that is attainable in this life, and which will enable me to bear chearfully all the misfortunes that may befal me; among which I shall always look upon the loss of your esteem as the greatest. I am, madam, with all due gratitude and respect, your obliged and very humble servant,
HENRIETTA COURTENEY.

"I must approve, nay admire your resolution, miss," said Mrs. Willis, returning the letter; "and if you persist in it, you will appear to me a wonder."

"Do you doubt my persisting in it?" replied Henrietta.

"When I consider," said Mrs. Willis, "your birth, your youth, your beauty, and the expectations you have been encouraged to entertain, I know it must cost you a great deal to throw away the advantages that are offered you, and which possibly you might secure by temporising[4] at least."

"Dissimulation," interrupted Henrietta, "on any occasion, is mean and scandalous; but in matters of religion it is surely a heinous crime; and I hope I am far enough from committing it; but I own I have many motives to stimulate my resolution.

"My own imprudence, and the treachery of others, have given a wound to my reputation, which a voluntary poverty can only repair. In this licentious age, she, who with youth and even the slightest advantages of person, dares to be poor, deserves surely to be thought virtuous; and I shall ever acknowledge the bounty of Providence, that, amidst the unjust censures which have been cast on me, has made an humble lot my choice."

"I am satisfied," interrupted Mrs. Willis: "reason, I see has a greater share in your so lately formed resolution, than the zeal of enthusiasm, or the suggestions of vanity; and you may believe me a true friend to your fame, when I heartily congratulate you on your present situation. And now, my dear miss, suffer me to assure you of my tenderest friendship; a friendship which cannot be contented with bare professions, and insists upon your putting it to some trial.

"Tell me how I can serve you? O! that you would honour me so far as to let this house be your asylum till fortune does justice to your merit. Condescend to live with me, my dear miss, and share my little income."

"You are very kind, dear Mrs. Willis," replied Henrietta, "but my circumstances will not permit me to continue your boarder, and no distress shall oblige me to be burthensome to a friend. I have already resolved how to dispose of myself, and, in the scheme I have formed, I shall need your assistance."

"Tell me, my dear," cried Mrs. Willis, eagerly, "how I can be of any use to you?"

"You must," replied Henrietta, blushing a little: "you must get me a service, my dear Mrs. Willis."

"A service!" exclaimed the good woman.

"I am very well qualified," resumed Henrietta, recovering from her first confusion, and smiling, "to wait upon a woman of fashion: for my mother gave me a useful as well as genteel education; and this station will be at once private enough to secure me from disagreeable accidents, and public enough to make my conduct acquit or condemn me.

"I will not," added she, observing Mrs. Willis continued silent, "offer myself to any place by my own name; that would look like an insult upon my great relations, and be perhaps an obstruction to my success. It is sufficient for me, that whenever I am discovered, it may be in circumstances at which they, not I, need be ashamed."

"When I first heard you mention this scheme," said Mrs. Willis, "I thought I could never be brought to approve it: but a little reflection has convinced me that it may have good consequences. You cannot be long concealed; that graceful form will soon draw notice upon you. Whenever you are known to be in a station so unworthy your birth and merit, the pride of your relations will be rouzed. How glorious then will this humiliation be for you! Methinks I see their confusion for their neglect of you, and their eagerness to repair it, by restoring you to the rank you was born in—Oh! my dear, you will certainly be happy yet, I am sure you will."

Henrietta smiled a little at the good woman's sanguine expectations; but in reality, the same thoughts had made a great impression upon her, and contributed more than she imagined, to allay the uneasiness she felt at being reduced to take such a step. By degrees she formed in her own mind so romantick a scene, that she grew impatient to enter upon it, and again intreated the assistance of Mrs. Willis.

The good woman telling her that a cousin of her husband's was a sack-maker, and in great vogue at the court end of the town, it was agreed that she should go to her, and engage her good offices towards recommending the young lady to a place; it being very likely that among her customers, who were mostly women of quality, she might hear of one that would suit her.

CHAP. IV.

Which contains very trifling matters.

Mrs. Willis succeeded beyond her hopes; the mantua-maker had been desired by a lady she worked for, to look out for a genteel young person to serve her in the quality of her woman; and promised her cousin, that she would mention her friend to the lady the next day, being to wait on her with some cloaths that were to be tried on. She added, that the lady was a citizen, but had an immense fortune, and that her place was certainly a very good one.

Henrietta seemed very well pleased with her landlady's success, though she was not free from some uneasy perturbations at the thoughts of the condition she was so soon to enter upon.

Mrs. Cary did not fail to visit her cousin the next day. "Well (said she) I have done the young gentlewoman's business: she has nothing to do but to wait upon miss Cordwain; and, if she likes her figure, she will hire her directly."

"Why, pray," replied Mrs. Willis, "what kind of figure will best please this lady?"

"Oh!" cried Mrs. Cary, "miss Cordwain's woman must be very genteel, and look like a gentlewoman; the richer she is dressed too, when she goes to wait on her, the better. Every thing about miss Cordwain must be magnificent. Well," pursued she, laughing, and taking a pinch of snuff, which produced several little pauses in her discourse, "it is really surprising to see these little cits, how they mimick people of quality—They must be so extravagantly in the fashion—I vow and protest the negligee I tried on miss Cordwain to-day, had a train three yards and a half long."

Henrietta that moment entering the room, Mrs. Willis, seeing her cousin was surprised at her appearance, said, this is the young gentlewoman who wants a place.

The mantua-maker, upon this information, resumed her familiar look and manner; and, throwing herself again upon her chair, took a full survey of the young lady, who thanked her, with some hesitation, and a blush that crimsoned over her face, for the service she had done her.

"I have just been telling my cousin," said Mrs. Cary, "that miss Cordwain, the lady I have recommended you to, ma'am, is very hard to be pleased. Her woman must look like a lady forsooth: she has refused three that went to see her place; one, because she had a red hand; it looked, she said, as if the creature had stood at a wash-tub; another, because she went to be hired in a linen gown; and the third, because she had lived with nobody of higher rank than a baronet's wife—But I am sure she can have no objection to you, ma'am, unless perhaps she may think you too handsome. Do you take snuff, ma'am?" offering her box, which Henrietta civilly declined.

"But dear ma'am," pursued the mantua-maker, "who makes your cloaths? I never saw any thing so frightful as the slope of that ruffle, then such a horrid sleeve: it is well you are naturally genteel."

Henrietta slightly bowed in return for this compliment; and asked her, at what hour it would be proper to wait upon miss Cordwain?

"About one o'clock in the forenoon," replied Mrs. Cary, "that's her breakfast time. Her father, honest man, is in his warehouse before six. But this is his only daughter; and he expects she will be a duchess, or countess at least—She has fifty thousand pounds."

"Where does the lady live?" asked Henrietta.

"Here in one of your filthy lanes," replied the mantua-maker; "I forgot the name of it, but every body knows Mr. Cordwain the packer."

She then rose up, made one of her best courtesies, and hurried into a chair that was waiting for her; for this polite mantua-maker was above visiting her customers in a hackney coach: and this insolence was such a proof of her excellence in her business, that few ever scrupled to pay for it.

Chap. V.

Which shews Henrietta in a new situation.

Henrietta having summoned all her resolution, that she might acquit herself with propriety of the task she had undertaken, prepared the next day to wait upon miss Cordwain. She remembered the mantua-maker's hint, and therefore avoided any studied simplicity in her dress; but no apparel, however mean, could have hid that noble air, or disguised that native elegance, so conspicuous throughout her whole person.

As soon as she was ready, she stepped in to Mrs. Willis's parlour, and, while a coach was sent for, assumed a more than ordinary chearfulness in her discourse with the good woman; for she was extremely desirous of concealing

the emotions she felt upon this mortifying occasion, and affected a most heroick indifference, while inly she suffered all that a mind, delicate and sensible
as her's, could feel.

Mrs. Willis followed her to the door with tears in her eyes. The young
lady stepped into the coach, smiled a farewel, and ordered the coachman to
drive to Mr. Cordwain's. A few minutes brought her to the house; and the
servant, of whom she enquired if miss Cordwain was at home, having shewn
her into a parlour, bowed and withdrew.

Miss Cordwain being informed that a lady enquired for her, ordered
her admittance; and the same servant returning, conducted Henrietta to her
dressing-room.

Miss Cordwain, who was still lingering over her tea-table with a female
acquaintance, rose up at Henrietta's graceful entrance, and, receiving her with
a low courtesy, offered her an arm-chair at the upper end of the room.

Henrietta, conscious of the error she had committed in not making use
of the mantua-maker's name before, blushed a little at this reception, which
was not suitable to the character she was to appear in, and, declining the chair;
"Mrs. Cary, madam," said she. She could utter no more than those two words;
but they were sufficient to give miss Cordwain to understand her business.

The haughty citizen was excessively shocked to find she had been betrayed
by the figure of Henrietta into so improper an instance of respect; and that
the person she took for a lady of distinction was the young woman who had
been recommended to her service, thought to recover the dignity which she
conceived she had lost from this mistake, by assuming an imperious air and
an insolent accent.

"Who did you live with last?" said she to Henrietta, throwing herself
again into her chair, and glancing her over with a supercilious eye; "I hope
it was with a woman of quality: you will not do for me, I can tell you, if you
have not been used to attend upon persons of rank."

Henrietta, notwithstanding the confusion she was under at acting so
strange a part, could not help being diverted with the pride of this daughter
of trade.

"I am afraid, madam," said she, "I shall not be worthy of your place; for I
never lived in the service of any woman of quality, nor indeed of any other."

"What you are a gentlewoman, I suppose," interrupted miss Cordwain,
drawling out the word *gentlewoman;* "and now I remember Cary told me you
had never been in service. Well, that does not signify: I have no objection to
your having been a gentlewoman; you may be the better servant for what I
know. For, to say the truth," said she, addressing herself to her companion,

"those sort of poor gentlewomen, when they are reduced, as they call it, to wait upon us, who could buy their whole generation, often know their distance better, and are more humble than such as have been bred to service."

"Oh!" said the other lady, with an applauding smile, "ever while you live, madam, chuse a gentlewoman for your maid. There is alderman Jennings the grocer's lady: I have heard her often declare she never was so well served as when colonel Noble's daughter waited on her. The colonel was killed in the last war; and, as those folks you know have seldom any thing to leave their families, his fine gay daughters were obliged to go to service after his death, and did very well; but some body left them ten thousand pounds a piece, and spoiled two excellent servants, by making them gentlewomen again."

"Nay, if they had fortunes left them," replied miss Cordwain, "why you know, then, they had a right to be called gentlewomen.

"Well, child," pursued she, turning to Henrietta, "as I told you before I have no objection to your having been a gentlewoman; for I am resolved never to have any other to wait on me: I shall take you upon Cary's recommendation, and the sooner you come the better."

Henrietta, who had really enjoyed the conversation that passed between these two ladies, told her that she would come whenever she pleased; and it being agreed she should come the following day, that she might dress her new lady for a city-feast, she courtesied profoundly low, and withdrew.

Henrietta, whose imagination was naturally lively, and not wholly free from those romantic notions which persons of her age readily admit, began to consider her transformation from the niece of lady Meadows, and a presumptive heiress, into the waiting-maid of a cit, as one of those caprices of fate which never fail to produce surprising effects. She could not help fancying herself the future heroine of some affecting tale, whose life would be varied with surprising vicissitudes of fortune; and that she would at last be raised to a rank as much above her hopes, as the station she was now entering upon was below all that her fears had ever suggested.

But these reflections were succeeded by others more reasonable, and which indeed afforded her a more solid satisfaction: she was going to refute the censures of an injurious world; to make that innocence which had been so vilely traduced manifest, in her chearful submission to poverty and servitude, at a time when a shining fortune was offered to purchase a change in her religious principles, and when perhaps a little dissimulation, or a temporary compliance with her aunt's proposals, might restore her to a rank in life suitable to her birth.

The satisfaction she felt from these pleasing ideas, diffused such a serenity over her fair face, as agreeably surprised Mrs. Willis, who had waited her return with impatience.

Henrietta repeated to her the dialogue that had passed between the two ladies with so much humour, and marked the pride of wealth, and aukward affectation of grandeur and distinction, in these opulent heiresses to the laborious gains of sordid thrift, and perhaps successful knavery, with such delicate strokes of satire, as convinced Mrs. Willis she would not be an injudicious observer of the manners of those whom it might be her lot to associate with, nor pass through this new scene of life, without drawing improvement from it.

The good woman was grieved to find that she must lose her so soon; but, being fully persuaded that this humiliating step would terminate in something happy for her fair friend, she disposed herself to part with her chearfully.

It was agreed between them, that the elder Mr. Damer should not be made acquainted with any part of his son's behaviour with regard to Henrietta, till his return from Holland, when the whole affair might be laid candidly before him; and that the younger should be told, that she was gone into service; but where, he was not to be informed.

The next day Henrietta, after taking a tender farewel of Mrs. Willis, repaired to her new dwelling. Miss Cordwain was just gone out to make some little purchases for the evening, and Henrietta, being directed to go into her lady's dressing-room, was met by her predecessor, who had lingered in the house to have an opportunity of speaking to her, that, according to the general custom of servants, she might prejudice her against her new mistress.

From this girl, who was not sparing in her invectives, she learned that miss Cordwain's temper, which was not naturally good, was extremely sowered of late by a disappointment in love; that the packer, her father, had been treating with a certain nobleman for a match between her and the nobleman's eldest son; but that it had been broke off, because the citizen had refused to lay down more than thirty thousand pounds with his daughter, and the nobleman insisted upon forty.

This little piece of history was followed by a thousand other family anecdotes; to all which Henrietta listened in silence, and was not sorry that the censorious waiting-woman, whose tongue had, during a whole hour, run with surprising volubility, was at length silenced by the arrival of miss Cordwain, whose voice when she heard on the stairs, she took a hasty leave, and retreated thro' a different door from that which the lady entered.

Miss Cordwain, as soon as she saw Henrietta, slightly inclined her head, in return to her respectful courtesy; and throwing some millenary trifles upon her toilet, sat down to her glass, and ordered her new woman to comb her hair, shewing a fretful impatience at her hairdresser's long delay; for she was to meet her company at nine o'clock, and it was now almost four: so that she had good reason to fear she should hardly have time enough to dress.

While Henrietta was acquitting herself handily enough of this task, her lady took up a collection of songs that lay upon her table, that she might improve her mind while her body was adorning; and after reading intently a few moments to herself, she hastily turned over the leaves to a place that was doubled down, and began to read aloud a most piteous complaint of a despairing nymph, whose lover had forsaken her for another: she concluded this doleful ditty with a deep sigh; and repeating the burden of it, *for men are as false as the changeable wind,* "Henrietta," said she, "was you ever in love?"

Our fair heroine, who understood this question as a prelude to a confidence from her mistress, was at some loss how to answer it, when she was relieved from her perplexity by monsieur Finesse, the French haircutter.

Miss Cordwain, immediately dropping her tender languishments, assumed a supercilious air; and, after haughtily interrogating the ingenious artist for not coming sooner, submitted her tresses to his forming hands, a settled gloom all the time clouding her face: for whether it was that her glass, on which her eyes were intently fixed, told her some unpleasing truths, or that her gentle bosom heaved with some secret discontent, it is certain that every thing displeased her; nor could all Henrietta's obliging attention to the adorning her person draw a smile of approbation from her.

After five hours labour, however, the lady was completely dressed. Her father, who had not seen her since dinner, which she had swallowed in haste, having so much business on her hands, now entered the room; and liking the shewy appearance she made, "Why, Molly," said he, "you are as fine as a duchess."

"As fine as a duchess," repeated she, pouting; "and why not?"

"Very true, girl," replied the father, "thou hast that which can make duchesses: but, Molly, I have something to say to thee in private; so send your waiting-maid away."

Henrietta immediately retired into her mistress's bedchamber; which being only separated from the dressing-room by a slight partition of wainscot, she could not avoid hearing every thing that passed.

"I have had a proposal made me this afternoon," resumed the father, "and I came to acquaint you with it. Mr. Harris has asked you in marriage; there's immense riches for you, girl: what say you?"

"Sure, papa," cried miss Cordwain hastily, "you have not given him any encouragement, have you? A fine match, indeed! so I must be called plain Mrs.

Harris all my days, and there's miss Jennings married to a viscount, and has coronets upon her coach: three weeks ago, miss Collins, the broker's daughter, became a countess: and but this very morning I heard that the duke of —— is courting miss Rogers, our neighbour the soapboiler's niece, and she has but twenty thousand pounds.—I can't bear it; so, I can't," pursued miss Cordwain, bursting into tears, "to see all my comrades at Hackney boarding-school married to right honourables, and I am not likely to be even a paltry baronet's wife."

Here her tears and sobs suppressed any farther utterance, and had such an effect upon the fond father that he also was ready to cry.

"Don't break my heart, Molly," said he, half-sobbing; "you know it is death to me to see you fret and grieve yourself: are you not my only child? is it not for you that I have been toiling and labouring for these forty years, up early and down late, scraping all I can together, gaining much and spending little, and all to make you a peeress of Great Britain, and a peeress you shall be; so don't cry, my girl, and spoil your complexion; neither neighbour Jennings, nor neighbour Collins's daughter, shall be greater than you. You shall be a countess, Molly, will that content you? I will lay down the odd ten thousand, that the earl of —— and I quarrelled about, and you shall have his son."

"I am obliged to you, papa," said miss Cordwain; "but—"

"Nay," interrupted the father, "I find nothing will please you: you were crying just now, because you were not a countess; and when I tell you that I will part with another ten thousand pounds, to make you easy, you come with your buts."

"Why, suppose I am a countess," replied miss Cordwain, "will not miss Collins be a duchess, and take place of me? I can never endure that."

"What signifies her taking place of you," said her father, "the duke's estate is not half so good as the earl of ——; besides, you refused a duke, you know, and you have often told me that you like lord B—— better than any man in the world, and how have you pined since the match was broke off!"

"Well, I confess," replied miss, "that I do like my lord B——, and would rather marry him than any duke in the land, provided that little odious thing, miss Collins, did not marry above me: she to be called her grace at every word, while I am only lady B——; I should die with vexation."

"Since it is so," said the father, "I shall lay aside my design, and make no advances to the earl."

"And then his son will marry some body else," cried miss Cordwain.

"What would the girl be at?" interrupted the good man, with some heat; "if you won't have him, need you care who has."

Miss Cordwain now burst into a flood of tears: she liked lord B——, but she could not bear the thoughts of miss Collins being in a rank above her; and love and envy raised such tumults in her breast, as made her seek a relief in tears.

"I wish you knew your own mind, girl," said the father half angry, and half concerned at her grief.

"I know my own mind well enough," replied miss, sullenly: "I would marry lord B——, and I would not have that proud minx be a duchess."

"Take my word for it," said the father, "she will never be duchess of ——; I know her fortune is not sufficient to clear the duke's estate of two mortgages that have almost swallowed it up."

"Nay, then," interrupted miss Cordwain, who eagerly admitted an argument that set her mind at ease, "I am sure the duke will not have her; for she is so ugly you know, papa, that nothing could charm him but her riches."

"Well," said the father, smiling with pleasure to see her in good humour again, "I am to meet a friend of the earl's to-night; shall this affair be brought on again?"

"As you please, papa," said miss Cordwain, courtesying; "you know it is my duty to be obedient."

"Aye," said the good man, kissing her, "you have always been one of the most dutiful children in the world; and I will make thee a lady, though I don't leave myself a shilling." With this wise declaration he quitted the room, leaving his daughter in high spirits; who, after she had called her maid to adjust whatever might be amiss in her dress, and taken a full survey of herself in the glass, stepped into her coach, with the air of a citizen who has a fortune of forty thousand pounds.

Chap. VI.

Contains an incident which the sagacious reader has probably foreseen.

Henrietta, when she was left alone, found sufficient matter for reflection in the sentiments and behaviour of this wealthy tradesman and his daughter; and as it was now become necessary for her own peace of mind to reconcile herself to the situation that fortune had placed her in, she endeavoured to extract useful lessons from every scene that passed under her observation.

Why have I lamented my poverty? said she to herself; riches neither give understanding to the mind, nor elegance to the person. How mean is miss

Cordwain with forty thousand pounds! what narrow notions! what selfish passions! how ignorant, how contemptible!—All the advantages her large fortune procures her, is a title and a coronet: honours how despicable, when such as miss Cordwain wear them!

Let me thank Heaven then, that made my father a younger brother; that he inherited the virtues and elevated sentiments of his noble ancestors, and wanted that allurement to upstart wealth, which might have given me a miss Cordwain for a mother, and have deprived me of those generous precepts, and those bright examples, by which I have been taught to think poverty a less evil than dishonour; and that a peaceful conscience is cheaply purchased with the loss of every worldly advantage.

These were her reflections, as she afterwards declared to her friend. It is not therefore surprising that with such sentiments, our fair heroine found herself tranquil in her humble station, and dignified misfortune by her graceful resignation to it.

If the woman she served had had judgment enough to distinguish merit, and goodness enough to love it, Henrietta must have engaged her attention and her kindness: but little minds like nothing but what resembles themselves.

Miss Cordwain sometimes condescended to enter into a conversation with her woman, but was quickly disgusted with the difference of their notions; and what she could not comprehend, she either despised as folly, or suspected as artifice.

They were upon these terms when Mr. Cordwain acquainted his daughter, that they were invited to spend a week at the earl of ———'s country-seat; for the contested ten thousand pounds being granted by the citizen, the treaty of marriage was renewed; and this visit was proposed in order to bring the young people together again with some kind of decorum.

Miss Cordwain, in high spirits, gave her woman notice to make preparations for this little journey; which done, Henrietta went to take leave of her faithful Mrs. Willis.

"What a triumph would mine be," said she to her friend, "if any of my relations should happen to be at this nobleman's seat, and behold me in the character of miss Cordwain's servant!"

"You have done right, my dear," replied Mrs. Willis, "to call it a triumph; for so indeed it would be, the triumph of virtue over pride and prejudice."

The good woman informed her, that her guardian was in a very ill state of health, and was gone to Montpelier, in consequence of his physician's advice: that the young man had been there to wait upon her; and that when he heard of the resolution she had taken, he affected to think himself extremely injured by her conduct, as it shewed the utmost contempt of his advice and friendship; but it was easy to perceive, added Mrs. Willis, that there was more grief than anger in the reproaches he threw out against you upon this occasion. He seemed much mortified at my refusing to tell him where you was, but owned that his wife made him very uneasy upon your account; and when I urged that as an argument against the propriety of your seeing him, his silence acknowledged me in the right.

Henrietta was sensibly affected with the news of her guardian's illness; and since his return was now uncertain, she resolved to write to him immediately, and give him an account of all that had happened to her since he went abroad, fearing that unless she explained the reasons of her conduct, he might be prejudiced against her by her aunt's representations of it. She would not give him any disquiet, by mentioning his son's behaviour, but left that to be unravelled by time.

Mrs. Willis having promised to get this letter safely transmitted to Mr. Damer, Henrietta took a tender leave of her, and returned home.

The next morning very early, the coach and six was at the door; miss Cordwain impatiently stepped in, for she thought every moment an age till she saw her noble lover again. Her face dressed in smiles of pleasing expectation, and her heart exulting with the consciousness of her own worth, which, by her father's concession of the disputed thousands, had received such a considerable addition: but being, as I have before observed, not very happy in the frame of her temper, this sun-shine of satisfaction was soon clouded at being obliged to wait a few minutes for her father, whose slowness but ill suited with her eager impatience.

Indeed the wary citizen, having wisely considered that they had a journey to perform of at least twenty miles, was busied in packing up some necessary refreshments, that they might not be famished by the way. For this purpose he had caused a neat's[5] tongue, a cake of ginger-bread, two or three pounds of almonds and raisins, and a bottle of sack,[6] to be provided; and he himself brought the basket in which they were deposited to the coach, directing Henrietta to get in first, that he might place it safely in her lap; which done, he took his seat next his daughter, and ordered the coachman to drive.

Miss Cordwain's ill humour insensibly wearing off, they pursued their journey with great satisfaction, not having baited[7] above three or four times on the road.

At length the young lady's eyes were delighted with the prospect of the magnificent villa, which she expected one day to be mistress of; but her attention was soon called off that object by the presence of her lover, who, being just returned from a little excursion on horseback, alighted as soon as he saw the coach stop, and advanced to help his mistress out.

The young lord presented his hand to miss Cordwain with an air of forced gallantry; but happening to glance his eyes towards Henrietta, he started back in great surprise.

Miss Cordwain, vexed at the attention with which he gazed upon her woman, jumped out of the coach, before he had sufficiently recovered himself to be able to offer her again the hand, which, in his confusion, he had withdrawn.

The lady having on a capuchin,[8] which she had wore during the journey, untied it, and, tossing it into the coach to Henrietta, bid her, in an imperious tone, to take care of it.

This action and these words gave the young nobleman to understand that our beauteous heroine was actually the servant of miss Cordwain: a circumstance which furnished him with new matter for wonder; and indeed this encounter gave him so much perplexity, and so entirely engrossed his thoughts, that the old tradesman (who enquired after my good lord and my good lady's health, with as many bows and scrapes as would have served any trader to express his acknowledgment to a customer whom he had just cheated) was obliged to repeat his questions several times before he could procure an answer.

As for Henrietta, she had, upon the first sight of this young nobleman, whom she immediately knew to be the same person that had lodged at Mrs. Eccles's, been under some confusion, lest he should accost her as an acquaintance before the lady on whom she attended; but observing that, from miss Cordwain's behaviour, he understood her situation, and took no further notice of her than by a side glance, which he gave her, full of passionate concern, she was relieved from her fears, and, far from being discomposed at the character she appeared in, she acquitted herself of the little duties of her station with the most graceful ease; gave her lady her fan, received her commands, and, with a little French trunk in her hand that contained some laces and linen, followed her to the house at a respectful distance.

Lord B——'s emotions at this unexpected meeting with Henrietta, having now in some degree subsided, he entertained his mistress as they walked with his usual vivacity and politeness, but could not help often turning to snatch a look of her fair attendant, whose charms in that humble station, a station so unworthy of her birth and shining merit, acquired a pathetic power that melted him to a tenderness he had never known before.

He conducted the lady and her father to the apartment of the countess his mother; and, taking the first opportunity to leave them, retired to his own, that he might be at liberty to reflect upon his adventure.

To know that the woman, whom all his most diligent enquiries for so many weeks could never discover, was in the same house with him, was a circumstance that afforded him infinite satisfaction; but he saw no probability of turning this circumstance to the advantage of his designs upon her. For, with what face could he plead his passion to one of her delicacy, while he was publickly addressing another.

The servile condition he saw her in was a bar to his hopes. She who, with such uncommon attractions, could resolve to be poor, must needs be incorruptible. What allurement could riches throw out for a woman, who knew no other pride but the pride of virtue?

He could not hope to make an impression upon her heart by the disguise of honourable love. She must needs know the terms he was upon with miss Cordwain; and was afraid that she already despised him for the meanness of such a choice.

It was indeed still in his power to throw such obstacles in the way of this match, as to defer, if not break it entirely, but he could not resolve to make such a sacrifice to love; he would have married Henrietta with half miss Cordwain's fortune, and was amazed at the violence of his passion, when he considered the prodigious disproportion between twenty and forty thousand pounds—Yet most sincerely did he wish his generosity could have been put to this trial; and, in the violence of his grief at the apparent impossibility that this should ever happen, a thousand times did he curse the malevolence of fate, that united so many virtues and graces in one lovely woman, and denied her wealth; which however, by his preference of miss Cordwain, he tacitly acknowledged was worth them all.

A whole hour's labour of thought and reflection, left lord B—— in the same state of anxious doubt and solicitude he was in when he first entered upon this examination of his own heart; and all he could be certain of, in this confusion of ideas and opposing sentiments, was, that the unexpected sight of miss Courteney had charmed him more than ever; and following the impulse of his passion, without knowing whither it would conduct him, or what it would terminate in, he anxiously lay in wait for some opportunity of speaking to her in private, which he found when he least expected it.

Chap. VII.

In which our heroine again appears very foolish.

Mean time our lovely heroine, who had been received by the countess's woman with prodigious ceremony, and had, during a whole hour, listened with smiling attention to all the impertinences she uttered, was at length relieved from the fatigue of such conversation, and, with a profusion of compliments, conducted to a chamber contiguous to that of her mistress. As soon as she was left alone, she began to consider how she should extricate herself from the difficulties her unexpected meeting with lord B—— had involved her in.

Her delicacy was shocked at the thoughts of remaining in the house with a man who had made an attempt upon her honour, especially in the situation she now was; a situation that would seem to invite his future attacks: and, though he might well impute their meeting to the fantastick effects of chance, yet he would not fail to construe her stay into a tacit encouragement of that passion he had professed for her at parting, the dishonourable purport of which was evident from the engagements he had entered into with miss Cordwain.

She reflected also on the censures under which her character laboured at present, and was justly apprehensive, that when this part of her story was known, the malicious world would not fail to insinuate that she threw herself into lord B——'s way, and the inferences that would be drawn from such a supposed conduct, must needs be highly disadvantageous to her.

But, on the other hand, how could she quit miss Cordwain's service so abruptly, without giving occasion for strange conjectures, and setting the tongue of malice loose to assign reasons for her behaviour, very different from the truth?

However, the inconveniencies, which might attend this step were light, compared with those she foresaw from exposing herself voluntarily to the pursuits of a young libertine, whose eyes in this last interview had spoken too plainly to leave her in doubt of his sentiments.

She therefore resolved to go away the next day; and, as soon as she was summoned to the toilet, acquainted miss Cordwain with her intention.

Henrietta was a scrupulous observer of truth, and would not on this occasion violate it, by forming any plausible excuse for her sudden determination; so that miss Cordwain, in whose breast the stings of jealousy had been rouzed by the passionate glances lord B—— had darted at her maid, began to entertain strange suspicions from so unexpected an overture; and, in a peremptory tone, demanded to know her reasons for quitting her service in such a manner.

Henrietta, with great sweetness, assured her that she did not desire to be dismissed in consequence of any discontent, but that the necessity of her affairs obliged her to return immediately to town.

"Your affairs!" said miss Cordwain, with a haughty sneer; "I vow it is mighty pretty to hear servants talk of their affairs, as if they really had any concerns of more consequence than the duty they owe their principals. I wonder you don't tell me you have half a dozen engagements in town," pursued she, laughing aloud; "such a speech would become you mightily: but prithee, go, creature; pack up your rags in a sheet of brown paper, and take yourself away. I suppose you have found out a new method of living, less mortifying to your pride of beggarly gentility than waiting upon a woman of fortune; and I doubt not but you will be shortly seen flaunting it in publick places with a flimsy sack, a painted face, and all the trappings of your trade."

To this coarse abuse Henrietta listened in silence, beholding her imperious mistress all the time with such a calm, but steady eye, as called up a blush in those cheeks which had been before overspread with a livid paleness.

Not that she felt any remorse for the reproaches she had uttered, or was ashamed of her indecent transports, but Henrietta's soft composure, the dignity of her silence, and the energetick expression in her eyes, struck a kind of awe into her mean-soul'd adversary; and, inly raging at the inferiority she was conscious of, she commanded her to be gone from her presence.

Henrietta instantly obeyed, and, meeting the countess's woman as she went out of the room, she begged her to send a servant to the nearest inn to hire a post-chaise for her, being resolved to return to London that very day.

This well-bred Abigail[9] expressed great concern that she was so soon to lose the honour of her company; and asked, with an appearance of anxiety, if she was not to return again?

Henrietta replied in the negative, at which the other seemed wonderfully surprised, though she was not ignorant of all that had passed between Henrietta and her lady; for, hearing miss Cordwain's voice very loud, she had applied her ear to the key-hole, and needed no further information.

Our fair heroine having evaded the artful questions of this prying woman, and discouraged her reflections on her own lady, whom, in her general invective against the pride and caprice of mistresses, she did not spare, told her, she would have the pleasure of viewing the fine gardens that belonged to the house, before she went away; and Mrs. Smith promised to join her, as soon as she had executed the commission she was charged with.

Henrietta accordingly repaired to the gardens, full of reflections upon the scene that had lately passed. She entered a little covered ally that led to a grotto, which she had an inclination to take a view of; when, hearing the sounds of steps behind her, she looked back, supposing it was Mrs. Smith; but was not a little surprised to find it was lord B——, who, seeing her cross the terrace from his chamber-window, had followed her thither.

Henrietta, rightly judging that this encounter was not meerly accidental, turned her steps from the grotto, and struck into a less private walk. Lord

B——, perceiving her intention, crossed immediately and met her, bowing profoundly low, and, with an air as respectful as if he was accosting a duchess, enquired after her health.

Henrietta, not at all flattered by this instance of respect, which he, by whom it was paid, considered as an act of supererogation, and that it would affect her accordingly, returned his compliment with the most graceful ease; and, smiling, told him, he must not now consider her as miss Courteney, but the servant of miss Cordwain.

"O that horrid appellation!" cried he; "What violence did I not do myself to behave to you as I did this morning! But tell me, for Heaven's sake, madam, what has occasioned this transformation?"

"My aunt's continued displeasure," replied Henrietta; "your lordship has perhaps heard what circumstances my father died in: the station therefore in which you see me, ought not to be called a transformation; it is what I was born to, since I was born in indigence."

"I cannot bear to hear you talk thus," interrupted lord B——; "how could you think of subjecting yourself to a condition so unworthy of you, when you knew there was a man in the world that would have died to serve you!"

"I am not of a temper," said Henrietta, "to be easy under great obligations; and servitude is, in my opinion, less shocking than dependence."

"Why, do you talk of obligations," said lord B——: "love knows no property; could you doubt that my fortune would be at your command. Suffer me, I conjure you," pursued he, "to snatch you from this unworthy situation; can riches be better employed, than in supporting her I love?"

"My lord," interrupted Henrietta, her face glowing with indignation, "this is an insult I could not have expected from one of your rank and politeness: I am fallen very low, indeed, when a man, who is upon the point of marriage with another, dares talk to me of love."

"There are certain engagements," replied lord B——, a little confused at the air with which she uttered these words, "in which the heart has no part."

"Very likely," interrupted Henrietta; "but it is sufficient for me to know, that the engagements your lordship has entered into, leaves you not the liberty of addressing me in this manner: and I look upon the professions you make me as the highest insult upon my distress."

Lord B——, notwithstanding he found in this justifiable haughtiness the ruin of his hopes, could not help admiring a mind so rightly turned; humble with such propriety, and proud only when condescension would be meanness.

"This is not a time," said he, "to tell you how far I am bound by those engagements you speak of; but, whatever they are, they ought not to deprive me of the happiness of doing you service."

"I am obliged to you, my lord," said Henrietta; "but, at present, the greatest service you can do me is to take no notice of me."

In speaking these words, she courtesied, and would have left him; but he, not able to part with her thus, snatched her hand.

"You must not leave me," said he, "till you promise to give me an opportunity of speaking to you more fully—Oh, how I love you!" cried he, gazing on her passionately.

"Again, this insulting declaration!" interrupted Henrietta, pulling her hand from him, and giving him a look full of scorn and anger, as she turned away.

"Hear me, madam," cried he, pursuing her: "suffer me in the character of your friend, to offer you my services. My mother was formerly acquainted with lady Meadows: if it will be of any use to you, I will engage her to renew it, and offer her mediation betwixt your aunt and you. You must not, by heaven you must not, continue longer in so shocking a situation."

This proposal, and the earnest manner in which it was made, drew Henrietta's attention: angry as she was, she thought it merited a civil return.

"Doubt not, my lord," said she, her charming eyes recovering their usual sweetness, "that I should be glad to consider you in the character of a friend: and the offer you now make me is so obliging, that I cannot dispense with myself from telling you my reasons for declining it."

She then, in a few words, acquainted him with the purport of her aunt's letter to her: "Such are the terms," added she, "upon which a reconciliation with my aunt can be only effected; therefore the countess's interposition in my favour, were she disposed to grant it, would be of no use."

Lord B——, having before fully informed himself of every thing relating to miss Courteney, no sooner heard that for so trifling a compliance as the change of her religion it was in her power to secure lady Meadows' estate to herself, which he knew to be very considerable, than he thought fit to alter his style, and declared that the affair between miss Cordwain and him was not carried so far to take from him the liberty of following his inclinations, and of offering her his hand; he begged her therefore to favour him with another interview in the morning, when he would explain himself further.

Henrietta perceiving the countess's woman approaching, and unwilling to leave him in doubt with regard to her sentiments upon this new proposal, thus answered hastily:

"My lord, this can never be: there are many obstacles against it; you will find it very difficult to surmount those your own family will throw in your way; but, suppose that could be done, my scruples will raise others less easy perhaps to be overcome."

She left him when she had said these few words, and went to meet Mrs. Smith, who told her she had procured a vehicle for her, and that it would be at the back gate in less than an hour; but, continued she, there is a strange confusion within, have you seen your lady?

Henrietta told her she had not.

"God knows what is the matter" said Mrs. Smith; "she went into the garden to look for you as I imagined, and returned a few minutes ago with a most wrathful countenance: her father and she confabulated together, and then went into my lord's dressing-room; and Mr. Jauvert, my lord's gentleman, told me that the old man seemed to be very uneasy."

Henrietta had no time to make any reflections upon what she heard; for a servant that moment came to tell Mrs. Smith, that her lady had sent him to look for her, and desired that she would bring miss Cordwain's woman to her apartment.

Henrietta, though a little surprised, followed Mrs. Smith with great chearfulness, who desired her to wait in the anti-chamber, while she went to acquaint her lady with her being there; where we will leave her for a few moments, till the reader is informed of the accident that occasioned this summons.

Chap. VIII.

Which contains a curious dialogue between the earl and the citizen.

Miss Cordwain, who in the notice lord B—— took of Henrietta, found matter sufficient for jealousy and uneasiness, entertained the most injurious suspicions, when she heard her woman's sudden resolution to return to London; and having driven her from her presence with a torrent of abusive language, vented her rage in tears as soon as she was gone.

She reproached herself with her folly, in dismissing her so readily; when, by obliging her to stay, she might have guessed her designs, or at least have obtained a more certain knowledge of them.

Her mischievous imagination being now upon the stretch to find some expedient for protracting her departure, at last presented her with one which she resolved to make use of.

She hid a diamond bracelet; and then rung her bell for Henrietta, with an intention to tell her, that she could not find it, and insist upon her producing it before she left the earl's.

Mrs. Smith, who was that moment passing by her apartment, and knew that Henrietta was not in the way, stepped in to know what she wanted. Miss Cordwain asked for her maid, and, being told that she was walking in the garden, hastened thither immediately, not more delighted with the opportunity she now had of putting a stop to her journey, than of affronting her with the suspicion of theft.

As she descended the terrace, her eyes were blasted with the sight of her maid at a distance in earnest discourse with her lover.

At this confirmation of her suspicions, she ran back like a fury into the house, and meeting her father, who had just left the earl in his dressing-room, told him, that they were invited only to be affronted: that Henrietta was lord B——'s mistress; that he had taken her out of her service; and that she was going back to London that very night, at his request.

The old man, without staying to enquire farther, or reflecting upon the extreme improbability of this story, swore that never a lord in the land should use his daughter ill, and strode back to the earl's apartment, while miss Cordwain retired to her own, meditating vengeance on those that had so cruelly injured her.

Mr. Cordwain, who had promised himself to speak to the earl in very high terms, was no sooner in his presence than he sunk into that littleness, which meer monied men are so conscious of, with persons of birth and politeness. However, he assumed courage enough to tell his lordship, that he had something to say to him in private.

The earl, observing that his features were ruffled, was a little surprised; but dismissed his gentleman immediately, though he was not quite dressed, and then, with a complaisant smile, desired the citizen to let him know his commands.

"I am a plain man, my lord," said Mr. Cordwain, "I don't understand fine compliments and breeding, though I don't want for manners neither; and I am sure I have always been very civil to your lordship; and I did not expect that your lordship would have invited my girl and I here to scoff at us. My lord, I can give my girl forty thousand pounds, which is what few lords can say, let me tell you that; and withal I am an honest man, tho' I have forty thousand pounds more in my pocket perhaps: but no matter for that, I am not proud of my riches."

"Mr. Cordwain," said his lordship, (wondering to what this eloquent harangue tended) "I hope nothing has happened to give you any disgust; upon my honour I have the highest esteem for you, and I think I give a proof of it, by being so desirous of your alliance; but I am at a loss to comprehend your meaning, when you talk of my having invited you and your daughter here to affront you.

Miss Cordwain is a most accomplished young lady, and my son has too much judgment not to be as sensible as he ought of her merits."

"Indeed," interrupted Mr. Cordwain, "my daughter is in my eye a very comely young woman; and I will never give her to any man, though he were a duke or a prince, that would keep a mistress under her nose, as one may say."

"You astonish me, Mr. Cordwain," replied his lordship; "have you any reason to suspect that my son is a libertine?"

"My lord," returned Mr. Cordwain, "I am no scholar, I don't understand hard words; I have had learning enough to scrape a few thousands together, and that is sufficient for me. Your lordship's son may be a libertine for what I can tell, that's neither here nor there; but I am sure he is a terrible rake: and what tender father," pursued he, almost in tears, "would marry his child to a rake, to have all the fruits of his toil and labour, for thirty years and upwards, squandered away upon lewd women?"

"Sure! Mr. Cordwain," interrupted his lordship, with a sterner accent, "you do not imagine my son capable of acting so dishonourably: his principles, Mr. Cordwain—"

"Nay, nay, my lord," resumed the citizen, "I have nothing to say against his principles; he is no Jacobite,[10] I dare engage: but he is a rake, my lord, that is my objection to him, and rakes are very bad husbands."

"My son," said the peer, "may have had some youthful follies; but I am sure miss Cordwain's beauty and good sense will fix his heart."

"And does your lordship really think my girl a beauty?" said the fond father, his eyes glistening with pleasure. "Indeed I always thought so; but fathers, my lord, are apt to be partial."

"She is both beautiful and witty," replied his lordship, who found every excellence in forty thousand pounds.

"Nay, as for her wit," said Mr. Cordwain, "I am the best judge of that, who have seen her growing up under my eye. She took her learning surprisingly, my lord, and by the time she was ten years old, she had read her Psalter quite through. Would it not grieve one then (continued he) to part with such a girl as this to one that will slight her, and keep mistresses?"

"Do me the favour, Mr. Cordwain," said his lordship, "to acquaint me with your reasons for suspecting that my son will keep a mistress, though he should be so happy as to have miss Cordwain for a wife?"

"Why, you must know, my lord," replied the citizen, looking extremely wise, "that I have made a discovery; and your son is actually carrying on an intrigue with my daughter's maid."

"Sure this must be some mistake," cried the peer.

"No, no, my lord," answered Cordwain, "it is no mistake, I am very sure of it."

"And you have discovered this intrigue, you say," resumed his lordship: "pray when, and by what means, did you discover it?"

"About half an hour ago," replied Mr. Cordwain; "my daughter told me of it."

"Oh! then it was your daughter that discovered it," said his lordship, smiling a little at the old man's absurdity.

"Ay, ay, my lord," cried he, construing that smile into an acknowledgment of his daughter's sagacity. "I told your lordship she did not want for wit."

"But miss Cordwain is certainly mistaken now," said the peer; "this is some pretty frowardness,[11] a love-quarrel; depend upon it we shall find it so: however, I will talk to my son, and I'll engage the countess to discourse your daughter upon this matter. Come, Mr. Cordwain, we who are the parents of these young people know their true interest better than they do, and must endeavour to make up this little breach between them. I will make an end of dressing," pursued his lordship, bowing low to the cit, "and join you in the garden a quarter of an hour hence, when I hope to clear up this affair to your satisfaction."

Mr. Cordwain immediately withdrew; and the peer having stepped to his lady's apartment to acquaint her with this strange story, left it to her to manage miss Cordwain, and went in quest of his son, who, when Henrietta left him, had retired to his study, and was revolving in his mind a scheme, which, by reconciling his interest to his love, would gratify all his wishes.

CHAP. IX.

In which Henrietta has an interview with the countess.

The countess, like a discreet matron, was resolved to see the young woman, of whom miss Cordwain entertained a jealousy, that she might by wholesome counsels fortify her against seduction; for she supposed that this suspicion took its rise from the girl's being pretty, and perhaps some little unmeaning gallantry of her son's, who, like all other young men, admired beauty wherever he found it.

She was willing also to know certainly whether miss Cordwain's fears were only imaginary, that she might the better effect a reconciliation between the lovers; for she passionately desired the completion of a match that would put her son into possession of forty thousand pounds.

When Mrs. Smith appeared, in consequence of her summons, and told her that Mrs.[12] Henrietta waited her ladyship's commands, the countess asked her what sort of a young woman she was?

Mrs. Smith replied, that she was an aukward sort of a body, mightily conceited of her beauty she believed; and Heaven knows, added she, she has not much to boast of.

"Well; tell her to come in," said the countess, beginning to believe, from this account of her, that miss Cordwain's fears were not without foundation; for vanity, she well knew, was the great underminer of chastity, from the duchess down to the chamber-maid.

When Henrietta entered the room, the countess, who expected to see a very different person, was so struck with her beauty and the dignity of her air, that she rose from her seat, and returned the graceful courtesy she made her with a complaisance that surprised her own woman, who, being ordered by her lady to leave the room, instantly obeyed, but went no farther than the door, where she stood listening, and heard all that passed.

"You appear to me," said the countess to Henrietta, with an engaging smile, "to deserve so little the suspicions that are entertained of you, that I really know not how to mention them to you, though it was for that purpose I sent for you hither."

Henrietta was a little surprised at this beginning; but conscious of the integrity of all her actions, she was wholly free from any apprehensions that could discompose her.

"I know not, madam (said she) the nature of those suspicions which I have incurred, but I am very sure I have no guilt to reproach myself with, which should make me fear to stand the strictest scrutiny."

"Upon my word I believe you," said the countess, charmed with the noble confidence of her answer, and the graceful manner in which it was delivered; "and it must be my son's imprudence that has given occasion for Mr. Cordwain's suspicions."

The countess was too delicate to make use of miss Cordwain's name upon this occasion; but Henrietta in an instant comprehended the whole mystery, and was now able to account for the injurious language she had given her.

"Own freely to me," pursued the countess, smiling, "has not my son been a little troublesome to you, and talked to you of love and such idle stuff?"

"It is some mortification to me, madam," replied Henrietta, blushing, "to own that I have been affronted in the manner your ladyship mentions: however it is certainly true, lord B—— has thought me weak enough to be dazzled with his professions."

"Then you have seen my son often," said the countess.

Henrietta, who thought it behoved her to be very explicit on this occasion, related to the countess the manner of her becoming acquainted with lord B——, his concealing himself in her chamber, and his behaviour afterwards.

"I did not know his lordship's name," pursued she; "and though I often heard him mentioned at Mr. Cordwain's, yet as I had no reason to suspect that he was the same young nobleman, whom I had such reason to avoid, I made no scruple to attend miss Cordwain hither."

"I am very much concerned," said the countess, "to hear this account of my son; it was a very shocking attempt. So you have acquainted your mistress with what happened?"

"No, madam," answered Henrietta, "that was not necessary; but when I discovered that lord B—— was the person who had treated me so freely, I desired miss Cordwain to dismiss me, because I did not chuse to throw myself in his way."

"That was very prudently resolved," said the countess; "and when are you to leave miss Cordwain?"

"Immediately, madam," replied Henrietta; "I have provided myself with a post-chaise to return to London, and I believe it is now waiting for me."

"Certainly!" said the countess (after a little pause) "this sudden resolution of yours must surprise miss Cordwain. What did she say when you acquainted her with it?"

"She was extremely angry, madam," replied Henrietta, "and said many severe things to me, at which I was then astonished; but if miss Cordwain entertained any unfavourable suspicions of me, her behaviour may be accounted for."

"Since you have not acquainted her," said the countess, "with my son's rude attempt upon you, what reason could she have to suspect you?"

"I know of none, madam," answered Henrietta, "except his lordship's speaking to me in the garden a little time ago, may have come to her knowledge."

"You have shewn so much candor in your answers to my questions," resumed the countess, "that I am persuaded you will tell me frankly the subject of my son's discourse to you in the garden."

"I was born to suffer indignities, madam," said Henrietta, her checks glowing with indignation: "My lord B——, though he must know that I was not ignorant of his honourable passion for miss Cordwain, yet dared to affront me with the mention of his love."

The countess was a little surprised at this sally, which escaped Henrietta in the warmth of her resentment, when she called to her remembrance a declaration, which she looked on as the highest insult, since lord B—— was acquainted with her birth. Had the countess known that it was the grand-daughter of the earl of ——, who expressed herself in such lofty terms, she would have admired that becoming pride, which suggested them; but in the waiting-maid of miss Cordwain, it appeared absurd and ridiculous, and she was ready to suspect her of artifice and dissimulation.

But when she cast her eyes upon Henrietta, and saw the emotion with which she was agitated, the deep blush that glowed on her cheeks, and the tears that trembled in her eyes, she reproached herself with the injustice she was guilty of, in so soon admitting doubts of her innocence.

Henrietta, supposing from the silence of the countess, that she had no more to say to her, courtesied to her respectfully, and was about to withdraw.

"You must not go," said that lady in an obliging accent, "till I know whether it is in my power to serve you. You have thrown up miss Cordwain's service upon my son's account, it is but just therefore that I should procure you another; if you are not provided for, I will recommend you to my sister, she will either take you herself, or settle you with another lady."

The countess, in making this offer, had another view besides serving Henrietta. She was not willing to lose sight of her, for she rightly judged that with so many charms in her person, and an understanding far above what was generally found in persons of her rank, this young woman was very likely to inspire a solid passion; and she dreaded lest her son should be so far captivated by her as to neglect the advantageous match that was now offered him.

If she placed her with her sister, or with any of her friends, it would not be easy, she thought, for her son to get access to her; or if he resolved to continue his pursuit, his designs, whatever they were, would be known soon enough to be prevented.

Henrietta penetrated no further into the countess's sentiments, than what served to give her a high idea of her benevolence. She accepted her offer with expressions of the deepest gratitude; and this the lady considering as a proof of her sincerity and right intentions, she, in the billet which she gave her for her sister, recommended her in very obliging terms to her favour.

Henrietta again politely thanked her, and, receiving the billet, upon which there was a full direction, she went out of the countess's chamber, with an intention to depart immediately.

Mrs. Smith, whom she found in the anti-chamber, informed her, that her chaise was waiting for her at the gate; upon which Henrietta took leave of her, and descended the backstairs, but was suddenly stopped by Mr. Cordwain, who had followed her, and, seizing her rudely by the arm, charged her with having robbed his daughter.

Chap. X.

Contains a discovery which it is hoped the reader will not be displeased with.

Good Heaven!" exclaimed Henrietta, in the utmost astonishment, "what can this mean?"

"Look you child," said the citizen, "my daughter tells me you have stole her diamond bracelet: any body but myself would send you to prison directly; but I am tender-hearted, and consider, that though I could hang you for this robbery, yet that would be poor satisfaction for such a loss: therefore in compassion I will spare your life, provided you immediately restore the bracelet."

Henrietta had by this time collected her scattered spirits, and comprehended the motive of this malicious accusation.

"May I not see miss Cordwain, sir?" said she, in a composed accent; "I am pretty sure that I can convince her she wrongs me greatly by this strange suspicion."

"See her! what should you see her for?" replied the old man, "unless you will give me back the bracelet: you must not think to move her with your whining; her intreaties shall not save you if you are obstinate; so look to it: but come, perhaps you will have the grace to repent, and return the bracelet; come along."

Saying this, he pulled her up stairs, and led her, with no great complaisance, into his daughter's chamber, who sat exulting in her successful mischief, and the disgrace she had fixed upon the creature that presumed to rival her: a blush however dyed her cheeks at the sight of Henrietta, who, with a look that at once expressed the highest contempt of her mean accuser, and calm confidence in her own untainted innocence, asked her how she had so far offended her as to make her seek her life?

"Offended me, creature!" said miss Cordwain, "have you the assurance to imagine that I am uneasy because—because—You vain saucy flirt—who told you that I could be jealous of you? and so you suppose—but you shall produce my bracelet."

"Ay, that she shall," cried the citizen; "I wish we were in town, I would carry her before alderman Grey-goose immediately. Come, girl, don't be a fool, but deliver up the bracelet, for this is hanging matter, let me tell you."

"Do you really intend, madam," said Henrietta, looking on miss Cordwain with a most contemptuous smile, "to go through with this malicious accusation? and are you resolved to perjure yourself, and swear that I have got your bracelet?"

"What does the creature mean!" interrupted miss Cordwain, colouring.

"My meaning is," said Henrietta, "that your bracelet is certainly in your own possession; and that you pretend to have lost it only to fix a scandal upon me."

"O my God!" cried miss Cordwain, putting her hand to her head: "the excessive insolence of this wench affects me so, I believe I shall faint—Dear papa, let her go about her business, I had rather lose ten bracelets than suffer so much uneasiness. Dear sir, let her go, one time or other she will meet with her deserts. She will not stop at this theft, but somebody else may bring her to justice; I will have nothing more to do with her."

"Base woman?" cried Henrietta, almost choaked with rage. "No, I will not take the liberty you offer me: has our laws, think you, no punishment for a calumny like this, that strikes at life as well as reputation? You shall be forced to prove your charge, and my fame shall be cleared to your everlasting confusion."

Miss Cordwain, conscious of her guilt, and apprehensive of the consequences of what she had done, knew not what answer to make to this menace. As for the citizen, he stared with stupid wonder upon the injured fair one: for the extraordinary emotion she was in, gave such vehemence to her utterance, and such fire to her eyes, that he even trembled, as if in the presence of some superior being. But poor Henrietta, after this sudden sally of rage, found her heart so oppressed with the indignity she had suffered, that she burst into a violent passion of tears.

Miss Cordwain was ready to renew her insults, when she found her so mortified, and her father being recovered from his pannic, again urged her to restore the bracelet; when a servant came in, and informed them, that dinner was going to be served, and that his lord and lady expected them in the dining-room.

Miss Cordwain immediately obeyed the summons, for she dreaded the conclusion of this affair. When she entered the room, the countess, who knew nothing of what had happened, seeing her look very pale, asked her, if she was well? and lord B——, who had promised his father to cure her jealousy by redoubled assiduity for the future, approached, and, with a well counterfeited tenderness, expressed his concern for her indisposition.

Miss Cordwain, who had been assured by her father that the earl earnestly desired the match between his son and her should go forward, resolved not to protract it by any shew of resentment at what was past, and therefore received his little assiduities with all the complaisance she was mistress of; but desirous of mortifying him in the person of her who had so greatly attracted his notice, as well as to give him an opinion of the softness of her disposition, she told him, that indeed she was prodigiously discomposed; that her maid had robbed her; "and my father," added she, "threatens the poor wretch with a prosecution, and I was weak enough to be excessively shocked with her blubbering."

"Has your maid robbed you, miss?" said the countess, extremely surprised.

"She has stolen a diamond bracelet from me this very morning, madam," replied miss Cordwain.

"Impossible!" cried lord B——, in a transport that deprived him of all consideration; "miss Courteney could not be guilty of any thing mean or scandalous."

These words were scarce uttered, when he discovered and repented of his indiscretion; but it was now too late to repair it.

"Miss Courteney!" repeated miss Cordwain, recovering from her surprise; "who is miss Courteney, my lord?"

The countess, perceiving her son was embarrassed, endeavoured to relieve him, by asking miss Cordwain some questions concerning her loss; but that young lady would not be diverted from her question.

"This creature has a variety of names, I suppose (said she): she hired herself to me by the name of Benson, and Courteney it seems is that she has been formerly known by. Sure I have been very unfortunate to get such a wretch to attend me."

"Madam," said lord B——, again thrown off his guard by his indignation at hearing a woman of Henrietta's merit so grosly abused, "you don't know who you are speaking of?"

"Why, do you know?" said the earl to his son, in an accent that shewed how extremely he was displeased with his imprudence.

"Yes, my lord (replied he) I do; and madam," pursued he, addressing himself to miss Cordwain, "I am sure you will have candor enough to excuse my engaging with some warmth in the defence of the unfortunate young lady, who is now your servant, when you shall know that she is the niece of the earl of ——, and that it is her firm attachment to the religion she was brought up in, which hinders her from succeeding to a very large estate, and makes it necessary for her to go to service for a subsistence."

This account brought tears into the eyes of the countess, who inly applauded herself for her discernment in the favourable sentiments she had conceived for Henrietta before she knew who she was.

The earl appeared moved, and was beginning to ask his son some questions concerning this fair unfortunate, when miss Cordwain fetched a deep sigh, and fell back in her chair.

Rage at this discovery of her rival's birth and extraordinary merit, and terror, lest the scandalous accusation she had forged against her, should end in her own disgrace, operated so powerfully upon her spirits, that she fainted away.

While the countess supported her, lord B—— rang the bell very deliberately for assistance; and the earl, not much concerned at an accident, which he imputed to a jealousy that proved her passion for his son, took that opportunity to remind him that it was his interest to improve the affection this young woman had for him.

The countess, who had in vain searched her pockets for a smelling-bottle, ordered a servant, who appeared at the summons of the bell, to bring one off her toilet; when Mr. Cordwain entered the room, and, seeing his daughter in that condition, made but one step from the door to the place where she sat, exclaiming, "Oh! my child, what ails my child? is she dead?"

"Don't be alarmed," said the countess, "it is only a fainting fit, she will recover presently."

Lord B——, who was ashamed to appear wholly inactive upon this occasion before his designed father-in-law, had presence of mind enough to take a decanter of water from the side-board, and sprinkle some of it on miss Cordwain's face.

This remedy was applied so successfully, that she immediately opened her eyes, but the first object they met had like to have closed them again; for her father, hearing a smelling-bottle called for, remembered that she always carried one or two about her, and, searching her pockets with trembling haste, pulled out, with a smelling-bottle, the bracelet which she had concealed there, as a place where it was likely to be most secure, being subject to no search but her own.

The old man made none of those reflections upon this accident, which were obvious enough to every one else; but, perceiving his daughter was beginning to recover, presented the bracelet, instead of the smelling-bottle to her, conceiving the former to be the best restorative.

"See, child!" cried he, in a transport, "I have found your bracelet—come, you must be well now—I don't wonder you was grieved: truly it would have been a great loss."

Miss Cordwain flattered herself from the words *I have found your bracelet,* that her father had wit enough to save her from any reproach, by giving some favourable turn to the discovery; but in this she greatly over-rated his abilities.

"And where dost think I found it, child?" pursued the old man: "even in thy own pocket, as all the company can witness."

"Very true;" said lord B——, maliciously.

"Was it found in my pocket?" said miss Cordwain. "Why then, to be sure, I pulled it off with my glove this morning, and forgot it: I protest I am sorry there has been so much noise made about it."

"It is a pity indeed," said the countess, "considering who the person is that was supposed to have stolen it."

"O la! papa," cried miss Cordwain, "you don't know that my maid Henrietta is discovered to be a great lady. Upon my word it is true," pursued she, seeing him look surprised.

"I am sorry to hear that," said the citizen, rubbing his forehead; "for if she has friends, who will support her, she may commence a suit against me for Scandalum Magnatum,[13] and what a power of money may I lose—See what comes of your heedlessness, girl. I protest I don't know what to do."

The countess, though she was vexed at the vulgar sarcasm of the daughter, was nevertheless desirous of freeing the old man from his uneasiness, as well as to have an excuse for visiting the injured young lady.

"I am persuaded (said she) that miss Courteney's delicacy will prevent her from seeking any publick reparation for the affront she has suffered; but I will see her myself, and, if necessary, dissuade her from taking any resolution to your prejudice."

Lord B——, who was talking to his father at a distant window, hearing this proposal, approached, and, by a look which he gave the countess his mother, seemed to bespeak her utmost tenderness and complaisance to the afflicted fair one.

Mr. Cordwain thanked her heartily for her kindness. "But, Odso![14] my lady," cried he, stopping her as she was going out, "I beg your ladyship's pardon, you must take the key up with you," continued he, fumbling in his pockets, and at last pulling it out; "for when I came down, I locked the door for fear the bird should fly away." With these words, he gave the countess the key, smiling and nodding his head in applause of his own sagacity.

The countess was extremely shocked to hear of this new indignity which the poor young lady had suffered, but she dissembled her concern, and silently withdrew.

Lord B—— again stole to a window to hide his emotions; and the earl, though greatly disgusted with the behaviour of both father and daughter, yet approached them with a complaisant air, and congratulated the latter on the recovery of her jewel.

Thus did these noble persons accommodate themselves to the manners of those whom they in secret despised; and, for the sake of a few paltry thousands, shewed the utmost solicitude to associate plebeian meanness in the honours of a noble ancestry, and to give title, rank, precedence, to one who would disgrace them all.

CHAP. XI.

Henrietta returns to London.

The countess, who was greatly affected with the cruel usage Henrietta had received, could with difficulty restrain her tears when she entered the room where the fair prisoner was confined: that air of distinction which she had observed in her before she knew her birth, seemed now more remarkable, and made the humiliating condition to which she was reduced, a subject of painful reflection to lady ——, who approached her with a look of tenderness and pity, and, taking her hand,

"I scarce know how to speak to you (said she) about an affair that miss Cordwain has much more reason to be ashamed of than you. She has found her bracelet."

Henrietta was a little surprised at the kind and familiar manner in which the countess accosted her; but still preserving that distant respect, which was due from the character she had assumed to a lady of her rank, she courtesied profoundly low, and thanked her for the honour she did her in condescending to bring this grateful piece of news herself.

"I must tell you also," said the countess, "that I am not ignorant of your name and family, nor of your motives for submitting to go to service; for which you deserve to be esteemed and admired by all the world. It was my son that betrayed your secret." pursued the lady, observing that Henrietta looked surprised; "I will not ask you now how you came to intrust him with it, some other time you shall, if you please, tell me all your story. I have now only leisure to assure you, that I am your sincere friend, and that I will serve you with all the interest I have in any way you shall desire."

Henrietta, after making a proper acknowledgment for this kind declaration, told the countess, that being determined to continue the way of life she had entered into, till her relations of themselves thought proper to alter it, the recommendation her ladyship had given her to her sister, was the greatest service she could possibly desire, and would be ever most gratefully remembered.

"I admire your resolution, miss Courteney," said the countess; "but I am grieved to think you should be in a situation so unworthy of you; something must be done to extricate you from it."

"I beg, madam," said Henrietta, "that your ladyship's kind concern for me may not lead you to take any steps in my favour with my relations. No;" pursued she, with some warmth, "their unnatural behaviour to me deserves the neglect I shew them, in not soliciting their assistance. I have already got over all those little passions and prejudices which might hinder me from being easy with my humble lot; and I freely confess to you, madam, that I find a secret pleasure in the thoughts of mortifying the pride of my lord ———, when some accident (for some accident it must be) shall shew him his niece in the quality of a servant."

"Consent at least," said the countess, "to my acquainting my sister with your birth, that she may endeavour to place you in such a manner as will be most agreeable to you."

"I do not wish, madam, to be known to the person I serve," replied Henrietta; "and I desire to have no other consideration shewn me than what my behaviour in the station I am placed in shall merit."

"Well," said the countess, "it shall be as you would have it; but I cannot express to you how much I esteem and admire you—You may judge of my good opinion of you, miss, when I tell you, that as to what regards my son's passion for you, I depend entirely upon your candor and generosity. You know our views for him; and this is all I shall say."

"I am obliged to you, madam," said Henrietta, "for the confidence you repose in me; I will endeavour to deserve it. And now, madam," pursued she, smiling, "since my imprisonment is at an end, I will, with your ladyship's permission, set out immediately for London; the chaise I had hired is, I suppose, still waiting for me. I hope to have the honour of presenting your letter to lady D——— to-morrow or next day at farthest."

"Take my kindest wishes along with you," said the countess, kissing her, and taking a diamond ring from her finger: "wear this for my sake," said she, giving it to Henrietta; "the intrinsick value of it is but small, but I hope you will consider it as a mark of my esteem for you."

The countess went out of the room as soon as she had spoken these words, leaving Henrietta extremely affected with her kindness; and all obstacles to her journey being now removed, she hastened to the gate, placed herself in her post-chaise which she found waiting, and in a few moments was out of sight.

Mean time, the countess returned to her company, and told Mr. Cordwain, smiling, that he had nothing to fear from Henrietta's vindictive resolutions. Upon which, miss Cordwain said, she would go up to her, and make her an apology for what had happened; but dinner was that moment served, which made it not necessary for the countess to tell her that Henrietta was gone, in order to prevent her intended civility: but as soon as a proper opportunity offered, she took care to let the young lady know, that her suspicions of Henrietta were very ill grounded; that she was perfectly virtuous; and likely to remain in the obscure condition of a servant, unless her relations, who were persons of rank and fortune, thought proper to do something for her.

She added, in order to remove all her uneasiness, that she had recommended her to a lady who would procure her a place, which was the least she could do for a young woman of her birth, in such unhappy circumstances.

Miss Cordwain was very well satisfied with what the countess had done; being persuaded, that since she was so desirous the treaty between lord B—— and her should go forward, that she would take care to hinder any thing from happening on the part of Henrietta, that might give her cause for disgust.

But poor lord B—— was in a truly pitiable situation: he was in love with the person of Henrietta, and the fortune of miss Cordwain; and these different passions by turns equally possessed him, so that it was impossible for him to form any fixed resolution.

When he reflected on the solid advantages that would accrue to him from a marriage with the packer's daughter, such as being enabled to play as high at Arthur's[15] as my lord ——, to bring as many race-horses to New-Market[16] as ——, to have as splendid equipages as the earl of ——, and several others, which make the envy and emulation of many of our present race of nobles, he was ready to sacrifice his inclinations to motives so just, so reasonable, so meritorious.

But when the image of Henrietta rose to his thoughts; her person so lovely, her manners so elegant, her birth not beneath his own, her virtue so eminent; how could he think of putting such a treasure out of his reach, by marrying her despicable rival! And indeed, so just were his notions of this treasure, and so high his value of it, that, provided any method could be found to reconcile her to her aunt, and secure to her the succession of her estate, he would willingly have renounced his pretensions to miss Cordwain, and have married Henrietta; though her fortune, as heiress of lady Meadows's estate, would be some thousands less than miss Cordwain's.

Such a proof of disinterestedness, he thought, must needs be very grateful to a young woman of Henrietta's fine understanding and enlarged sentiments; and, having brought himself to this point, his next care was to procure a private interview with her, that he might acquaint her with his designs, and engage her concurrence with them.

But this scheme being defeated by her sudden departure, which he learned from his mother, he was plunged into new perplexity and uneasiness. He asked the countess, with an air of indifference and unconcern, where she was gone, and how she intended to dispose of herself? But that discerning lady, who observed his sudden emotion at the news of Henrietta's departure, would give him no other satisfaction than telling him, that she supposed she would again go to service; for she seemed to have no expectations of any favour from her relations.

Lord B——, after a little reflection, comforted himself with a hope, that some accident or other would again throw her in his way; and that the disgust she must necessarily entertain, to a way of life so unworthy of her, would induce her to embrace his honourable proposals: for such he conceived them to be, since all the sacrifice he should expect from her, was a temporary compliance with her aunt's inclinations with regard to religion: but however, he thought it would be prudent not to break off with miss Cordwain, because in her fortune he would always find wherewithal to comfort himself, if he was disappointed in his love.

In pursuance of this wise resolution, he behaved in such a manner to the citizen's daughter, as gave her no cause to be displeased with him; so that every thing in this noble family, and their designed allies, was upon the same footing as before Henrietta, with mischief-making beauty, came in the way.

HENRIETTA.

BOOK THE FOURTH.

CHAP. I.

Atheists have been but rare, since Nature's birth;
Till now she-atheists ne'er appeared on earth.
Ye men of deep researches, say, whence springs
This daring character in timorous things!
Who start at feathers, from an insect fly,
A match for nothing—but the Deity.
*—*YOUNG'S UNIVERSAL PASSION.

Mean time our fair heroine, having performed her little journey without any unfortunate accident, arrived late in the evening at the house of her friend Mrs. Willis, who, in her astonishment at her sudden return, asked her a hundred questions in a breath.

Henrietta satisfied her eager curiosity with a succinct detail of all that had happened to her that day, which had indeed been a very busy one.

The honest heart of Mrs. Willis was variously affected with the different parts of her story. She wept for her sufferings: she execrated the malicious miss Cordwain; she praised the countess; and was exceedingly solicitous about the purport of lord B——'s designs, which, from what she had heard of his behaviour, appeared to her very mysterious. But Henrietta, who had a thorough contempt for that young lord, declared, that although he should break with miss Cordwain, and address her upon honourable terms, yet she could not bring her heart to approve of him.

"He is mean (said she) and sordid in his temper. His principles are bad: he is a lord, but he is not a gentleman; and I am sure I could never esteem him. Besides, the countess, who is more alarmed about the sentiments he has for me than I think she has reason, depends upon my honour not to encourage any overtures from him, and I will not abuse her confidence.

"It is easy (pursued she, smiling) to be just when our own inclinations do not oppose it. I shall pretend to no merit in making this sacrifice, if ever it be in my power to make it; because in reality it will not be a great one. If riches and splendor could have made me happy, I would have married sir Isaac Darby; for it was not his age that I objected to most, but to those qualities and manners which made his age contemptible."

"But, surely, my dear," said Mrs. Willis, "your gratitude would be engaged, should lord B——, in the present inequality of your circumstances, make you an offer of his hand."

"Not at all," replied Henrietta, with some warmth: "no man has a right to the love or esteem of a woman on whom he has entertained dishonourable designs, and, failing in them, offers marriage at last. The lover, who marries his mistress only because he cannot gain her upon easier terms, has just as much generosity as the highwayman who leaves a traveller in possession of his money, because he is not able to take it from him."

"Well, well, my dear miss," said Mrs. Willis, smiling, "I can collect this at least from the nice distinctions you make, that your heart is absolutely free; you would not reason so well, were there any secret passion in the case."

"Surely," replied Henrietta, "you do not imagine that I should become less delicate in my notions for being in love: that passion, like some plants, derives its qualities from the soil it grows in; for instance, in lord B——, it is mean, selfish, wavering."

"And what would it be in you?" interrupted Mrs. Willis.

"Ah! no matter," cried Henrietta; "I am not in love yet, and never will be with a man who has such sentiments as lord B——; he had best be constant to miss Cordwain. Plebeian lords and the nobility of the shop and warehouse are equal matches."

To this remark Mrs. Willis, who was pleased with the vivacity of her fair friend, assented only with a smile: for supper was now placed upon the table; and, as she knew Henrietta had not dined, she was extremely solicitous to make her eat, and with the same maternal fondness hurried her soon to bed, that she might recover the fatigue she had suffered during the day.

The next morning at eleven o'clock, our fair heroine set out in an hackney-coach for —— square, where lady D—— lived, to whom she was to deliver the recommendatory letter which the countess had given her.

The lady was at her toilet when she read her sister's letter, which Henrietta had sent in to her, and immediately ordered her admittance. Surprised at the elegant figure which met her eyes in the glass upon our fair heroine's entering the room, she hastily turned her head, and gazed on Henrietta so intently, that she blushed; which lady D—— observing, obligingly desired her to sit down, and said, she would talk to her presently.

Henrietta modestly placed herself at a distance, but so luckily for the lady's curiosity, that she could have a full view of her in her glass, without renewing her confusion.

"My sister," said lady D——, breaking silence at last, "has mentioned you very advantageously, Mrs. Benson, I wish it may be in my power to serve you."

Henrietta bowed respectfully.

"You are very young," pursued the lady; "I suppose miss Cordwain's was the first service you ever lived in?"

At the word Service Henrietta blushed again; and indeed the lady did not pronounce it without some hesitation, for having a sensible and ingenuous mind, she felt the impropriety of the term when used towards a person, who, notwithstanding the humility of her deportment, had a dignity in her looks and air, which commanded respect. She took notice of this emotion, and the more because she saw it endeavoured to be suppressed; and being desirous of gaining some further knowledge of her, she asked her a hundred little questions, which she thought would lead her to an explanation of her circumstances.

Henrietta avoided making a discovery of herself, but answered in such a manner, as, without satisfying the lady's curiosity, gave her a very good opinion of her candor and her sense: but she was particularly struck with the graceful ease with which she talked; and observed such a perfect politeness in her manners, as persuaded her she was born in a much higher rank than her present situation allowed the probability of.

Lady D——'s daughter now entered the room, and asked her mamma, if she desired to hear her take a lesson from her singing-master that morning?

The lady ordered the master to be admitted, upon which Henrietta rose up to go away; but the lady told her with a benevolent smile, that she should stay and hear miss D—— perform, and desired her to resume her seat.

While the young lady was singing, lady D—— kept her eyes fixed on Henrietta's face, and, from the sweet expression in it, supposing that she had a taste for music, asked her, if she had ever been taught?

Henrietta, though not willing to make a display of talents which were not necessary to her present condition, yet owned, that she had a little knowledge of music.

Lady D—— immediately desired to hear her sing, and the young lady at the same time presenting her guitar to her, she was obliged to comply. Her air, her attitude, the exquisite grace with which she touched the little instrument, the sweetness of her voice, and the sensibility in her fine eyes, charmed lady D——, who was an enthusiastic admirer of the art, so that she cried out in a kind of transport, "Mr. Minime! would you not be proud of such a scholar?"

"Madam," said the master, bowing, "the young gentlewoman has a very pretty voice and manner, to be sure: but if miss D—— applies closely to music for seven or eight years longer, and does not suffer her mind to be distracted with the study of other sciences, I shall have more reason to be proud of my scholar than any master in the world."

This speech forced a smile from Henrietta, who the third time rose up to be gone, upon hearing a female visiter announced; but lady D——, conceiving that she was not obliged to a strict observation of ceremony with the person now entering, (who was of a very low birth, but had a competent fortune left her by a father who had held it as a maxim of sound wisdom, that money should be got by any means;) again insisted upon Henrietta's staying, telling her, she had thought of something for her, and that she would acquaint her with it as soon as the lady was gone.

Henrietta had but just time to express a grateful acknowledgment of her kindness, when the visiter was introduced. She was a woman of a very mean aspect, but had a great deal of self-sufficiency in her air. After the usual compliments were over, she threw herself into an easy chair, and examined Henrietta with such extreme attention, that she blushed.

The lady, who took consequence to herself from the power of throwing an ingenuous mind into confusion, finding that Henrietta was oppressed by her looks, gazed at her the more earnestly: and having indulged herself several minutes in this exertion of her superiority, thought it was now time to make the poor bashful girl stare in her turn, and began to display her wit and learning; the former in an inundation of words that swallowed up her meaning, and the latter in French words and phrases, brought in to supply the deficiencies of her own native tongue.

Lady D——, who was used to divert herself with the ridiculous singularity of this woman's character, listened to her with complaisance. But Henrietta, who began to conceive a very mean opinion of a lady who seemed to value herself so highly upon the knowledge of a language, which was now become a part of every cobler's daughter's education, beheld her with an indifference that sensibly wounded her pride, and made her have recourse to other methods to impress her prodigious consequence upon her; and since she could not make her stare at her learning, she was resolved to make her wonder at her principles.

"You know, lady D—— (said she abruptly) I do not often go to church."

"I know it, and I am sorry for it," replied her ladyship.

"Upon my word (said she) I have too much reverence for the Deity to go to a place where it is ten to one but I shall hear him blasphemed."

Henrietta now began to stare indeed. The wonderful lady proceeded,

"I never pretend to deny that I am a deist."[17]

"You must pardon me, Mrs. ——," interrupted lady D——, "if I tell you that I really think you often declare that very improperly; I have heard you say so before your children and servants."

"Madam," replied Mrs. ——, "I take care that my servants shall not think me an atheist. They know my principles better: they know I am a deist; they have heard me declare that I believe there is an intelligent cause which governs the world by physical rules. As for moral attributes, there is no such thing; it is impious and absurd to suppose it. The arbitrary constitution of things in the human system produces happiness and misery; that is to say, misery and happiness is productive of—Or rather, as I said before, the arbitrary constitution of things, vice and virtue, is necessarily produced by—that is, necessarily brings on happiness or misery.—Prayer, and such like artifices of religion, is foolish: for whatever is, is right. To talk of imitating God, is blasphemy. His Providence is extended to collective bodies only; he has no regard to individuals: nor is the soul a distinct substance from the body. There is no future state; it is all a fiction. To argue from unequal distributions is absurd and blasphemous. Whatever is, is best. The law of nature is sufficiently clear; and there is no need of any supernatural revelation."

"I must entreat you, madam," interrupted lady D——, seeing her eldest daughter that moment enter the room, "to change the discourse now, miss D—— has not been used to such deep reasoning on these aweful subjects, and may perhaps mistake what you are saying for blasphemy."

"More absurd mistakes than that may be made, madam," replied Mrs. ——, "when persons are not allowed to exercise their mental faculties—but your ladyship is going to dress—I interrupt you." Saying this, she rose up, and lady D—— making no efforts to detain her, took her leave.

"I have always hated that woman," said miss D——, as soon as she was gone, "ever since I heard her ridicule parental affection, and call it brutal instinct."

"Oh!" said lady D——, laughing, "it would ill become one of her elevated understanding, to have natural affections: those she treats as vulgar prejudices. Her own sex are the objects of her scorn, because they are subject to such weaknesses as tenderness and pity. She reads Seneca on friendship in the morning; and exclaims, O the exalted passion! how divinely he treats it! what noble sentiments! In the afternoon she over-reaches her friend, and applauds her own wisdom. Epictetus is studied with great care. She will preach a moral sermon out of Epictetus that will last two hours. Epictetus teaches her to curb her passions. She reads him intently while her maid is combing her hair, and closes her book to storm at the poor trembling creature for accidentally hurting her with the comb."

Chap. II.

In which Henrietta makes a very fantastick distinction.

Henrietta could not help smiling at lady D——'s satirical manner of exposing the follies of the lady who had just left the room: but a female free-thinker was, in her opinion, so shocking a character, that she would much rather have seen it the object of abhorrence than mirth.

Lady D—— put an end to her reflections: for, turning towards her, "Mrs. Benson (said she) it is time to think of you now." Henrietta immediately rose from her seat.

"There is a lady of my acquaintance," pursued lady D——, "to whom your accomplishments of singing and playing will make you a very acceptable companion: and indeed I think it is a pity a young woman of your appearance and genteel education should remain in the condition of a servant, which I am persuaded you was not born to."

Henrietta blushed; which lady D—— observing, "come," said she, smiling, "be ingenuous, and confess that the proposal I have made you will suit you better than being a servant."

"Indeed, madam, it does not," replied Henrietta; "I am extremely obliged to your ladyship for your kind intentions, but I had rather be recommended to the lady as a servant than in any other character."

"You surprise me," said lady D——, after a little pause; "what objections can you have to a situation so much to be preferred to servitude?"

"I am very sure, madam," said Henrietta, "that I have not too much pride to be a servant, since it is necessary I should be one: but I am afraid I cannot so easily submit to be a dependent."[18]

Lady D——, a little disappointed to find herself so far below this obscure young person in delicacy of sentiment, answered gravely,

"Well, since it must be so, I will serve you in your own way; let me see you again a few days hence, by that time I may possibly have heard of something for you."

Henrietta again politely thanked her ladyship, and withdrew, leaving lady D—— and her daughter differently affected with her behaviour in this last instance: for young minds are apt to be struck with uncommon sentiments, and to admire such as seem to possess them; while persons advanced in years, either from experience of the world, or the natural depravity of the human heart, ascribe every thing to affectation and design, that contradicts certain received maxims in life.

However, Henrietta's peculiarity made lady D—— extremely desirous to know who she was, and whether there was any thing extraordinary in her circumstances. She wrote to the countess her sister, expressing her curiosity: but that lady was resolved to keep Henrietta's secret, as well in regard to the promise she had given her, as because she really thought an unseasonable discovery of her true name and family would be disadvantageous to the plan she had laid.

She therefore contented herself with telling her sister, in answer, that Mrs. Benson was a very deserving young woman, who had been well brought up, but, by misfortunes in her family, reduced to go to service.

Lady D—— was satisfied with this account; and when Henrietta, in obedience to her commands, waited on her again, she received her with great benevolence; told her, she had recommended her to a lady of great fortune, whose place she believed would be an advantageous one; and ordered her own woman to go with a message to the lady, and introduce her.

Henrietta having a hackney-coach waiting, lady D——'s woman and her, after some ceremonies which our fair heroine would gladly have dispensed with, seated themselves in it; and, as soon as it drove from the door, the Abigail began,

"Well, madam, you are certainly very fortunate, Mrs. Autumn's place is one of the best in Christendom: you have nothing to do but to flatter her, and you will gain her heart for ever."

"Is the lady fond of flattery then?" said Henrietta.

"Oh! immensely," cried the other; "but for fear you should mistake, and compliment her in the wrong place, you must know (and I think it is very lucky that I had an opportunity of instructing you) you must know that though she is between forty and fifty years of age, she affects to be thought extremely young; and having been handsome in her youth, as my lady says, she forgets she is no longer so now she is old.

"Now, dear madam, this is your cue. Be sure to praise her bloomy complexion, and the brightness of her eyes; and, if she bids you guess how old she is, as 'tis ten to one but she will some time hence, don't exceed twenty years, I charge you.

"The poor simple girl that lived with her last, lost her place, by saying, when she asked her how old she believed her to be, that she took her ladyship to be about the same age as her mother. She was a vulgar creature, to be sure. You, madam, are in no danger of speaking so improperly. But on certain occasions you may contradict her rudely, and she will be the more pleased; as for instance, when she says she looks horridly! tell her in a surly way, as if you were vexed at her perverseness, that you never saw her look so handsome."

"Mighty well," said Henrietta, smiling, "I perceive you are excellent in this art; I am—"

"Oh! no thanks, dear madam," interrupted lady D——'s woman, "I am fond of doing good offices."

"I was going to say," replied Henrietta, "that I am afraid these wise documents will be thrown away upon me."

"I hope not," said the other, gravely. "Come, take courage, you are but a young beginner; these things come of course. I should be sorry you were not capable of taking good counsel."

They were now arrived at Mrs. Autumn's house: lady D——'s woman sent up word, that she was come with the person her lady had recommended to her ladyship; upon which both were ordered to go up stairs.

They found the lady giving audience to a millener, a mantua-maker, and a mercer.[19] Several pieces of silk lay unrolled before her, and a vast variety of ribbons, lappets,[20] egrets,[21] and other fashionable trifles, were spread upon a table, on which she leaned, in a thoughtful posture, as unable to determine her choice.

When Henrietta and her companion entered, she raised her eyes, and nodding familiarly at lady D——'s woman, who approached her, courtesying; "you find me excessively busy, Mrs. Ellis (said she) well, what has lady D—— sent me—Oh! a good likely body," pursued she, looking at Henrietta; "my compliments, Mrs. Ellis, and thanks—You see I have hardly time to speak to you—The young woman may stay, I'll talk to her presently."

Mrs. Ellis withdrew; and the lady resuming her contemplative posture, gave Henrietta an opportunity of considering her at leisure.

If lady D——'s woman had not fixed her age at somewhat more than forty, she would have concluded her to have been older, by the deep furrows in her face, her fallen cheeks, and the poor shrivell'd hand that supported her head: but her dress spoke her scarce fifteen; a French fillet[22] supplied the place of a cap, and served to bind the few straggling hairs that graced her temples, to a tête;[23]

which was so loaded with hair, that her head seemed to be of an enormous size. The rest of her dress was suited exactly to the childish ornaments of her head; and though no object could be more ridiculous, yet Henrietta beheld her with a serious concern; for, true benevolence compassionates those follies which unfeeling hearts sacrifice to mirth.

Mrs. Autumn at length rose up; "that must be the thing," said she pointing to a pink and silver.[24] She then gave some directions to her millener; and, suddenly interrupting herself, turned with a lively air to the mercer, and asked him, why he had not cut off the silk?

"Your ladyship did not tell me how much you wanted," replied the tradesman.

"Lord! I am the giddiest creature," exclaimed Mrs. Autumn. This matter, however, was soon settled, and the important business with the millener dispatched, she dismissed her trades-people, and, throwing herself with an affected air upon a settee, ordered Henrietta to come forward.

"I was afraid (said she) that lady D——, who is very fond of seeing grave solemn faces about her, had sent me some antiquated creature that would have frightened me; but you seem to be a sprightly young body: we shall agree very well, I hope."

Henrietta courtesied.

"I hate old people," pursued the lady; "they are generally obstinate and surly. God help us, we shall all be old if we live—but when one is in years one's self it is time enough to be plagued with the humours of those that are; you will suit me extremely well."

Henrietta courtesied again.

"You are no talker, I find," said Mrs. Autumn, a little chagrined that the hints she had thrown out, had produced nothing which could flatter her extreme desire of being thought young. "Well, there is no great harm in that; I shall take you upon lady D——'s recommendation. As for terms—"

"Madam," said Henrietta, who now for the first time opened her mouth; "they shall be whatever you think proper."

"Very well," said the lady, "we will talk no more about them then; if you can find out how to please me, which will be no difficult matter I assure you, my place may prove a very advantageous one, and the sooner you come the better."

Henrietta told her, she was ready to come whenever she pleased. Upon which, Mrs. Autumn, with the pretty impatience of youth, asked her, if it would be any inconvenience to her to come that very night?

Henrietta, who was naturally obliging, assured her it would not; and was dismissed with a gracious smile for her ready compliance.

Mrs. Willis, who had flattered herself that she should enjoy the company of her amiable friend for a few weeks at least, was greatly disappointed when she found she was to lose her so soon; and gently blamed her for being so precipitate.

Henrietta gave her the character of the lady she was going to live with, and repeated what she had said to her. "You may be sure (added she) that I shall never please Mrs. Autumn in the way she expects to be pleased. Flattery is always mean; but to flatter folly, is, in my opinion, criminal. However, I gladly embraced the first opportunity that offered to shew my willingness to oblige, though I would not flatter her. You will hardly believe me, perhaps (said she, smiling) when I tell you, that one of the greatest bars to my happiness in my present humble situation is, the difficulty of pleasing without wounding my own delicacy and candor. It is not easy to live well with our superiors, and preserve our integrity, but it is not impossible; and, if I fail in that attempt, I shall at least have this satisfaction, that I suffer in the cause of virtue."

"It requires all that sweetness of temper which you possess," said Mrs. Willis, "to live with a woman of Mrs. Autumn's fantastick turn, without being disgusted with it. What an absurdity! at fifty years to expect to be thought young; and to imagine that, by affecting the follies of youth, she shall have the bloom of it also. Our sex have been reproached with never cultivating our minds till we can no longer please by our persons; but here is a woman who has not judgment enough to know when she ought to resign the hope of pleasing by her person. Take my word for it, you will be very unhappy with her, unless you resolve to accommodate yourself to her humour, and sooth her in her ridiculous folly."

"That I will not do," replied Henrietta; "and since I have learned not to fear poverty, my happiness will never depend upon others."

Mrs. Willis, finding she could not prevail with her fair friend to alter her resolution, acquiesced in it at length; and Henrietta, taking an affectionate leave of her, repaired to her new habitation.

CHAP. III.

Which shews Henrietta in her new service, where she acquits herself extremely ill.

The lady being engaged with company when Henrietta arrived, she did not see her till late at night, when she was summoned to undress her.

"Come hither, Henrietta," said she, as soon as she entered the room; "I have seen lady D—— since you was here—She has given me such an advantageous account of your understanding, that I am resolved to make you my confidant."

At the word Confidant Henrietta looked a little confused: but the lady, who did not observe her emotion, reclined her head upon her hand, and fixing her eyes on her glass to see how this pensive attitude became her,

"I am certainly (pursued she, sighing) the most unfortunate woman in the world—Benson, if you would be happy, never marry."

"I have no thought of marriage at present, madam," said Henrietta.

"Ah, how I envy your freedom!" said the antiquated fair; "you are plagued with no unreasonable jealousy. Benson, you will not be here long before you are a witness to my persecutions. I wish I could conceal them, but that is impossible."

"I am sorry, madam," said Henrietta, who was under a necessity of saying something in answer to this strange stuff, "to hear that you have any thing to make you uneasy."

"It does not signify," exclaimed the lady, with an emotion which she herself took to be real; "I shall be choaked if I don't speak; may I depend upon your prudence, Benson!—But I am sure I may. Well then, you must know there is a poor young fellow who pretends—But why do I say pretends—who is desperately—what shall I call it—who has an unconquerable, invincible, hopeless, fatal, dying passion for—for me, in short. Is not this a shocking thing?"

"Indeed! madam," replied Henrietta, with great truth, "I pity you extremely."

"Ay, am I not greatly to be pitied, child?" said the lady. "Then the poor wretch cannot conceal his folly; and it makes Mr. Autumn so uneasy, that really his temper is intolerable."

"Pardon me, madam," said Henrietta; "but I am not surprised that Mr. Autumn is uneasy at such folly as you justly call it."

"Why, to be sure it is folly," said Mrs. Autumn: "but then if one reflects a little—It is not folly neither—for love, you know, is an involuntary passion. So that—but you have a very unfeeling heart, Benson; and yet, to judge by your looks, you should have great sensibility. Pray, have you never felt the tender passion?"

"If you mean love, madam," replied Henrietta; "indeed I cannot say I have."

"Well, you will be a happy creature," said the lady, sighing, "if you can always maintain this indifference: but poor Languish must not expect to meet with much compassion from you. Poor wretch! (continued she, laughing) I cannot help triumphing a little. I have nick-named him Languish from his eternal sighing, and the melancholy roll of his eyes. Mr. Autumn cannot endure to hear me call him by this name; but I love to plague him a little now and then: what signifies power, if one does not shew one has it. Yet he ought to be satisfied with me for what I did this evening, when Languish indiscreetly betrayed the violence of his passion, by eagerly running (though there were two gentlemen nearer) to take up my glove which I had dropped: I took no notice of the dying air with which he presented it to me; but, as if his touch had polluted it, I received it haughtily from him, and threw it aside. Sure this instance of disdain was enough to satisfy a jealous husband; yet mine, instead of looking pleased, coloured with jealousy and rage, and gave me such furious glances—however, this will always be the case, where there is so great a disproportion in age; Mr. Autumn is not less than forty. But hey day! is the girl asleep?" continued she, looking at Henrietta, who stood fixed in thought; for the absurd affectation of her mistress gave her matter enough for reflection. "Come, undress me; Mr. Autumn will wonder at my long stay, and as he is ingenious in tormenting himself, he will possibly suspect that I have been reading a letter from this rival of his; but there he over-rates his presumption, he has not ventured to write to me yet, his passion is only expressed in sighs and looks."

Henrietta made haste to obey her, her patience being almost exhausted; for Mrs. Autumn had got on a subject which she knew not how to quit, and her women being the only persons to whom she could utter these extravagancies, without any danger of being mortified with sarcastick hints of age, and such envious and unjust reflections, she made herself amends with them, for the reserve she was much against her will obliged to maintain with others.

Henrietta was at length ordered to wait on her to her chamber, and soon after retired to her own, greatly out of humour with her mistress, and not a little displeased at herself, to find that her philosophy, by which she was enabled to bear the change of her fortune with patience and resignation, could not guard her against fretfulness and disgust at the follies she was forced to be witness to.

Mrs. Autumn, like other modern ladies, lay in bed always till it was very late: this being one of those happy expedients for killing time (as the fashionable phrase is) which, to discover, employs the inventions of persons of rank and fortune. Henrietta had attended three whole hours in her lady's dressing-room, in expectation every moment of being summoned to assist her to rise, when Mr. Autumn at length entered the room.

His servant, while he was dressing him, had told him, that his lady's new woman, whom he had a glympse of as he passed by her on the stairs, was the

greatest beauty he ever beheld; so that being curious to see her, he came to breakfast with his wife that morning.

Henrietta rose up at his entrance; Mr. Autumn bowed, looked at her attentively, and thought his man had taste. But he was still more struck with
her noble air than the charms of her face, and felt an uneasy emotion when
he saw her continue standing, with that humble respect, which, although it
became her situation, seemed little suited to the dignity of her appearance.
"Is not Mrs. Autumn up, madam?" said he, not being able to forbear using
that respectful style. Henrietta, supposing he did not know her rank in his
family, replied,

"I expect my lady will ring every moment, sir."

"Pray let her know that I am come to breakfast with her," said Mr. Autumn.

Henrietta went immediately into her lady's chamber, and, finding her
awake, delivered her message.

"Lord bless me!" said Mrs. Autumn, "what new whim is this? He does not
use to invade my apartment in a morning: I suppose he is come to teaze me with
some of his jealous fancies. Well, since it must be so, order breakfast to be sent
in, and come to me directly."

What a ridiculous woman is this, thought Henrietta, as she went out of
the room, to torment herself at her age with the notion of her husband being
jealous of her.

The good lady, when she returned, charged her not to leave the room while
they were at breakfast. "Your presence (said she) may perhaps be some restraint
upon him."

She then slipped on a night-gown, and went in a frightful dishabille[25] to
attend her complaisant spouse; for she was one of those ladies who dress for every
body but their husbands.

Henrietta was not sorry that she was directed to wait, for she was extremely
desirous of knowing whether her lady had any reason for the uneasiness she expressed. Mr. Autumn's good humour and complaisance soon put that matter out
of doubt; but Mrs. Autumn was resolved to persuade her maid that her husband
was jealous, and laughing affectedly, cried,

"Well, don't be chagrined, Mr. Autumn, but I protest I dreamt of poor
Languish last night."

The husband shook his head, winked at his wife, and pointed to Henrietta,
as if he had said, don't expose yourself before your new servant.

"Why, how you frown now!" pursued Mrs. Autumn; "I knew you would
be angry. Lord! what does it signify of whom one dreams: one does not always
think of the persons one dreams of. I wish I had not told you."

"I wish you had not," said Mr. Autumn, biting his lip with vexation at her folly. The lady then lowering her voice, as if she was not willing to be heard by Henrietta, tho' she took care not to make it impossible, repeated,

Trifles, light as air,
Are to the jealous, confirmations strong
As proofs of holy writ.[26]

"You are well read in Shakespear, madam," said Mr. Autumn, who was willing to give another turn to the discourse.

"Oh!" exclaimed she, "he has touched the passion of jealousy finely in his character of Othello; I think the Moor was uneasy about a dream too."

Just then somebody tapped at the door, Henrietta opened it; one of the footmen delivered a message from one lady, enquiring how Mrs. Autumn did, and a sealed-up card from another.

While the servant was speaking, Mrs. Autumn called out, what makes the fellow whisper in that manner, as if the message he brings was a secret! Henrietta delivered her the card, which she threw upon the table without opening it. "I am resolved (said she) to turn that blockhead away; his mysterious manner is enough to put strange fancies into people's heads."

"The strange fancies are all your own," said Mr. Autumn, peevishly.

"I thought it would be so," cried the lady, "you are out of humour. What is this sealed up card the grievance? come, we will open it, and you shall know the contents."

"Indeed I will not," said Mr. Autumn rising; "I have not the least curiosity about the contents—Good morning to you, my dear, I am going out."

"Well, Benson," said Mrs. Autumn, as soon as her husband had left the room; "is not this a comfortable life I live? what a passion that poor man is in!"

"Was Mr. Autumn angry, madam?" said Henrietta.

"To be sure he was," said the lady; "did you not observe it?"

"Indeed, madam," replied Henrietta, "Mr. Autumn did not seem to me to be angry."

"No, really!" said Mrs. Autumn; "you have a great deal of penetration, it must be confessed—You think you are very discreet now, but you are mistaken. However, I charge you, don't gossip among your companions about Mr. Autumn's unhappy jealousy; I don't want the world to know what I suffer upon that account."

"I never will mention it, madam, to any body," replied Henrietta.

"Nay, for that matter," said Mrs. Autumn, "you might mention it without any bad intention, by way of pitying me, or so; and perhaps I should not think the worse of you. But if you can be silent, Benson, you will oblige me; reports of this kind, you know, should not be circulated."

"They never shall by me, madam," said Henrietta.

"Enough, enough," cried Mrs. Autumn, hastily; "I hate long speeches."

Henrietta was pleased with a declaration which enjoined her silence; for if it be tiresome to listen to the sallies of affectation and impertinence, it is much more so to be obliged to answer them.

Chap. IV.

Gives the reader hopes of a favourable change in the circumstances of our fair heroine.

Henrietta had exercised her patience for some weeks in the service of Mrs. Autumn; but every day producing new instances of her folly, she resolved to quit her as soon as the countess came to town. She conceived she was in some degree accountable to that lady for her actions, since it was through her recommendation, that she had been introduced to Mrs. Autumn; and she thought it necessary for the justification of her conduct, to have so considerable a witness of its being irreproachable.

Her lady, though she found herself always disappointed in that complaisance to her whims which she endeavoured to exact from her, yet ventured to make her a proposal, which her own want of delicacy hindered her from seeing the impropriety of.

She had taken it into her head to try her supposed lover's constancy, and therefore wrote a letter to him, in the character of a lady unknown, on whose heart he had made a deep impression, but who was resolved not to discover herself till she knew whether his was wholly disengaged.

This letter, she doubted not, would produce a declaration that would afford matter of great triumph to herself, who she suspected was the secret object of his adoration.

She acquainted her woman with her scheme, and gravely desired her to copy the letter, for Languish, she said, knew her hand.

Henrietta blushed with surprise and shame at this improper request, and very frankly begged to be excused from complying with it.

"What!" said Mrs. Autumn, a little confused; "you dispute my commands then!"

"I never refused to obey any of your commands, before, madam," replied Henrietta; "but this, (pardon me, madam,) appears so strange."

"You do not dare to suspect my virtue, I hope," said Mrs. Autumn, in a lofty accent.

"It does not become me, madam," said Henrietta, "to censure your actions."

"No certainly," replied the lady, "nor to refuse to do any thing that I order you to do: but I would fain know if you, in your great wisdom, think there is any thing improper in this little piece of gallantry."

"My opinion is of no consequence, madam," replied Henrietta; "I only beg to be excused from copying it."

"Well, no more of the letter," cried Mrs. Autumn, hastily: "perhaps I had only a mind to try your discretion; perhaps too I shall like you the better for your steadiness—Be modest and reserved, and you will be sure of my approbation. Were you the best servant in the world, you would not do for me, unless you were extremely modest. And now you know my mind, be cautious how you behave: modesty is a sure recommendation to my favour; I can pardon any fault in my servant but want of modesty."

Henrietta, from this declaration, had reason to think herself pretty sure of her lady's favour: for the severest prude that ever declaimed against the monstrous levity of her own sex, could not have objected to the propriety of her behaviour; but, unhappily for her, she was that very day guilty of a fault by which she incurred very shocking suspicions: for having neglected to fill her lady's smelling-bottle with some fresh Eau de Luce, Mrs. Autumn declared that such heedlessness must necessarily proceed from her having her thoughts continually employed upon fellows; and telling her, that she could not endure such a creature in her sight, ordered her to be gone immediately.

Henrietta did not think proper to offer any answer to this strange charge; but quitting her presence immediately, and her house a few moments afterwards, she returned to Mrs. Willis, who, seeing her alight at her door, eagerly flew to receive her.

"I have great news for you, my dear miss," said she, "I was this moment preparing to set out in a coach to bring you a letter, which was left here by one of your uncle's servants." "It is very true," pursued she, seeing Henrietta look surprised. "I asked the young man, who he came from? and he said, the earl of ——. You may believe I am impatient to know the contents of this letter. Come, my dear, and read it; I hope all your troubles are over now."

Henrietta receiving the letter from her, which she took out of her pocket, followed her into the parlour, and breaking the seal,

"It is my uncle's hand, indeed (said she) and this is what he writes."

'Mrs. Courteney is desired to call at the earl of —— , to-morrow morning at twelve o'clock: he has something to propose to her for her advantage.'

"Did I not tell you, miss," said Mrs. Willis, exultingly, "that the step you had taken would produce a favourable change in your fortune?"

"Don't be too sanguine in your expectations, my dear Mrs. Willis," said miss Courteney; "who knows but my uncle may have another sir Isaac Darby to propose to me: however, I will certainly wait upon him, and, if possible, will be punctual to the hour he has prescribed me; but if nothing should come of this overture of his lordship's, I shall be your guest again for some time. I have left Mrs. Autumn."

She then related to her some circumstances of that lady's extravagant folly, and the cause and manner of their parting, which, together with their comments on lord ——'s message, furnished them with matter sufficient for discourse during the remainder of the day: what happened to our fair heroine the next, will be found in the following chapter.

Chap. V.

Destroys the expectations raised by the foregoing chapter.

Henrietta was at her uncle's house exactly at the hour prescribed her; and, upon sending in her name, was desired to walk into his lordship's library.

The earl was there to receive her: he had with him two of his daughters; but these young ladies withdrew immediately, after saluting her in a very distant manner, which she returned with equal reserve and coldness.

"Miss Courteney," said his lordship, as soon as they were alone, "I have been very angry with you for leaving your aunt in the strange manner you did."

"I am extremely obliged to your lordship," replied Henrietta, "for taking so much interest in any thing that concerns me."

"You certainly acted very indiscreetly," said the earl; "but what is past cannot be helped. You have had the good luck to make yourself friends, notwithstanding this wrong step. You have been at the countess of ——'s seat, I hear."

"Yes, my lord," answered Henrietta; "I was there with ——"

"The countess is very much your friend," interrupted his lordship, hastily, "but her son is more so."

Henrietta blushed, and was silent.

"I will not," pursued his lordship, "examine into your motives for leaving lady Meadows; but I will, if possible, accommodate matters between you, provided you will concur with me in my endeavours for that purpose."

"I desire nothing more earnestly than to be reconciled to my aunt," replied Henrietta.

"I believe it will be your own fault if you are not," resumed his lordship; "and if you recover her favour, your good fortune will not stop there—To keep you no longer in suspence then, lord B—— has declared a passion for you, has solicited my interest towards effecting a reconciliation between your aunt and you, that he may pay his addresses to you in a proper manner."

"I am surprised that lord B—— should make such a proposal," said Henrietta, "he is engaged to the daughter of a rich citizen."

"No, not engaged," replied the earl; "the match has been proposed, and he has visited the young woman."

"Indeed, my lord," replied Henrietta, "the affair is much farther advanced."

"Well, well," interrupted his lordship, "we will suppose that the writings are drawn and every thing settled; but they are not married, nor engaged neither.

"His inclinations, you find, have taken another turn: you have no reason to blame him for this, I am sure; and it would be strange indeed if a man of his rank and fortune was to mind the censures of the vulgar."

Henrietta was silent. His lordship proceeded,

"Lord B—— will find it difficult, no doubt, to prevail upon the earl to break off this treaty, and consent to his marrying you, though lady Meadows should offer to make you her heir; because in that case your fortune would be still less than that of this citizen, whom he has chosen for him. Nevertheless, he does not despair of effecting this, provided your aunt will do for you what it is expected she would before you was so unhappy as to disoblige her. In this lord B—— sufficiently shews the sincerity and ardor of his passion; it is your part now to convince him that you are not ungrateful."

"What would your lordship have me to do?" said Henrietta.

"I would have you submit to your aunt," said the earl, "and regain her affection, if possible. Lord B—— has reason to expect this compliance from you."

"I will do every thing I ought to do," replied Henrietta, "to recover my aunt's favour, and this without any view to lord B——'s offers."

"Well, we shall not examine too nicely into that matter," interrupted his lordship, smiling. "All that remains to be done, is this; I will see lady Meadows myself, she will be in town soon, I suppose; lord B——'s proposal, which I will acquaint her with, will captivate her attention, and be your best justification. As for what little concessions she may expect from you, I shall leave them to be settled by yourselves."

"There are certain concessions, however," said Henrietta, "which it is impossible for me to make, and which, if my aunt insists upon as the necessary conditions of a reconciliation between us, I must still continue under her displeasure, and hazard all the consequences of it."

"I am afraid you are going to say some silly thing or other," interrupted his lordship, rising from his seat; which motion Henrietta understanding as a hint for her to hasten her departure, rose also.

"I will detain your lordship no longer," said she, "than just to tell you that some time ago my aunt proposed to me to settle all her fortune upon me, provided I would embrace the Roman catholic religion."

"A noble offer, upon my honour!" said his lordship, "and did you refuse it?"

"Would your lordship have had me accept of it?" said Henrietta.

"What signifies what I would have had you do," replied the earl, peevishly. "What did the consideration of your own interest suggest to you?"

"To refuse it, my lord," answered Henrietta, "and I did so."

"I find you are a very romantic girl," said his lordship; "I am resolved to trouble myself no more about your affairs."

"I hope it will not be imputed to me as a crime," said Henrietta, "that I could not be bribed to change my religion."

"Change your religion!" repeated the earl, "what necessity was there for changing your religion: you might have humoured the old woman, have gone with her to mass, and conformed to some of her superstitious ceremonies, and be a good protestant in your heart notwithstanding; the world, knowing your motives, would have commended you for such a prudent conduct—I see there is nothing to be done with you," pursued he, after a little pause. "For the sake of the unfortunate man, who was your father, I would have been glad to have seen you well married; but lord B—— is not such a fool as to take you without a fortune; and as you cannot reasonably have any expectations but from lady Meadows, who has no children, and may leave her fortune to whom she pleases, without doing any body injustice, you know best whether it is worth your while to make a proper submission to her or not."

"I will never make an improper one," said Henrietta.

"To be sure," said his lordship, "your own wisdom is to be judge of that."

"No, my lord," replied Henrietta; "you shall if you please be judge—if my conscience—"

"Pray, let me hear nothing about your conscience," interrupted the earl; "it is not my business to set matters even between you and your conscience: your aunt's popish confessor, who is likely to be her heir, is skilful in those things; yet I would not advise you to consult him neither, for he is an interested person: but remember, that you may either secure to yourself a good estate, and marry a very deserving young nobleman, or continue in the obscurity and want your father left you in, which is all the legacy he bequeathed you. Think well of this, and then let your conscience determine. I do not advise you to do any thing against it."

"My resolution is already fixed," said Henrietta: "my conscience will neither permit me to change my religion, nor to counterfeit a change of it."

"Do you insinuate by that," said his lordship, hastily, "that I advised you to do either the one or the other?"

"My aunt already knows my mind," said Henrietta, evading a question which she could not answer truly without offending him; "I have nothing to hope for from your lordship's interposition, unless she has been pleased to give up this point; and I shall chearfully return to that poverty my father bequeathed me, since with it he bequeathed me piety and virtue."

"It is a pity he did not leave you prudence also," said the earl, who found something very provoking in this last speech, "you would not then have disobliged your aunt by your scandalous elopement from her, which has reduced you to the miserable condition you are now in, so that your friends know not how to take notice of you."

"Friends! my lord," replied Henrietta, rising in her temper; "I have no friends, I have only relations."

"That is likely to be their misfortune," said his lordship, who was very angry at this sarcasm: "your undutifulness to your aunt makes you unworthy of the notice of your relations; and I declare to you plainly, that from this moment I will never concern myself about you."

Henrietta disdained to make any answer to this unjust and cruel speech; but courtesied in silence, and withdrew; leaving the earl very well satisfied with himself for the tender and parental part he had acted towards his brother's daughter, and furnished with excellent reasons for never seeing her more.

"I had provided a match for her," said he, that very evening, to an humble friend, who he knew would not fail to spread the report, "not unworthy of a daughter of my own. She rejected my proposal. She refused to make any submission to her aunt, whom I would have prevailed upon to be reconciled to her. Let her suffer the consequences of her obstinacy and folly; I have done all that I ought to do, and am justified to the world."

His lordship forgot to add, that the submission which was expected from her was nothing more than the change of her religion, and the match she so obstinately refused, could not be effected without she purchased a fortune by an impious hypocrisy. Nevertheless the omission of these trifling circumstances gave such a colour to Henrietta's behaviour, that she was considered by all, who heard her uncle's account of it, as an unhappy young creature, who would ruin herself, and be the blot of a noble family.

As for our fair heroine, she foresaw that her uncle would justify his neglect of her at her expence. She had every thing against her; rank, fortune, power; that general prejudice which prevails against the unfortunate, and that as general servility which adopts the passions of the great. But these reflections filled her with no uneasy apprehensions; for there is this advantage in virtue, that it is sufficient for itself, and needs not the applause or support of others, its own consciousness is its best reward.

CHAP. VI.

In which lord B—— shews himself a true modern lover.

Henrietta, before she went home, waited upon lady D——, to acquaint her that she had left Mrs. Autumn. She avoided mentioning that lady's peculiarities which had made it impossible to please her; but with great simplicity related the error she had been guilty of, and the suspicions she had incurred by it, which occasioned her dismission.

Lady D—— diverted herself for some time with the extreme delicacy of her whimsical friend, and then told Henrietta, that having still a good opinion of her prudence and modesty, notwithstanding the reasons Mrs. Autumn had to suspect her, she would place her about a young lady, a relation of her own.

Henrietta thanked her in very respectful terms, and took her leave, after she had, at lady D——'s desire, left her a direction to her lodgings, that she might know where to send for her when it was necessary.

At her return, she found the faithful Mrs. Willis full of anxious impatience to hear the success of her visit to the earl. Henrietta, thro' respect to her uncle, concealed the greatest part of his discourse to her, but owned that she had no expectations from him.

Mrs. Willis shrugged up her shoulders: "Then it was as you suspected (said she) your uncle has proposed some absurd match to you, and you have forfeited his future favour by not complying with it."

"You will be surprised to hear that lord B—— has made an application to my uncle," said Henrietta.

"Surprised!" repeated Mrs. Willis; "why, to be sure, considering how your affairs are circumstanced, this is a generous way of proceeding. Well, I hope you begin now to have a favourable opinion both of his love and honour."

"I am sure I think highly of his prudence," replied Henrietta, smiling: "only mark the caution with which he acts in this affair; my poverty gave him hopes that I should be an easy conquest, and that passion which first manifested itself in an open attempt upon my honour, sought afterwards to allure me with bribes. It is not strange that persons who hold money to be the greatest good, should think it more than an equivalent for virtue. Here, however, he was disappointed again, to his great astonishment, no doubt, and marriage is this honourable lover's last resource; but this he does not offer till he is sure I shall have a fortune, if not equal to that of my rival the packer's daughter, yet at least sufficient to justify his choice in the opinion of the prudential part of the world; and perhaps he expects I should purchase the mighty blessing of his hand by the sacrifice, the temporary sacrifice at least of those principles, for which I have already suffered so much."

"Have you any reason for this shocking suspicion?" interrupted Mrs. Willis.

"I think I have," replied Henrietta: "a reconciliation with my aunt is, it seems, a necessary preliminary to his addresses; and yet he heard from myself upon what condition that reconciliation could only be effected." Henrietta, suddenly interrupting herself, cried out, "There he is; there is lord B——."

"Where? where?" said Mrs. Willis, running to the window. "It is certainly he," said Henrietta, "he passed by in a chair."

That instant they heard a loud rap at the door.

"As I live," cried Mrs. Willis (in a violent flutter) "he has come to visit you. I hope you will see him, miss Courteney; hear what he has to say, pray do; there can be no harm in that, I am sure."

"Well, well," said Henrietta, smiling at her solicitude; "I will see him; let him be shewn into the other parlour, if you please."

Mrs. Willis, curious to see this young lord, went herself to open the door. He bolted out of the chair; and, with a look and accent full of impatience, asked her, if the young lady that lodged there was at home?

"Miss Courteney, sir?" said Mrs. Willis.

"Yes," replied he, hastily; "is she at home, can I see her? Pray tell her a gentleman from —— enquires for her."

Mrs. Willis desired him to walk into the parlour, said she would acquaint the young lady with his being there; and a few moments afterwards Henrietta appeared.

Lord B—— flew to meet her, with the air of a lover conscious of the right he had to be well received; and, taking her hand, which he respectfully kissed,

"Now," cried he, exultingly, "can you doubt the ardor of my passion for you? and will you not at length confess that it is possible for a man to deserve you?"

"Certainly, my lord," replied Henrietta, "it is very possible."

"May I perish if I think so (said he) but how poorly would words express my adoration of you! Judge of the purity, the ardor of my love, by what I have done to make you mine—Have you not seen your uncle, miss Courteney?"

"I have, my lord," replied Henrietta.

"You have!" repeated his lordship; "and in that grave cold accent too. Surely my sentiments and designs are still unknown to you: it is impossible else that you should be thus insensible, nay ungrateful, I will say—for I have given no common proofs of love, I think."

"Indeed, my lord" replied Henrietta, who had a mind to teaze this generous lover a little, "you shall not suffer for your noble disinterestedness—you shall not resign miss Cordwain and her immense fortune for me."

"Name not her fortune," cried lord B——; "were it millions I would refuse it for you."

"Nay, now your lordship is quite romantic," said Henrietta, "to prefer to a rich heiress an unhappy young woman, deserted by her relations, and reduced to seek a subsistence by her labour."

"Call not my passion romantic," interrupted lord B——, "because it soars above common conceptions: a mind so elevated as yours might give it a juster epithet."

"Were my aunt," pursued Henrietta, "to leave me her whole estate, you would still make no inconsiderable sacrifice by quitting miss Cordwain for me, since my fortune would then be inferior to her's. But you know, my lord, I have no expectations from lady Meadows: I have declared to my uncle the hard conditions upon which she offers to make me her heir, conditions that I never will accept of; and therefore I may well call your passion romantic, when, under such circumstances, you could think of making an application to my uncle."

"To be sure, madam," said lord B——, whose countenance expressed at once surprise, confusion, and disappointment—"I did apply to the earl, not personally indeed. I contrived it so that a friend of mine, who is very intimate with his lordship, should give him a hint of your situation, and the sentiments I entertained for you: and, from the account my friend gave me of his success in his negotiation, I conceived that you might be prevailed upon—that is, that you would consider—For might I not hope, my dear miss Courteney, that you would not be insensible of my affection."

Here his lordship paused, and looked on Henrietta with a languishing air, seeming to wish and expect that her tenderness would spare him a further explanation; but our fair heroine, who did not chuse to collect his meaning from the abrupt and unconnected sentences he had uttered, continued maliciously silent, as if she waited for the end of his discourse.

"I see (resumed he) that I have not been happy enough to inspire you with any tender sentiments for me. Pardon me, miss Courteney, but I must be so free as to tell you that if you were not prepossessed in favour of another person, the proofs I have given you of my affection would not be received with such indifference."

"There needs not any such prepossession," replied Henrietta, vexed at this hint, "to make me receive with indifference the proofs you have hitherto given me of that affection your lordship boasts of. Am I to reckon among these proofs, my lord, the insult you offered me at Mrs. Eccles's, and the strange declaration you made me in the country?"

"Ah, how cruel is this recapitulation now!" cried lord B——: "do I not do justice to your birth, your beauty and virtue, by my present honourable intentions?"

"It is not enough for me, my lord," said Henrietta, "that your intentions are honourable now; to have merited my esteem, they should always have been so: but, to speak plainly, I am still doubtful of your intentions."

"Doubtful still of my intentions!" repeated lord B——: "have I not declared them to your uncle, madam? have I not solicited his interest with you?"

"Suppose that obtained, my lord," said Henrietta, "and that it has all the weight with me you could wish."

"Why then we shall be happy, my angel," cried he, taking her hand, and pressing it to his lips. "You will be reconciled to your aunt, and I may hope for my father's consent to our union."

"A reconciliation with my aunt is impossible," said Henrietta, withdrawing her hand.

"Say not that it is impossible," replied lord B——, "but that you have not complaisance enough for me to attempt it."

"Did I not know it to be impossible," resumed Henrietta, "I would attempt it for my own sake; but nothing less than the sacrifice of my religion will satisfy my aunt: on this condition indeed she promises to settle her whole estate upon me; I think I once told your lordship so."

"You did, my dear miss Courteney," interrupted lord B——; "and I adore you for your steady adherence to your principles."

Henrietta was a little startled at so unexpected a declaration; but lord B—— did not suffer her to remain long in the error his last words had occasioned.

"If lady Meadows was not such a bigot," pursued he, "excuse my freedom, miss, we might expect that she would receive my proposals with pleasure, and make such concessions in favour of her niece, as might engage my father's consent to our marriage: but since this is hopeless, is it reasonable that you should be the victim of her obstinacy? By seeming only to comply with your aunt's desires, all obstacles to our union will be removed; a temporary compliance is all that is necessary to secure to you a fortune, and a rank in life suitable to your birth. Do not imagine that I wish to see you a proselyte to the religion she professes: no, if any thing could weaken my passion, your being capable of such a change, upon interested motives, would do it. I love you; I repeat it again, I love you for your piety."

"Then, to be sure, my lord," replied Henrietta, "you think that a little dissimulation in this case would be a virtue."

"In your circumstances," resumed lord B——, "it certainly would; for while your principles are unchanged, what do you sacrifice, in yielding to your aunt, but externals only? this sacrifice your interest, your happiness demands of you: let me add also that you owe it to a man who loves you with the ardor I do. And surely, to industriously seek occasions of suffering for a religion, which, if you could be contented with secretly professing, you would be happy yourself, and make others happy also, is to give the world reason to suspect that ostentation has a greater share in your resolves than piety. Therefore, my dear miss Courteney, you see it is not the sacrifice of your religion that I require of you, but of the reputation of suffering for it."

"Well, my lord," replied Henrietta, who had listened to him with great calmness, "if ever I was in doubt of your intentions, you have clearly explained them now; of them, and of the sentiments you have avowed, you may collect my opinion, when I declare to you, that if you had worlds to bestow on me, I would not be your wife."

"Is this your resolution, miss Courteney?" said his lordship.

"It is, my lord (she replied). A resolution justifiable upon your own great principle interest. It is my interest I consult, when I prefer poverty and servitude to the fortune my aunt can give me; because the silent testimony of a quiet conscience is, in my opinion, of infinitely more value than riches. It is interest by which I am influenced, when I refuse your offered alliance, because I am sure I could not be happy with a man whom I cannot esteem."

"Hold, madam, hold," interrupted lord B——, "this is too much: I have not deserved this treatment, but I thank you for it; yes, from my soul I thank you for it: it has helped to restore my senses; I have been foolish, very foolish, I confess."

His lordship indeed looked foolish enough when he pronounced these words, which were succeeded by a pause of several minutes: then suddenly starting from his seat, and bowing with an affected negligence,

"The best apology I can make, madam (said he) for the importunate visit I have paid you, is to assure you I never will repeat it."

Henrietta courtesied gravely without answering him; and having rung the bell for a servant to attend him to the door, went into the room where her friend was sitting. Lord B—— stopped, looked back, and, finding she had withdrawn, he rushed out hastily, and flung himself into his chair, glad of his escape, and congratulating himself upon the victory he had gained over his passion; for, in the first emotions of his grief at parting, he had almost resolved to declare he would marry her without any fortune: but her disappearing so suddenly, gave him time for a moment's reflection, and that was sufficient to hinder him from being guilty of an imprudence which he now trembled at the thoughts of.

It is so difficult for mean and selfish persons to conceive that any thing but private advantage can influence the resolutions of others, that notwithstanding the proof Henrietta had given of her attachment to her religion, and her inviolable regard to truth, yet still lord B—— supposed there must be some other latent motive for a conduct, in his opinion, highly ridiculous, and very inconsistent with that good sense which it was apparent she possessed.

Sometimes he fancied he had a rival; and then, to clear a doubt so tormenting, he was upon the point of returning to her to offer her his hand upon her own conditions: but his avarice restrained him from making so dangerous a trial: she might accept his offer; and with all the passion he felt for her, he could not resolve to marry her without a fortune.

To stifle a thought which suggested to him designs so destructive to his interest, he endeavoured to persuade himself that her obstinacy, in refusing to temporize a little when such mighty advantages were in view, was the effect of female vanity, which sought distinction at the expence of solid happiness. In this opinion he was confirmed by his friend, whom he had employed to sound the earl her uncle with regard to his proposals, and to whom he now communicated the result of his interview with Henrietta.

"Depend upon it," said this sagacious person, "your goddess will descend from her romantic flights, when she finds she has almost soared out of human ken; and is much more likely to be laughed at for her extravagant folly, than admired and applauded for her extraordinary piety. Follow my advice (pursued he) suffer your mistress to believe you have broke her chains; if interest does not make her wish to recal you, vanity will. Few women can endure that a lover should escape them; and, to recover their influence, they often make concessions, which, in the zenith of their power, they would have thought impossible."

Lord B—— improved a little upon his friend's scheme, and resolved to continue his addresses to miss Cordwain, to pique Henrietta, he said; but in reality, he was as much in love with her fortune, as with the person of our fair heroine; and was not willing to hazard the loss of the one, while it was yet doubtful whether he should ever possess the other.

CHAP. VII.

Which concludes the fourth book of this history.

Henrietta having acquainted Mrs. Willis with what had passed in her interview with lord B——, the good woman who had flattered herself that the affair would have ended more happily (though more honourably it could not) for her fair friend, conjured her, with tears of anxious tenderness, not to think of going to service again, but to allow the countess, whom her conduct with regard to her son must necessarily oblige very highly, to employ her good offices with lady Meadows in her favour, that a reconciliation might be effected, without those shocking conditions which had at first been proposed to her.

"If I thought such an application would be successful," replied Henrietta, "I would readily consent to it. For you may easily imagine, my dear Mrs. Willis, that this low condition is not my choice: but I know my aunt's temper; whatever she desires, she desires with ardor; and makes a merit of persisting obstinately in a resolution she has once formed. Her pride will be a more powerful advocate for me, than any thing the countess can urge; to that

I formerly owed my deliverance from dependence, more mortifying than servitude. This pride will no doubt be sensibly wounded, when she finds that I am determined in my choice; if any thing can make her recede from her purpose, it will be the shame of seeing her niece reduced so low. But surely it is not the way to convince her I am really determined, if I allow my friends to teaze her with solicitations, when she has already declared her resolution in such strong terms: she will believe that I have engaged them to make this trial; she will be offended with their interposition, and perhaps be the less inclined to raise me from this obscure condition, as she will not have the merit of doing it from her own generosity and tenderness, but at the instances of others: time only, my dear Mrs. Willis, can produce any favourable change in my circumstances; it will either soften the hearts of my relations, or it will blunt my sense of the meanness of my condition, by familiarizing me to it. This I am sure of at least, that, in the consciousness of doing right, I shall always find an unfailing source of happiness, however Providence may think fit to dispose of me."

"Ah, never doubt but you are the care of Providence, my dear miss," cried Mrs. Willis, "such virtue and piety must sooner or later be happy: Heaven and your own prudence direct you."

"I have not always been prudent," said Henrietta, sighing; "but misfortunes, as you once told me, teach us wisdom."

Mrs. Willis, observing an unusual pensiveness stealing over the sweet features of Henrietta on this reflection, changed the discourse to a less interesting subject, and employed her utmost assiduity and tenderness to make the time she stayed with her pass agreeably.

A week being elapsed, and no message coming from lady D——, Henrietta began to apprehend that she should be disappointed of a place, in which she expected more satisfaction than she had found in those she had hitherto been in, when she was surprised with a visit from the countess of ——.

She flew to receive her with respectful joy. The lady tenderly pressed her hand—

"I had business in the city (said she) and I took this opportunity to call on you—and how do you do, my dear good girl? (pursued she) have you any agreeable news to tell me? has your family relented yet?"

"I have no reason to think they have, madam," replied Henrietta.

"Shocking insensibility!" exclaimed the countess, lifting up her eyes; "you have been very ill used too by Mrs. Autumn, my sister tells me."

Henrietta smiled, but was silent.

"Well, miss Courteney," resumed the countess, "will you come and live with me as my friend and companion. I know your generous scorn of dependence; but it is the unworthiness of the donor only, that can make benefits sit heavy on a mind like yours: there is often as much greatness of soul in receiving as in conferring benefits; and when true friendship is the motive for giving, it is pride, not generosity, to refuse."

"Do me the justice to believe, madam," replied Henrietta, "that I receive this instance of your goodness with the deepest gratitude, but there is—"

"I understand you," interrupted the countess—"my son; but I hope, when he is married, you will have no objection to living with me as my friend."

The countess, in speaking these words, looked earnestly on Henrietta.

"No, certainly, madam (cried she, eagerly) I shall think myself happy in living with you in any situation."

"I know not what to think of my son's conduct in this affair," resumed the countess; "every thing is settled between my lord and the young lady's father; but he still finds pretences to delay the match." Her eyes, as she pronounced these words, seemed to demand an explanation of Henrietta.

"I am afraid, madam (replied she) that I have been partly the cause of these delays."

"That is candidly said," interrupted the countess; "have you seen my son lately?"

"I have, madam," answered Henrietta; "but your ladyship may be entirely easy."

"Easy!" repeated the countess; "why do you imagine that I am so insensible of your merit—but you know, my good girl, lord B—— is in honour engaged to miss Cordwain."

"His lordship's partiality for me," said Henrietta, "has induced him to carry this matter further than (as he is circumstanced) I think he should have done. He has caused my uncle to be applied to; but this has produced nothing, madam. I told lord B—— upon what conditions my aunt had offered to settle her estate upon me; and his lordship is convinced that I cannot comply with them. My resolution is fixed, my lord B—— knows it is so, and you have nothing to fear, madam, from any imprudence on his side, or any ungenerosity on mine. I ventured to promise that I would deserve the confidence you was pleased to place in me on this occasion, and I hope I have and shall continue to deserve it."

Notwithstanding the delicate manner in which Henrietta stated the affair between her and lord B——, yet the countess discovered that her son had shewn more prudence than generosity, or even love in his behaviour; and, by a strange contradiction in the human heart, she at once approved and condemned, was pleased with, yet ashamed of his conduct; but charmed with

Henrietta's noble disinterestedness, her candour and sincerity, she embraced her with the tenderness of a mother, and perhaps with the more tenderness because it was not likely she should be her mother.

"I am impatient (said she) till I can have you with me, that I may have it in my power to shew you how greatly I both love and esteem you."

Henrietta thanked her with great politeness; and then told her of lady D——s intentions to recommend her to a young lady, a relation of her's.

Oh! miss Belmour, you mean," said the countess; "my sister mentioned it to me: she is an agreeable young woman, has a very good fortune, and is entirely mistress of herself. She will be much better pleased to receive you in the character of a companion than a servant, when she knows your birth and merit."

"I will owe obligations of that kind to none but yourself, madam," replied Henrietta; "and I beg this young lady may know no more of me than what is just necessary to recommend me to her good opinion as a servant."

The countess contested this point with her for some time; but finding her not to be dissuaded from her design, "Well!" said she, kindly, "you shall be indulged this once, but remember I claim your promise to come to me when a certain objection is removed; in the mean time we will settle you with miss Belmour in the way you chuse. She will be with my sister to-morrow morning; and if you come likewise, lady D—— will introduce you to her."

Henrietta said she would not fail to attend lady D—— Upon which the countess rose up, kissed her at parting, and desired she would look upon her as one of her most faithful friends.

Our fair heroine had reason to be satisfied with the kind manner in which lady D—— recommended her to miss Belmour, as well as with the reception that young lady gave her. She carried her home with her in her coach, and behaved to her with an affability that Henrietta could no otherwise account for, than by supposing the countess had discovered her true name and circumstances to her—In this, however, she was mistaken: her young mistress was in love; she had occasion for a confidant. Henrietta's youth and gentleness promised her she would be an indulgent one: besides, her good sense and the elegance of her person and behaviour so lessened the distance between the mistress and servant, that her pride was not wounded by the familiarity with which she condescended to treat her, as the necessary prelude to the confidence she was resolved to repose in her.

Henrietta listened with complaisance to the overflowings of a heart tender by nature, and wholly possessed, as she thought, by a deserving object; but when miss Belmour, in the course of frequent conversations on this exhaustless theme, gave her to understand that this lover of whom she boasted was the husband of another lady, from whom he had been parted several years, surprise, horror, grief, were so strongly impressed on her countenance, that her lady began to repent of a confession she had made, in full confidence that her sentiments, whatever they were, must needs be approved by her servant.

But it being now useless as well as dangerous to retract what she had said, she was under a necessity of submitting to the mortifying task of defending her conduct to one whose duty as well as interest she had a moment before conceived it to be, to acquiesce in, or rather applaud all she did.

She began with telling Henrietta, that Mr. Morley had, when very young, been forced, by an avaricious father, to marry a woman whom he could not love, and with whom he had been so miserable, that a separation was agreed to by the relations on both sides.

Henrietta sighed sympathetically at this account. Miss Belmour, encouraged by this mark of her sensibility, proceeded with great fluency of language, to expatiate on the resistless power of love: her lover's sophistry had furnished her with arguments to prove, that the marriage he had been forced into was not binding in the sight of heaven, and that he was at liberty to bestow his affections elsewhere. She treated marriage as a mere human institution, adopted the sentiments of Eloisa,[27] talked of an union of hearts, eternal constancy, generous confidence—Henrietta heard her with patience; but being out of breath at last, she stopped, and seemed to expect a reply.

Our fair heroine, with all the humility becoming her station, but at the same time with all the firmness of virtue, opposed the specious arguments she had urged with others, which reason, religion, and the purity of her own sentiments suggested to her: these, however, made very little impression on miss Belmour. She yawned, smiled contemptuously, and was several times ready to interrupt her with an authoritative air, but refrained, from the consideration that her woman was now, by the participation of her secret, become her companion, if not something more.

Henrietta, despairing to rescue her unhappy mistress by motives of piety, from the snares that were laid for her, sought even to interest her passions in the cause of virtue.

"You depend, madam (pursued she) upon your lover's constancy; but what security can you have that he will be constant?"

"What security!" interrupted miss Belmour, roused to attention by so interesting a question; "his vows."

"These vows, madam (said Henrietta) will expire with the passion that caused them: he will be constant as long as he loves, but how long he will love, is the doubt."

"I am really vain enough to imagine," replied miss Belmour, bridling, "that those few attractions I have received from nature, since they have gained, will fix his heart: I am quite free from any apprehensions of that sort, I can assure you."

"You have charms, madam," said Henrietta, "that entitle you to a worthier conquest than of a man, who, not having it in his power to marry you, yet dishonourably seeks to ensnare your affections."

"It is natural to wish to be beloved by those we love," replied miss Belmour: "I am convinced Mr. Morley loves me."

"If he loved you sincerely, madam," said Henrietta, "he would not make you unhappy; true love never seeks the ruin of its object: disinterestedness is the test of love; try Mr. Morley's by that."

"Mr. Morley has no mean, selfish designs upon my fortune," cried miss Belmour.

"His designs are mean and selfish in the highest degree," replied Henrietta, "since he expects that to make him happy you should sacrifice your peace, your honour, and your reputation; and should he succeed in these designs, which heaven forbid, the neglect he will soon treat you with will convince you, that love, when not founded on esteem, cannot be lasting: for the contempt which even libertines feel for those whom they have seduced, is a proof of that secret homage which all men pay to virtue."

"If I thought Mr. Morley would ever fail in the respect and adoration he pays me now," said miss Belmour, "I should hate him."

"The only way to preserve that respect, madam," replied Henrietta, "is not to allow him to encourage any presumptuous hopes: if you wish to keep his heart, engage his esteem; he may one time or other, perhaps, be at liberty to offer you his hand."

"Ah, Henrietta!" interrupted miss Belmour, sighing, "that time is very distant, I fear: but you have put strange thoughts into my head; I have been to blame to suffer Mr. Morley to talk to me so freely of his passion: indeed I think he has been less respectful, since I suffered him to perceive that I prefered him to all the men I ever saw. I own to you freely that it was my apprehensions of losing him that made me listen to his arguments; for I thought, if I reduced him to despair, he would conquer his passion for me: but what if the very means I have used to keep his heart should prove the cause of his slighting me!—Oh! you do not know what anxious, uneasy doubts you have raised in my mind!—However, I am resolved to behave with more reserve to him for the future. I will try whether his passion is strong enough to subsist of itself; for you have convinced me that the hopes with which I have hitherto fed it, have been less likely to nourish than to cloy."

Henrietta would have been better pleased if sentiments more pure had suggested this design; but it was a great point gained to prevail with her on any terms to discourage the addresses of a man whose love was a crime. She flattered herself likewise that this unexpected severity in miss Belmour would produce an alteration in her unworthy lover's behaviour, which might favour her views of exciting her resentment against him; and in this she was not mistaken.

Mr. Morley thought fit to be offended at the new plan of conduct miss Belmour had laid down for herself, and complained of it at first with that mixture of haughtiness and submission which a man, who is sure he is beloved, thinks he has a right to use; but, finding this had not the effect he desired, he had recourse to a personated indifference, in order to alarm her with the fear of losing him.

Henrietta, whom she acquainted with every change in his behaviour, told her that this was the time to humble her imperious lover. "You must either give him laws, madam (said she) or be contented to receive them of him: his aim was to degrade you to a mistress; he will love you, you see, upon no other condition."

"I see it! I see it plainly!" interrupted miss Belmour, bursting into tears; "where is now that aweful love he professed for me, when a look, a smile, was a sufficient reward for all his sufferings!—Dear Henrietta, tell me what I shall do to shew him how much I hate and despise him."

"Avoid him, madam, as much as possible," replied Henrietta. "When you happen to meet him in company, suffer him not to speak to you apart, and receive no letters from him; persist in this conduct, and you will convince him that you are resolved not to purchase the continuance of his affection by the sacrifice of your honour. If he is capable of a sincere and generous passion, he will esteem and reverence that virtue which opposes his desires; and his esteem will strengthen his love."

"Yes," cried miss Belmour, "he shall find that he is not so sure of me as he has the presumption to imagine. I will tell him so myself, and see him again, but it shall be only to declare that I will never see him more—Give me pen and ink, my dear Henrietta: I will appoint him a meeting at lady D——'s this evening; and while the company is engaged at cards, I shall have an opportunity to tell him the resolution I have formed, and doubt not but I will speak to him in the severest terms my resentment can suggest: he shall know, to his confusion, that I am in earnest."

"Indeed, madam," said Henrietta, "that is not the way to persuade him that you are in earnest; let your actions speak for you; shun him carefully, and then he must be convinced that you do not feign."

"I have thought of a way to torment him," said miss Belmour, after a little pause; "I will go to Paris. Last year some ladies of my acquaintance proposed to me to go there with them, and I had almost consented; but the wretch, who braves me so insolently now, declared then that he could not support my absence, and seemed so overwhelmed with grief that I put off my journey for that time: but now were he to offer to stab himself at my feet, it should not alter my purpose. I will write to him this moment, and let him know my design."

"Let me intreat you, madam," said Henrietta, "not to do that; go first, and write to him afterwards—And yet I could recommend a better way of punishing this insolent lover."

"Tell me what better way," cried miss Belmour, eagerly.

"It is to marry, madam," replied Henrietta; "chuse out of that crowd of lovers who address you, him whom you think most deserving. Marriage will secure your peace, your honour, and reputation, and effectually punish the man, who made the sacrifice of all these, the necessary condition of his love for you."

This expedient was not at all approved of by miss Belmour. She declared she hated the whole sex for Mr. Morley's sake; and Henrietta had no difficulty to believe her: however, she prevailed with her to promise that she would keep her intended journey secret till she was just ready to depart, that it might not seem as if she meant only to alarm her designing lover. This promise she observed so ill, that she declared that very day at lady D——'s her intention to spend a few months in Paris. Mr. Morley, who was there, and who still kept up his assumed indifference, instead of endeavouring to alter her purpose, as she expected, coldly congratulated her on the pleasures she would enjoy in that enchanting metropolis. Miss Belmour came home ready to burst with rage and disappointment.

"I knew how it would be madam," said Henrietta, "if you talked of your design. Mr. Morley thinks he sees through the artifice of it: all you can do now is to hasten your departure."

"I am resolved I'll set out to-morrow morning," said miss Belmour. "No matter for preparations; pack up a few necessaries to take with us in the coach, and leave directions for my trunks to be sent after. When we come to Dover, if there is not a packet-boat ready to sail, I'll hire one at any price: I shall not be at rest till I have convinced this man I am really determined to avoid him."

Henrietta kept up this spirit; and after she had given proper directions to the housekeeper, and sent orders for the coach to be ready early in the morning, she busied herself in packing up, her lady assisting, in a violent flutter of spirits, and wishing impatiently for the hour of departure.

Our fair heroine had some objections to taking this journey herself, but her concern for miss Belmour over-ruled them all. She was not willing to leave unfinished the good work she had begun; and she was apprehensive that, if the young lady was left to the guidance of her own passions, this sudden sally of resentment would end in a reconciliation fatal to her virtue.

She would have been glad to see the countess before she went, but there was no time for this visit; therefore she contented herself with writing to that lady, and to her friend Mrs. Willis. The countess received the news of this journey with great pleasure, because she hoped that absence would effectually cure her son's passion for Henrietta, the consequences of which she was still apprehensive of, notwithstanding he had shewn an extraordinary prudence in the conduct of it.

But Mrs. Willis was very uneasy, lest any thing should happen that might make her repent the removing herself thus from all her friends, and putting herself entirely in the power of a stranger. Had there been time for it, she would have endeavoured to dissuade Henrietta from going; but, recollecting that Mr. Damer was in France, and that they might possibly meet, she resolved to write to the old gentleman, and give him a full account of every thing relating to the situation of his fair persecuted ward, not even omitting his son's doubtful behaviour with regard to her; for she knew, that if they met, Henrietta would be silent upon that article, and yet it was necessary he should know it, that he might be convinced her misfortunes were chiefly owing to his son's treachery; and this consideration she hoped would produce something to her advantage.

HENRIETTA.

BOOK THE FIFTH.

Chap. I.

Contains an adventure, in which our heroine is more than ordinarily interested.

In the mean time, our fair travellers, having regulated their affairs in the best manner the extreme hurry they were in would admit, set out for Dover in miss Belmour's coach. That young lady, still agitated with the violence of her resentment, which Henrietta took care should not abate, and elated with the hope of reducing her lover to despair, by thus leaving him, thought the horses went too slow for her impatience. She wished for wings to convey her at once far from him, and declared that she never desired to see him more; yet Henrietta observed that she frequently looked out of the windows with an air of anxious expectation, and would sigh when she drew in her head again, as if she had been disappointed—Doubtless she had conceived hopes that her lover would follow her; and considering this neglect as a new proof of his indifference, it redoubled her rage, and strengthened a resolution in which reason and virtue had very little share.

This thought gave Henrietta extreme concern: her conversion promised no great permanency, since it was founded on such motives; but all she could now do was to manage her passions, for the time was not yet come, to touch her heart by sentiments of piety and virtue.

On their arrival at Dover, they found the Calais packet-boat ready to sail. Miss Belmour, who would fain have lingered at Dover a day, was not much pleased with this circumstance, but her pride was concerned not to betray any irresolution; accordingly she embarked with a tolerable good grace; and the wind continuing fair, they soon landed at Calais.

Miss Belmour having made the journey before, was under no embarrassment how to conduct herself. She proceeded to the inn she had formerly been at; and having hired a post-chaise for herself and Henrietta, and a horse for her servant, she set out immediately after dinner, and reached Boulogne that evening.

As the chaise stopped at the inn they put up at, two gentlemen alighted at the same time; one of whom hearing they were English ladies advanced, and respectfully offered them his hand to help them out. Miss Belmour, pleased with the graceful appearance of this stranger, politely accepted his assistance, which he likewise tendered to Henrietta, whose charms, at the first glance, made a powerful impression on his heart.

His eyes told her this so intelligibly, that she was under some confusion; yet she found in herself a kind of satisfaction at the attention with which he gazed on her, and was now for the first time sensible to the pleasure of charming: but, accustomed to watch carefully over the motions of her own mind, she checked this rising vanity; and a little ashamed of the folly she discovered in herself, she hastily withdrew her hand, which he still held, as not being master enough of himself to part with it, though she was already out of the chaise; and thanking him by a graceful courtesy for his civility, she followed miss Belmour into the room the landlady had conducted her to.

The young gentleman stood gazing after her as long as she was in sight; then turning to his friend, who was giving some orders to their footmen,

"Oh, Charles!" cried he, with a look half serious, half gay, "my fatal hour is come."

"What! I'll warrant you," said the other, "you are shot through the heart with the glances of the younger of those ladies; I observed how you gazed on her."

"Is she not a charming creature?" exclaimed the first; "what features! what a complexion! what elegance in her whole form!—I am sure she has wit; I saw her soul in her eyes."

"Faith! I am half concerned for you," interrupted Charles, with an affected seriousness: "this will be an unfortunate encounter, I am afraid."

"Can we not think of some method to introduce ourselves to them?" cried the other, without minding what he had said: "I shall not rest till I find out who they are."

"What will it signify to you to know," replied Charles: "they are going to Paris, and we to London."

"Why aye, that is true," said the other, "we shall go different ways in the morning; and yet—what think you, my dear Charles, of going back to Paris for a few days, and we shall have an opportunity of escorting these fair travellers?—Come, it will be but a frolick, and I know you are no enemy to them."

"I don't like this frolick," replied Charles; "it has too serious an air: sure you are strangely charmed with this girl—Just upon the point of seeing your father and your family, after a long absence, and so suddenly to resolve upon protracting your stay from them—I don't half like it I confess; and this once, my lord, I must oppose your inclinations."

"Oh, sir, you are grave!" replied his lordship, a little sullenly, "you have a mind to exert the governor[28] too; but let me tell you, that, considering the equality of our years and the terms we have hitherto lived upon, this wisdom is very unseasonable."

The young lord, having said this with some emotion, hastily entered the house; and calling to the inn-keeper to shew him a room, went away, without taking any farther notice of his governor, who stood musing for some time after he was gone, and then followed him with an intention to bring him, if possible, to reason.

Upon his entering the room, he found his pupil leaning on a table, with a discontented air. He just raised his head to see who it was that came in; and immediately resumed his former posture, without speaking a word.

The governor looked at him a moment in silence; at last,

"This pensiveness (said he) and this causeless resentment; are they not strong arguments against my complying with your proposal? The impression this girl has made on your heart must needs be very great, since it can make you already forget that friendship you have vowed for me, and in which I placed so much happiness."

"It is you, not I, who seems to have forgot our mutual friendship," replied the young nobleman, melted at those last words: "Why did you, my dear Charles, lose the beloved friend and companion in the austere governor? is not this strange affectation!"

"Indeed, my lord," replied the governor, "I should be unworthy the title of your friend, if I was not attentive to your interest."

"Was there ever any thing so absurd," interrupted his lordship, "to make a serious affair of a little idle curiosity!"

"Don't you make a serious affair of it," replied the governor, "and I shall be contented."

"Well, then, you consent to go back to Paris with me," said the pupil.

"If you are resolved to go," answered the governor, "to be sure I will go with you."

"Now you are my friend again," said the young lord, hugging him: "I promise you, I will not stay long in Paris; but we must be Freeman and Melvil once more, my dear Charles—Ah, how many pleasant adventures have we had under those names!"

"If this proves of no greater consequence," resumed the young governor, "I shall not regret coming into your scheme; but I confess I am alarmed at your eagerness to follow this young woman. She seems to have made no slight impression on your heart: there is danger in these sort of attachments; how do you know how far this may lead you?"

"What strange notions have entered your head!" said the young nobleman; "it is hardly worth while to make a serious answer to them: but this you may depend upon, that I never will follow my inclinations in opposition to the duty I owe my father. And now, what do you think will become of this dangerous attachment? but (added he, smiling) we must make our fellow-travellers a visit; these inns are charming places for shortening the ceremonies of a first introduction." He rang the bell, without waiting for his friend's answer, and, one of his servants appearing, he ordered him to present Mr. Freeman's and his compliments to the two English ladies, with a request that they would permit them to wait upon them.

Henrietta felt her heart flutter at this message; yet her natural reserve made her wish miss Belmour would decline the visit of these young gentlemen. However, that lady returned a civil answer, and permission for them to come.

Henrietta, sensible of an agitation which she had never known before, would have chosen not to have shared this visit; but it was not possible to avoid it: miss Belmour had obliged her to throw off the character of a servant, and to live with her upon the footing of a friend and companion; to which Henrietta was induced to consent, by the hope she had, that this familiarity would furnish her with opportunities to guard her unhappy mistress against the evils into which her blind passion was hurrying her.

To this mark of consideration and esteem miss Belmour added a most affectionate behaviour, which entirely won the heart of the tender and grateful Henrietta: for nothing so much resembles true friendship, as those connexions which lovers form with persons whom they make the confidants of their passion.

Thus circumstanced, Henrietta was obliged to receive the compliments of Mr. Melvil and his friend, as well as her lady, who, soon after, fell into a fit of musing, that made it necessary for our fair heroine to keep up the conversation with the two gentlemen, which she did with that sprightliness and vivacity so natural to her.

The graces of her wit, the easy elegance of her manners, and the modest dignity of her deportment, formed new chains for the heart of Melvil. He looked on his friend with an exulting air: his eyes challenged his admiration of the woman, whose merit justified the sentiments he entertained for her.

At parting, he told the ladies, that, since he was going to Paris, as well as they, he hoped they would allow him the pleasure of escorting them; and that he would regulate his journey entirely by theirs.

Henrietta, who well remembered to have seen these travellers taking the very contrary route, was a little surprised at this declaration; but miss Belmour, absorbed in her own reflections, was wholly ignorant of that circumstance; and, considering this offer in no other light than that of general politeness, she received it with her usual complaisance.

The youth and beauty of the two ladies made their apparent independent situation a matter of curiosity to Mr. Freeman, as well as the profound melancholy in which one of them seemed buried.

Melvil was little concerned in these enquiries; all his thoughts were taken up with the perfections he found in her who had charmed him; and he was much less solicitous to discover who she was, than how to make himself agreeable to her. He found she was not married, by the other lady's giving her the title of miss when she spoke to her; and he was perfectly satisfied with this knowledge. Conscious of the ardor with which he already loved this fair stranger, he was apprehensive of awakening the fears of his friend, by dwelling too long on her praises; but he received the testimony, which Freeman could not help giving to her merit, with such an undisguised transport, as drew from him some serious admonitions, which he rallied off with a sprightly air, and then changed the discourse to a less interesting subject.

CHAP. II.

Which shews that it is easier to be wise for others than ourselves.

Though miss Belmour's melancholy had hindered her from taking any great share in the conversation during this visit, yet her mind was still free enough to observe, that Henrietta had made an impression upon the heart of Mr. Melvil. She congratulated her, smiling, upon her conquest; nor did her raillery even spare her: for Henrietta, who, for a full hour, had appeared animated with an extraordinary vivacity, became all on a sudden pensive and silent. This change exactly commenced at the time Mr. Melvil went away; but she did not perceive it herself, and started, as from a dream, when miss Belmour reproached her with it.

Concerned that she had given room for a suspicion of this nature, she began, as soon as she was alone, to examine her own heart: miss Belmour had praised the personal graces of Mr. Melvil, and it was but justice to own, that he was eminently handsome; but was she weak enough to be dazzled with the beauty of a man? No, certainly; his countenance pleased her, because it was a picture of his mind; candor, sweetness, benevolence, shined in every feature: the politeness of his address, his gentle manners, that air so noble, yet so peculiarly soft and engaging, his good sense, and, above all, the justness and purity of his sentiments, which she had time enough to discover during their conversation; were not these qualities which a modest young woman might esteem? and is love a necessary consequence of esteeming one of that sex? Must she deny herself the pleasure of approving virtue and merit, for fear of loving it too much? It was thus she argued, and soon dispelled those doubts which miss Belmour's raillery had raised in her mind.

While Henrietta, under the notion of barely esteeming what was indeed truly worthy of esteem, was insensibly giving way to more tender sentiments, Mr. Melvil, who loved with all the tenderness and ardor of a first passion, as his really was, burned with impatience for the hour when they were to join the fair travellers: Freeman directed his attention to miss Belmour, which gave the young lover an opportunity of employing his whole care and assiduity about his mistress, who ascribed all to his natural politeness, and remained in a perfect tranquility, as well with regard to his sentiments as her own. Miss Belmour's experience, however, soon let her into the secret of their hearts. Melvil's passion was indeed apparent enough, notwithstanding the pains he was at to conceal it, thro' fear of his friend's troublesome remonstrances; but Henrietta's, tho' hid from herself, was open to miss Belmour's discerning eyes, and she exulted in the discovery.

This rigid censurer of her conduct; this inflexibly virtuous maid, was entangled in the snares of love. She perceived that she herself was ignorant of her own danger, and she was resolved not to draw her out of this false security by any unseasonable railleries: for, however useful the strict principles of Henrietta had been to her, yet she could not bear the superiority they gave her; and she rejoiced in the hope, that a passion, perhaps as unfortunately placed as her own, would reduce her to an equality with her.

Their journey now drew near a period: Melvil trembled at the thoughts of parting; he had indeed laid the foundation of an intimacy with the two ladies, which would give him a right to visit them in Paris; but he had been used to see the object of his passion continually, from the first moment of his acquaintance with her: and altho' they never separated till the evening, yet he thought the time amazingly long till they met again. How then would he be able to support an answer of two or three days, which decorum would oblige him to make the interval of his visits? besides, she was still ignorant of the sentiments she had inspired him with. Hitherto he had never found an opportunity of speaking to her alone; but if one should offer, how could he declare himself to a woman, for whom he felt as much respect as love? yet one, whose birth he was ignorant of, who seemed to be in a dependent situation, whom he could not think of marrying, and whom he durst not wish to seduce.

The difficulties he could not remove he endeavoured to banish from his thoughts; and, without considering what must be the event of the passion he was thus indulging, he for the present confined all his wishes to the pleasure of seeing her.

Miss Belmour had often wondered that this young lover shewed so little solicitude to make opportunities of speaking to his mistress in private. She could not impute this behaviour to want of ardor; every look he gave her was expressive of the tenderness his soul was filled with: it was then respect, it was awe, it was fear of offending, that laid him under this restraint. How glorious this for Henrietta! how humiliating for her, who had scarce escaped falling a sacrifice to the dishonourable attempts of her lover! Was she then less capable of inspiring a respectful passion than her woman? or did her charms act more powerfully on the heart she had subdued, than those of Henrietta? This question her self-love easily decided; and, from the same sentiment, she was persuaded that Henrietta, with all her boasted virtue, would defend herself as weakly against the lover her inclinations declared for, as she had done. Her present triumph, she thought, was less oweing to her own strength than her lover's weakness, who had not yet made a formal attack upon her heart: curiosity to know what effect the declaration of his passion would have, made her resolve to give him an opportunity of speaking to her in private. They were now within a day's journey of Paris. On their arrival at the house where they were to dine, Mr. Freeman, as usual, went to give orders for their entertainment, and left Melvil with the two ladies. Miss Belmour, pretending that she had a mind for some particular dish, ran after him, and kept him in conversation, that he might not interrupt the lovers, who being now for the first time alone together, were both equally embarrassed.

Henrietta cast down her eyes, surprised at the confusion in which she found herself, and shocked at the intelligence this new emotion gave her of the true state of her heart. Mr. Melvil approached her trembling; he could not resolve to lose so favourable an opportunity of declaring his sentiments to her: but the natural goodness and rectitude of his mind suggesting to him, that it was a kind of fraud to seek encouragement of a passion, the design of which he was not himself able to answer for, he remained a few moments in suspence.

This silence increased Henrietta's embarrassment, but suddenly reflecting upon the advantage it gave Mr. Melvil over her, she turned her eyes towards him, with a look, in which she endeavoured to throw as much indifference as possible, but which, nevertheless, had an unusual coldness in it; so that Melvil, partly with-held by his extreme delicacy, and partly by the awe which this severe glance inspired him with, dropped, for that time, all thoughts of declaring his passion, and immediately entered into an indifferent conversation.

Henrietta seemed as if relieved from a painful load; her countenance resumed its former sweetness, and she talked to him with her usual vivacity; yet miss Belmour, at her return, saw some remains of her late uneasiness in her eyes: she observed too, that she spoke less to Mr. Melvil, and more to his friend than she did before; that she studiously avoided the looks of the former; and that her behaviour to him was less free and obliging than it used to be. All this she looked upon as the play of coquetry; and in Mr. Melvil's apparent melancholy she saw its purpose and effect.

But Henrietta taught by what passed in her own heart, during the few moments she was alone with Mr. Melvil, that she not only considered him as a lover, but a lover formidable by his engaging qualities, resolved not to strengthen her prepossession in his favour, by continuing to see and converse with him. Lord B——'s behaviour had given her no high idea of the disinterestedness of men. She trembled at her own imprudence, in so far forgetting the humble station that Providence had placed her in, as to entertain sentiments of tenderness for a man, who, from the inequality there was between them, might think himself authorised to form expectations injurious to her honour: tho' her weakness was so lately known to herself, yet she fancied it had been perceived by others before, and that even Mr. Melvil had discovered the preference with which she regarded him. It was this thought which made her so suddenly alter her behaviour; but as indifference is, of all dispositions of the mind, the hardest to feign, Melvil imputed the apparent constraint in her manner to some disgust he had unhappily given her, and miss Belmour to the artifice of a coquet.

Henrietta, who was far from imagining she over-acted her part, continued, during the whole time they were at dinner, to avoid her lover's looks, so carefully that he had no opportunity to make her comprehend by them, how much he was concerned at her extraordinary coldness. However, she could not, without affectation, refuse him her hand when they left the inn; but they followed Mr. Freeman and miss Belmour so close, that it was not possible for him to speak to her without being overheard; and he in vain sought her eyes: they were always directed another way. He sighed when he helped her into the chaise; and if she had not turned her face from him that moment, the blush with which it was overspread, would have shewn him that she took but too much notice of that sigh.

"You are melancholy, Henrietta," said miss Belmour, after looking at her in silence for a long time, attentive to the motions of her mind, which might be easily read in her countenance.

"Am I, madam?" replied she, with a sigh half suppressed, and a gentle smile.

"Yes, indeed, are you," resumed miss Belmour, mimicking the languid accent in which she spoke; "and I don't remember that I ever saw you so before."

"And yet I have many causes for melancholy, madam," replied Henrietta, whose heart was full, and she eagerly grasped at this opportunity to relieve herself by tears; tears, which she supposed she gave to the remembrance of her misfortunes, without asking herself, why that remembrance was more poignant now than before.

"Ah! Henrietta," said miss Belmour, shaking her head, "your heart has undergone a great change within these few days—You are in love, my dear." "Is it possible, madam," cried Henrietta, hastily, her fair face all crimsoned over, "that you have discovered?—Do you think that—Then, to be sure, Mr. Melvil."—She stopped abruptly, and cast down her eyes: the mention of that name seemed to lead her to a consciousness, that she had betrayed herself.

Miss Belmour was affected with her beautiful simplicity. "Don't be ashamed, my dear Henrietta," said she, taking her hand, "to speak freely to me. From me, (added she, sighing) you may be sure of indulgence."

"No, madam, no," interrupted Henrietta, with great earnestness, "I would not seek indulgence for my weaknesses: but I conjure you, madam," pursued she, with tears that in spite of her endeavours would force their way, "suffer me to return to that humble station, from which your partial kindness raised me—You have made me forget I was a servant—It does not become me to view with sensibility the merit of persons so greatly above me. But you shall find, madam, that I will repair this error, and that my conduct shall be such as may render me not unworthy your esteem."

Notwithstanding the delicate turn which Henrietta gave to a declaration, which shewed she was determined early to conquer her passion, yet miss Belmour considered it as a triumph over her, who had not been capable of acting with equal prudence.

"It is happy for you (said she, coldly) that you need no assistance to help you to keep your passions in subjection; but I owe you too many obligations for the good counsel you have given me, to permit you to appear in any other character than that of my friend."

Henrietta's mind was in so much agitation, that she did not take in the full sense of this answer, but struck with the obliging purport of the last words of it, she expressed her gratitude in terms full of tenderness and respect.

The sight of Paris drew them both out of a long silence, which had succeeded a conversation with which neither had been pleased: Henrietta, because it had discovered so much weakness on her side; miss Belmour, because it had shewn so little.

Their chaise, as miss Belmour had directed, stopped at the house of her banker in Paris. The two gentlemen were already at the side of it: Mr. Melvil, as if he was afraid Henrietta would refuse him her hand, seized it with trembling haste; and, as he led her into the house, ventured to press it with his lips, unperceived by any one else. Henrietta, imputing this boldness to the discovery he had made of her sentiments, pulled her hand away hastily, giving him a look at the same time that expressed her resentment; but all her anger could not prevent her from being affected with the soft languor that appeared in his face, and the submissive manner in which he had yielded to the effort she made to withdraw her hand.

Miss Belmour, at parting, told them, she hoped to see them again in a day or two, when she should be settled. Her Parisian friend soon procured her convenient lodgings, and, at her desire, recommended to her a Femme de Chambre,[29] among the other servants he provided her, which Henrietta in vain opposed; but fixed in her design to avoid Mr. Melvil, she took care to be seldom in the way when he came.

Miss Belmour blamed her for this conduct. "You will make the man think you love him, and are afraid of him (said she) by flying him."

"If I loved him, madam," replied Henrietta, blushing, "is it not prudence to avoid him?"

"Why, I don't know," said miss Belmour, "Mr. Melvil certainly loves you; and, whatever inequality there may be in your conditions, yet love is a great leveller: he may possibly intend to marry you."

"It is not fit I should suppose he has any such design, madam," resumed Henrietta, "since it is highly improbable; and I will not expose myself to the danger of being deceived. I have some-where read (added she, smiling) that in love flight is victory; and this way at least I shall be sure to conquer."

Miss Belmour, who knew how difficult it was to be in love and be wise, laughed at a resolution, which she did not think it would be always in her power to maintain. Poor Henrietta, who had so artlessly laid open her heart, was often exposed to the most poignant raillery from her; but at length she was delivered from this kind of persecution by a surprising alteration in miss Belmour herself.

This young lady, who had fled from her lover, rather with a hope of stimulating his passion than of subduing her own, though she endeavoured to impose upon herself in believing the latter to be the true motive of her conduct, fell into a most violent despair, when she found that, far from following her, he did not even seek a reconciliation by writing to her. Sick of herself, the world, and tired of her existence, she mistook the agitations of a heart tortured by jealousy, disappointment, and the pangs of slighted love, for the motions of grace, and the genuine marks of repentance. She neglected her dress, took no pleasure in any amusement, avoided company, and spent whole hours in her closet, where she wept and prayed by turns.

She told Henrietta, that the world and all its pleasures were grown insipid to her; that her whole soul was filled with divine love; and that the thoughts and exercises of religion made up all her happiness. She then passionately regretted that there were no religious communities among the protestants, where a mind that was weaned from this sublunary world, and all its vanities, might freely indulge its pious contemplations, and devote itself entirely to Heaven. "Oh, how happy are the nuns!" she exclaimed; "how I envy them! Sure nothing can be more delightful, when persons are truly pious, than to live in a religious society excluded from all commerce with a world they must certainly despise. I think I should be perfectly contented if I was in a cloister."

Henrietta congratulated her upon her new sentiments, but endeavoured to prove that there was more merit in passing through life with innocence, and in rightly performing all its duties, than in flying to the gloomy solitude of a cloister, where virtue is secured by bolts and bars, and the exercises of religion performed as a penance. She recommended to her the study of the scriptures, and put some practical treatises of religion written by the best authors, into her hands: but the zeal of this new convert was so flaming, that nothing would serve her but a total retirement from the world; and she made such frequent visits to a convent, where a friend of her's had lately taken the veil, that Henrietta was apprehensive the nuns would discover the true state of her mind, and take advantage of her passions to pervert her principles, and secure her to themselves.

While these whims possessed her, she was so inaccessible to all visiters, that Mr. Melvil could with difficulty get admittance. Freeman saw the progress of his passion with great uneasiness, and, finding that he could not be prevailed upon to leave Paris, resolved to write to his father, and give him a hint of the dangerous attachment his son had formed, that he might send him a peremptory command to return to England; but before he could execute this design, Melvil, to his great surprise, told him, that he would leave Paris in two days. The poor youth expected his friend would have expressed some joy at this news; and, being disappointed at his receiving with indifference what had cost him so many pangs to resolve upon,

"You make me no compliments," said he, with a tender smile, "upon the conquest I have gained over my inclinations: do you think I can banish myself from miss Benson without concern?"

"I am sure I cannot hear you speak in this manner without concern," replied Freeman. "Is it fit for a young man of your rank to entertain a serious liking for a woman, to whose birth and character you are an absolute stranger?"

"There is not a man in the world," resumed Melvil, eagerly, "who need to blush for loving miss Benson; her person, beautiful as it is, is the least of her charms; that mingled sweetness and dignity in her manners, that graceful modesty which distinguishes every word and action of her's, exalt her above all the women I have ever seen. You have heard her talk, and you could not help owning that you thought her very sensible."

"Well, but what is all this to the purpose?" interrupted Freeman, "what signifies attributing such goddess-like perfections to an obscure girl, whom, if you were at liberty to dispose of yourself, you would not, I suppose, be so mad as to marry: your fortune enables you to make other proposals, less unworthy of yourself, though advantageous enough for a young woman in her dependent situation; own freely then that this is your intention."

"May I perish," replied Melvil, with some emotion, "if I would degrade such excellence to a mistress; but if I were capable of such a design, her virtue, I am sure, is incorruptible. Have you not observed with what care she shuns me? She knows I love her; but she knows not with what purity I love her; and, conscious of her situation, she is afraid I should take advantage of it to declare myself in a manner that would wound her delicacy.—Charming creature, I love her! I adore her!—Indeed, my dear Freeman, it is time to be gone."

"I see it plainly," replied Freeman, "you are grown quite romantic—We will set out to-morrow, if you please; for, with the strange notions you have entertained, I think you ought not to trust yourself here any longer."

The lover consented with a sigh; but at the same time put his friend in mind, that civility obliged them to go and take leave of the ladies. Freeman could not reasonably oppose his making this visit; and, after he had given proper directions to the servants for their journey the next day, he accompanied him to miss Belmour's lodgings.

Chap. III.

In which miss Belmour acts the part of a true female friend.

They found the two ladies together: Henrietta could not, without affectation, avoid her lover that day, as she was in the room when he came in; and he, who had not been so fortunate for several days before, found so much delight in looking at her and hearing her speak, that he forgot he came to pay a farewel visit, which Mr. Freeman observing, took care to mention their design of leaving Paris the next day.

Melvil's gaiety was immediately over-cast, Henrietta turned pale, Freeman was attentive to his friends emotions, and only miss Belmour had freedom of mind enough left to speak. She said some civil things upon the occasion, which Freeman answered; for Melvil continued silent, with his eyes fixed upon Henrietta, who had bent her's towards the ground: conscious of the emotion with which she had heard the news of their intended departure, she durst not look up, lest the person, from whom she was most solicitous to hide her concern, should read it too plainly in her countenance.

Recovering herself at length, upon miss Belmour's taking occasion to thank them anew for the civilities she had received from them during their journey from Calais, she added a few words to her compliment; but, in doing so, her eyes slightly glanced over Mr. Melvil, and directed their looks full upon his friend.

The conversation was dull enough during two hours that they stayed; and Freeman, perceiving the young gentleman wanted resolution to put an end to the visit, rose up first, Mr. Melvil did so likewise, though with apparent reluctance; and having saluted miss Belmour, approached Henrietta, trembling. She turned pale and red successively; a soft sigh stole from her. Melvil was in too much emotion to observe her's: he saluted her with an air of solemn respect; but, as she retired a step back, a sudden impulse, which he could not resist, made him take her hand; he pressed it to his lips with passionate tenderness, and, sighing, quitted the room with the utmost precipitation.

Henrietta's eyes overflowed; she made haste to wipe them before miss Belmour, who attended the gentlemen as far as the door of her anti-chamber, returned.

"Ah! my poor Henrietta," said that young lady, who perceived she had been weeping, "I pity you—What sordid wretches are these men! Melvil loves you, and yet he is able to leave you; nay, I am persuaded he has discovered your tenderness for him—What monstrous ingratitude! you ought to hate him, my dear."

"You bid me hate him, madam," replied Henrietta, smiling, "yet say every thing that can confirm me in a favourable opinion of him. If he loves me, and has seen any weakness in me, he gives the best proof of his love in not seeking to take advantage of that weakness."

Miss Belmour, who thought this a strange way of reasoning, answered no otherwise than by a significant smile, which seemed to say she was resolved to justify him at any rate; while Henrietta, finding in her lover's behaviour a delicacy which agreeably flattered her esteem of him, cherished his remembrance with a tender grief, and perhaps, for the first time, repined at her unhappy fortune, which had placed such a distance between them.

As soon as the two gentlemen had left their lodgings, Melvil, who found himself very low-spirited, proposed to his friend to spend the evening at a noted Hotel, with some young Englishmen of fashion, who were newly arrived: Freeman consented; but observed with uneasiness, that his pupil, who till then had been remarkably abstemious, pushed about the bottle with great velocity, and could not be persuaded to go home till the night was far advanced.

Mr. Freeman saw him in bed, and then retired to his own chamber, full of apprehensions lest this sudden intemperance should have any bad effect on his health. As soon as it was light, he went to his bed-side, and found him with all the symptoms of a feverish disorder upon him, to which the agitations of his mind had contributed more perhaps than the liquor of which he had drank so freely.

All thoughts of their journey were now laid aside; physicians were sent for, who pronounced that he was dangerously ill: Freeman, full of anxiety, sat close to his bed, holding one of his burning hands tenderly pressed between his. He heard him sigh frequently, and from thence took occasion to ask him, if any secret uneasiness occasioned his indisposition?

The young gentleman attributed his illness entirely to the excess he had been guilty of the night before; but his fever increasing, he grew delirious, and then the name of miss Benson was continually in his mouth.

Freeman, judging by these ravings of the deep impression this young woman had made on the heart of his pupil, blamed himself for so obstinately opposing his passion, and, judging from Henrietta's situation that she would not refuse to listen to such proposals as his fortune enabled him to make her, he resolved to attempt something in his friend's favour.

His curiosity having led him to make some enquiries concerning miss Belmour of several persons that had lately arrived from England, he found she had but a doubtful character; her connexions with Mr. Morley having exposed her to great censure: of her companion he could learn nothing; but, concluding from the friendship there appeared to be between them, that she was her confidant in this amour, he flattered himself that she would not be a very difficult conquest.

He shut his eyes upon all that was wrong in this proceeding; and, considering nothing but the interest of his friend, for whom he had the most passionate concern, he thought it less dangerous to give him a mistress, than to trust him to the fantastic power of his passion, which might hurry him on to a clandestine marriage.

The young gentleman was in a few days entirely out of danger from the fever; but his sighs, and the pensive air of his countenance, shewed that his mind was not at ease.

"If you were able to go abroad" said Freeman to him, "we would visit our English ladies once more before we leave Paris. They imagine we are in London by this time, and will be strangely surprised to see us again."

"Then they do not know I have been ill," replied Mr. Melvil.

"Not yet," said Freeman; "but if you wish they should know, I will wait on them this afternoon, and tell them what has kept us in Paris so much longer than we intended."

Melvil affected to receive this proposal with indifference; but his friend observed, that he was more chearful than before, and doubted not but he expected the news of his illness would have some effect on Henrietta.

He went at the usual hour, and was immediately admitted: "you are in Paris still, then?" exclaimed miss Belmour, in a joyful accent, as soon as Freeman entered her apartment, "I am excessively glad of it, I hope your agreeable friend is with you."

Freeman, a little disappointed at not seeing Henrietta with her, answered coldly, that Mr. Melvil had been indisposed, which obliged them to delay their journey.

"I fancy," said miss Belmour, with an arch leer, "that the air of Paris is mighty necessary for your friend at this time; you are in the wrong to hurry him away."

"You have a great deal of penetration, madam," replied Mr. Freeman, smiling, "you have guessed the cause of his illness, I believe."

"I believe I have," resumed miss Belmour, "and perhaps I could tell him something that might contribute to forward his recovery."

Freeman began now to think his scheme was in a hopeful way. "To be sincere with you, madam," said he, with a graver look and accent, "Mr. Melvil is desperately in love with miss Benson."

"Poor man!" cried miss Belmour, laughing, "he is to be pitied truly, for miss Benson is most desperately in love with him likewise."

"How happy would this news make him!" exclaimed Freeman. "Am I, madam, at liberty to tell him?"

"Certainly," replied miss Belmour, "I told you for that purpose; and now what do you think of my frankness?"

"I adore you for it, madam," said Freeman, taking her hand, which (encouraged by her behaviour) he kissed with great liberty. "Ah!" pursued he, looking at her tenderly, "what additional charms does kindness give to beauty!"

"I hear miss Benson on the stairs," said miss Belmour, withdrawing her hand; "I will give you an opportunity to plead your friend's cause: remember what I have told you, and don't be discouraged by a little affectation."

She stopped upon Henrietta's entrance, who started at the sight of Mr. Freeman, and immediately after her fair face was covered with blushes.

"You see we have not lost our good friends yet," said miss Belmour. Henrietta only smiled. "I must desire you, my dear," pursued that young lady, "to entertain Mr. Freeman; I ordered some trades-people to attend me about this time."

She hurried out of the room when she had said this, not without some confusion for the part she had acted; to account for which, it is necessary the reader should know that the mind of this young lady had undergone another revolution, within the few days of Mr. Melvil's illness.

A letter from her lover, filled with tender complaints, and new assurances of everlasting fidelity, had banished all thoughts of devotion and a convent. She had answered it immediately without communicating it to Henrietta; her transport at finding herself still beloved, and the fear of disgusting him by any new coldness, hurried her on to the most fatal resolutions. She invited him to come to Paris to her; and, not doubting but he would instantly obey her summons, she was now only solicitous how to reconcile Henrietta to her conduct, and oblige her to keep her secret.

The unexpected news of Mr. Melvil's being still in Paris, and Mr. Freeman's acknowledgment of his friend's passion for Henrietta, answered all her views. She imputed the reserve Henrietta had been enabled to maintain, less to her own virtue than to the unenterprising temper of her lover; and was persuaded that the discovery she had made of her tenderness for him, would put the affair upon such a footing, as to make her less rigid in her remonstrances with respect to Mr. Morley.

Chap. IV.

Which contains a very interesting discovery.

Freeman, though persuaded that miss Belmour was a woman of intrigue, and by consequence entertaining no elevated idea of her companion, yet found himself so awed by the modesty that shone in her countenance, and the dignity of her person and manner, that he was at some loss how to introduce the subject which had brought him thither. Henrietta, however, innocently led him to it, by expressing her surprise to see him still in Paris.

"You say nothing of my friend, madam," said Freeman; "and this indifference with regard to him is a very bad omen."

"I hope Mr. Melvil is well," said Henrietta, gravely, without seeming to take any notice of the strange speech he had made.

"He is better than he was three or four days ago," replied Freeman, "when his physicians despaired of his life."

"Bless me!" cried Henrietta, with an emotion she could not suppress, "has Mr. Melvil been so ill then? I am extremely concerned to hear it."

"You would, no doubt," said Freeman, "be more concerned if you knew you were the cause."

"This kind of raillery, Mr. Freeman," replied Henrietta, a little confused, "is not at all agreeable to me, I assure you."

"By Heaven I am serious," resumed Freeman; "my friend loves you with the utmost ardor: I am a witness to the birth and progress of his passion, and to his fruitless endeavours to conquer it. The effort he made to leave Paris, has almost cost him his life; he was taken ill the evening before our intended departure. Oh, miss Benson! had you heard with what tenderness he called upon your name, when the violence of his fever had deprived him of his senses, I am sure you must have pitied him."

Freeman perceived by the changes in Henrietta's countenance, that she did not hear him without emotion. He paused, in expectation of some pretty affected answer, that would give hope while it seemed to destroy it; but Henrietta, with a composed look and accent, replied,

"If I am to believe this account of your friend's illness not exaggerated, permit me to ask you, sir, what is your design by making me acquainted with his sentiments, and what you expect from me on this occasion?"

Freeman was a little disconcerted by this speech, and at the manner in which she delivered it; but, relying on the intelligence he had received from miss Belmour,

"I expect you will have compassion on my friend (said he) and give him an opportunity to declare to you himself the passion you have inspired him with."

"I will be very free with you, Mr. Freeman," replied Henrietta; "your ready concurrence with your friend in the liking you say he has entertained for me, is not consistent with your good sense and prudence. Mr. Melvil is a young man of rank and fortune; I am poor and dependent; my birth perhaps greatly inferior to his. Will his parents, think you, approve of such a choice?"

"What have parents to do with a tender engagement?" interrupted Freeman; "an engagement in which the heart only is consulted."

"Were my heart ever so well disposed in favour of your friend," resumed Henrietta, not willing to understand him, "I would not receive his addresses without the sanction of his parents consent."

Freeman could hardly help smiling at this formal declaration; and, supposing that the best way to drive these strange notions out of her head, was to acquaint her with Melvil's quality, which he likewise expected would have no small influence over her,

"It is not fit (said he) that you should be any longer ignorant of the rank of him whom your charms have subjected. Melvil is not the name of my friend; he is the heir of an illustrious title and a great estate: he loves you, he will make your fortune; do not throw away this opportunity of freeing yourself from poverty and dependance, nor let a romantic notion of virtue deprive you of the advantages that are offered you."

"Hold, sir," interrupted Henrietta, rising from her chair, "this insult is too plain; I ought not to have listened to you so long." She spoke this with tolerable composure; but, finding her tears begin to flow, she turned aside to conceal them, and hastily wiping her eyes, she looked on him again with a kind of calm disdain.

"I know not, (said she) what weakness you have discovered in my behaviour to encourage you to make me such shocking proposals; but I may venture to tell you, though I am not the mistress of this apartment, that the doors of it shall never be open to you again."

She was hurrying out of the room when she had spoke this, leaving Freeman in so much confusion, that he knew not what to say to her, when miss Belmour entered with a letter in her hand.

"Do you know a gentleman of the name of Damer, (said she to Henrietta) who is at present at Montpelier?"

"I do, madam," replied she, looking eagerly at the letter.

"Then this letter is for you, I suppose," said miss Belmour, "it was inclosed in another to me, and directed to my banker's: but is your name Courteney? you see the superscription is for miss Courteney?"

"The letter is certainly for me, madam," said Henrietta, blushing.

"Oh! then," replied miss Belmour, smiling, and giving it to her, "I have discovered a secret, I find."

Henrietta retired immediately; and miss Belmour approached Mr. Freeman, who stood leaning over his chair, with his eyes fixed on the ground,

"What is the matter with you? (said she) you look excessively pale."

"Where is miss Benson, madam?" said he, starting out of his reverie at the sound of her voice.

"She is in her own chamber, I believe," replied miss Belmour; "but did you take notice of what passed about the letter? I delivered it to her before you on purpose: you see she in a manner owned that Courteney is her true name; is not this strange?"

"I must beg leave to speak to her again," said he, interrupting her, and making towards the door, "which way, pray madam?"

Miss Belmour followed him, surprised at the agitation he appeared to be in; and, pointing to a room just opposite, "you will find her there," said she.

Freeman opened the door without any ceremony; Henrietta, who was reading her letter, looked up at the noise he made in entering: "this is extremely rude, sir (said she) I desire you will instantly be gone, and trouble me no more." But, apprehensive that he would not quit her so easily, she rushed by him, and was running to the room in which she had left miss Belmour: he took hold of her hand, to prevent her leaving him; and she was upon the point of expressing her resentment at the insolence of this treatment, in harsher terms than any she had yet used, when she saw tears gush in great abundance from his eyes. Moved at this sight, she stood still, but endeavoured to disengage her hand, looking at him earnestly, and in the utmost astonishment.

"O my sister!" cried he at last, bursting into a fresh flood of tears; "my dear, dear sister"—He was not able to utter a word more, but led her gently back to her chamber, which she permitted, trembling, confused, and full of anxious expectation.

"How strangely you look upon me!" said he, "do you doubt whether I am your brother?"

"I know not what to think," replied she, shrinking from his embrace; for he had folded his arms about her.

"Dear girl!" cried he, "how amiable is this sweet reserve—these modest doubts—but it is certain I am your brother, my Henrietta: is it possible your memory retains no traces of my features? in your's, methinks I see a lively resemblance of my dear mother. How dull was I that I did not discover it before! but how could I expect to meet you in France, in such a situation, and under a disguised name! Oh! my dear sister, these circumstances distract me—Good Heaven! what a part have I acted—I perceive you are still perplexed," pursued he, after a little pause; and, taking a miniature picture out of his pocket, "You will certainly be able to recollect your mother's picture (said he) which she gave me at parting."

Henrietta looked at the picture, kissed it, and then threw herself in tears upon her brother's neck—"Forgive my doubts (said she) it is many years since I have seen you; we were children when we parted, but now I am convinced you are my brother: my heart tells me so without this dear testimony," pursued she, kissing again the picture of her mother, which she still held; then suddenly clasping her hands together, and lifting up her fine eyes, which were swimming in tears, "I thank thee, O my God! (said she) for restoring to me my brother:" and, turning again to him with an affectionate look, "a few moments ago (said she) I thought myself very unhappy, but now you will be a friend and protector to me."

He tenderly kissed her cheek—"What a wretch have I been!" said he, sighing—"Indeed, my dear sister, I never shall forgive myself for having ignorantly practised on your virtue."

"Oh! that my brother," replied Henrietta, "would be taught by this accident never more to form designs against innocence; and, in cases like mine, to consider every virtuous young woman as a sister."

Mr. Courteney, for so we shall now call him, was extremely moved at these words. He gazed at her some moments with mingled tenderness and delight; but all on a sudden, as if struck with some painful reflection,

"Henrietta," said he, with a look and accent greatly altered from his former sweetness, "why came you to France? and how has it happened that you are so intimately connected with this woman, this miss Belmour?"

"Why, do you know any harm of miss Belmour?" said Henrietta, frighted at his sternness.

"You don't answer my question," replied he, peevishly.

"Alas! my dear brother," said Henrietta, "I have a long and melancholy story to tell you: I have been reduced to great distress; my aunt, with whom you supposed me so happily settled, has treated me unkindly: I must confess, indeed, I have not been wholly free from blame; but you shall know all some other time. As for miss Belmour, I was recommended to her—I would not shock you, brother; but I have been obliged to go to service, and I was recommended to miss Belmour by two ladies of quality, her near relations."

Mr. Courteney sighed deeply at this account, and remained for several moments silent; at length recovering himself,

"Miss Belmour, it seems (said he) did not always know your real name— You appear to be on the footing of a companion."

"Miss Belmour was pleased to take a liking to me," said Henrietta; "and, though ignorant of my birth, would not suffer me to continue with her in the character of a servant—I have been greatly obliged to her."

"Yes, you are obliged to her," interrupted Mr. Courteney, kindling into rage at the remembrance of what had passed between them; "infamous wretch! she has done her part towards betraying you to ruin. You have been very imprudent, Henrietta; you have talked to her of Mr. Melvil too freely: she believes you are in love with him, and told me so, to encourage my attempts upon you."

Henrietta blushed at the mention of Mr. Melvil, and presently after burst into tears at this discovery of miss Belmour's baseness and ingratitude, but uttered not a word of complaint or resentment.

"I will not suffer you to remain any longer with her," resumed Mr. Courteney; "I will go directly and provide you lodgings in the house of a worthy English family: I suppose you can have no objection to this proposal."

"Why do you look and speak so coldly, my dear brother?" said Henrietta: "to be sure I can have no objection; dispose of me as you please, you are in the place of my father, I will obey you as such."

"Forgive me, my dear," said he, tenderly pressing her hand, "my temper is warm; I have spoke to you harshly: indeed I am greatly alarmed at the disagreeable circumstances I find you in: you have been to blame, you own. Alas! my dear sister, what have you done to be thus abandoned by your aunt? I shall be on the rack till I have heard all your story; but this is not a proper place—Take a civil leave of miss Belmour, but do not acquaint her that you have discovered your brother, for I know not yet what measures I shall take; I will call for you in less than an hour in a coach."

Henrietta promised to be ready; he took a tender leave of her, and departed.

CHAP. V.

The history continued.

O ur fair heroine continued some time alone in her chamber, so transported at this unexpected meeting with her brother, that she sometimes doubted whether her happiness was real, and whether all that had past was not an illusion of her fancy. When her spirits were a little composed, she began to consider what reason she should give miss Belmour for quitting her so suddenly: she rightly judged that the secrecy her brother had recommended to her, proceeded from his embarrassment with regard to Mr. Melvil; and she resolved, however strange her going away might appear to miss Belmour, to follow his directions punctually.

The treachery this young lady had been guilty of towards her, excited less resentment than grief for the conviction it brought her, that her principles were not changed. Several circumstances now rushed upon her memory, which served to convince her she was relapsing into her former indiscretions; and she doubted not but miss Belmour would be rejoiced to be delivered from her presence. This thought gave her courage to go to her immediately, and acquaint her with her intention.

"A strange alteration has happened in my affairs, madam," said she, entering her apartment, "within this hour."

"That letter has brought you some good news, I suppose," said miss Belmour, coldly.

"It came from a dear and worthy friend, madam," replied Henrietta; "and I have indeed heard some good news, which I little expected: but I am obliged to leave you, and so suddenly, that I am afraid you will think me ungrateful for your kindness, in submitting to this necessity."

"Pray make no apologies," interrupted miss Belmour, with great indifference, "you are entirely at your liberty."

Henrietta, who thought she had reason for this behaviour, was studying for some answer, which, without revealing the secret motive of her conduct, might tend in some measure to excuse it; when a servant introduced a gentleman into the room, who, though she had seen but once, she knew immediately to be Mr. Morley. She turned eagerly to observe how miss Belmour was affected by this visit; and discovering no signs of surprise or anger in her countenance, but an excess of joy and satisfaction, she concluded this meeting was concerted, and retired immediately, in great concern, to her own room.

Here, while she waited her brother's return, she employed herself in writing to miss Belmour. In this letter she repeated what she had often urged before, to guard her against the base designs of her lover: she recalled to her remembrance the resolution she had made, and the vows with which she had sealed it, never more to listen to his destructive addresses; and conjured her, by every motive of religion, honour, and virtue, to banish from her sight a man whose only aim was to ruin her.

She had scarce finished her letter, when a servant came to tell her that some company waited for her in a coach. She made haste to seal it, and gave it to miss Belmour's maid, with orders to deliver it to her lady. At the door she found her brother, who helped her into the coach, and came in after her. He asked her, smiling, how she had parted with miss Belmour?

Henrietta told him, she had left her with company. "It is indifferent to me what company she sees now you are not with her," said he: "but my heart will not be at rest till I hear all your story, sister."

Henrietta promised to satisfy him when they were arrived at her new lodgings. "I am also impatient (said she) to know your adventures; why you called yourself Freeman, and what was the cause of your not writing to me for so many months past."

"To say the truth, my dear sister (said he) I have been guilty of a little neglect in not writing to you oftener: however, some of my letters must certainly have miscarried; for I wrote to you both from Brussels and Genoa, and I don't remember I had any answer. The account you gave me of Mr. Damer's kindness in taking upon him the office of your guardian, and your happy settlement with lady Meadows, made me perfectly easy with regard to you. I had informed you that I was appointed governor to the marquis of ——: this young nobleman had contracted a friendship with me during his stay at Leyden, where his governor dying, he wrote to his father the duke of ——, in such pressing terms in my favour, which, joined to the knowledge of my birth, and very high recommendations from the university, had so much weight with him, that his grace, notwithstanding my youth, appointed me governor to his son, with a salary of five hundred pounds a year. I have endeavoured to acquit myself faithfully of this trust; my pupil and I have always lived together like brothers; and I flatter myself his father will have no cause to repent his having consigned him to my care."

"But why did you take the names of Melvil and Freeman?" interrupted Henrietta.

"The marquis," replied Mr. Courteney, "had an inclination to travel without the parade of quality, that he might, as he wrote to his father, make nearer and more useful observations upon men and manners; and, being indulged in this scheme, we have travelled through France and Italy under those names, and with a very small equipage. And now, Henrietta, that you know the quality of my friend, I expect you will not entertain any ridiculous hopes from the liking he has expressed for you. I will do him the justice to own that he never formed any dishonourable designs upon you. The character of the woman you lived with, encouraged me to make you some shocking proposals. You behaved very properly; but, my dear sister, no words can express my anguish and confusion, when I heard you own the name of Courteney, and your connexions with Mr. Damer—Good Heaven! what did I not suffer at that moment—What a wretch did I seem in my own eyes!"

"Let not this cruel remembrance disturb you now, my dear brother," said Henrietta; "I am so happy in finding you, that I forget all my past uneasinesses."

Her looks bore delightful witness to the truth of what she said. Joy sparkled in her charming eyes, heightened the rosy bloom of her complexion, and animated her whole air: but, dearly as she loved her brother, the assurance he gave her, that her lover had no part in the dishonourable proposals he had made her, was a circumstance that greatly increased her satisfaction in this meeting.

Mr. Courteney looked at her with admiration and delight, while a tender sense of the misfortunes she had been exposed to, almost melted him into tears. As soon as the coach stopped, he told her, that the master of the house they were going into was a very worthy man, with whom he was intimately acquainted, and whose prudence he could depend upon. "His wife (pursued he) is a virtuous, sensible woman: I know no family so proper to place you in as this; and it was extremely lucky that I thought of them upon this occasion, for it was not fit you should stay with miss Belmour, and in so short a time it was difficult to dispose of you properly."

As soon as they alighted, Mrs. Knight came to receive Henrietta, and presented her husband to her. Both seemed greatly charmed with her appearance, and politely thanked Mr. Courteney for bringing them so agreeable a guest.

After a few compliments they withdrew, supposing the brother and sister would be glad of an opportunity to converse together in private. Mr. Courteney immediately drew his chair near his sister's, and, with a look of impatience, demanded the account she had promised him.

Henrietta blushed, and begged him not to judge her errors too severely. She then gave him a candid relation of all that had happened to her, from her mother's death till the time she met him at the inn, concealing nothing from him but miss Belmour's passion for Mr. Morley.

Mr. Courteney was variously affected during the course of her little story. He often changed countenance, but would not interrupt her. He observed with pleasure, that she laid no stress upon any part of her conduct, which might with justice challenge esteem and admiration, but appeared nicely conscious of every little imprudence; and, when she had ended, waited for his reply, with an anxiety that shewed she rather expected censure than praise.

"My dear Henrietta," said Mr. Courteney, at length, with tears in his eyes; "you have acted nobly; you cannot imagine how much your sufferings endear you to me, since you have behaved under them with such becoming fortitude."

"How happy you make me," cried Henrietta, "by your approbation—Indeed I was afraid you would have chidden me severely for leaving my aunt in the manner I did."

"It was a rash step," replied Mr. Courteney, "but your subsequent conduct has effaced it; and I see not how you could have otherwise avoided being in the power of that villain-priest."

After some farther conversation on different parts of her story, he looked at his watch: "How fast the minutes fly!" said he, smiling. "My dear Henrietta, I must leave you now, yet I have a thousand things to say to you: but I will see you to-morrow morning. You will be very happy (continued he) with Mrs. Knight, and I shall have no scruple to trust you to her care, till I have conducted the marquis to London: we shall go in a day or two: and, after I have delivered my charge safe to his father, I will come back to Paris, and fetch you."

Henrietta turned pale at these words: "Then we are to part again soon!" said she, in a melancholy accent.

"It would be highly improper for you (replied he) to take this journey with us, on several accounts: I shall be concerned to leave you, but it must be so."

"Could you not stay till Mr. Damer comes?" interrupted Henrietta; and, taking his letter out of her pocket, "see here how affectionately he writes to me (added she): he proposes to be in Paris in three weeks, and insists upon my going to England with him."

Mr. Courteney read the letter with great pleasure. Mr. Damer addressed her in it by the tender name of daughter; and assured her, that he would in every respect act like a father towards her. He praised her conduct in terms of the highest admiration, and begged her not to be uneasy at her aunt's desertion of her; since it was in his power to make her easy, and he was resolved to do so.

"This letter," said Mr. Courteney, after a pause, "will make some little alteration in my plan: I had resolved not to take any notice to the marquis, that I had discovered you to be my sister, but to make some excuse for your disappearing; however I see it will be necessary to wait for Mr. Damer. I congratulate you, my dear Henrietta, on the friendship of so worthy a man."

"But will you stay till he comes to Paris?" interrupted the tender, anxious Henrietta.

"May I depend upon your prudence, sister?" said Mr. Courteney. "It is possible the marquis may talk to you of love: if you give him the least encouragement, you will forfeit my esteem for ever; it shall never be said, that I took advantage of his youth to draw him into a marriage with my sister."

"Oh! do not suspect me of such meanness," said Henrietta, blushing: "if the marquis was a thousand times more amiable than he is, and were I ever so much prejudiced in his favour, I have too just a sense of what I owe to my birth, to your honour, and my own, to admit of a clandestine address—You may be entirely easy upon this article."

"I am satisfied," replied Mr. Courteney, tenderly pressing her hand; "and now, my dear Henrietta, adieu for this evening."

"Don't fail to come, to-morrow," said she, following him to the door. He smiled assentingly; and having taken leave of Mrs. Knight, who met him as he was going in search of her, he hurried home to his pupil, by whom he was expected with extreme impatience.

Chap. VI.

Farther continuation of the history.

The marquis, as soon as he entered his chamber, perceived that something extraordinary had happened to him.

"Sure, (said he, smiling) you have met with some strange adventure, Freeman; you look pleased, and yet there is a thoughtful air in your countenance."

"I have had an adventure indeed," replied Mr. Courteney (entering abruptly into an affair which could not be concealed from him) "I have met with my sister here in Paris."

"Your sister!" repeated the marquis; "you did not expect her, did you?"

"No, faith," replied Mr. Courteney; "nor did I know her when I saw her."

"That is not surprising," said the marquis; "she was very young when you parted, I have heard you say: I hope you will allow me to pay my respects to her; but (added he, impatiently) how does miss Belmour and her fair friend?"

"Her fair friend, as you are pleased to call her (replied Mr. Courteney) is my sister, whom for so many weeks I have seen almost every day without knowing her."

"Is it possible! (cried the marquis, surprised) miss Benson your sister! Sure you are not in earnest."

"Indeed I am (said Mr. Courteney) I discovered her by the oddest accident: miss Belmour herself did not know who she was; but while I was there, she brought her a letter, which had been inclosed to her; it was directed for miss Courteney, and came from Mr. Damer, my sister's guardian: she owned the name, and by that means I found out my sister. I see you are astonished (added Mr. Courteney) poor Henrietta has told me all her story; the repetition would be tedious, but——"

"How can you think so?" interrupted the marquis, eagerly: "can you doubt that I am extremely interested in every thing that concerns you."

"Excuse me, my dear marquis (said Mr. Courteney) I really cannot enter into particulars just now—Fortune still persecutes my dear father in his children. I thought my sister was happily settled with her aunt lady Meadows, who has no child, and adopted her; but the old lady, being a rigid Roman catholic, pressed her very much to change her religion, and was at last so strangely influenced by an artful priest, who is her chaplain, that she had formed a design to send my sister under the conduct of this fellow, to be shut up in a nunnery. The poor girl, who was, as I can collect by her account, extremely apprehensive of being so entirely in the power of this sly priest, had no way to avoid this misfortune, but by leaving her aunt privately, who absolutely refused to be reconciled to her on any other condition than her changing her religion. Thus deserted, her guardian being abroad, and having nothing to expect from her relations, she chose to go to service, and was recommended to miss Belmour, by the countess of ——, her kinswoman."

"What a wretch must your uncle be!" said the marquis, with tears in his eyes, "to permit such excellence——" He stopped a moment; then suddenly grasping his hand, "O my dear Freeman (pursued he) you have it in your power to make me happy—You know how ardently I love your charming sister——"

"This I was apprehensive of," interrupted Mr. Courteney. "I beg, my lord, that you will banish these thoughts."

"What!" cried the marquis, hastily; "have you any objection to my passion for your sister?"

"Indeed I have, and a very strong one," replied Mr. Courteney, "and that is the certainty of the duke your father's disapprobation of it."

"It is possible indeed," said the marquis, after a little pause, "that in the choice of a wife for me, my father will be influenced by the same motives that most fathers are: he will expect a large fortune with the person I marry; therefore, my dear Charles, you see the necessity there is for not consulting him in this case."

"Sure you forget, my lord," interrupted Mr. Courteney, coolly, "what you once declared, that you would never enter into an engagement of this kind, contrary to the duke's inclinations."

"I remember I said so (replied the marquis); and were I to make a choice which he could reasonably object to, certainly it would be wrong, very wrong to disobey him: but if the want of a fortune can make my father disapprove of my affection for a young lady of miss Courteney's birth and merit, must I be governed by such sordid motives?"

The marquis went on to prove, by a great many arguments common enough on such occasions, that in the article of marriage, a parent had no right to lay any restraint upon the inclinations of his child. Mr. Courteney did not think proper to enter into a dispute with him upon this subject: the patience with which he listened to him, made the young nobleman conclude he was not unwilling to come into his measures.

"My dear Charles (added he, after a short pause) will you not be my advocate with your charming sister? I die with impatience to throw myself at her feet, and offer her my heart and hand."

"You cannot doubt, my lord (said Mr. Courteney) but that I think my sister highly honoured by the esteem you express for her; but she would be very unworthy of it, if she was capable of admitting your addresses, either unknown to your father, or in opposition to his will. I may venture to answer for her, that she will not, by so unjustifiable a conduct, expose her brother to censure: and it gives me great concern to find you are no better acquainted with my sentiments, than to imagine I will so basely betray the trust the duke has reposed in me, and be accessary to your disposing of yourself in a manner which I am very sure he will not approve."

"Then I am to expect nothing from your friendship on this occasion, Mr. Courteney!" replied the marquis, with an air of displeasure: "you are determined to raise difficulties to my design, instead of removing them; is this acting like a man whom I have loved like a brother, and whom it would be my highest happiness to call so."

"To call you brother with your father's consent, my lord (said Mr. Courteney) is an honour I cannot hope for, and which without it I do not wish."

"As noble and disinterested as you imagine this conduct to be (said the marquis, rising) it will have another name perhaps with persons less romantic in their notions than you are. However, sir, you are no more than the brother of miss Courteney; if I am happy enough to prevail with her to receive my addresses, I shall not think your consent necessary." He passed by him with a cool bow, as he pronounced these words, and retired to his own chamber.

CHAP. VII.

In which we are afraid some of our readers will think Mr. Courteney
acts a very silly part.

Mr. Courteney saw plainly, that by refusing to comply with his pupil's desires, he should entirely lose his friendship, but in a case where his honour was so greatly concerned, this consideration had no weight with him: and although he had a high opinion of his sister's candor and integrity, yet the intimation miss Belmour had given him of her regard for Mr. Melvil, made him apprehensive that she might be prevailed upon to listen to the vows of the marquis of ———. He resolved therefore to keep the place of her abode a secret (for he knew he could depend upon the prudence of Mr. Knight and his wife) and to use his utmost endeavours to hasten the young lord's departure from France.

The marquis, mean time, was forming very different designs. It is so rare a thing for a man in love to be either reasonable or just, on occasions where the interest of his passion is concerned, that it is not surprising the marquis should impute his governor's conduct with regard to his sister to peevishness and caprice, and think himself extremely ill used by his not accepting his offers. He conceived miss Courteney to be equally injured by the opposition her brother made to the advancement of her fortune; and flattering himself that, if his person was not disagreeable to her, he should soon overcome any scruples Mr. Courteney might have suggested on account of the duke his father's disapprobation, he determined to consult him no further in the affair, but to address himself directly to her.

He spent part of the night in writing a letter to her, in which he declared his passion in the most tender and respectful terms, and begged she would allow him to wait upon her. The remaining hours were not spent in sleep, but in impatient longings for the morning, which was to confirm or destroy his hopes. As soon as it was light, he rose and walked about his room. He read over the letter he had written; he thought it but poorly expressed the ardor of his love: he sat down and wrote another, which he liked still less, and had recourse again to the first, after adding a postscript, in which he earnestly repeated his request to be indulged with a few moments private discourse with her.

He sealed up his letter, and directed it for miss Courteney. Her brother had not mentioned to him his having removed her from miss Belmour: he supposed she was still with her; but a doubt occurring to him, whether she was willing to assume her real name yet, he thought it best to put it in another cover, superscribed for miss Benson.

It was still too early to send to a lady's lodgings; he counted the hours with anxious impatience, and at length rung his bell for his servant. As soon as he appeared, he gave him the letter, recommending secrecy, and charging him not to return without an answer.

The valet, when he came back, brought him word that miss Benson was gone; and this was all the intelligence he could get. Miss Belmour's woman indeed had added with a sneer, that she went off with Mr. Freeman, and it was strange that his friend Mr. Melvil should not know where she was. This part of the message the fellow prudently suppressed; for he judged the business to be an amour, and that the young gentlemen were rivals, and he was afraid of making mischief.

The marquis, however, easily guessed that this sudden removal of miss Courteney was her brother's act: he dismissed his servant; and beginning now to be sensible how much it was in his governor's power to traverse his designs, and how obstinately he was bent upon doing so, he resigned himself up to the most violent transports of rage; and, during a few moments, all his thoughts ran upon revenge.

Mr. Courteney came into his chamber while he was under these agitations; and, seeing him walking about with a furious pace, "For Heaven's sake, my lord (said he) what is the matter with you?"

The marquis turned short upon him, and, with a voice broken with passion, exclaimed, "May I perish, Courteney, if I forgive you."

Mr. Courteney, who supposed this resentment was the consequence of their conversation the night before, replied calmly, "You are angry, my lord—This is no time to talk."

He was going out of the room, but the marquis, hastily stepping between him and the door, shut it with great violence.

"If it is not your time to talk, sir, it is mine," said he.

"Very well, my lord," replied Mr. Courteney, with a composed look and accent, "I am ready to hear you."

The young nobleman continued to walk in a sullen silence, as if resolved to be angry, and knew not well what cause to assign for it; when suddenly stopping,

"I insist upon your telling me, sir (said he) why you have secreted your sister? Do you suspect I have dishonourable designs upon her?"

"Dishonourable designs upon my sister!" repeated Mr. Courteney, kindling at the expression: "my lord, no man, while I have life, shall incur such a suspicion with impunity."

"This spirit becomes one of your birth," replied the marquis; "but let me tell you, Mr. Courteney, your conduct is not altogether consistent; why must your sister be hurried, no body knows whither, and concealed with such wonderful caution?"

"Are you sure this is the case, my lord?" said Mr. Courteney.

"Yes, very sure," answered the marquis, hastily.

"Since it was not I who gave your lordship this information," resumed Mr. Courteney, "you must have taken some trouble to come to the knowledge of it; and the motive that set you upon these enquiries sufficiently justifies my caution with regard to my sister."

"Then I am not worthy, it seems, to pay my addresses to your sister," said the marquis, peevishly.

"Indeed, my lord, this is a very childish speech," replied Mr. Courteney; "you know your addresses would do honour to any woman: but the depressed state of my sister's fortune leaves her no right to expect a man of your quality for a husband; and she has too just a pride to submit to make a clandestine marriage; nor will I be branded with the imputation of having seduced my pupil into a marriage with my sister."

"What have you to do with the affair at all?" replied the marquis, eagerly: "leave miss Courteney to act as she thinks proper; you need not make yourself answerable for my conduct on this occasion: I loved her before I knew her to be your sister; cannot your romantic honour satisfy itself with being passive in this business?"

"I should but ill perform my engagements to your father, my lord," interrupted Mr. Courteney, "if I did not use my utmost endeavours to prevent you from displeasing him in a matter of so great importance as your marriage."

"How are you sure my father will be displeased?" said the marquis; "miss Courteney's merit will justify my choice."

"Put it upon that issue," replied Mr. Courteney; "ask his consent."

"Well, sir, I will ask his consent," resumed the marquis; "and now am I at liberty to visit your sister?"

"If you intend, my lord, to be governed by the duke's advice (said Mr. Courteney) you will certainly be contented to wait his answer; and you cannot suppose, that knowing your sentiments so well as I do, I will permit my sister to receive your visits while we are ignorant of the duke's intentions."

The marquis lost all patience at this unreasonable obstinacy, as he conceived it. "I renounce your friendship from this moment (said he) for ever; and, had you not a sister, I would resent this behaviour in another manner."

He flung out of the room when he had said this; and, shutting himself up in his study, gave his valet orders to allow no body to disturb him.

Mr. Courteney was not so much offended at the harshness of his language, as to hinder him from feeling great concern for the uneasy state of his mind; and, notwithstanding his own temper was vehement enough, yet he was able to make some allowances for the transports of a young man, who saw himself so resolutely opposed in a point he had set his heart upon: but despairing to pacify his pupil without entering into his design, he determined to place his sister effectually out of his reach; and then, if he could not prevail upon him to return to England, nothing remained but to make the duke his father acquainted with the whole affair.

He waited some time in expectation that the marquis would come down to breakfast as usual; but, finding that he had ordered his chocolate to be brought to him in his study, he went to visit his sister, as he had promised.

The marquis heard him, as he passed by his door, call for his hat and sword; and, his valet entering a moment afterwards with the chocolate, he asked him, if Mr. Freeman was gone out! Being answered that he was, it suddenly came into his head, that he was going to see his sister.

"Follow him instantly (said he to the fellow) and bring me word to what place he goes, and here is something to purchase your secrecy and diligence."

The sight of five Louis d'ors, which the marquis gave him, left the valet no inclination to be discreet any longer. He ran out of the room with officious haste, fully determined to execute his commission with the utmost exactness. When he got into the street, he perceived Mr. Courteney walking leisurely on: he followed him at a distance, took particular notice of the house he entered; and, after waiting a few moments to see whether he came out again, he went back to the marquis with his intelligence.

The young lover did not doubt but he had discovered his mistress's abode; and in the joy this thought gave him, he bestowed many praises on his valet's ingenuity, together with a reward of five Louis d'ors more, which he liked still better. He then ordered him to give directions for his chariot to be got ready, while he assisted him to dress. His looks discovered such an excess of satisfaction, that the valet, under no apprehensions that what he had done would produce any disagreeable consequences, entered with vast delight upon his new post of confidant to his master. The marquis ordered him to stay at home till Mr. Freeman came in, and then immediately to come to him at the Hotel de ——.

Chap. VIII.

In which Mr. Courteney gives more instances of his folly.

While Henrietta thus innocently sowed the seeds of discord between the two friends, she herself enjoyed a perfect composure of mind, and indulged the most pleasing reflections on the happy change of her fortune.

She was no longer in the humiliating condition of a servant; or, what to her was far more mortifying, a dependant upon the bounty of another; an unknown wanderer, without friends or protectors. She was now under the care of a brother, whom she tenderly loved, whose merit could not fail of distinguishing him, and of forcing that respect and consideration due to a noble birth, and which he, though in a deprest fortune, so nobly supported.

She was assured that her guardian was not only free from any unfavourable prejudices on account of her aunt's desertion of her, but that she might expect all the tender offices of a parent from him; and, what afforded the nice sensibility of her soul a more delicate satisfaction than all this, the only man in the world whom she was capable of regarding, with a preference to the rest of his sex, though, in so elevated a rank, had loved her in indigence and obscurity with honour, and justified the tender sentiments she entertained for him.

Her smiles, when she saw her brother appear, and the gaiety of her behaviour, convinced him, her mind was at ease; but his features still retained that impression of chagrin he had so lately felt from the marquis's causeless rage; and there was a solemnity in his manner, that, in an instant, changed the innocent chearfulness of Henrietta into anxiety and concern.

The presence of Mrs. Knight was a restraint upon them both. She perceived it; and as soon as the tea-table was removed (for the ladies were at breakfast when Mr. Courteney came in) she retired and left them at liberty.

The moment she was gone, Henrietta eagerly asked him, if any thing had happened to give him uneasiness since she saw him?

"Yes (replied he abruptly) the marquis and I have quarrelled."

"Quarrelled!" repeated Henrietta, trembling and pale as death, "have you quarrelled?"

Mr. Courteney, who observed her emotion, continued to look at her so earnestly that she blushed and cast down her eyes. "You seem greatly affected with this accident (said he at last) I wish I had not mentioned it to you."

"Could you suppose," said Henrietta, in an accent which had at least as much of grief as tenderness in it, "that I could hear with indifference what must necessarily be very afflicting to you?"

"Your indifference, perhaps, on this occasion (said Mr. Courteney) would be more welcome to me than the concern I see you under."

Henrietta having pondered a little on the meaning of these words, replied in a firmer tone, "place some confidence in me, brother, you will find I shall deserve it."

"My dear Henrietta," resumed Mr. Courteney, affected with the manner in which she spoke, and her expressive look, "you ought to forgive my doubts, when you reflect on what miss Belmour told me; the merit of my noble pupil has made an impression on your heart; but your marriage with him, sister, will bring everlasting infamy upon me."

"Have I not already declared my resolution to you upon this head?" replied Henrietta.

"The marquis loves you," resumed Mr. Courteney: "he is rash and inconsiderate; he has no hope (and indeed it would be strange if he had) that the duke his father will consent to such an unequal match; yet he presses me to introduce him to you as a lover, and to favour his designs of marrying you privately. You may easily imagine what answer I gave him; the consequence is, that he has declared himself my enemy. We are upon very bad terms. But this is not my greatest concern: the marquis, if he can get access to you, will teaze you with solicitations; and, disposed as you are in his favour, have I not cause to apprehend you will listen to him but too readily?"

"Although I should confirm your suspicions," said Henrietta, with tears in her eyes, "yet I must again repeat I am grieved at this difference between your pupil and you. Nay I will own," pursued she, avoiding with a sweet bashfulness the earnest looks of her brother, "that I am not insensible of this young nobleman's affection for me; but, after this candid confession, you ought to believe me, when I assure you, that I will enter into no engagement with him without your approbation; and to make you easy, I will comply with any measures you think proper, to avoid his pursuits."

"I see I may rely upon you," said Mr. Courteney, charmed with her amiable frankness; "but, my dear Henrietta, I hope you will not allow this prepossession to take too deep root in your heart: sure your good sense and the delicacy of your sentiments, will hinder you from giving way to a hopeless passion."

"I beg you not to talk to me on this subject," interrupted Henrietta, tears, in spite of her endeavours to restrain them, flowing fast down her face; "only tell me what you would have me do to avoid the marquis: have you formed any plan? Doubt not of my readiness to comply with it."

"Have you any objections to boarding in a convent till Mr. Damer comes?" said Mr. Courteney.

"No (replied Henrietta, half smiling) for I cannot suspect you have a design upon my religion, as my aunt had, and mean to confine me all my life."

"No, really," resumed Mr. Courteney, smiling likewise; "but it will be more difficult for the marquis to get access to you in a convent than here; and as it is probable enough that this affair will make some noise, it will be more for your reputation to have it known that you lived in such a respectable society, where there were so many witnesses of your conduct, and such exact regularity required, than in private lodgings, where you were accountable to no body for your actions."

"Then you intend to leave me before Mr. Damer comes?" said Henrietta, sighing.

"To be sure (replied Mr. Courteney) I will force the marquis away if possible; and if I find all my remonstrances ineffectual, the duke must interpose his authority."

"You intend to write to him then?" said Henrietta.

"Certainly (replied he) don't you think I ought to do so, sister?"

"Indeed I do," answered she.

"I am glad of it (resumed Mr. Courteney) yet this procedure will embroil me more with the marquis; but I see no help for it, unless Mr. Damer should happen to come sooner than we expect, and take you with him to England. I hope to prevail upon my pupil to leave Paris in two or three days; and if I have not the satisfaction to leave you under Mr. Damer's care, a convent is the fittest place for you to retire to."

Henrietta, having reflected on her brother's proposal, found it so reasonable, and so much to the advantage of her reputation, that she readily yielded to put it in immediate execution.

Mrs. Knight being desired to return, Mr. Courteney told her their design, and requested her assistance. She expressed some concern at being so soon to lose her agreeable guest, but undertook to transact the affair; and it was resolved that she should go that day, and procure the young lady to be admitted as a pensioner in the Augustine nunnery of English ladies in Paris.

Mr. Courteney, having promised his sister to come and conduct her to the convent the next day, took leave of her, highly satisfied with her docility, and returned home. He was surprised to hear that the marquis was gone abroad; but having no suspicion of his intention to visit Henrietta, whose abode he concluded was still a secret to him, he was only concerned lest his health should suffer, by venturing out before it was fully re-established.

The marquis's valet no sooner saw Mr. Courteney return, than he ran immediately to acquaint his master, who set forwards, with a beating heart, to visit his mistress. The valet had given so exact a direction, that the coachman had no difficulty to find the house. The marquis alighted the moment the door was opened, and asking the servant for miss Courteney, was instantly introduced into a parlour, where Henrietta was sitting alone, Mrs. Knight having just left her to go and execute her commission.

The sight of the marquis threw her into the utmost confusion. She rose, however, and received him with great respect: he approached her bowing, and made her a genteel compliment upon her happy meeting with her brother.

Henrietta would not suffer this subject to be dwelt upon long, lest it should lead to circumstances too interesting. She changed the conversation to indifferent matters, and took care that it should not flag a moment; so that the marquis, partly embarrassed by that awe which always accompanies a sincere passion, and partly by the prudent management of Henrietta, found he had protracted his visit to a considerable length, without drawing any advantage from it.

Alarmed at the thoughts of losing an opportunity, which the rigid and inflexible temper of his governor might prevent him from meeting with again, he suddenly assumed courage to make her a declaration of his passion, but in terms the most tender and respectful, and with an explicitness that became one of his rank and fortune, to use towards a young lady in her delicate circumstances, whom he would not for a moment leave in doubt of the sincerity of his professions, and his firm resolution to adhere to them.

Henrietta listened to him with a graceful modesty; and when he earnestly pressed for her answer, she assured him, that she was very sensible of the honour he did her, and should always think herself obliged to him for having entertained such favourable sentiments of her, as could make him overlook the inequality there was between them. As for the rest, she referred him to her brother, who, she said, was in the place of a father to her, and by whose advice and direction she was determined to be governed entirely.

The marquis would have had no reason to be dissatisfied with this answer, if he had not known that he had nothing to expect from an application to her brother; and the apprehension that she also knew it, and therefore took this method to free herself from his importunities, gave him so much concern, that he turned pale, and sighing, fixed his eyes upon the ground. His air, his attitude, his looks, were all so moving, so expressive of tenderness, anxiety, and grief, that Henrietta durst not trust herself to behold him, lest he should turn his eyes towards her, and discover in her's the too great interest she took in his uneasiness.

Some moments passed in an affecting silence on both sides, during which the marquis remained immoveably fixed in the same pensive posture, till rouzed by the opening of the door, and the appearance of Mr. Courteney. Henrietta's face was in an instant covered with blushes: the marquis seemed greatly embarrassed. Mr. Courteney shewed some surprise at first; but, recovering himself, he spoke to his pupil with an easy air, and relieved both him and his sister from their confusion, by entering immediately into an indifferent conversation.

The marquis drew a favourable omen from this behaviour: his looks resumed their usual sweetness and vivacity; and, during a whole hour that they continued together, nothing could be more spirited and lively than the discourse between three persons, who had the most perfect tenderness for one another, yet, from their several circumstances, were obliged mutually to oppose and give pain.

The marquis at length, with apparent reluctance, put an end to his visit, as did Mr. Courteney likewise, though he was very desirous of talking to his sister in private. When they were in the chariot together, the young lord was several times upon the point of pressing his governor again upon the subject of his love, as he seemed to be less inclined than formerly to oppose him; but he was restrained from entering into any explanation, by his apprehension of destroying those hopes he had so lately begun to entertain, and of rendering his access to Henrietta more difficult for the future: Mr. Courteney also had his reasons for preventing any such explanation, and industriously amused him with other discourse.

The marquis could not help thinking it strange that he took no notice of the visit he had made his sister: but as love is ever ready to flatter its own wishes, he began to imagine that Mr. Courteney had relaxed in the severity of his resolutions, but knew not yet how to yield with a good grace; he favoured his embarrassment therefore for the present, and they passed the remaining part of the day in their usual company and diversions.

When they came home at night, the marquis desired to have an hour's conversation with him; but Mr. Courteney, complaining of a sudden head-ach, excused himself, and retired to his own chamber.

The next morning, before his pupil was up, he repaired to Mrs. Knight's. She told him, that every thing was agreed on for the reception of the young lady; and he had the satisfaction to find his sister making preparations for her removal, without any appearance of discontent. She acquainted him with what had passed in the conversation between the marquis and her.

"I have no doubt of his affection for you," said Mr. Courteney; "we must leave the event of it to Providence, and act so as that whatever happens, we may not incur censure."

As soon as breakfast was over, Henrietta, accompanied by Mrs. Knight and her brother, went in a coach to the convent, where she was very civilly received by the superiour. Mr. Courteney promised to visit her soon, and took leave of her, to wait upon Mrs. Knight home; after which he returned to the marquis, who had enquired for him several times.

Chap. IX.

In which the reader, it is presumed, can make no discoveries concerning the event of this history.

The marquis, when he saw him enter his chamber, approached him with an obliging air, and affectionately pressing his hand,

"May I hope, my dear Courteney (said he) that you have overcome your fantastic scruples, and that you will favour my pretensions to your charming sister. I will make you no apology for stealing a visit to her; you would, I am sure, have done the same in my situation. Indeed, Charles, you must either resolve to give me miss Courteney, or to see me miserable. She referred me to you; my happiness depends upon a single word of your's: can you be so cruel to refuse me this instance of your friendship?"

"You know, my lord," replied Mr. Courteney, "that there is not any thing you can desire of me, consistent with my honour, which I would refuse; but, unless I would make myself infamous, I cannot yield to your marrying my sister without the duke's consent. Hear what I have to propose," continued he, perceiving him to be in a violent emotion; "let us return to England immediately. You have often told me, that the duke is a most tender father; you are an only child: it is possible he may be prevailed upon to yield to your desires, if you tell him you cannot be happy without my sister. Let us make the trial at least."

"I agree to it," interrupted the marquis, eagerly, "provided you will promise me, that if my father is so unreasonable as to refuse his consent, you will no longer oppose my marriage. I am of age; it is fit that, in a matter of such importance to the future happiness of my whole life, I should be at liberty to follow my inclinations. Speak, Charles, will you make me this promise?"

"Indeed, I will not, my lord," replied Mr. Courteney, "you must not expect it."

"Detested obstinacy!" cried the marquis, flinging his hand away, which he had held till this moment, "what a wretch am I to have my happiness depend upon the will of a capricious man, who mistakes his romantic whims for honour! But observe what I say, Courteney," added he, turning hastily towards him, "you shall not hinder me from visiting your sister; nothing but her absolute commands shall prevent my seeing her."

"My sister (said Mr. Courteney) will stay no longer in France, than till Mr. Damer (to whose care her mother left her at her death) returns from Montpelier: he is to conduct her to England; and she is gone to board in a convent till his arrival."

"Gone to a convent!" repeated the marquis; "this is your scheme, I suppose."

"I hoped to prevail upon you," said Mr. Courteney, "since you are quite recovered, to leave Paris immediately; and I thought a convent the properest place for my sister to reside in till her guardian comes."

The marquis instantly running over in his thoughts the use that might be made of this intelligence, replied, that he had no inclination to leave Paris yet; and broke off all farther conversation by quitting the room.

In effect, he had resolved to make an application to Mr. Damer, supposing, that since he had not the same foundation for scruples as his governor, he would readily listen to an offer so advantageous for his ward.

Mr. Courteney penetrated into his views, and doubtful how Mr. Damer would act, and whether his sister, having the sanction of his approbation, might not give way to the motions of her own heart, and encourage the addresses of the marquis; he concluded it necessary to make the duke acquainted with the whole affair, that he might take such measures as he judged proper to restrain his son from an action which would incur his displeasure.

He wrote accordingly that day, and having thus discharged his duty, his mind was more at ease.

The marquis, full of hope that his new scheme would be successful, made no effort to see Henrietta, for fear of raising suspicions in her brother: but the coldness and reserve with which he treated him, sufficiently shewed how much he resented his conduct.

Henrietta was soon reconciled to a retirement, in which she had full liberty to indulge her reflections; for she was in love enough to find more satisfaction in being alone, than in the gayest and most agreeable society. Her brother did not fail to visit her every day: he found her satisfied with her situation; and, in appearance, no otherwise affected with his approaching departure, which he gave her room to expect, than what her tenderness for him might well allow of.

In the mean time the duke of ——, having received Mr. Courteney's letter, was greatly pleased with the nobleness and generosity of his behaviour. He wrote to him immediately, in terms of the highest friendship and regard; and, acquainting him with the purport of his letter to his son, recommended it to him to hasten his departure, assuring him, he had the firmest reliance upon his integrity and honour.

The packet, to avoid suspicion, had been directed as usual to the marquis, who was not surprised to find a letter in it for Mr. Courteney, to whom his father was accustomed to write often: he sent it to him immediately; and, after reading his own, he went to Mr. Courteney's chamber, holding it still in his hand.

"My father writes to me (said he) to leave Paris as soon as possible. He does not expressly say that he is ill; but, from some hints in his letter, I can collect that this is the cause of his extreme earnestness to see me. You cannot imagine how much I am affected with this accident (pursued he, sighing). I love my father: I did not know how much I loved him, till I feared his loss. I am determined to set out to-morrow from Paris; but I must see your sister first, Courteney, nor ought you to refuse me the satisfaction of telling her, that I depart with a firm resolution never to be but her's."

"Well, my lord," replied Mr. Courteney, after a little pause, "we will go together, and take leave of my sister."

"I was to blame (said the marquis) to expect any indulgence from you; we will go together then, since it must be so." He retired again to his own apartment to write to his father; and in the mean time Mr. Courteney gave the necessary orders for their journey the next morning.

Henrietta had been prepared by a billet from her brother, for the visit that was intended her. The news of their departure had cost her some tears; but when she was informed they waited for her in the parlour of the convent, she appeared before them with all that soft composure and dignity of manners, which never forsook her in the most trying situations.

Mr. Courteney watched the turn of her countenance when the marquis accosted her, and was pleased to see it equally free from embarrassment and affectation; and that, notwithstanding all the expressive language of her lover's eyes, she had so much command over herself, as to seem the least interested person in the company.

Politeness obliged the marquis to shorten his visit, that the brother and sister might be at liberty to take a private leave of each other. He rose from his seat, and approached Henrietta, with an air that left her no room to doubt of his intention to say something particular to her; and now, for the first time, her looks betrayed some little confusion.

"I cannot go away, madam (said he) without renewing the declaration I made you some days ago; and I take this opportunity to assure you, before your brother, who knows the sincerity of my heart, that my sentiments for you will ever be the same: and, if you do not forbid it, I will carry away with me the dear hope of being able one day to merit your esteem."

Henrietta courtesied in silence; but her blushes, and the soft confusion she was in, seemed no unfavourable omen for the marquis: he bowed respectfully, and retired.

Mr. Courteney, affecting not to perceive his sister's concern, entered immediately after his pupil's departure into other discourse. He recommended it to her to improve her guardian's esteem for her, and assured her he would visit lady Meadows, and use his utmost endeavours to remove her prejudices, and restore her to the place she formerly held in her affection: at her desire likewise he promised to call upon Mrs. Willis, to whom she had been so greatly obliged. He charged her to keep up no sort of intimacy with miss Belmour, though she should seek it, but permitted her, in company with Mr. Damer, to pay her a farewel visit; and, indeed, the conduct of that young lady, since the arrival of Mr. Morley, justified these precautions.

Henrietta promised to follow all his directions. He said a thousand affectionate things to her; and then, desiring to see the superiour, he tenderly recommended his sister to her care; took a short leave, and went home; while Henrietta retired to her chamber to weep.

The marquis was not visible till the next morning, when he was informed that the post-chaise was at the door. His extreme melancholy during the whole journey, gave his governor great concern: but he in vain attempted to amuse him; for though the marquis behaved to him with all imaginable respect, yet he was so cold and reserved, that he found it impossible to renew his former freedom with him.

The duke of —— had informed them, that he should be at his country-seat; and, immediately upon their landing in England, they repaired thither: the duke received his son with the most tender transports, and his governor with every mark of esteem and regard.

The morning after their arrival, he sent for Mr. Courteney into his closet, and thanked him in very affectionate terms for having so faithfully and honourably discharged his trust. He politely avoided mentioning the affair of the young lord's passion for his sister, because she was his sister; but said enough to convince him, that he had the most grateful sense of his disinterested conduct upon that occasion. He settled on him, during his life, the sum he had allowed him while he travelled with the marquis; and offered him, in the most cordial manner, all his interest towards procuring him an establishment suitable to his birth.

Mr. Courteney received these instances of the duke's friendship for him with respect and gratitude; but he was more touched with the old nobleman's delicacy with regard to his sister, than with all the favours conferred on himself.

The interest of this sister, whom he loved with the most tender affection, made him hasten his departure from the duke's seat, that he might wait on his aunt, who he had heard was in London. The duke embraced him tenderly at parting, and obliged him to promise that he would return as soon as possible. The marquis lost all his reserve and coldness, when he took leave of his governor, his friend, and, what was more than all, the brother of his adored Henrietta.

"You have used me unkindly," said he in a low voice; yet pressing him tenderly to his breast, "but I shall always love you."

Mr. Courteney let fall some tears, but made no answer; and immediately after mounting his horse, he set out for London, attended by his own servant, and one of the duke's, whom his grace had ordered to escort him.

Chap. X.

Which leaves the reader still in doubt.

Mr. Courteney, when he came within a short distance of London, dismissed the duke's servant, with compliments to his grace and the marquis, and proceeded on his journey. It came into his head to alight at the house of Mrs. Willis, from whom it was possible he might receive some intelligence that would be of use to him. The good woman received him with great civility; but, when he told her his name, she was in transports, and enquired for her beloved miss Courteney with the tender anxiety of a mother.

Mr. Courteney told her, that his sister would soon be in London with her guardian. He took occasion to thank her for her friendly care of her, which Henrietta had mentioned with the utmost gratitude; and assured her, he should always consider himself as highly obliged to her.

"How largely do I share in my dear miss Courteney's joy (said she) for so happy a meeting with her beloved brother! Heaven will, I doubt not, shower its blessings on her; for sure if ever mortal deserved them she does. O! sir, your sister is an angelic creature—"

Mrs. Willis, indulging the tender effusions of her heart, continued to expatiate on Henrietta's virtues, till Mr. Courteney, though not displeased to hear her, interrupted her, to ask some questions concerning his aunt.

"I was going to write to miss Courteney today sir (replied she) for I have great news to acquaint her with: that vile priest, who was the cause of all her uneasiness, has at length shewn himself in his true colours. The sanctified hypocrite was detected in an amour with lady Meadows's woman: this affair has opened her eyes; she thinks her niece has been greatly injured by the mis-representations of this wretch, whom she has discarded with infamy; and the first proof she has given of her favourable disposition towards miss Courteney, was her taking again her former woman, whom she had dismissed on account of her attachment to the young lady. I had this intelligence from Mrs. White herself; for so your aunt's woman, sir, is called. She says she does not doubt but her lady will write to miss Courteney in the most tender manner, and invite her home again."

This news gave Mr. Courteney great satisfaction: he resolved not to delay a moment visiting his aunt; his portmanteau had been carried into a chamber, by Mrs. Willis's directions, and thither he retired to dress. As soon as he was ready, he got into a hackney-coach, and fraught with a thousand kind wishes from this faithful friend of his sister, he proceeded to the house of lady Meadows.

He was so lucky as to find her at home, and sent in his name without any hesitation. The old lady, in a violent flutter of spirits, advanced as far as the door of her apartment to meet her nephew. His graceful form and polite address prejudiced her instantly in his favour; and she received him with all the tenderness he could have wished, and with much more than he expected.

Her first enquiries were for Henrietta. Mr. Courteney was pleased with this solicitude; but he observed that, during the course of their conversation, her attention with regard to his sister, decreased considerably. He praised her with all the modesty, yet with all the affection of a brother.

Lady Meadows, who had heard a very advantageous account of her niece from the countess, her good friend, assured him that she knew his sister's merit, and had restored her to that tenderness and esteem, which some little errors of her's, and some unjust suspicions of her own, which had been artfully infused into her, had robbed her of. She expressed great satisfaction at hearing of her guardian's kindness: but her words, "I hope he will do something for her," gave Mr. Courteney great concern; who, from the first moment that he had heard Henrietta was likely to recover her favour, had formed a scheme to make her and the marquis happy.

Lady Meadows perceived that he was affected with that expression: she therefore added, that his sister might depend upon a welcome reception from her, whenever she returned to England.

Though there was nothing to object to the words of this declaration, yet there was a great deal to the manner of it. In the coldness with which she made it, he saw the disappointment of his hopes. In reality, lady Meadows had begun to entertain a prodigious fondness for her nephew; and Henrietta had now but the second place in her affection. The longer she conversed with him, the more this fondness increased. Women are ever readier to discover merit in the other sex than their own. Henrietta had as many amiable qualities as her brother; but lady Meadows was not so sensible of them: and Mr. Courteney made as great a progress in her affections in three hours, as his sister had done in as many months.

When he rose up to take his leave, she declared with some vehemence, that he must have no other home than her house. "You have an aunt (added she, smiling) tho' you have no uncle, nor any other relations." Mr. Courteney reddened with indignation at the mention of his unworthy uncle; but, recovering himself, he made her suitable acknowledgments for her kindness, and, at her desire, immediately dispatched a messenger to Mrs. Willis, to acquaint her that he should not return, and at the same time sent orders to his servant to bring his portmanteau.

Lady Meadows having given directions for an apartment to be prepared for Mr. Courteney, they passed the evening together with great satisfaction, particularly on the part of the old lady, who thought herself extremely happy in having so accomplished a youth for her nephew. All her thoughts ran upon the pleasure she should have in shewing him to her friends and acquaintance, and of piquing his unnatural uncle, by openly professing her regard for him.

More than a week after his arrival was spent in a continual succession of visits, to all which he attended her; and so absolutely had he won her heart in that time, that she determined on nothing less than the making him her sole heir. Mr. Courteney, who was desirous of improving the favour he was in to his sister's advantage, took all opportunities to revive his aunt's affection for her; so that to please him, she expressed an impatience to see her. He received letters from her, and from the duke of ——, the same day. Henrietta informed him, that she had heard from Mr. Damer, and that she expected him in Paris in a few days: that the affairs he had to settle there, would detain him but a short time; after which they were to set out immediately for England. She added, that the marquis had wrote to her, and gave him a brief recapitulation of his letter, which seemed to be dictated by the most ardent affection, and the strictest principles of honour.

The duke's letter contained only an earnest request to see him as soon as possible. Lady Meadows was very unwilling to part with him, though he assured her, he would return in two or three days. He spent part of the night in answering his sister's letter, and set out the next morning in a post-chaise for the duke's seat: he reached it in the evening at supper time.

He found only the duke and his son at table; in the countenance of the latter, he observed a profound melancholy, which sensibly affected him. The duke received him with great kindness. The marquis spoke little, but seemed pleased to see him. The next morning the duke sent for Mr. Courteney into his closet.

"What shall I do with my son?" said he to him abruptly, as soon as he entered, "you see the way he is in; he will certainly break my heart. I made him a very advantageous proposal three days ago; he tells me positively his heart is engaged; yet he knows I am very desirous the match I mentioned to him should take place. This is such an instance of obstinacy and disobedience, as I know not how to pardon. Little did I imagine that his return, which I so passionately wished for, would be productive of so much uneasiness to me."

The duke paused here, and looked earnestly at Mr. Courteney, who, not knowing what it was he expected from him, or to what aim his words were directed, continued silent, with his eyes fixed on the ground.

"I see you are concerned," resumed the duke, "for the trouble this un-lucky affair gives me."

"Indeed I am, my lord, most sincerely," replied Mr. Courteney.

"Then I may depend upon your readiness to assist me in removing it (said his grace) hear what I have to propose—Your sister, allowing for the warmth of an admirer's imagination, appears to me, by my son's account of her, to have a great deal of merit: such a young lady cannot be without pretenders to her heart. It would give me great pleasure to contribute to her establishment: if you have a match in view for her, let me know if I can forward it, either by my purse or my interest. I candidly confess to you, that meer generosity is not my motive for making you this offer: my son's passion is strengthened by hope; when your sister is married, I may find it less difficult to prevail upon him to yield me the obedience I require, and which I have a right to expect.—You do not answer me, Mr. Courteney," added his grace, after a little pause, "is there any thing disagreeable in this proposal?"

"Thus pressed, my lord," replied Mr. Courteney, "it becomes me to speak with plainness and sincerity—I have no power over my sister's inclinations, and no consideration whatever should oblige me to hurry her into a marriage, which her own choice did not direct her to. Besides, I am not without suspicions, that the merit of the marquis has made some impression on her heart; and, though she has sacrificed it to her honour and duty, yet it will for some time, no doubt, render her deaf to any offer that could be made her. I am very certain, my lord, that she will never encourage the addresses of the marquis without your grace's consent; but were she capable of acting differently from my hopes and expectations, my honour is concerned to prevent it: and I most solemnly assure your grace, that my sister shall never be the wife of the marquis without your express approbation."

The duke could not help being pleased with the candor and spirit of this reply. "We must leave this affair then as we found it," said he: "I am so well convinced of your integrity and honour, that I rely upon you entirely to prevent any consequences that may be disagreeable to me."

The duke that moment perceiving his son crossing the terrace opposite to his window, desired Mr. Courteney to join him. "You have still great influence over the marquis, (said he) try what your persuasions can do to make him alter his behaviour; this obstinacy of his both afflicts and offends me."

Mr. Courteney bowed, and quitted the duke's closet immediately. The marquis, when he saw him coming towards him, stopped to wait for him.

"You have been closeted with my father," said he to him, smiling, "may I know the subject of your conversation?"

"I dare engage your lordship guesses," replied Mr. Courteney, smiling likewise.

"I believe I do (said the marquis) the duke has been complaining of me for my disobedience, has he not?"

"His grace tells me he has made you a proposal, my lord, which you have rejected (answered Mr. Courteney) and he is under great concern about it."

"Well, I am sorry for his uneasiness," interrupted the marquis: "but there is no help for it."

"Ah, my lord (said Mr. Courteney) have I not cause to be very uneasy also? I who know your motive for disobliging the duke, in a point he seems to have so much at heart?"

"You are mistaken," resumed the marquis, "I should act as I do, tho' I had never seen miss Courteney. But tell me, my dear Charles, have you heard from your sister?"

"I have, my lord," replied he.

"She is well, I hope," resumed the marquis, sighing.

"She says nothing to the contrary," answered Mr. Courteney; "but I find your lordship has wrote to her."

"Then she mentions me in her letter?" cried the marquis, eagerly: "I did indeed write to her, but she would not favour me with an answer. But, dear Charles (continued he) have you not miss Courteney's letter about you? let me see that part where I am mentioned. Shew me only my name, written by her dear hand, you know not what pleasure it will give me to see it."

"Upon my honour I have not her letter here," said Mr. Courteney. "Why, why, my lord," pursued he, in great concern, "will you indulge this fatal passion for my sister? you must by this time be convinced that it can produce nothing but uneasiness to the duke, yourself, to me, and even to her."

"To her!" repeated the marquis. "O! Charles, your sister is wrapped up in indifference and reserve; she has not the least sensibility for what I suffer upon her account."

"You are too generous, my lord, (replied Mr. Courteney) to wish my sister should encourage any sentiments for you but those of respect and esteem. It would be presumption in her to hope for the duke's approbation of your passion; and were she too sensible of it, she must be unhappy."

"It is enough for me to be unhappy," resumed the marquis, sighing; "unhappy in the avarice of my father, to whom I have laid open my whole heart. The want of a fortune is all the objection he has to miss Courteney; for he appeared charmed with her character, and her birth he knows. Unhappy too, in a rigid friend, who sacrifices me to the fantastic notions he has formed of honour. O! Charles, little did I imagine once that you would have contributed all in your power to make me miserable."

"Indeed, my lord (replied Mr. Courteney) this reflection is cruel: this very moment all my thoughts are employed on the means to make you happy."

"Now you are again my friend," interrupted the marquis, embracing him eagerly: "will you then at last give me your charming sister. All that duty can require I have performed: I have implored my father's consent; he has had the cruelty to refuse it me; and this on a motive so sordid, that I am justifiable in following my inclinations without soliciting him any more."

"You mistake my intentions, my lord," interrupted Mr. Courteney: "no, never expect that I will consent to your marrying my sister without the duke's approbation."

"What then did you mean (said the marquis) by the hopes you gave me just now!"

"To prevail, if possible, upon the duke to consent to your marriage," replied Mr. Courteney.

The marquis sighed, and cast down his eyes, as if hopeless that this expedient would succeed; but would not say any thing to divert him from his purpose: yet he thought it strange that he should undertake a task, which, interested as he was, seemed less proper for him than any other person.

Mr. Courteney guessed his thoughts, but would not explain himself any farther. In reality, what the marquis had said of his father's having no other objection to his choice but the want of a fortune, confirmed him in his design of using the favour he was in with lady Meadows to the advantage of his sister; and he was not without expectations of prevailing upon her, by the prospect of so honourable a match for her niece, to do as much for her as she had formerly promised, in case she had married the old baronet.

The marquis, who beheld him earnestly, perceived something was labouring in his mind, and he began to entertain hopes of success, tho' he knew not on what reasonably to found them. "I cannot," said Mr. Courteney, observing the tender solicitude with which he gazed on him, "communicate to you the scheme I have formed to reconcile the duke to your wishes, for reasons which will be obvious enough hereafter. Only thus much I will say to satisfy you, that I think it is highly probable I shall succeed; but there is one condition which you must yield to, and which I tell you plainly is the price I set upon my endeavours to serve you in this affair."

"Name it," interrupted the marquis, eagerly, "it must be a strange one indeed if I do not comply with it."

"You must give me a solemn promise, my lord (resumed Mr. Courteney) not to seek my sister's consent to a clandestine marriage, if I should fail in my endeavours to procure the duke's approbation, and you must make the same promise to his grace likewise.—Nay, my lord," pursued he, observing that he hesitated, "you risk nothing by entering into this engagement, for I am bound by oath, as well as by honour, to prevent my sister from being your's upon any terms but the duke's express consent; and, depend upon it, you will never gain her's but on the same condition."

"Well (replied the marquis) you have my promise, and I will make the same declaration to my father: it will be time enough to tell him, if your scheme proves unsuccessful, my fixed resolution never to marry at all, if I do not marry miss Courteney."

Mr. Courteney had already gained so important a point, that he did not think it necessary to combat this resolution at that time. They walked together into the house; and the marquis conceiving that it might be of some advantage to Mr. Courteney's scheme to take an early opportunity of making the promise he required of him, the duke had that satisfaction in his next private conversation with his son, and was charmed with this new instance of Mr. Courteney's integrity.

The marquis, after having long puzzled himself with conjectures about the design Mr. Courteney had formed, at length concluded that he had some expectations from the earl of ——, his uncle, in favour of his sister; and he was so unfortunately circumstanced between his father's avarice and Mr. Courteney's strict principles of honour, that he was reduced to wish earnestly for the success of an expedient, which he would have disdained, if he had been master of his own actions. Mr. Courteney at parting, which was in a few days, begged him to rely securely upon his friendship, and to be mindful of the promise he had given him, which the young lord again confirmed.

CHAP. XI.

In which the history draws near to a conclusion.

Mr. Courteney found his short absence had rather endeared him to his aunt, than lessened the ardor of her fondness; encouraged by her behaviour, he was several times upon the point of laying open to her the whole affair of his pupil's passion for Henrietta, and the difficulties which obstructed so advantageous a match; difficulties which she could so easily remove: but he hoped a great deal from the presence of Henrietta, which it was highly probable would revive the old lady's tenderness for her, and from the interposition of Mr. Damer, who, it was not to be doubted, would enter heartily into the interest of his ward, for whom he expressed so tender an affection.

While he waited in anxious expectation of a letter from his sister, to acquaint him when she was to leave Paris, with her guardian, he was pleasingly surprised with a billet from Mr. Damer himself, requesting him to meet miss Courtney and him at the house of Mrs. Willis, where they were just arrived.

Mr. Courteney, without communicating this news to lady Meadows, hastened to see his beloved sister. The moment he entered the room, where she was sitting with her guardian and Mrs. Willis, she flew to receive him with a transport of joy. He embraced her tenderly; and Mr. Damer advancing to salute him, he in the politest manner, thanked him for his generous care of Henrietta.

Mr. Damer was extremely pleased to hear that she might depend upon an affectionate reception from her aunt. "And now, my child," said he; for so he tenderly affected to call her, "since I have delivered you safe into the hands of your brother, I will leave you, and a day or two hence I will visit you at your aunt's, and settle your affairs in a manner which I hope will not be disagreeable to you."

Henrietta, who, from some past conversations with him, well knew the kind purport of these words, by a grateful look and a respectful courtesy, expressed her acknowledgment. Mr. Courteney, seeing him prepare to leave them, begged he would favour him with a few moments private conversation. Mr. Damer readily consented; upon which Mrs. Willis shewed them into another room, and returned to load her dear miss Courteney with a thousand tender caresses.

Mean time Mr. Courteney gave the friendly guardian of his sister a brief account of the marquis's passion for her, and the conduct he had observed in that affair. He added, that he believed it would be easy to engage the duke's consent to his son's marriage with Henrietta, provided her aunt would act as generously towards her, as she had formerly given her reason to expect.

"From several hints (said he) which lady Meadows has thrown out, and from the great kindness she expresses for me, I am apprehensive that she intends to transfer her bounty from my sister to me; but as my circumstances, though not affluent, are easy, and as I have nothing so much at heart as the happiness of my friend and my sister, I will most chearfully relinquish in her favour all my expectations from lady Meadows. The prospect of so advantageous a match will probably have some weight with her aunt; and the mention of it will come with propriety from you, sir, as the guardian of Henrietta. Lady Meadows will then explain herself clearly; and we shall have an opportunity given us of pressing her to remove, by her generosity, the only obstacle that obstructs my sister's advancement."

Mr. Damer was prodigiously affected with the uncommon nobleness of this proceeding. He took the young gentleman's hand, and, giving it an affectionate shake, "I shall love and honour you while I live (said he) for this generous proposal: doubt not of my ready concurrence in every measure for your sister's advantage. I love her as well as if she was my own daughter; and the inconveniencies she has suffered through the folly and imprudence of some of my family, require that I should make her amends, by doing every thing in my power to make her happy."

"I will wait upon lady Meadows," pursued he, "to-morrow in the afternoon, and then we will talk over this affair." Mr. Courteney told him, he would prepare his aunt for the visit he intended her. After which, Mr. Damer went away, and he joined his sister and her friend. A coach being ordered, they took leave of Mrs. Willis, whom Henrietta promised to visit again very speedily. Mr. Courteney had some discourse with his sister as they went, concerning the marquis; but carefully avoided mentioning his design to her, lest he should raise hopes which might be unhappily disappointed.

Henrietta was under some perturbation at the thoughts of appearing before her aunt, whose displeasure against her, and unjust suspicions, all recurred to her memory; but the reception the old lady gave her, immediately effaced those impressions: it was perfectly kind and affectionate, without the least mixture of upbraiding or reproach.

"I had a mind to surprise you, madam," said Mr. Courteney, who with infinite pleasure beheld his sister so tenderly embraced by her aunt. Lady Meadows assured him, that he had surprised her very agreeably; and, again embracing Henrietta, told her, that her good friend, the countess of——, had been very lavish in her praise, and had acquainted her with several circumstances of her conduct, which had raised her highly in her opinion.

"I suppose you will not be very much grieved (added the old lady, smiling) to hear that your former lover lord B—— is married to the citizen's daughter."

"No, indeed, madam," replied Henrietta, "they seemed to be formed for each other."

"They are not very happy, I hear," said lady Meadows; who, having fallen upon the article of domestic news, related a great number of anecdotes concerning her acquaintance, some of which Henrietta had often heard before. The old lady's fondness for talking at length gave way to her curiosity to hear every thing that had happened to her niece during their separation.

Henrietta gratified it with discretion, suppressing whatever might tend to revive disagreeable remembrances. She was now put into possession of her former apartment, and had an opportunity that night to congratulate her old friend Mrs. White (who assisted her to undress) upon her being reinstated in the favour of her lady.

Chap. XII.

Which concludes the history.

The next day Mr. Courteney informed lady Meadows, that Mr. Damer intended to wait on her, and hinted that he had a match to propose for Henrietta, which he hoped she would approve.

Lady Meadows, who had already taken her resolution with regard to both brother and sister, told him, that she was very desirous of seeing her niece settled; and that she was determined never to oppose her inclinations, being convinced that her virtue and prudence were to be entirely depended upon.

Mr. Damer came according to his appointment, and, being soon after left alone with lady Meadows, he acquainted her with the whole affair between the marquis of —— and Henrietta, as he had received it from Mr. Courteney; and, observing that the old lady was dazzled with the prospect of her niece becoming a dutchess, added, that the want of a suitable fortune should not hinder the advancement of Henrietta: "for whatever you design for her, madam (said he) I will double; so great is my regard for her, and admiration of her virtues."

Lady Meadows with reason thought this a very generous proposal. She complimented him upon it; and, stepping to her cabinet, took out a box that contained her will, and another deed which had been drawn up, while Mr. Courteney was in the country with the duke of ——, but were not yet executed. She put these papers into Mr. Damer's hands, and desired him to read them, saying, "you will there see, sir, what I intend to do for my nephew and his sister."

Mr. Damer opened the first, which was the will. He found she had constituted Mr. Courteney her heir, leaving him her whole estate, charging it only with the sum of five thousand pounds, to be paid his sister on the day of her marriage. The other paper contained a settlement of three hundred pounds a year upon Mr. Courteney during her life.

Mr. Damer, who knew the young gentleman's sentiments, proposed to lady Meadows to send for him, and acquaint him with her intentions. To this she readily agreed. Mr. Courteney turned pale when he heard the moderate sum designed for his sister; and, after expressing his gratitude to lady Meadows for the favour she shewed him, in terms the most respectful and affectionate, he earnestly conjured her to let Henrietta be at least an equal sharer with him in her kindness. He urged, as a motive to her to comply, the very advantageous match that was proposed to his sister. He expatiated on the marquis's tender and faithful passion for her; and touched with great delicacy upon the sentiments Henrietta could not avoid entertaining for a young nobleman, who had loved her with honour, even when ignorant of her birth, and when she was under very humiliating circumstances.

Lady Meadows interrupted him with the most flattering praises of his disinterestedness; but declared that her resolution was unalterable. "Your sister will have ten thousand pounds," said she; "this is no despicable fortune: and since there is so much love on the side of the marquis, there is no doubt but it will be thought sufficient."

Mr. Damer explained the old lady's meaning, by telling him what he proposed to do for miss Courteney, and preventing the young gentleman's acknowledgments: "You have sufficiently shewn your regard for your sister (said he) and I am of opinion we ought not to press lady Meadows any more on this subject; she has acted nobly by you both."

The lady was extremely flattered by the praise Mr. Damer gave her; and, to prevent any more solicitations from her nephew, she signed the papers immediately, which Mr. Damer, at her request, witnessed.

Mr. Courteney said every thing that gratitude and politeness could suggest, upon her presenting him the settlement; yet there was an air of concern upon his countenance, which Mr. Damer observing, took an opportunity to desire him, in a whisper, to meet him at a coffee-house (which he named to him) that evening, having something to say to him, which he hoped would make all things easy.

Mr. Courteney promised to attend him. He then begged lady Meadows not to let Henrietta know what had passed with regard to the marquis. "At present (said he) she considers this marriage as impossible to be effected, and so I would have her consider it, till I am sure that the duke will make no objection to the fortune that is designed her." Lady Meadows approved of his caution; and Mr. Damer was desired to visit her in her own apartment, and acquaint her with the dispositions made by her aunt.

Henrietta expressed the highest satisfaction at what had been done for her beloved brother, and, with the greatest sweetness, acknowledged her obligations to her aunt for the provision she had made for her; but when Mr. Damer acquainted her with the addition he designed to make to the fortune her aunt would give her, tears of tenderness and gratitude overspread her face, and she could utter no more, than, "O! sir, how generous—how kind is this—how shall I repay such unexampled goodness—"

Mr. Damer interrupted her soft exclamations, to lead her down stairs to her aunt, to whom she paid her acknowledgments with inimitable grace, and congratulated her brother with so sincere a joy, that he, who knew how much she was likely to lose by his good fortune, was moved almost to tears.

Mr. Damer a short time afterwards took his leave, and went to the coffee-house, where he had appointed Mr. Courteney to meet him. He was soon followed by the young gentleman, whose mind was under great agitations on his sister's account.

"One would hardly imagine," said Mr. Damer to him, smiling, "that you have just been declared heir to a good estate, you look like one disappointed and unhappy."

"I am indeed disappointed, sir," replied Mr. Courteney; "I had laid a plan to make my sister and my friend happy: but my aunt's partiality has broke all my measures for the present."

"Then you intend," said Mr. Damer, who had taken particular notice of his last words, "to make some addition to your sister's fortune, when the estate comes into your hands?"

"Certainly, sir, (replied Mr. Courteney) I should but ill deserve it, if I did not."

"It must be confessed (resumed Mr. Damer) that you are a very good brother."

"All that I can do for my sister, sir, (said he) will be but bare justice; but your generosity to her can never be enough admired."

"No more of that," interrupted Mr. Damer. "I love your sister: she is a worthy young woman; I am grieved to think so noble a match for her, should meet with any obstruction for the want of a fortune. What do you think the duke will expect?"

"The lady he has proposed to his son, sir," said Mr. Courteney, "has twenty thousand pounds; and it would have been my pride and happiness to have prevailed with my aunt to make my sister's fortune equal to that."

"Is it possible!" cried Mr. Damer, surprised. "Why fifteen thousand pounds is at least one third of your aunt's fortune?"

"My sister," said Mr. Courteney, "has a right to expect it. The whole would have been her's but for some unlucky accidents, and the strange partiality of lady Meadows for me. All that I can now do is, to let the marquis know, that my sister will have ten thousand pounds paid on the day of her marriage, and ten thousand more on the death of her aunt. The duke loves money; and I greatly doubt whether all his son's solicitations will make him relish this reversionary ten thousand pounds."

"We will not put it to the hazard," interrupted Mr. Damer, "since you are determined to act thus generously by your sister, I will lay down the money myself, and all the security I require, is your bond for the re-payment of it, when your aunt's estate comes into your possession."

Mr. Courteney was so overwhelmed with surprise, joy, and gratitude, for this unexpected, noble offer, that, during some moments, he was unable to utter a word. But this silence, accompanied with looks the most expressive that can be imagined, was more eloquent than any language could be. Recovering himself at last, he was beginning to pay the warmest acknowledgments; but Mr. Damer would not suffer him to proceed.

"I am impatient (said he) for the conclusion of this affair. Write to your friend immediately, and let him know that your sister's guardian will treat with the duke his father, whenever he pleases."

Mr. Courteney, at his reiterated request, took leave of him, and went home, in order to communicate this joyful news to his friend. Hearing that lady Meadows and his sister were engaged in company, he went to his own apartment, and wrote a short letter to the marquis, in which he acquainted him, that his sister being restored to the favour of her aunt, he had it now in his power to assure him, that if he continued in the same sentiments towards her, and could prevail with his grace to authorise them by his consent, he was impowered by her aunt and her guardian, to declare that her fortune would be twenty thousand pounds.

Having sealed and dispatched this letter to the post, he joined the company below stairs, with looks so full of satisfaction, and a behaviour animated with such extraordinary gaiety, that lady Meadows was more than ever delighted with him, concluding that the noble provision she had made for him, was the source of his joy: but Henrietta, who knew her brother better, and who besides saw something particular in those looks, which he from time to time gave her, felt strange flutterings in her gentle bosom: hopes checked as soon as formed; wishes suppressed as they rose. In these perturbations, she passed that night and the three following days.

Mean time the marquis, having received Mr. Courteney's letter, was so surprised at this sudden change in the fortune of Henrietta, that he read it over several times before he could persuade himself what he saw was real. His first emotions were all transport: every obstacle to his marriage was now removed; and he might solicit his father's consent, with a certainty almost of not being denied. Yet a sentiment of delicacy and tenderness made him regret, that it was not in his power to convince Henrietta of the disinterestedness of his love, and for some moments rendered him insensible of his present happiness.

The duke came into his chamber, while he was reading the letter the twentieth time, and so intently, that he did not perceive his entrance. When suddenly raising his eyes, and seeing his father, who, suspecting that this letter, which he seemed to read with so much emotion, came from his mistress, was looking earnestly on him.

"O! my lord (cried he) there is nothing wanting to make me perfectly happy, but your consent to my marriage with miss Courteney. See, my lord, what her brother writes: her brother, who till now has so obstinately opposed my passion!"

The duke took the letter out of his hands, and having read it, returned it to him again without speaking a word, and walked to the other end of the room. The marquis, who saw nothing unfavourable in his looks, followed him, and, throwing himself at his feet, conjured him not to oppose his happiness any longer. The duke desired time to consider; but his son would not give over his solicitations, till he had obtained leave of him to visit miss Courteney, and to declare that his addresses had the sanction of his consent.

The happy marquis gave orders instantly for his post-chaise to be got ready, which his father at first did not oppose; but, after reflecting a little,

"Can you not rein in your impatience for a few days?" said he to him; "I intend to be in town next week: I shall then have an opportunity of seeing the young lady (and, since you are so obstinately bent upon the match) of talking to her aunt and her guardian."

The marquis would not disoblige his father, by making any objections to this little delay, grievous as it was to him; but retired to write to Mr. Courteney, whom he acquainted with the duke's intentions, and, anticipating the tender name of brother, poured out his whole heart in the warmest expressions of love, friendship, joy, and every soft emotion with which he was agitated.

Mr. Courteney having communicated this letter to Mr. Damer, he agreed that it was necessary to make lady Meadows acquainted with the steps they had taken in the affair. She entered with a good grace into the generous designs of her nephew in favour of his sister.

"If I had done more for her," said she to him, smiling, "you would not have had an opportunity of doing so much." Mr. Courteney kissed her hand with a tender and respectful air.

"Go," said she, with a look that shewed she was highly pleased; "go, and tell your sister this good news; and tell her also that I am impatient to embrace and congratulate her."

Mr. Courteney willingly obeyed her. He went to Henrietta's apartment, and, seeing her sitting pensive and melancholy, he began to rally her upon her tenderness for the marquis. She bore it with great sweetness, but not without some surprise; for her brother was used to be very delicate and reserved upon that subject. By degrees he assumed a more serious tone; and at length gave her to understand, that the marquis was now permitted by his father to pay his addresses to her.

Henrietta blushed and trembled from the moment her brother began to speak to her in a serious manner. Her emotions increased as he proceeded; yet she laboured to conceal them, till Mr. Courteney, explaining to her what Mr. Damer had done for her, which necessarily included his own generous gift, that innate delicacy, which had forced her joy to be silent, suffered her gratitude to shew itself in the most lively expressions. Lady Meadows came into the room, and gave a seasonable interruption to these tender effusions of her heart, which Mr. Courteney had listened to with a kind of painful pleasure. She embraced her niece, and congratulated her on her happy fortune.

Miss Courteney, who had now reason to expect a visit from the marquis, was not much surprised a few days afterwards to see his equipage at the door. After a few moments conversation with Mr. Courteney, he was introduced to lady Meadows, who received him with great respect. Henrietta blushed a little when he appeared, but recovered herself, and received the tender and respectful compliment he made her with her usual grace.

A great deal of company coming in soon afterwards, he found means to engage her apart for a quarter of an hour. Their conversation was such as might be expected between persons of their sense and politeness, who loved each other with the utmost tenderness, and now for the first time saw themselves at liberty to declare their sentiments. Henrietta did not scruple to own to the man, who had so nobly merited her esteem, that her heart had received a most tender impression for him; and this soft acknowledgment completed her lover's felicity.

Mr. Courteney waited upon the duke the next morning, and had the pleasure to hear from his own mouth, that he was entirely satisfied with his son's proceedings. His grace visited lady Meadows the same day; and was so charmed with Henrietta, that he scarce discovered less impatience than his son, for the conclusion of the marriage. Every thing being agreed on between the duke and Mr. Damer, with regard to settlements, the writings were drawn up with all convenient speed, and a day appointed for the marriage.

Lady Meadows, though a Roman catholic, allowed the ceremony to be performed at her house: after which the new-married pair, with the old lady, the duke, Mr. Damer, and Mr. Courteney, set out for his grace's country-seat.

The charming marchioness did not make her first public appearance in town till late in the ensuing winter; when her beauty, her sufferings, her virtue, and her good fortune, were for a long time the subjects of conversation.

Mr. Courteney, happy in the conscious integrity of his heart, happy in the ardent affection of his sister and the marquis, and the esteem of all who knew him, was, by the death of lady Meadows, which happened a few months after his sister's marriage, enabled to discharge his obligations to Mr. Damer. His generosity was not long unrewarded: an opulent heiress fell desperately in love with him; she was related to the duke, who interested himself so warmly in the affair, that the marriage was soon concluded.

Lord B——, as has been observed already, lived very unhappy with his plebeian lady. The sight of the charming Henrietta renewed his passion.

Tortured with remorse, disappointment, and despair, he had recourse to the bottle, and fell an early sacrifice to intemperance.

Miss Woodby, who had always a violent passion for a red-coat, listened to the sighs of a young cadet, and married him in a week after their first acquaintance. Her excuse for this precipitancy was, that the *lovely youth* would certainly have stabbed himself, if she had delayed his happiness any longer. With part of her fortune he bought a commission, and spent the rest in a few months. After which, he went abroad with his regiment, leaving her, in an obscure retirement, to bewail his absence, and sooth her love-sick heart with hopes that he would return more *passionate* than ever, and lay all his laurels at her feet.

Miss Belmour, forsaken by her lover, became a proselyte to the Roman catholic religion, and retired to a convent, where the nuns wrought her up to such a degree of enthusiasm, that she settled her whole fortune upon the community, and took the veil; but soon afterwards, repenting of this rash step, she died of grief, remorse, and disappointment.

Mrs. Willis was generously rewarded by the marchioness, for the many kind and faithful services she had received from her: and Mr. Damer, who highly esteemed her for her behaviour to his beauteous ward, settled her husband in such an advantageous way, that in a few years he made a considerable fortune.

The younger Mr. Damer found, in the incessant clamours of a jealous wife, a sufficient punishment for his treacherous designs on Henrietta; and it was not without great difficulty that he was restored to his father's favour.

Every branch of the Courteney family made frequent advances towards a reconciliation with the marchioness and her brother: but generous as they were, they had too just a sense of the indignities they had suffered from them, to admit of it; and, in this steady resentment, they had, as it usually happens with successful persons, the world on their side.

THE END.

APPENDIX I

VARIANTS BETWEEN THE 1758 AND 1761 EDITIONS

The following list of substantive variants is keyed to the page number of the present edition. Readings from the 1758 edition are on the left of the square bracket, beginning with the first few words of the paragraph; readings from the 1761 edition are given on the right. Any editorial explanations are given in bold type within brackets.

VOLUME I

7	About the middle	road; and,] road; and
7	Fellow me	Fellow me! no fellows] *Fellor* me! no *fellors*
7	Sit closer	dame, and,] dame, and
7	Who am I	saucy] fancy
8	Good lack-a-day	would-be gentry] would-be-gentry
8	Very likely	woman"] woman."
8	Very likely	coachman, I] coachman." I
8	Nay, since you	young lady] young woman
8	A young gentlewoman	window] widow
9	The passengers who	however] however,
9	The fair stranger	nature] sort
10	The melancholy	good will] good-will
10	The passengers being	madam, said] madam," said
10	This exclamation	conceived there] conceived that there
10	This exclamation	it be] it is
11	Oh heavens	lady] lady in an affected tone
11	Oh heavens	I was] Yes
11	You have	confidence.] confidence!
11	You have	meeting.] meeting!
11	You have	our's] ours
11	Courteney is a very	name;] name,
12	I was christened	Courteney] Courteny

12	Alas! said the	to relate] to talk of my
12	Alas! said the	as to the manner in which] tell me in what manner
12	Dear madam	Clelia."] Clelia?
12	I beg your pardon	ten years] several years
13	I would not	dictract] distract
13	I would not	Heaven?] Heaven!
13	I would not	prudent friends] prudent; friends
13	This young lady	marvelously] marvellously
13	Lord! my dear	And,—] And,"—
14	That's well	well,"] well"
14	Well, well	please,"] please."
15	The letter being	with] from
16	No really	No, really] No really
16	I have indeed	lady;] lady,
16	How all	relations?] kinsfolks?"
16	Oh, Oh	Well;] Well,
16	The old gentlewoman	going to,] going, to,
16	The old gentlewoman	should] intended to
16	The chairman	question;] question,
16	The chairman	millener he enquired for lived] millener for whom he enquired, lived
17	The fellow	returned] returned,
17	I have a letter	yours,] yours:
17	Oh!	I dare say they are good enough,"] they are good enough, no doubt,"
18	Henrietta followed	miss Courteney] she
19	You will no doubt	easy till] easy here till
19	Miss Courteney	laid] found
20	This account was	millener,] millener
20	When the clock	up] up,
20	As soon as	time] time,
21	La!	ma'am,"] ma'am,
21	La!	directed,] directed;
21	La!	coffee] chocolate
21	In about a quarter	appeared,] appeared
21	After the tea-things	her own apartment] her apartment
21	After the tea-things	long'd] longed
21	The book however	new Atlantis] New Atlantis

22	I am sorry	sorry,] sorry?
22	I am sorry	she,] she
22	I assure you	she,] she
24	Oh Heavens!	creature"] creature,"
25	The widow, by a	subsistence,] subsistence;
25	The widow, who knew	atttend] attend
25	The earl's youngest	My father] The earl's youngest son
25	Mr. Courteney, as he	blushing] blushing,
26	Mr. Courteney received	father, hoped] father; he said he hoped
26	The lady was so	and,] and
26	The lady was so	mere] meer
26	She remembered	gentleman] gentleman,
27	Mr. Courteney began	politeness] politeness,
28	This interview	He] he
28	Amazed to find	hopes] hopes,
28	Amazed to find	resolved nevermore to expose himself to the danger] resolved to expose himself no more to the danger
28	Mr Courteney was	content] consent
30	Resolutions are so	trifle] trifle,
30	Resolutions are so	fortune] fashion
30	His fortune indeed	Besides] Besides,
31	Early the next	ago] before
31	Mr. Courteney, who	and acquainted] and had acquainted
31	Mr. Courteney, not	however] however,
31	He left him	borne with] sustained
32	He walked down the	Mall,] Mall:
32	He walked down the	and,] and
32	In a few minutes	for love if it hopes all, fears all likewise,] (for love if it hopes all, fears all likewise,)
32	In a few minutes	ladies?] ladies!
32	O my God!	sir] Sir
33	Mrs. Carlton lay	in] on
33	Miss Carlton was	Her daughter] Miss Carlton
33	Miss Carlton was	cheeks. It] cheeks, and hastily turning to her mother, it
33	Oh! Sir, said Mrs. C	sir] Sir
33	Mr. Courteney threw	you.] you?
34	What do you say	But] Then

34	That young lady	which,] which
34	That young lady	it. For] it: for
34	Surprise and joy	London] London,
35	As soon as he	having] having,
35	As soon as he	inpulse] impulse,
35	As soon as he	concurrence;] concurrence:
35	As soon as he	object:] object;
35	This difficult task	he had solicited] he was soliciting for
35	After a few hours	again] again,
35	I am dying	with difficulty] with great difficulty
36	As soon as it was	spirits,] spirits
36	As soon as it was	delicate] delicate,
36	Mr Courteney, stung	house that was] house which was
37	Having given directions	is] is,
38	The countess durst	hundred] hundred pounds
38	What a romantic	it is not at all like] there is no resemblance in it
38	What a romantic	sound] word
38	What a romantic	taken] mistaken
39	I have not come	which] such as
39	Proceed, my dear	"I] I
39	Proceed, my dear	two hours and a half] two hours
39	Proceed, my dear	manner.] manner:
40	My father, who	conciliating at least his brother's affections, wrote to him] conciliating his elder brother's affections, at least wrote to him
40	My father, who	convinced him] proved
40	My father, who had	a] an
40	My father, now	under,] under
41	My mother, being	Five hundred] Eight hundred
41	My mother, being	However] however
41	My mother having	four hundred and fifty pounds] eight hundred
41	My mother having	merchant,] merchant a man of birth and liberal education,
42	My mother shed	her son showed himself] appeared her son
42	I was so much	affection] affection,
43	At her return	an asylum] a retreat

43	The tears,	which ran] flowed
45	I sent her an	wrote] sent
45	About three days	wrote] written
45	About three days	servants;] servants:
45	O yes, replied	footman,] footman.
46	I was as much	however] however,
46	I was as much	and,] and
46	Lady Manning was	nothing] a trifle
46	Lady Manning was	fortune] *fortune*
47	You have guessed	of having me] to have me
47	The governess, who	for] to
47	The governess, who	parler françoise] *parler françoise*
47	Nay, my dear	merely] meerly
47	Nay, my dear	boarding-schools,] boarding-schools
48	Truly, said miss	agreeable,] agreeable:
48	Truly, said miss	Her own] These were her
48	When there was	instance] instances
49	My surprise was	pray] pray,
50	Such a proposal	proposal] proposal,
50	Such a proposal	likely] likely,
50	In my first emotions	them, and that is riches] them; they are rich
51	Yes, said lady Meadows	cousin] niece
51	It is not to be doubted	quittted] quitted
51	Thus, my dear Miss	pleadings] soft pleadings
52	Lady Meadows gazed	weep] weep,
52	I was very unwilling	Meadows's] Meadow's
53	Lady Manning, according	all the rest] the rest
53	I thought it became	church:] church;
53	I thought it became	that I] I
53	This chaplain, whose	dependence] dependance
54	[chapter intro]	jesuit] Jesuit
54	She then desired	time, said she, we] time," said she, "we
54	Miss Courteney was	her."] her.
55	Henrietta, a little	sprightliness,] sprightliness
55	Miss Woodby was	form,] form
55	The chair had been	longer,] longer
55	She was now summoned	Mrs] Mr
55	She was now summoned	wil] will
55	She was now summoned	him—"] him—."

56	Mrs. Eccles	though] tho'
56	Oh! exclaimed Miss	grace] grave,
57	You are in a gay	discovered,] discovered;
57	You are in a gay	anxious to get out of] desirous of leaving
58	But, my dear Miss W	But] But,
58	But, my dear Miss W	furnish] funish
58	Well, said Henrietta	Well] "Well
58	I must confess, said	gave him] furnished him with
59	I have heard it observed	jesuit by his insidious praises] jesuit, by his insidious praises,
60	It is certain, that	her,] her
61	My aunt, having thus	miserable,] miserable
61	I smiled, courtesied	out of the] out of the room
62	In Sir Isaac Darby	When we were placed at table, I found myself opposite to him; and observing that he chewed his meat with great difficulty, for want of teeth, I was resolved to mortify him, by letting him perceive that I observed it, looking at him several times with a kind of sensibility for this so unavoidable a misfortune.] **[deleted]**
63	Oh, good sir	sir!] sir,
63	Oh, good sir	but,] but
63	How admirably	But] But,
63	Was there ever	dear?] dear,
63	I really think	honour] honour,
63	I went out of	teeth,] teeth
64	Full of these	that] the
64	Full of these	deference,] deference
64	I had been writing	three] two
64	I had been writing	raillying] rallying
64	So, Henrietta	sir] Sir
65	How did I	railly] rally
65	I considered that	that I listened] of my listening
66	I was so terrified	misfortune] misfortune,
66	My aunt looked	looked like] had the appearance of one
67	You hesitate, Henrietta	I not see it,] not I see it
68	Mrs. White repeated	that] which
68	When breakfast was	different] indifferent

69	No indeed, interrupted	Windsor-forest] Windsor forest
69	No indeed, interrupted	courtisied] curtesied
69	This thought, and	that] who
69	We set out next morning	Windsor,] Windsor:
70	To all this I answered	tho'] though
70	To all this I answered	O my dear, how difficult it was for me to forbear laughing here;] (O my dear, how difficult it was for me to forbear laughing here);
70	Here (continued she)	fellows;] fellows!
70	Here (continued she)	or] nor
70	I was going to speak	give] allow
70	I was going to speak	I have hitherto] Hitherto I have
71	It was indeed	again,] again;
71	It was indeed	resentment] resentment,
71	My brother was	Darby's hand,] Darby,
71	My imagination	aunt's favour,] aunt's favour;
71	My imagination	but] but,
71	My imagination	ones] ones,
71	Towards evening Mrs	to-morrow] the next day
72	When she was gone	considered] considered,
72	I left the garden	countenance] countenance,
72	I confess I	there;] there,
73	Ah! cried miss C	Woodby,] Woodby
73	My aunt seemed	and, in a rapture of joy, I told her how] and told her, in a rapture of joy, how favourably
74	In the end my	use,] use
74	That is impossible	will,] will.
74	Good God! cried	extremity?] this extremity!
74	The latter part	but,] but
75	My perplexed mind	headach] head-ach
76	There is certainly	one's self] one's self,
76	There is certainly	the peculiar care of Providence on certain] on certain occasions the peculiar care of Providence
76	There is certainly	Roman catholic] Roman Catholic
76	There is certainly	However] However,
78	I assure you my	interruption;] interruption:

78	I assure you my	terror] perplexity
78	I assure you my	catholick] catholic
78	I assure you my	there,] there;
78	Mrs. White	and,] and
79	Having thus got	treatment] usage
79	Having thus got	or] nor
79	Having sealed	very,] very:
80	Wretches!	my dear] my dear,
81	Envy will	it's] its
82	Is not Mr. Damer	sir?] sir!"
82	My father, madam	gentleman,] gentleman
82	Pardon, me, madam	It is sir,] It is, sir,
82	Dear miss, said	yet, perhaps,] yet, perhaps—
83	Ah! the wretch	match] husband
83	Ah! the wretch	husband] person
84	The cloth was	came] came,
84	Miss Courteney, who	lordship] lordship,
85	The young nobleman	milliner] millener
85	The conversation	milliner] millener
85	This is a strange	handsome;] handsome!
85	This is a strange	love-mystery] love mystery
85	Your lordship	yet,] yet
85	Your lordship	way,] way
86	Oh! very fond	Eccles.] Eccles,
87	Mrs. Eccles	possible. He] possible, he
87	Mrs. Eccles	reflexion] reflection
87		Chap. IX.] Chap. VI.
87	Henrietta,	but, hearing] but hearing
87	Henrietta,	her's] hers
88	I will not flatter	Bale,] Damer.
88	I hope, sir	foundation:] foundation;
88	Henrietta,	him for a a solicitude] for a solicitude
89	I hope	objection to lodging] objection to lodge
89	She had	an whole] a whole
90	Mr. Damer	and, meeting] and meeting
90	Oh!	was distorted] were distorted
90	Oh!	acted] acting
90	Oh!	intoxicated] intoxicated,
91	That is bad	for,] for

91	Indeed!	communicative:] communicative!
92	I think I hear	him,] him
93	His lordship	was a very short] was but a very short
93	In the mean time	lord] lord,
93	In the mean time	of an agreeable air] had an agreeable air
93	A young woman	controll] control
94	In the mean time	eleven o'clock,] eleven o'clock
94	This motion was	crimson'd] crimsoned
95	Amidst the melancholy	which] whence
96	Dear heart	lain in it] lain it
96	And why pray	Eccles,] Eccles
96	And why pray	choose] chuse
96	Will you order	farther] further
96	Insulted, indeed	door.] door,
96	Perhaps not	me!] me?
97	I hope	Courteney:] Courteney,
97	Henrietta was	sighing:] sighing,
97	Henrietta was	behaviour to you to-day] behaviour to-day
97	I have something	secret,] secret
98	I am contented	Courteney] Courteney,
98	My lord	he;] he:
98	My lord	rejoiced] rejoiced,
98	He is the guardian	own] own,
98	He is the guardian	merchant,] merchant
99	Henrietta answered	courtesy] courtesey
99	I was going out	Indeed!] Were you!
99	You have a great	she,] she
100	The young nobleman	any hazard] all hazards
100	The young nobleman	great] greatest
100	The young nobleman	fifty thousand pounds] forty thousand pounds
100	The great point	success. For] success: for
101	Our lover	with advantage to his passion] with more advantage
101	Our lover	further] farther
103	As soon as	folly,] folly
104	While her aunt	action?] action;
105	Remember, miss	No,] No
105	These considerations	miss] miss,

106	Indeed I have	not] not:
106	Henrietta had	behaviour] behaviour,
107	Mr. Damer	Courteney,] Courteney
108	I would not alarm	more] more,
109	Compose yourself	by] with
109	That moment	Possibly] Possibly,
109	That moment	to you] to you,
109	Pert creature	stranger,] stranger
110	Pert creature	dressing-room,] dressing-room
111	Insolent trollop	life] life,
112	The word *abuse*	further] farther
112	To be sure	was] is
112	Yes, said Mrs. Willis	love,] love
112	And this man	still,] still
113	It is no flattery	beauty,] beauty
113	It is no flattery	domestick] domestic
113	I was a little surprised	situation,] situation;
113	I was a little surprised	friends;] friends,
113	I was a little surprised	you awakened suspicions:] you, awakened suspicions:
113	I was a little surprised	it] it,
114	I am persuaded	house] house,
114	She must either	case,] case

Volume II

123	These melancholy	enquietude] inquietude
124	Mrs. White, when	Courteney, enquiring] Courteney enquiring
124	Oh! miss,	time] time?
125	Treachery!	surely] surely,
125	Aye, Woodby	dressing-room] dressing room
125	Aye, Woodby	service] service,
125	Nay, for that	you, and a great clutter she made with that word,] you (and a great clutter she made with that word),
126	Did Mr. Damer	say] say,
126	Well, and what is	a melancholy air] an air of despondence
126	The two ladies	silence] silence,

127	In this manner	[footnote to "an ingenious writer"—The author of maxims, characters, and reflections, etc. Printed for J. R. Tonson.] **[deleted]**
127	Oh no!	strange indeed] strange, indeed,
128	I should say	opinion] opinions
128	That is to say	that] this
128	But it is not	meritorious;] meritorious:
128	But I will keep	suspense] suspence
129	To be sure I	greatly,] greatly
129	Doubtless I had	reason.—] reason—
129	Bless us!	Bless us,] Bless us!
129	Truly,	Truly sir,] Truly, sir,
130	I told you that this	told] related
130	You must know	proposal] proposal,
130	To one of her	reach] reach,
131	For niece I	for, whether] for whether
133	I am satisfied	see,] see
134	When I first	it;] it:
134	Henrietta smiled	contributed,] contributed
135	Mrs. Willis	citizen;] citizen,
136	But, dear	well,] well
137	What you are a	For] For,
138	Henrietta, who	that had passed] that passed
139	Henrietta repeated	satire] satire,
139	The next day	evening;] evening,
139	This little piece	Cordwain;] Cordwain,
139	Miss Cordwain	toilet, she sat down] toilet, sat down
141	Sure, papa	countess;] countess:
141	Here her tears	father,] father
141	Don't break	half sobbing] half-sobbing
141	Nay, interrupted	you you] you
142	Well, said the father	pleasure,] pleasure
142	Aye, said the good	had] has
144	Henrietta was	and,] and
145	At length	advanced to hand] advanced to help
145	This action and these	imposed upon] cheated
145	As for Henrietta	person who] person that had
145	As for Henrietta	that] that,

146	To know that the	another?] another.
146	A whole hour's	lord B——'s mind in the same state]
		lord B——'s in the same state
146	A whole hour's	it] he
147	Mean time	such a conversation] such conversation
147	However, the	step, were] step were
147	However, the	spoke] spoken
148	Henrietta accordingly	sound] sounds
149	Lord B——,	proud only,] proud only
150	You must not	Ah] Oh
150	Again, this	Henrietra] Henrietta
150	Hear me	me,] me
150	Doubt not, my	not,] not
150	Doubt not, my	friend;] friend:
151	God knows what	matter,] matter
152	Mrs. Smith	woman] maid
152	As she descended	woman] maid
152	At this confirmation	night] night,
152	Mr. Cordwain, who	lordship] lordship,
152	Mr. Cordwain, said	harrangue] harangue
153	My lord, returned	leud] lewd
153	Sure!	dishonourably,] dishonourably:
155	When Mrs. Smith	appeared] appeared,
155	The countess	that lady] she
156	Certainly	your's] yours
157	The countess	recalled] called
157	The countess	niece] grand-daughter
158	Offended me,	Cordwain;] Cordwain,
158	Offended me,	And] and
159	Ay, that she shall	is a hanging] is hanging
159	Do you really	propose, madam?] intend, madam,
159	O my God!	head;] head:
159	Base woman	woman!] woman?
159	Miss Cordwain was	pannick] pannic
160	Yes, my lord	earl of ——;] earl of ——,
161	This account	she conceived] she had conceived
161	This remedy	again:] again;
162	I am sorry	friends] friends,
162	Mr. Cordwain	madam] my lady

163	I must tell you also	secret,] secret.
164	I admire your	resolution," said] resolution, miss Courteney," said
164	I beg, madam	for an accident] for some accident
164	Well, said the	you, when] you, miss, when
164	I am obliged	lady C——] lady D——
166	In pursuance	that young lady] the citizen's daughter
167	Atheists have been	'Till] Till
167	He is mean	Besides] Besides,
168	It is easy	but those] but to those
169	Lady D——'s	asked [with a long s]] asked [with a modern s]
169	The lady ordered	her,] her
169	While the young	collecting] supposing
169	While the young	musick] music
169	Henrietta, though	musick] music
169	Lady D——	D——] D——,
170	Lady D——	enthusiastick] enthusiastic
170	Madam, said the	musick] music
170	This speech	the person that was now entering, again] the person now entering, (who was of a very low birth, but had a competent fortune left her by a father who had held it as a maxim of sound wisdom, that money should be got by any means;) again
170	This speech	her;] her,
170	Henrietta	a mean] a very mean
170	Lady D——, who	the singularity] the ridiculous singularity
171	I must intreat you	miss has not] miss D—— has not
171	Oh	Oh,] Oh!
172	Oh, said Lady D——	regulate] curb
173	She therefore	in her answer] in answer
175	Lord!	matter however was] This matter, however, was
176	Henrietta gave	opportunity] opportunity
177	At the word	and,] and
177	Ah, how I envy	freedom,] freedom!
177	It does not signify	know] am sure
177	Why, to be sure	but then,] but then
178	Well, you will be	lances:] glances—

180	While the servant	secret?] secret!
182	I never refused to	this, pardon me, madam, appears] this, (pardon me, madam,) appears
183	Mrs. Courteney is	o'clock,] o'clock:
183	Miss Courteney, said	extremely] very
183	You certainly acted	past,] past
184	I believe it will be	you, and has] you, has
184	Indeed, my lord	further] farther
184	Lord B——	greatly below] still less than
184	Lord B——	it was expected] it is expected
184	Lord B——	passion,] passion;
185	I will detain your	catholick] catholic
185	I find you are	romantick] romantic
185	Change your religion	for your changing] for changing
186	My resolution	Henrietta;] Henrietta:
189	Yes, replied	from ——, enquires] from —— enquires
189	Lord B—— flew	lover] lover,
189	Indeed, my lord	lord,"] lord"
189	Indeed, my lord	relinquish] resign
189	Nay, now your	romantick,] romantic,
189	Were my aunt	romantick,] romantic,
189	Call not my passion	your's] yours
190	Here his lordship	inconnected] unconnected
190	Suppose that	obtained my lord,] obtained, my lord,
191	Say not that	for me, to] for me to
191	In your circumstances	you;] you:
193	Depend upon it	romantick] romantic
193	Depend upon it	recall] recal
193	Lord B—— improved	the fortune of that young lady,] her fortune
193	Henrietta having	woman,] woman
193	Henrietta having	tho'] though
193	If I thought	merit at persisting] merit of persisting
195	Well, miss Courteney	your's] yours
195	I have, madam	have madam,] have, madam,
196	Notwithstanding	tenderness,] tenderness
196	Notwithstanding	Because she was not likely she should not be her mother] because it was not likely she should be her mother
196	Henrietta thanked	lady D——'s] lady D——s

196	Our fair heroine	her.—] her—
197	Henrietta sighed	a union] an union
197	Henrietta, despairing	mistress,] mistress
199	I see it!	Henrietta] Henrietta,
200	It is to marry	man] man,
203	In the mean time	and,] and
203	In the mean time	resolution which reason and virtue had very little share in.] resolution in which reason and virtue had very little share.
203	This thought gave	great] extreme
203	Miss Belmour	The customary ceremonies at landing being over, she proceeded] She proceeded
204	As the chaise	gentlemen alighted from their horses at the same time] gentleman alighted at the same time
205	I don't like	confess,] confess;
205	The young lord	possible] possible,
205	It is you, not I	friendship,] friendship!
205	Now you are my	again] once more
206	Henrietta,	chose] chosen
207	At parting	their's] theirs
207	Though	Tho'] Though
208	Their journey now	an absence] an answer of
209	Miss Belmour	self love] self-love
209	Miss Belmour	From me] From me,
213	This young lady	grace] grace,
213	She told Henrietta	perfectly happy] perfectly contented
213	Henrietta congratulated	religion,] religion
213	Henrietta congratulated	written by the best authors on that subject] written by the best authors
214	Well, but what is	Freeman;] Freeman,
214	Well, but what is	enable] enables
214	Well, but what is	situation.] situation; own freely then that this is your intention."
214	May I perish	her,] her;
214	May I perish	Charming creature, how I love her!] Charming creature, I love her! I adore her!
214	I see it plainly	romantick] romantic
214	The lover	sign,] sigh;

215	Melvil's gaiety	friend's] friends
216	The young gentleman	the debauch he had made the night before] the excess he had been guilty of the night before
217	He shut his eyes	friend, he] friend, for whom he had the most passionate concern, he
217	If you were able	abroad,] abroad
217	He went at	then!] then?
217	I fancy	time,] time;
220	What have parents	has] have
220	Were my heart	parents'] parents
220	I know not	not] not,
220	Do you know	Damer] Damer,
221	Then this letter is	Courteny."] Courteney?"
221	She is in	letter,] letter?
222	Henrietta looked	you,] you;
223	Forgive me,	in,] in:
223	Forgive me,	aunt.] aunt?
225	The marquis	thro'] through
227	My dear Henrietta	eyes,] eyes;
227	After some farther	you;] you:
227	After some farther	two;] two:
228	Sure,	Sure] Sure,
229	Excuse me,	Belmour] Belmour,
229	It is possible	indeed."] indeed,"
230	I remember I said	(replied the marquis;] (replied the marquis);
233	What have you	occasion,] occasion:
234	Mr. Courteney was	reach,] reach;
234	The marquis heard	out?] out!
234	The sight of five	two Louis d'ors] five Louis d'ors
234	The young lover	two Louis d'ors] five Louis d'ors
235	She was assured	sex;] sex,
236	I see I may	sense,] sense
238	The marquis would	brother,] brother;
239	The marquis at	began] begun
240	As soon as	prioress] superior
240	I agree to it	fit, that] fit that,
241	Detested obstinancy	mikakes] mistakes
241	Mr. Courteney penetrated	which might incur] which would incur

242	I was to blame	you:] you;
242	Mr. Courteney	in company] in the company
243	Henrietta promised	prioress] superiour
243	Henrietta promised	care,] care;
244	You have used	he,] he
245	I was going	today,] today
245	This news gave	portmantua] portmanteau
246	Lady Meadows perceived	expression.] expression:
246	Lady Meadows perceived	added] added,
249	You are too	lord] lord,
254	Mr. Damer came	appointment;] appointment,
255	Henrietta expressed	her:] her;
255	Mr. Damer interrupted her	he] she
256	Certainly, sir,	sir] sir,
256	All that I can do	sir] sir,
259	Lady Meadows	which,] which
260	Miss Woodby	heart,] heart

APPENDIX II

CORRECTIONS TO THE 1761 EDITION FOR CLARITY

The following is a list of our editorial corrections keyed to the page numbers of the present edition. The first few words of the paragraph are also provided. The original text from the 1761 edition appears to the left of the square bracket, and the corrected text is given on the right.

VOLUME I

7	About the middle	17,] 17——,
7	Well, said a tall	the the] the
7	Well, said a tall	bu-ness] business
12	I was christened	Courteny] Courteney
13	I would not terrify you	prudent; friends;] prudent friends;
19	Henrietta had just	supperbeing] supper being
46	I was as much pleased	as as] as
55	She was now summoned	Mr] Mrs
58	But, my dear miss Woodby	funish] furnish
82	Is not Mr Damer	bu-ness] business
85	This is a strange girl	Gad] God
93	His lordship	no] not
109	No, *madam*	mikaken] mistaken

VOLUME II

153	She is both beautiful	fifty thousand] forty thousand
162	The countess	sarcasmo f] sarcasm of
238	Henrietta listened	them] him

NOTES TO THE NOVEL

VOLUME I

1. *Hammersmith* Area outside of London proper, north of the Thames and directly west of Kensington.

2. *Which illustrates* Paraphrased from *Moral Maxims by the Duke de la Roche Foucault*, which was first translated into English in 1694. In the 1748 Dublin edition the maxim reads, "In the Adversity of our best Friends, we find something that doth not displease us" (131). In the 1751 Dublin edition it reads, "In the Adversity of our Friends, we always find something that don't displease us" (58).

3. *guineas* To translate eighteenth-century pounds into today's dollars, multiply by 100. A guinea equaled a pound and a shilling, making it worth 105 dollars. The modern equivalent of these lodgings would be approximately 210 dollars. A certain prestige was attached to the guinea, which was a high-status pound. "The [guinea] was so named because the gold from which it was made came from the Guinea coast of Africa and because it was first struck to celebrate the founding in 1663 of the slave-trading monopoly known as the Royal Adventurers into Africa" (Vincent Carretta, *Equiano: The African* [Athens: University of Georgia Press, 2005], xxiii).

4. *sack* A general name for a class of white wines formerly imported from Spain and the Canaries (*Oxford English Dictionary*).

5. *chair* For those with money there were several kinds of transportation possible within the city of London at midcentury: post chaise, post coach, stagecoach, hackney coach, or chair. A post chaise was a traveling carriage, either hired from stage to stage or drawn by hired horses. It usually had a closed body and seated two to four people. The driver, or postilion, rode on one of the horses. A post coach was a stagecoach used for carrying mail. A stagecoach ran daily or on specified days to convey passengers or parcels. A hackney coach was a four-wheeled coach kept for hire. It was drawn by two horses and seated six people. A chair was an enclosed chair or covered vehicle for one person, carried on poles by two men (*OED*).

The post chaise or post coach was the most expensive form of long-distance coach because it was fast and private. The stagecoach was cheaper because it was slower and more crowded. Coaches were a common form of transportation, although they tended to be bumpy and very noisy. At two-thirds the cost, the chair offered some privacy as a passenger could embark from home. Chairs were uncomfortable for women since "their hoop petticoat has to be squeezed in by bending it up on each side." However, "their construction was ingenious. The roof was hinged so that you could walk in from the front without stooping and sit down. The roof was closed, and you shut or perhaps locked the door in the front. In cold weather you might have a foot-warmer ready on the floor" (Liza Picard, *Dr. Johnson's London* [New York: St. Martin's, 2001], 27). Chairs were sometimes taken even short distances just to avoid being muddied by the dirty streets of London. (Also see Kirsten Olsen, *Daily Life in Eighteenth-Century England* [Westport, Conn.: Greenwood, 1999]).

6. *lie-in* Give birth.

7. *chocolate* In the 1758 edition Henrietta drank coffee rather than chocolate. Simon Varey explains the relationship between the medicinal and exotic qualities particularly associated with chocolate. "Coffee tended to be served the same way almost everywhere: black, in a dish, with a stick of cinnamon and some sugar, but chocolate was more likely to be prepared with a greater sense of adventure" (21); it was consistently associated with Mexico and it "was considered an aphrodisiac [as opposed to coffee and tea], and therefore dangerous" (42). He also explains that "Quaker families, who pioneered chocolate manufacture in England, . . . cornered the market [and] retailed their product as beneficial to health" (31). "Three Necessary Drugs," in *1650–1850; Ideas, Aesthetics: An Inquiry in the Early Modern Era*, vol. 4, ed. Kevin Cope (New York: AMS, 1998).

8. *New Atlantis The New Atalantis* was a novel published in 1709 by Delarivier Manley. Its publication led to the arrest of Manley and her publisher on charges of *scandalum magnatum* (libel). A political satire, the novel deals with the sexual escapades of courtiers, courtesans, politicians, and aristocrats of early eighteenth-century England. The book tells of the goddess of justice, Astrea, who comes to earth to gather information about public and court life on the mythical island of Atalantis. Manley herself described it as a "publick attempt made against those designs & that [Whig] ministry which have been since so happily changed" (cited in Ruth Herman, *The Business of a Woman: The Political Writings of Delarivier Manley* [Newark: University of Delaware Press, 2003], 69). She is thought to have been instrumental in bringing about this change. (See G. M. Trevelyan, *England under Queen Anne* [London: Collins, 1965], I:194, II:62; Gwendolyn B. Needham, "Mary de la Riviere Manley, Tory Defender," *Huntington Library Quarterly* [1948–1949]: 263.) Ros Ballaster argues that "Manley concealed the 'transgression' of representing and embodying female political ambition beneath the 'lesser' transgression of representing and embodying active female sexual desire" (*Seductive Forms: Women's Amatory Fiction from 1684 to 1740* [Oxford: Clarendon, 1992], 116).

9. *Adventures of Joseph Andrews . . . Mrs. Haywood's Novels Joseph Andrews* was Henry Fielding's first novel (1742), satirizing Samuel Richardson's *Pamela*. Eliza Haywood (1693–1756) was a popular and prolific early novelist. Henrietta's choice of *Joseph Andrews* over Haywood's works indicates her preference for classical learning and references over the popular and perhaps scandalous. Haywood is condemned unfairly in Pope's *Dunciad* (1729) as a "shameless scribbler" of "profligate licentiousness." Her writing ranges from her explicitly erotic fiction of the 1720s to the more morally decorous prose and didactic fiction of the 1740s and 1750s.

10. *sell his commission* Officers had to buy their position in the army from a

retiring officer or from one who had gotten a promotion. The only men able to do this were from the landed and aristocratic classes. This purchase did not include uniform and other equipment, which an officer also needed to buy himself. A commission was considered an investment, since the officer could sell it when he retired, when it would be worth the same if not more money. (H. C. B. Rogers, *The British Army of the Eighteenth Century* [New York: Hippocrene, 1977]). An ensigncy at midcentury would have cost about 400 pounds, while a lieutenant colonelcy was worth about 3,500 pounds (Roy Porter, *English Society in the Eighteenth Century* [New York: Penguin, 1990], 114, 136). Purchasing a commission would be the modern equivalent of purchasing a medical practice (Barnett Correlli, *Britain and Her Army, 1509–1970* [New York: William Morrow, 1970], 137).

11. *Absence . . . more fiercely* From the Duke de la Rochefoucault's *Maxims*. It seems that Lennox translated this quotation from the French herself, as early eighteenth-century English editions offer different translations.

12. *elegant writer* Sir John Suckling (1609–1642), Cavalier poet. The quote, partly misremembered, comes from the fifth act of Suckling's comedy *Goblins*.

13. *wedded-love . . . miserable with it* Samuel Johnson's *Rasselas* (1759) echoes this sentiment: "Marriage has many pains, but celibacy has no pleasures" (*The History of Rasselas, Prince of Abissinia*, edited by J. P. Hardy [Oxford: Oxford University Press, 1999], 64).

14. *pin-money* An annual sum allotted to a woman in her marriage settlement for personal expenses in dress, etc.

15. *citizen* Usually applied, more or less contemptuously, to a tradesman or a shopkeeper as distinguished from a gentleman. Samuel Johnson: "a pert low townsman; a pragmatic tradesman."

16. *young girls of quality* As a result of Louis's revocation in 1685 of the Edict of Nantes, which had granted religious toleration to French Huguenots, as many as fifty thousand Protestant refugees fled to England, where they became textile manufacturers, goldsmiths, glassmakers, and wine merchants and lived in ghettos. Not only did they provide the British with additional reasons to oppose France, but these refugees also fought in England's armies (William Willcox and Walter Arnstein, *The Age of Aristocracy* [Lexington, Mass.: Heath, 1996], 15; Porter, *English Society in the Eighteenth Century,* 157; also see Robin D. Gwynn, *Huguenot Heritage* [London: Routledge, 1985]).

17. *corn-factor* A dealer in grains—all grains, such as oats, barley, and wheat, are called "corn" in England.

18. *cit* Short for citizen; contemptuous designation for a tradesman, merchant, or shopkeeper.

19. *Parade* A public square or promenade.

20. *staring with astonishment at him* This passage omitted here: "When we were placed at table, I found myself opposite to him; and observing that he chewed his meat with great difficulty, for want of teeth, I was resolved to mortify him, by letting him perceive that I observed it, looking at him several times with a kind of sensibility for this so unavoidable a misfortune."

21. *Spring-Gardens* In the 1750s there were two sites that might be invoked here. One was at Spring Garden, Stoke Newington, which was visited on Whitsunday evening by Londoners of the lower classes (Thomas Legg, *Low-life; or, One Half of the World, Knows Not How the Other Half Live*, 3rd ed. [London: J. Lever, 1764], 74). However, the most famous pleasure garden in London was Spring Gardens at Vauxhall. It came to be known simply as "Vauxhall" and offered a pleasant place to walk, with manicured gardens, walkways, arbors, nightingales, and orchestras. Admission was one shilling. "Tom Brown declares that in the close walks of the gardens 'both sexes meet, and mutually serve one another as guides to lose their way, and the winding and turning in the little Wildernesses are so intricate, that the most experienced mothers have often lost themselves in looking for their daughters.'" All levels of society frequented this place, but "even Bishops have been seen in this Recess without injuring their Character" (Warwick Wroth, *The London Pleasure Gardens of the Eighteenth Century* [London: Macmillan, 1896], 288, 292).

22. *jointure* An allowance written into the marriage articles to be settled on a woman for her maintenance if she outlived her husband.

23. *saints of Whitefield's or Wesley's creation* George Whitefield (1714–1770), Methodist preacher famous for his oratory. John Wesley (1703–1791) was the founder, along with his brother Charles, of Methodism, which was an expression against the rise of the dominant Anglican tradition of moral and rational religion. Orthodox Anglicans attacked Wesley for "enthusiasm" (claims to special revelations), teaching salvation by faith, and breaches of church order. Women held more prominent positions in the Methodist church (*Dictionary of National Biography*; also see Isabel Rivers, *Reason, Grace, and Sentiment: A Study of the Language, Religion, and Ethics in England, 1660–1780* [Cambridge: Cambridge University Press, 1991–2000]).

24. *Yet a writer . . . a very good return to it* The writer described here is Samuel Richardson. In *Sir Charles Grandison* (1753–1754), Mrs. Jervois/O'Hara, a woman of "abandoned character," is converted by Methodists. Lady G explains, "[t]hose people [Methodists] have really great merit with me . . . I am sorry that our own Clergy are not as zealously in earnest as they. They have really. . . . given a face of religion to subterranean colliers, tinners, and the most profligate of men, who hardly ever before heard either of the word, or thing" (vi, 32). Richardson was known to be a Dissenter and to be supportive of many women writers, including Lennox.

Sir Charles Grandison came out in a third edition in 1754.

25. *mussulmen* Muslims.

26. alcoran The Koran, or Quran.

27. *Envy will . . . the substance true* Alexander Pope's *Essay on Criticism* (1711), ll. 466–67.

28. *White's* In 1758 this was a well-known private gaming club where annual subscription fees were paid to the proprietor. It had formerly been associated with gallantry and intrigue, and even called "a den of thieves" (H. B. Wheatley, *London Past and Present* [London: Murray, 1891]).

29. *Ranelagh* Ranelagh Gardens were public pleasure gardens located in Chelsea,

then on the outskirts of London, to which all classes resorted.

30. *piquet* A card game played by two persons with a pack of thirty-two cards (the low cards, from "two" to "six," being excluded), in which points are scored on various groups or combinations of cards and on tricks.

31. *cardinal* A short cloak worn by ladies, originally of scarlet cloth with a hood (*OED*).

32. *factors* Agents.

33. *packer* A tradesman whose business is to pack goods for shipping.

34. *the faults . . . justified* From John Dryden, *Fables Ancient and Modern Translated into Verse from Homer, Ovid, Boccace, & Chaucer, with original poems by Mr. Dryden* (London: Tonson, 1700), 174.

VOLUME II

1. *premune* Colloquial contraction of *praemunire:* a difficulty, scrape, predicament, fix.

2. *ingenious writer* Footnote omitted in 1761. Fulke Greville, *Maxims, Characters, and Reflections, Critical and Satyrical, and Moral* (London: J and R. Tonson, 1756), 84. The 1756 edition reads: "Despair is the shocking ease to the mind that mortification is to the flesh." There was also a 1758 edition.

3. *spark* A youngblood, beau, single young man.

4. *temporising* Equivocating.

5. *neat's* Bovine animal such as an ox or cow.

6. *sack* Sweet wine.

7. *baited* Giving food and water to horses, especially on a journey.

8. *capuchin* A lady's hooded cloak, in imitation of that worn by Capuchin friars.

9. *Abigail* Designation for a maid.

10. *Jacobite* A supporter of James II or his son, the Pretender; loyal to the deposed Stuarts. In this context a code for political sedition.

11. *frowardness* The quality of being "habitually disposed to disobedience and opposition" (*Merriam-Webster's Collegiate Dictionary,* 11th ed., s.v. "froward").

12. *Mrs.* The use of this term here connotes respectfulness. Mrs. could be used to signal respect rather than as a marital designation.

13. *Scandalum Magnatum* A malicious libel upon a social superior.

14. *Odso* Contraction of "godso" or "oh god"; an exclamation of surprise.

15. *Arthur's* A gaming house; a London coffeehouse that started out as a social club for the elite with gambling.

16. *New-Market* A racecourse.

17. *deist* One who does not believe in revelation but whose belief in God comes only from reason; e.g., one common deist position was that God was the original cause of creation, setting the world in motion, because that is all that reason could

demonstrate. Deists did not believe in the immanence or omnipresence of God, and did not believe that he affected individuals but only collective bodies such as the church or the state.

18. *dependent* In this context, a lady's companion, or a "toad eater," one who is given room and board in return for being pleasing and accommodating.

19. *mercer* A person who deals in textile fabrics, especially silks, velvets, and other fine materials.

20. *lappets* Streamers attached to a lady's headdress.

21. *egrets* From *aigrette,* a tuft of feathers, spray of gems, or similar ornament worn on the head.

22. *French fillet* A headband used to bind the hair, to keep the headdress in position, or simply for ornament.

23. *tête* From the French "head"; a woman's head of hair, or wig, dressed high and elaborately ornamented.

24. *pink and silver* Colors of the pattern on the silk.

25. *dishabille* A state of undress, as in wearing nightclothes.

26. *Trifles, light as air . . . Othello,* III, iii, line 323.

27. *Eloisa* Heloise (also known as Eloisa) and Abelard's twelfth-century love letters are a well-known example of early romantic love. Abelard was of a noble class, which he had renounced to become a philosopher and teacher. Heloise was of a lower social standing and his student. Their illicit relationship resulted in a child, a secret marriage, and ultimately, Abelard's castration and life as a monk. Heloise became an abbess. The couple continued their correspondence, which at first was passionate but eventually became philosophical.

28. *governor* Tutor and guide.

29. *Femme de Chambre* A chambermaid. The implication is that a French chambermaid is more easily suborned, either because French morals are looser or because she is a new servant in Miss Belmour's pay and hence less responsive to Henrietta's wishes.

BIBLIOGRAPHY

SELECTED WORKS BY CHARLOTTE LENNOX

Original Editions

The Life of Harriot Stuart. London: J. Payne and J. Bouquet, 1750.
The Female Quixote. London: A. Millar, 1752.
Shakespear Illustrated. London: A. Millar, 1753–1754.
Henrietta. London: A. Millar, 1758.
Sophia. London: J. Fletcher, 1762.
Eliza. London: J. Dodsley, 1767.
The Sister. London: J. Dodsley, 1769.
Euphemia. London: T. Cadell, 1790.

Modern Editions

Euphemia. Facsimile edition, with an introduction by Mary Anne Schofield. New York: Scholars' Facsimiles, 1989.
———. Facsimile edition, with an introduction by Peter Garside. London: Routledge/Thoemmes, 1992.
The Female Quixote. Edited by Margaret Dalziel, with an introduction by Margaret Doody and chronology and appendix by Duncan Isles. Oxford and New York: Oxford University Press, 1989.
———. Edited with notes by Amanda Gilroy and Wil Verhoeven, with an introduction by Amanda Gilroy. New York: Penguin, 2006.
The Life of Harriot Stuart. Edited with an introduction by Susan Kubica Howard. Madison: Fairleigh Dickinson University Press, 1995.
Sophia. Edited with an introduction by Norbert Schürer. Peterborough, Ontario: Broadview, 2008.

SELECTED FURTHER READING

Bannet, Eve Tavor. "Charlotte Lennox." In *The Oxford Encyclopedia of British Literature,* edited by David Kastan. Oxford: Oxford University Press, 2006, 3:271–75.
———. "The Theater of Politeness in Charlotte Lennox's British-American Novels." *Novel: A Forum on Fiction* 33, no. 1 (Fall 1999): 73–92.

Bartolomeo, Joseph. "Female Quixotism V. 'Feminine' Tragedy: Lennox's Comic Revision of *Clarissa*." In *New Essays on Samuel Richardson,* edited by Albert Rivero, 163–76. New York: St. Martin's, 1996.

Batchelor, Jenny. "The Claims of Literature: Women Applicants to the Royal Literary Fund, 1790–1810." *Women's Writing* 12, no. 3 (2005): 505–21.

Berg, Temma. "Getting the Mother's Story Right: Charlotte Lennox and the New World." *Papers on Language and Literature* 32 (Summer 1996): 369–98.

———. *The Lives and Letters of an Eighteenth-Century Circle of Acquaintance.* Aldershot, U.K., and Burlington, Vt.: Ashgate, 2006.

Carlile, Susan. "Charlotte Lennox's Birth Date and Place." *Notes and Queries,* n.s., 51 (December 2004): 390–92.

———. "Expanding the Feminine: Reconsidering Charlotte Lennox's Age and *The Life of Harriot Stuart.*" *Eighteenth-Century Novel* 4 (2004): 103–37.

Chaplin, Susan. "Femininity and the Law of Romance: Charlotte Lennox's *The Female Quixote.*" In *Law, Sensibility, and the Sublime in Eighteenth-Century Women's Fiction: Speaking of Dread,* 61–80. Burlington, Vt.: Ashgate, 2004.

Clarke, Norma. *Dr. Johnson's Women.* London and New York: Hambledon and London, 2000.

Doody, Margaret Anne. "Shakespeare's Novels: Charlotte Lennox Illustrated." *Studies in the Novel* 19 (Fall 1987): 296–310.

Ellis, Lorna. "Reacting to Romance and Building the Bildungsroman: *The Female Quixote* and *Betsy Thoughtless.*" In *Appearing to Diminish: Female Development and the British Bildungsroman, 1750–1850,* 63–87. Lewisburg: Bucknell University Press, 1999.

Gallagher, Catherine. "Nobody's Credit: Fiction, Gender, and Authorial Property in the Fiction of Charlotte Lennox." In *Nobody's Story: The Vanishing Acts of Women Writers in the Marketplace, 1660–1820,* 145–202. Los Angeles: University of California Press, 1994.

Gardiner, Ellen. "Writing Men Reading in Charlotte Lennox's *The Female Quixote.*" *Studies in the Novel* 28 (Spring 1996): 1–11.

Gordon, Scott Paul. "Charlotte Lennox's *Female Quixote* and Orthodox Quixotism." In *The Practice of Quixotism: Postmodern Theory and Eighteenth-Century Women's Writing,* 41–66. Basingstoke: Palgrave MacMillan, 2007.

Green, Susan. "A Cultural Reading of Charlotte Lennox's *Shakespear Illustrated.*" In *Cultural Readings of Restoration and Eighteenth-Century English Theater,* edited by J. Douglas Canfield and Deborah C. Payne, 228–57. Athens and London: University of Georgia Press, 1995.

Hanley, Brian. "Henry Fielding, Samuel Johnson, Samuel Richardson, and the Reception of Charlotte Lennox's *The Female Quixote* in the Popular Press." *ANQ* 13 (Summer 2000): 27–32.

Howard, Susan Kubica. "Seeing Colonial America and Writing Home about It: Charlotte Lennox's *Euphemia,* Epistolary, and the Feminine Picturesque." *Studies in the Novel* 37 (Fall 2005): 273–91.

Isles, Duncan. "Johnson, Richardson, and *The Female Quixote.*" In *The Female Quixote,* by Charlotte Lennox, edited by Margaret Dalziel, 419–28. Oxford and New York: Oxford University Press, 1989.

———. "The Lennox Collection." *Harvard Library Bulletin* 18, no. 4 (October 1970): 317–344; 19, no. 1 (January 1971): 36–60; 19, no. 2 (April 1971): 165–86; 19, no. 4 (October 1971): 416–35.

Kramnick, Jonathan. "Reading Shakespeare's Novels: Literary History and Cultural Politics in the Lennox-Johnson Debate." *Modern Language Quarterly* 55 (December 1994): 429–53.

Labbie, Erin. "History as 'Retro': Veiling Inheritance in Lennox's *The Female Quixote.*" *Bucknell Review* 42, no. 1 (1998): 79–97.

Langbauer, Laurie. "Diverting Romance: Charlotte Lennox's *The Female Quixote.*" In *Women and Romance: The Consolations of Gender in the English Novel,* 62–92. Ithaca: Cornell University Press, 1990.

Levin, Kate. "'The Cure of Arabella's Mind': Charlotte Lennox and the Disciplining of the Female Reader." *Women's Writing* 2, no. 3 (1995): 271–90.

Looser, Devoney. "Charlotte Lennox and the Study and Use of History." In *British Women Writers and the Writing of History, 1670–1820,* 89–118. Baltimore: Johns Hopkins University Press, 2000. Lynch, James. "Romance and Realism in Charlotte Lennox's *The Female Quixote.*" *Essays in Literature* 14 (Spring 1987): 51–63.

Mack, Ruth. "Quixotic Ethnography: Charlotte Lennox and the Dilemma of Cultural Observation." *Novel: A Forum on Fiction* 38 (Spring–Summer 2005): 193–213.

Malina, Deborah. "Rereading the Patriarchal Text: *The Female Quixote, Northanger Abbey,* and the Trace of the Absent Mother." *Eighteenth-Century Fiction* 8 (January 1996): 271–92.

Marshall, David. "Writing Masters and 'Masculine Exercises' in *The Female Quixote.*" *Eighteenth-Century Fiction* 5 (January 1993): 105–35.

Martin, Mary. "'High and Noble Adventures': Reading the Novel in *The Female Quixote.*" *Novel: A Forum on Fiction* 31 (Fall 1997): 45–62.

Maynadier, Gustavus. *The First American Novelist?* Cambridge, Mass.: Harvard University Press, 1949.

"Memoirs of Mrs. Lenox." *Edinburgh Weekly Magazine,* October 9, 1783, 34–36.

Motooka, Wendy. "Coming to a Bad End: Sentimentalism, *The Female Quixote,* and the Power of Interest." In *The Age of Reasons: Quixotism, Sentimentalism, and Political Economy in Eighteenth-Century Britain,* 125–41. London: Routledge, 1998.

Nussbaum, Felicity. "The Empire of Love: The Veil and the Blush of Romance." In *Torrid Zones: Maternity, Sexuality and Empire in Eighteenth-Century English Narratives,* 114–34. Baltimore: Johns Hopkins University Press, 1995.

Palo, Sharon Smith. "The Good Effects of a Whimsical Study: Romance and Women's Learning in Charlotte Lennox's *The Female Quixote.*" *Eighteenth-Century Fiction* 18 (Winter 2005–2006): 203–28.

Ross, Deborah. "Mirror, Mirror: The Didactic Dilemma of *The Female Quixote.*" *Studies in English Literature, 1500–1900* 27 (Summer 1987): 27–38.

Roulston, Christine. "Histories of Nothing: Romance and Femininity in Charlotte Lennox's *The Female Quixote*." *Women's Writing* 2, no. 1 (1995): 25–42.

Runge, Laura. "Aristotle's Sisters: Behn, Lennox, Fielding, and Reeve." In *Gender and Language in British Literary Criticism, 1660–1790*, 121–67. Cambridge: Cambridge University Press, 1997.

Schellenberg, Betty. "The (Female) Literary Careers of Sarah Fielding and Charlotte Lennox." In *The Professionalization of Women Writers in Eighteenth-Century Britain*, 94–119. Cambridge: Cambridge University Press, 2005.

Schürer, Norbert. "A New Novel By Charlotte Lennox." *Notes and Queries*, n.s., 48 (December 2001): 419–22.

Séjourné, Phillipe. *The Mystery of Charlotte Lennox: First Novelist of Colonial America*. N.s., 62. Aix-en-Provence: Publications des Annales de la Faculté des Lettres, 1967.

Small, Miriam Rossiter. *Charlotte Ramsay Lennox: An Eighteenth Century Lady of Letters*. New Haven: Yale University Press, 1935. Reprint, Hamden, Conn.: Archon, 1969.

Spacks, Patricia Meyer. "The Subtle Sophistry of Desire: *The Female Quixote*." In *Desire and Truth: Functions of Plot in Eighteenth-Century English Novels*, 12–33. Chicago and London: University of Chicago Press, 1990.

Thompson, Helen. "Charlotte Lennox and the Agency of Romance: Ingenuous Subjection and Genre." In *Ingenuous Subjection: Compliance and Power in the Eighteenth-Century Domestic Novel*, 152–71. Philadelphia: University of Pennsylvania Press, 2005.

Todd, Janet. "Re-Formers: Eliza Haywood and Charlotte Lennox." In *The Sign of Angellica: Women, Writing, and Fiction, 1660–1800*, 146–60. New York: Columbia University Press, 1989.